System Failure

ALSO BY JOE ZIEJA

Epic Failure Trilogy
Mechanical Failure
Communication Failure

EPIC FAILURE TRILOGY
BOOK III

WITHDRAWN

System
Failure

JOE ZIEJA

SAGA  PRESS

LONDON SYDNEY NEW YORK TORONTO NEW DELHI

SAGA PRESS
AN IMPRINT OF SIMON & SCHUSTER, INC.

1230 AVENUE OF THE AMERICAS, NEW YORK, NEW YORK 10020

SAGA PRESS and colophon are trademarks of Simon & Schuster, Inc.
For information about special discounts for bulk purchases, please contact Simon & Schuster Special Sales at 1-866-506-1949 or business@simonandschuster.com.
The Simon & Schuster Speakers Bureau can bring authors to your live event. For more information or to book an event, contact the Simon & Schuster Speakers Bureau at 1-866-248-3049 or visit our website at www.simonspeakers.com.
Interior design by Michael McCartney
The text for this book was set in New Baskerville.
Manufactured in the United States of America
First Saga Press trade paperback edition September 2019
10 9 8 7 6 5 4 3 2 1
CIP data for this book is available from the Library of Congress.
ISBN 978-1-4814-8693-4
ISBN 978-1-4814-8695-8 (eBook)

**To Aevalyn and Ellawyn,
for ensuring my profanity
generator will never be broken**

System Failure

Galactic Takeover Wasn't in the Job Description

Lucinda Hiri was pretty sure taking over the galaxy hadn't been in the job description when she was offered this intern position six months ago. Then again, it wasn't impossible. The Snaggardir corporation's paperwork was notoriously long and detailed, vetted by droves of lawyers at every level of approval to make sure that the language had all the right loopholes in all the right places. Lucinda supposed that somewhere on page 356 there could have been a small asterisk that said "in the event a nascent people rise up after two hundred years of secret collusion, you will be required to take detailed notes at their strategy meetings."

It had seemed like a dream come true at the time. Sal Snaggardir and his family's company were arguably the most powerful economic force in the galaxy. The possibilities for her career as a businesswoman were endless. Not like interning at some space technology company on Urp, where she would likely move laterally for the entirety of her disappointing, coffee-supported life. Snaggardir's was the place to make it big.

In retrospect, though, Lucinda should have noticed that Mr. Snaggardir was trying to conceal just how big his company had gotten. Subsidiary corporations, literally thousands of banks all across the galaxy holding funds under different names, and that nondisclosure agreement she signed threatening to eradicate her family line if she ever told anyone anything about the company. The legal department said that was boilerplate, and, really, what did she know? She was just a thirty-year-old unpaid intern with three advanced degrees in business arts.

Mr. Snaggardir was looking at her.

"Uh, yes, sir?" Lucinda asked.

"I asked if you got all of that," Mr. Snaggardir said. He was a fine-featured, wiry man with a receding hairline and the beginnings of liver spots, and his beady eyes were always just a bit too narrow to not be actively judging you.

Lucinda felt her face go hot as she looked down at her notebook. For some reason the Snaggardir corporation was adamant about its internal dealings being recorded on old-fashioned pencil and paper, then transcribed to the data networks later. Right now, however, she realized that the page she was writing on was blank, and she hadn't heard a word anyone had said for a solid five minutes.

"I'm sorry, sir," she said, looking down at the paper to avoid his eyes. She knew it looked stupid, like she was blaming the paper for her negligence, but she couldn't hold Mr. Snaggardir's gaze. Waving at the notepad, she fumbled for an excuse, and, unable to come up with one, settled on honesty.

"I guess I'm just finding it hard to focus, given, um, everything that's happened."

That was easily the understatement of the last two hundred years. The entire Fortuna Stultus galaxy had practically collapsed—though she would never use that term in front of the Snaggardirs—in the wave of the Jupiterian uprising. The figures at the table—practically all members of the Snaggardir family—had been the last leg in two hundred years of planning and plotting. Snaggardir's used to just be a place that sold great snacks and industrial equipment. Now the catchphrase "until all the chairs are empty" was popping up on leaflets and posters all over the place, referring to the War of Musical Chairs in which the Jupiterians had been denied a place in the galaxy.

"Are you sure having her around is a good idea, Uncle Sal?" Sara Alshazari said, looking between Lucinda and her boss with open suspicion. Every time the woman talked, Lucinda couldn't help but hear the voice of all the Snaggardir products in her head. Lucinda had been offered countless free nachos and bowling games by this woman, and now she came to find out that Sara Alshazari was in reality a master of manipulation and propaganda, the leader of all the subtle information campaigns conducted by the Jupiterians in the last twenty years. In her mid-forties, she had touches of gray appearing in her short brown hair, but her face showed no wrinkles.

"It's fine," Mr. Snaggardir said, his lips cresting in a small smile. He was a demanding man to work for, but not unreasonable and certainly not unkind. It made the fact that he was currently murdering thousands of people all over the galaxy in revenge seem not so bad.

Wait . . . that didn't feel right.

"Ms. Hiri is a trusted ally to the cause who has proven herself many times over the last half year. She has no Jupiterian blood, so I am sure she's a little . . . taken aback by all that's gone on. Isn't that right, Ms. Hiri?"

Lucinda nodded emphatically and realized that she was writing down Mr. Snaggardir's excuses for her on her notepad, which seemed pointless. Also, she'd spelled "Jupiterian" wrong. Not a word she was used to writing.

"Yes, sir," she said. "I am fully behind the Jupiterian cause."

The statement was true, of course. There was something about being on the moral high ground that Lucinda enjoyed, particularly because she'd always disapproved of the way the Jupiterians had been forced to scatter when mankind had traveled to the Fortuna Stultus galaxy. Of course, it had supposedly been the scientifically ambitious Jupiterians' fault for collapsing the Milky Way in the first place, but those were small details.

"See?" Mr. Snaggardir said, gesturing to the other three people at the table—Sara Alshazari, General Szinder, and Dr. Mattic. "No problems. Now, perhaps for my intern's edification we could quickly recap the status of our plans. General Szinder, if you would?"

For everything that Mr. Snaggardir was, General Szinder was not. Pompous, loud, brash, and unrefined, the military genius of the Jupiterian movement was all bark and even more bite. Broad shouldered and dark skinned, he was from a different Jupiterian family line than the Snaggardirs. At least Lucinda thought he was. It was difficult getting up to speed on Jupiterian genealogy when she hadn't really known they'd existed until a short while ago. General Szinder looked at her, clearly upset with having to repeat himself, and Lucinda made a great show of staring at her notebook.

"Of course," he said, his voice having that rough quality that comes with spending one's youth shouting over people at bars. "We waited two hundred years for this; what's the harm in wasting another few minutes repeating myself?"

Lucinda's face reddened even further. If she could have crawled into the lined yellow paper she was holding, she would have made an elaborate tent and gone into hiding for days. How did she get herself into this?

Dr. Mattic, the only person in the room to have said nothing during the entire meeting, stared off into space like he always did. Perhaps it was stereotyping to characterize a scientist this way, but the man always reminded Lucinda of an egg, both in shape and in personality.

General Szinder went on. "Grandelle and New Neptune are

well in hand. The propaganda campaign that Sara came up with worked beautifully in New Neptune."

The "propaganda campaign" that General Szinder was referring to was really just some fake newspaper articles informing the New Neptunians that they were now under the rightful control of the Jupiterian uprising. New Neptunians were notoriously both gullible and averse to any sort of conflict. Composed of immigrants from former communist countries on Old Earth, they were mostly used to life being terrible and thought doing anything about it was a waste of their time and effort.

"Grandelle's planetary governments are well aware of the sway that we hold in their system," the general said. "At any point, simply freezing the assets we control would cause their entire societal structure to collapse. They are playing nice for now, but I still suggest setting up a network of regional ambassadors to keep them in line." He grinned. "At the first hint of resistance, we could burn them to—"

"Stop," Mr. Snaggardir said, holding up a hand. "Let's stick to the topic."

General Szinder looked displeased, but didn't argue. "Merida and Thelicosa are where we have the most problems, thanks to the brilliant doctor's half-baked plan." He shot a look at Dr. Mattic, who either wasn't listening or didn't care. Lucinda had seen the general harangue the doctor so many times now that it would have seemed like an empty meeting without it. She scribbled down the insult.

"The good doctor's experiments with artificial intelligence aren't the only reason things have failed to take shape in those two systems," Mr. Snaggardir said. Sara was nodding. "There was quite a large network of sleeper cells all throughout Thelicosa that failed to activate. We lost Zergan before he was able to carry out most of his plans, and the rest of the Colliders' ships are now back in the control of the Thelicosans."

"More will activate as the information gets out," General

Szinder said, sitting back in his chair and scowling. "It's just a matter of getting the right messages—"

"There is also the issue with the cyber warfare failings . . . ," Sara said.

"That was not my fault!" the general shouted.

Lucinda wasn't actually sure what either of them were talking about now. There had been some other plan in the works, something that the general had cooked up because he thought he could do technological warfare better than Dr. Mattic. Whatever it was, it hadn't gone well.

"Whatever the failings," Mr. Snaggardir said, letting his voice hang on the word, "we need to focus on what to do next. Dr. Mattic—the construction?"

The doctor, pale and specter-like despite his sizable girth, finally made eye contact, but only to deliver a few words.

"Ahead of schedule."

Mr. Snaggardir nodded, as if that was all the information he needed to know.

Construction? Lucinda wrote down. Another mystery for her. They clearly weren't as trusting of her as Mr. Snaggardir had let on.

"By next week I want to know about the calibration efforts of the device, and a final completion date. Given that things unfolded in such a . . . disorganized fashion, we may need to activate our contingencies."

Sara looked very uncomfortable at the prospect of whatever contingencies Mr. Snaggardir was referring to.

"What about our blockades?" Sara said, perhaps just to change the subject. "If we allow the rest of them to organize, we could have problems."

"The blockades are perfect," the general said, recovering some of his haughtiness. "We have enough native forces to scatter all throughout the galaxy, plus all the defectors. My blockades are perfect—you have never seen such amazing blockades.

If anyone tries to break them . . ." He paused for a moment. "We will burn them to—"

"Stop," Mr. Snaggardir said again, this time sharply. He was about to say something else, but someone knocked at the door. The conversation came to an abrupt halt; nobody ever knocked at the door. This was a meeting of the highest echelon of the most powerful economic—and maybe now military—force in the world. You don't just knock on their door like a salesman.

No one seemed to be doing anything about it, though. Everyone just sort of sat and stared. At Lucinda. Like she was an intern, or something.

"Right," Lucinda said, moving quickly over to the door. "Sorry."

She shuffled through the fancy conference room, the white, paneled walls making everything feel sterile and critical. It also probably felt critical because Lucinda was constantly being criticized.

She opened the door to find a young man actually wringing his hands like some sort of cliché, milquetoast servant. Lucinda could relate, though she was very careful about not wringing her hands. She had very dry skin, and it hurt.

"I'm sorry to interrupt," he said, his voice thin. Lucinda tried to place him—she was certain she'd seen him before—but ultimately he was just another face in the sea of Snaggardir employees. He stood there like he expected some sort of answer to his apology, but the people at the table merely looked at him. General Szinder's face contorted like he was going to start chewing on the edge of the table if this man didn't begin talking immediately.

"I have some news," the visitor said.

"We gathered that," Mr. Snaggardir said, just a touch of edge in his voice.

"It's the blockades. Someone is breaking through them."

All eyes turned to General Szinder, who, to his credit, hid his disbelief under a thin veil of anger.

"That's not possible! The strategy is perfect. We know everyone's military secrets. What kind of military genius do they have on their side to help them through something like this?"

The young man, not at all liking his current position as the target of the general's ravings, looked down at a piece of paper he was holding.

"It says something here about a Captain Rogers?" he said, his voice going up way too high for a normal question.

Everyone went quiet. So quiet, in fact, that the messenger looked up as quickly as if someone had started shooting a disruptor rifle. He stared around the room at all the expressions with something approaching wonder, and Lucinda could understand why. Even Dr. Mattic looked disturbed.

"You've heard of him before?" the young man said.

The question rang out like a shot echoing down a dark alleyway.

"We're familiar," Mr. Snaggardir said flatly.

"So," Rogers said, idly flicking the end of a fork.

"So," the Viking said. She looked around the room aimlessly, as though something interesting was going to magically manifest itself in the middle of the empty dining hall.

The problem with being on the Meridan *Flagship* rather than the Thelicosan *Limiter* was that when you invited someone to have a drink with you, you were really inviting them to an austere dining hall that didn't serve alcohol. Rogers hadn't been able to resupply the *Flagship* with any drinks, and Grand Marshal Keffoule had destroyed the bar on the *Limiter* with a spinning back kick. His stateroom was, he supposed, an option, but something about it felt very inappropriate for a first date. As a result, Rogers and the Viking's rendezvous was relegated to the Peek and Shoot, which Rogers had used his admiral-like powers to close for a little bit, ordering that they not be disturbed.

Unfortunately, he neglected to take into account the utter

awkwardness of being in a completely silent, completely empty warehouse-sized dining hall with only one other person. He could have sworn that his heartbeat was echoing throughout the cavernous room, hammering out the drumbeat of all of his romantic failures.

Neither of them were really dressed for the occasion, either. Rogers had at least put on a clean uniform, but it was still a uniform. The Viking had also put on a clean uniform, which was both nice and a little disappointing.

"Not really the perfect first date," Rogers blurted.

"Nope," the Viking said simply.

After a moment, Rogers realized that she'd allowed him to call it a date without any violence, which he supposed was a good thing. She could have, for example, stood up, flipped the table, and berated him for being so presumptuous. Maybe pushed him around a little, cursed . . .

"But hey," he said, tugging at his collar and suddenly feeling a little hot. "It could be worse, right? We could be swarmed with droids trying to kill us or being threatened by a Jupiterian uprising." He forced out a laugh, which sounded like a gunshot in the echoing room.

The Viking looked at him squarely, squinting one eye in a way that made Rogers squirm in his seat.

"Speaking of which," she said, "are you sure there's nothing that you should be doing on the bridge?"

Rogers waved a hand dismissively, which collided with a fork and sent it ricocheting off tables and benches until it came to rest on the other side of the room.

"Nah," he said. "Totally boring space travel. We'll be back at Merida Prime before you know it."

She was going to be *so* pissed when she found out that there was a huge space battle going on outside right now in the Furth sector of Meridan territory. At the same time, Rogers had put an awful lot of effort into disabling the battle station alarms in the dining halls and making sure nobody would talk to him until the date was concluded. That was romantic, right? Besides, he'd left Deet in charge. His robotic deputy could certainly handle a little space battle.

"I guess," the Viking said. "As long as you're not blowing off something important for this."

Yep. She was going to kill him.

But really, could she blame him? This was the first moment of peace they'd gotten since they'd wrapped things up with the Thelicosans and gotten recalled back to headquarters. He'd tried so many times to approach her about making good on her promise to have a drink with him, but there always seemed to be some triviality blocking his love life. Things like a minor resurgence of droids randomly waking up and wanting to kill everyone, or Deet becoming uncomfortably obsessed with doing research on his own programming, or some of the cooks who had been marines wanting to go back to the marines because people shot at them less. Being the acting admiral of the 331st really was not all it was cracked up to be. Why did he want this job again?

Oh, that's right. He didn't.

"This is important," Rogers said. "At least, it is to me."

The Viking frowned. "Like, collapse-of-the-free-galaxy kind of important?"

"Sure," Rogers said, nodding emphatically. "Absolutely. Yes."

Looking at him for a long moment, the Viking displayed one of her considering faces. Rogers always took these to mean that she was considering what kind of violence to visit on him, but lately it seemed like she was trying to control herself a bit more. She had told Rogers that she didn't want him to think face-hitting was her only method of communication, and it really seemed like she was trying in earnest to find other ways to talk to him.

"Not making fun of me?" she asked finally.

"Nope," Rogers said.

Come on, man, he thought. *Can you come up with anything more than one-word answers? How long have you been waiting for this?*

Something that felt suspiciously like a direct hit from plasma cannons sent vibrations throughout the room.

"What the hell was that?" the Viking said, looking up at the ceiling.

"Outgassing," Rogers said. "Don't worry about it."

The Viking frowned. "Are you sure?"

"Absolutely. I'm an engineer. So tell me about yourself."

"What do you want to know?"

"Anything," Rogers said. "Where did you grow up? What is your favorite food? What are your thoughts on heavy petting?"

"What?"

"Maybe just answer the first two," Rogers said.

The Viking chewed on the inside of her cheek—or maybe she had a piece of leather tucked away in there, Rogers couldn't be sure—and shifted in her seat. He wasn't used to her looking so uncomfortable. Maybe he'd come on too strong with the personal questions, or maybe the Viking had an itchy butt.

"Well," she said, "I grew up on Parivan, near the Jikkarn salt mines. Kind of a backwater town, not a lot going on. It was—are you *absolutely* sure there's nothing going on?"

She was probably referring to the light fixture that had just fallen from the ceiling; Rogers wasn't totally sure. She might also have been concerned with the alternating red-and-amber light that had started blinking in the corner of the room. Rogers must have missed that one.

"Positive," Rogers said, feeling his face involuntarily contort into what may have been the guiltiest smile he'd ever given. Wasn't he supposed to be good at conning people? "Peaceful open space out there for sure. I would know, right? I'm the captain of the ship and the acting admiral of the fleet and all that, right?"

The Viking didn't look particularly convinced. She put her

hands on the edge of the table and made to get up. "I dunno, Rogers, maybe we should go check it out—"

"Wait!" Rogers said, just a touch too desperately. He paused a moment to compose himself. For some reason he felt like if the Viking walked out that door, he would lose her forever. Which was kind of a silly notion: they all lived together on a contained ship in free space; her room was still only a few doors down from his own.

Something inside him was just on the verge of being about to tell him to begin considering the possibility of telling her the truth when the door opened, and Corporal Tunger stole the chance from him.

"Captain Rogers," he said, thankfully in an accent Rogers could understand, "we can't figure out who's on Furth!"

"What?" the Viking barked. "We're in Furth?"

"Yes," Rogers said, holding up his hands. "I was just about to tell you that. Tunger, what do you mean you don't know who's on Furth?"

"It's probably better that you come up to the bridge. Since you're the only person who knows how to fight space battles and all."

"What?" the Viking barked. "We're in a space battle?"

"Yes," Rogers said, unable to hold up his hands any more than he was already holding up his hands. "I was about to tell you that, too."

The Viking narrowed her eyes and stood up. "You told me there was nothing going on out there."

"There isn't!" Rogers declared, too loudly, and stood up as well, his hands now really, really held up, to the point where it looked like he was doing the wave at a concert. It probably no longer looked like the placating expression he'd hoped for. "There's nothing going on at all."

"There's definitely something going on, sir," Tunger said. "And now we don't know who's on Furth."

"*Tunger,*" Rogers hissed. "I do not *care* who is on Furth."

"You probably would if you were up on the bridge with the space battle."

"Rogers . . . ," the Viking warned. "Are you blowing off a space battle?"

In the ensuing silence, there really was no denying the loud alarms going off all over the rest of the ship calling everyone to their battle stations. It seemed kind of silly, because the battle in the Furth sector had been going on for quite a long time. If there were people still not at their battle stations this far in, they were in trouble.

Rogers dimly realized that he was not at his battle station.

Sighing, Rogers hung his head. "Yes, I am blowing off a space battle."

"You swore to me," the Viking said. "You told me I wasn't missing anything."

In reality, she wasn't missing anything. Unless they were going to get boarded, or going to board someone else, the marines were just going to stand around stroking their disruptor rifles and making everyone else around them more nervous. But more than that, Rogers had never heard anyone refer to war as something that one might "miss" in a negative way.

He turned to apologize to her, to explain that it was just his way of trying to make sure they got to spend time together, but she was already stomping out of the room. The mesmerizing vision of her walking away from him was enough to stop his tongue in his mouth, especially when she was angry, but as she vanished from sight, Rogers knew he'd made a grave error. He'd forgotten to lock the damn door.

"Tunger," Rogers said slowly. "One of these days, I am going to kill you."

Tunger shrugged. "I'm not a tactician, sir, but I'm pretty sure you're going to kill *all* of us if you don't get to the space battle."

Who's on Furth?

"Alright," Rogers said as he stormed onto the bridge, waving his arms like a monkey looking for something to throw. "Someone had better tell me *very quickly* what is so goddamn important up here!"

The whole bridge went silent, only the beeping of consoles and random bursts of communications from other ships in the fleet making any noise. Everyone on the bridge stared at him, and there was no slow-salute thing this time at all. In fact, most of them looked pretty upset.

"Oh, I don't know," the dour, serious Commander Belgrave said, looking up from his helmsman console. "Maybe the unraveling of the entire galaxy?"

Rogers cleared his throat and felt heat rise to his face.

"Right," Rogers said. "Okay. Yes. Fine. Tunger said something about not knowing who's on Furth, whatever the hell that means. What's going on?"

He settled into the chair on the command dais and tried to

get a sense of what was actually happening. Maybe ditching a pitched battle hadn't been a great idea; he had a lot of catching up to do in a very short amount of time. There were lots of things on screens, and things that were beeping, and people who were pushing a lot of buttons. The panic button didn't appear to be pressed, but the THEY'RE ATTACKING US button was blinking like a pagan yuletide tree on the winter solstice. Rogers didn't really need the THEY'RE ATTACKING US button to know that, though. There was a small group of ships making an attack run directly at the window of the bridge right now.

"Duck!" Rogers screamed, and immediately realized how little sense that made.

Just as he was vanishing below the thin railing of the command platform that would not at all have protected him from any munition, he saw the incoming fighters get swept away by a barrage of cannon fire from the defensive systems on the *Flagship*. Right—of course they had defensive systems specifically designed to prevent a couple of small fighters from blowing a hole in the side of their command ship.

Space warfare was really stressful.

"If you're finished with that," Commander Rholos, the defensive coordinator, said as she moved the microphone of her headset away from her mouth. Her windbreaker, which was definitely not standard-issue Meridan clothing, looked sweaty. "I can give you an update."

"That would probably be a good idea," Rogers said.

Rholos moved around the outside of the platform and climbed up so she could stand next to Rogers. She held a datapad in one hand and a laminated card of *The Art of War II: Now In Space* by Sun Tzu Jr. in the other.

Rogers wasn't used to people climbing on his platform. He also wasn't used to being bothered by it.

"What are you doing?" he asked. "Can't you just show me on all of these giant, expensive displays we have all around the bridge?"

Rholos looked at him flatly. "They're a little busy prosecuting a war at the moment."

Rogers glanced up and noticed that, indeed, the expensive displays were showing expensive images from expensive sensor arrays located all over the ships of the 331st Anti-Thelicosan Buffer Group. As was the case when he'd been fighting the now-deceased Commodore Zergan, he really didn't understand what almost any of them meant. It looked like a lot of blue and red lines and blue and red dots to him. Though, now that he was looking at it, he realized that most of the dots and lines weren't either of those colors anymore, but an ambiguous-looking amber.

Holding up her datapad, Rholos began an incredibly fast, incredibly complicated rundown of the disposition of their forces in the battlespace. The words she was using were both foreign and scary, and Rogers felt himself clutching the armrests of his chair as his anxiety built.

"Hang on," he said, finally not able to take anymore. "I'm pretty sure we've gone over the fact that I have no education or practical experience in commanding a space battle, and the only reason it works is precisely because of this." He thought for a moment. "Come to think of it, I was pretty sure none of you knew what you were doing either."

"We learn fast," Rholos said. She put the datapad down. "Here's the real problem, Skipper. Something is going wrong with the IFF. The Jupiterians have been integrated into so many different forces, it's impossible to tell who is who. Somehow they seem to be able to avoid shooting each other, but whatever decoder they have, we don't. Most of our ships are firing glancing blows and just trying to maneuver effectively because they're too scared of blowing up friendlies."

Rogers frowned. "You're saying they know who the enemy is, but we don't?"

"Exactly," Rholos said. She pointed to the screen, and now Rogers understood why everything was colored amber. "There's a mixture of Thelicosan and Meridan ship classes out there that seem to be fighting against us, so we can't even isolate the enemy visually. Except for that ship right there. Starman Brelle, zoom in please."

"Yes, ma'am," Starman First Class Brelle, the communications tech, said.

A button press or two later, one of the ships appeared close-up on the screen. So close, in fact, that Rogers could see right into the main viewing window of the bridge. There was a small, hand-drawn sign in the window, facing outward, that said *Get Outta My Chair, Muthafucka!*

"I see," Rogers said. "Yeah, that's probably a Jupiterian. There's no chance all of them have signs like that, is there?"

Rholos shook her head.

"Well can we at least blow *that* ship up?"

Rholos looked like she was about to answer, but they were interrupted by the frantic yelling of Commander Zaz, the offensive coordinator.

"Goddamn it, Jackal two five! That's holding! Open your damn eyes! I'm starting to think you don't really want this."

He paced in a thin racetrack-like pattern across the bridge floor, waving his laminated sheet above his head, his face redder than a ripe tomato. Coming from someone who was normally a quiet, if not aloof man, Zaz's anger took Rogers by surprise.

"I'm not sure I want this either," Rogers muttered.

"What was that?" Rholos asked.

"Nothing." He rubbed his eyes. "Okay, so we need to figure out who to kill before they kill all of us, right?"

Commander Belgrave just sighed.

"Not now, Belgrave," Rogers said. "You just get ready to dodge all the missiles and torpedoes they're launching at us from every direction."

Belgrave sighed again.

Commander Rholos nodded. "We're not going to be much good if we can't start clearing up the IFF. Starman Brelle is doing all she can, but every time she thinks she's decoded something it seems to reset itself."

Rogers thought for a moment. If only they had a mildly intelligent automaton who could automatically process this information, cross-check it, and take human input in real time.

"Wait a minute," Rogers said slowly, looking around the bridge. "Where the hell is Deet? Didn't I put him in charge while I was romancing . . . uh, dealing with other matters?"

Commander Belgrave looked at Rogers meaningfully. S1C Brelle waved at Commander Rholos, and she excused herself momentarily to see what was going on.

"What is it, Belgrave?"

"Oh," the helmsman said. "Am I allowed to talk now?"

Rogers put his hand on his forehead. "I feel like I never know if you are a helmsman, a philosopher, or a fourteen-year-old girl."

"Humph," Belgrave said, as if to emphasize Rogers' point. "Well, if you must know, Deet left the bridge almost immediately after we became engaged. He said something about going down to IT so he could get something off the larger network now that we're not jammed anymore."

That goddamn robot is going to get us all killed, Rogers thought, completely ignoring that he should have been the one on the bridge this whole time. Then again, even if he had been on the bridge, there was a greater chance of him screwing things up than pushing them toward victory. He certainly couldn't have decoded the IFF by himself. This sort of thing was precisely why he kept the prototype droid around.

"Someone put IT on the line," Rogers said.

A few moments later, a bored, flat, female voice came across the channel. She introduced herself as an S1C.

"Hi," Rogers said. "This is your boss's boss's boss's boss. Is there a stray robot plugging himself into random things in your office?"

Nobody answered for a moment—they seemed to be having a

muffled discussion over whether or not Deet was a stray or if he was owned by someone—but they didn't have to. After a few seconds, Rogers heard a familiar voice in the background yelling.

"I am not an [EXPLETIVE] stray! Nobody owns me! I am the master of my own [MATERNAL FORNICATION] destiny!"

"Yep," Rogers said. "That's him. Let me talk to him."

"You're on speaker, sir," the S1C said.

"Deet," Rogers said. "Do you want to explain to me what you're doing down there instead of up on the bridge where I told you to be?"

"No, I don't," Deet said.

Rogers put his hand on his forehead. "I didn't actually mean that as a question."

"Then why did you ask it like one?" Deet beeped.

"What are you doing there, Deet?"

"This is the first time since the jamming net was lifted that I have access to the greater Meridan network," Deet said. "I'm trying to do some research, Rogers, which you may not be familiar with since you don't seem accustomed to doing your job."

Rogers ignored the barb. Why did Deet sound so snippy all of a sudden? Could a robot really be snippy?

"I don't know what you're researching, but we need you up on the bridge," Rogers said. "We're all going to die if you can't help us sort out this IFF thing."

"For the love of all that is good," Belgrave said, "can you please stop saying those things out loud?"

"Shut up and fly the ship, Belgrave," Rogers barked. "And Deet, get your metallic ass up here on the double."

"How can I get up there more than once?" Deet asked.

"Expression!" Rogers yelled. *"Come to the bridge!"*

Deet was quiet for a moment. Only faint mechanical and electronic noises came in through the speaker. All around the bridge, the chaos of battle seemed overwhelming. Everyone looked as though they were at the end of their patience, their talent, and their sanity. Two marines were holding back a defensive-systems technician who was frantically seeking the actual, physical panic button, the effects of which were still sort of a mystery to Rogers.

"I don't want to," Deet said finally.

The bridge seemed to quiet down a bit. For reasons that Rogers could not understand, Commander Belgrave gave him a smug smile. Was this weird self-actualization and defiance Belgrave's fault? Rogers would keelhaul him. Which, he guessed, meant kill him if the keelhauling was done in space. Rogers might have been okay with that.

"I'm not giving you an option," Rogers said slowly. "I'm giving you an order. I don't care if you think you've discovered some sort of consciousness inside that circuitry of yours—you are still a member of my crew. Now get back here before I have you thrown in the robot brig for dereliction of duty."

"Kind of like when you were just off having a date with—" Belgrave began.

"*Shut up!*" Rogers yelled. "Deet, I am your boss, and I am telling you to get up here."

"You're not my boss," Deet said.

"I am your boss in so many different kinds of ways I don't know where to start explaining that to you," Rogers said. "I put you together from the fibers of the universe—"

"The trash pile," Deet said.

"The trash pile," Rogers conceded. "I rescued you from certain destruction at least three times, and I taught you how to tell jokes. I am basically God to you."

"Fine," Deet said. "I'm on my way."

The line cut out abruptly, and Rogers sat back in his chair. His brain felt tired. Having a contest of wills with a droid was not the way he should have been spending his time during a decisive space battle. If they couldn't get past this blockade and get back to Meridan headquarters, they might as well scuttle all their ships and go work for Snaggardir's.

"Brelle," Rogers said. He saw the young woman pop her head up over her console. "As soon as Deet gets onto the bridge, plug him into the system and have him start running whatever algorithm he can to try and clear this up."

"Yes, sir!" she called, then vanished behind her console.

"Until then, can we like, uh, do some kind of delaying tactic where we run around in circles and neither shoot at anyone nor get shot at?"

Commander Rholos, done with whatever business she had with S1C Brelle, was halfway back to the command platform. She conferred with Zaz for a moment, who was sweating profusely as he shouted into his microphone, using terms that Rogers was pretty sure had nothing to do with space warfare.

"Sweep left, Hound five four!" he yelled. "Get into the pocket and wait for the damn snap!"

Apparently, Hound five four didn't know what the hell Zaz was talking about either, since he promptly exploded. Recovery crews were working overtime trying to pick up all the ejection capsules. Rogers felt a grim seriousness settle over him as he looked out the window of the bridge at the eerily bright and colorful display that was modern space warfare.

Rholos approached him, uncomfortably close, and put her laminated sheet over her mouth as she spoke to him. This resulted in Rogers not being able to understand anything she was saying. When Rogers gave her a blank look, she got the picture and moved the sheet to the side.

"Captain," she said softly. "We can't sustain this for much longer. I'm not trying to be a doomsayer, but we're losing ships left and right. It's not like the battle with the Thelicosans, either; ships are being destroyed and there's not much we can do to help them."

Looking past Rholos out the window again, Rogers felt sick. This really wasn't what he wanted. He cleared his throat and tried to focus.

"What about the Thelicosan fleet?" he asked. "The Colliders. Has Grand Marshal Keffoule been in touch?"

"She checked in maybe an hour ago, but it's been mostly radio silence," Rholos said. "I'm not sure there's much she can do either."

The remnants of the Thelicosan fleet that had nearly blown them all to pieces were intermixed with the Meridan fleet outside, all fighting together to try to stop this amorphous ex-culture from visiting destruction on the galaxy and getting their revenge. The whole thing was a little surreal. They still didn't know what the Jupiterians really wanted—though anyone with any level of intelligence could probably guess—and, worse than that, they still didn't know who was on Furth.

"Any ideas?" Rogers asked quietly.

Rholos shook her head. "If we can't get the IFF fixed, the best thing I can come up with is just to shoot everyone."

"That doesn't seem very productive. What about a secret communication code that we can broadcast to only our ships?" Rogers raised his voice and repeated the suggestion to S1C Brelle.

"Not going to work, sir," she said. "Most of those ships are stolen, including all the cryptography inside the communication systems. It'd take longer than we have to reprogram the encryption and then somehow get all of the other ships in the fleet the new codes without also giving them to the enemy."

"Damn it," Rogers said. Where the hell was Deet? The minutes it was taking him to get to the bridge—if he hadn't gotten distracted and plugged himself into anything with a power outlet, the lecher—were costing them lives. There had to be something else they could do. Everyone but the Jupiterians was scared to shoot anyone. It might have been better if everyone just did nothing at all.

Rogers' eyes widened. It *would* be better if everyone just did nothing at all.

"I have an idea. Brelle, get Grand Marshal Keffoule on the line. I want her to hear this."

"Yes, sir."

As much as he didn't want to hear the voice of the former enemy commander who desperately wanted to marry him, it was important that they do this together.

"You've called me at one point six one minutes past the hour," her voice crooned over the speaker.

That goddamn ratio, Rogers thought. Just because everything between Keffoule and Rogers seemed to line up with the Golden Ratio, Keffoule thought it was destiny that they be together forever. But Rogers couldn't really stand to be in the same room as the cryptic, math-crazy woman for more than about one point six one seconds.

"Not now," Rogers said. "Not ever really. We've been over this."

"So you think," Keffoule said slowly. He could hear the crooked smile in her voice, and it made his skin crawl.

"Right. I've got an idea, Alandra, and I'll need your help. I'm about to tell everyone here."

"Go on," she said.

"Everyone listen up!" Rogers said, standing. Eyes started to turn to him. He took a deep breath and delivered his nugget of brilliance, to which he expected applause and cheers and hopefully not another promotion; the only thing above captain was admiral, and admirals were always getting hit by asteroids.

"We are going to employ my most practiced technique: sitting and doing absolutely nothing."

The unified blank stare of the bridge wasn't quite what he'd been going for.

"Sir," Commander Rholos said, "*The Art of War II: Now In Space* says 'inaction is the crow's meal . . . in space.'"

"You and I both know Sun Tzu Jr. is an idiot," Rogers said. "Hear me out. They know who to shoot, and we don't, right?"

"I'm getting some new ideas of who to shoot," the Viking said.

He hadn't even realized she'd made her way up to the bridge. How long had she been standing there, looking at him like she wanted to destroy him in not the good kind of way? Dimly, he realized the depth of his mistake by trying to keep her away from the battle, but he couldn't deal with it right now. Apologies and bootlicking could come later. The small but deadly Sergeant Mailn, who had become the Viking's de facto second in command despite not being an officer, had come as well, but she was already busy talking to some systems technicians about something Rogers couldn't hear.

Clearing his throat, Rogers tried to look away from her. "If they know who to shoot, and we don't, we simply stop shooting. I want orders transmitted to the entire fleet that everyone is to stand down and assume patrol patterns."

"You want us to just sit here and die?" Keffoule asked, her voice thin and icy.

"No, I want us to sit here and get shot at," Rogers said. "Shields can take a few blows if they need to, and that will give us what we need. The instant a ship opens fire, I want you to tag it manually and concentrate our fire on it until it *stops* shooting."

"That might actually work," Commander Belgrave said.

"Don't sound so shocked," Rogers shot back.

"They're going to hear us transmit these orders," S1C Brelle said. "No encryption, remember?"

"So what?" Rogers said. "What's the worst they can do—try to camouflage themselves further by also not doing anything at all? Then we all just become floating space junk for a little while until we can really decode the IFF and get back to running the blockade. At least nobody dies that way."

Despite not giving him the rousing, cheering response he wanted, everyone seemed to be on board with the idea. Without asking any further questions, Brelle started processing the order, and Zaz and Rholos started conferring quietly away from the command platform. Belgrave continued to fly the ship by pressing a button every few minutes to make sure they stayed out of the way, and the defensive systems continued to shoot out bursts of fire at incoming ships.

"Set a time for it all to happen at the same time," Rogers called over to Brelle. "Is five minutes enough time?"

"I'll need ten, Captain."

"Fine," Rogers said. "As long as we can synchronize." He squinted at nothing in particular, thinking. They'd need a good way to keep up with what would likely be a hell of a lot of note taking. Who would be good for that kind of mindless grunt work?

His eyes fell on the Viking and for a few seconds he forgot about the battle happening all around them. He kind of wished she could too, but the fact that she had one hand on her disruptor pistol and was clenching her teeth told Rogers that he was living in a pipe dream. It took a lot of courage to actually motion her to come toward him. Whether the courage was for confronting his own demise or confronting a very angry version of the woman of his dreams, he had no idea. Probably a bit of both.

"I'm glad you're here," he said as she approached, "because we're going to need some help. Bring up some of the marines to the bridge to help take notes. Marines can read, right?"

"Rogers . . . ," the Viking growled.

"Just checking," Rogers said. "I need them to help keep track of the ships that attack so we can mark them as enemies manually. Have them work with the defensive-systems team to get their datapads patched in so there's no lag time between figuring out which ship is an enemy and getting that information on our datalink."

"You want *my* marines to take notes?"

"I want them to help win a space battle—one that I totally swear I had no idea was going on while we were talking in the Peek and Shoot," Rogers said. "Look, you know as well as I do that if we don't get boarded, you're not going to see any action. At the first indication that we're going to see any fighting that doesn't involve giant spaceships, I'll let you know, alright? I promise. If that happens, you will be able to shoot *so many things*."

This seemed to brighten the Viking's spirits a bit. She didn't say anything, but she did take her hand off her holster and leave the bridge, ostensibly to go and get some troops to help with the tracking. They weren't signal analysts, of course, but without some automation—such as the kind that could have been provided by Rogers' *utterly useless* deputy droid—they could at least help speed up the process and slow down the casualty rate.

Casualty rate. He was sitting in a commander's chair thinking about casualty rates. What had his life become? He wished he could have deployed something like his antisalute sling that would have functioned as an anticommand sling. Or maybe he could try hanging himself in the zero-g room again. If Zergan could do it, so could he.

But then who was going to do this job? Was that what duty was? In comparison, death was lighter than a feather, duty heavier than a *mountainous, steaming pile of shit.*

In the following minutes, things seemed to move along just fine without Rogers' input. Zaz and Rholos were busy coordinating the fighters and heavy ships into positions where they'd be able to respond quickly to the first aggressor they marked. Brelle was calling ships frantically and giving specific time codes for the cease-fire. Marines were filing into the bridge and talking to the display technicians to get their datapads set up for input. The Viking was desperately trying to hide the fact that she was teaching one of them how to sound out words slowly—but, to her credit, it was only one of them and he was a water support technician. Nobody could really be responsible for those guys.

"Two minutes!" called Brelle. "Orders are out and acknowledged, sir."

Rogers shifted in his seat. He hated moments like these. They were the moments that a commander was really supposed to get the hell out of everyone's way, but he wanted very badly to be doing something. Drinking, mostly. Where the hell was Deet? When he found him, he was going to strangle him. Well, he didn't breathe, so maybe he'd like . . . slowly cut the power to

Deet's processors or something. He definitely should have been on the bridge by now.

"Get ready," Brelle shouted. The bridge got very quiet. Marines dutifully held their styluses over their datapads. The water-purification guy licked the tip of his.

"Implementation in three, two, one . . . ," Brelle called.

Suddenly war stopped. Meridan and Thelicosan ships completed their maneuvers, and the bright, colorful display of disruptor and plasma-cannon fire came to an abrupt and eerie halt. It was like someone had just unplugged the master transformer to a really twisted circus, and all the figurines and holograms suddenly died away. For a moment, it seemed that Brelle was right—the Jupiterians had intercepted the orders and were mirroring them to avoid being discovered. Ships were intermingling anew in ways that made even visual identification of them impossible.

"Well that didn't work," the Viking said.

"Wait," Rogers said.

"For what?" the Viking barked back.

"There's always that *one* guy . . . ," he said, his voice trailing off as he peered intently at the screen.

Seconds later, a medium-sized attack frigate, near the fringe of the battlespace, suddenly turned and fired.

"Hut, hut, hike!" Zaz screamed, his voice cracking.

Instantly the entire force of friendly ships opened fire. Shields crackled and died, and the Jupiterian vessel was torn apart in a puff of space dust that was as good of an explosion as there ever could be in a vacuum.

"Every fleet has their Flash," Rogers said.

"Did you call for me, skipper man?" the pilot not-very-affectionately known as Flash came over the radio. Rogers was surprised he was out there. Not because he wasn't certified to fly or anything, but Rogers was continually in disbelief that any of the Meridan Ravager spacecraft were big enough to hold the man's ego.

"No," Rogers said. "You can always assume the answer to that question is no."

Following the destruction of one of their ships, another few Jupiterian ships began to open fire as well. Marines and the communication troops began working furiously as the strategy of focusing fire on one ship at a time disintegrated. Within minutes, a cascading effect of panic wormed its way over the Jupiterian fleet. Rogers couldn't imagine what their radios sounded like now. The battlespace display stopped showing so many amber dots and started showing green and red ones as the manual IFF made its way into the datalink.

They were going to turn this around! Rogers could feel it.

"Wait," one of the marines said. "Damn it, I pressed the wrong button! How do I undo?"

"You can't undo," another marine said.

"No, not that button," Brelle said, pointing to the wrong marine's datapad. "This butto—"

"That's my lunch order!"

"Why are you ordering lunch?"

"Uh, because I'm hungry?"

They were absolutely not going to turn this around! Rogers could feel it. Human error started to creep into the system as things got more and more out of control. Even with the added help of the marines, there was simply too much data to handle, and every time someone made a mistake it took ten times as long to undo it than it had to mark the ship in the first place. As Rogers fought the rising urge to have a stroke, he stared at the display to find that they only had one-third of the ships identified. It was better than nothing, he supposed, but he really, *really* needed—

"Deet!" someone yelled.

Rogers whipped around to find his awkwardly built droid deputy sauntering onto the bridge like there wasn't a giant battle going on outside. His mismatched limbs, compiled from various components Rogers had found in the junk heap where he'd originally discovered Deet, made his gait somewhere in between a sugar-high zombie and a drunken gymnast.

"What?" Deet said. "What is everyone so panicked about?" He looked around the bridge, his horse-like head swiveling a full rotation, which always sort of creeped Rogers out. He made a few nondescript beeping noises and walked casually to where S1C Brelle was starting to sweat rather profusely.

"Are you serious right now?" Rogers asked. "I wanted you on the bridge hours ago, and you come in asking what everyone is so panicked about? What the hell were you doing down there?"

"Asking questions," Deet said cryptically. Rogers didn't really have time to dig into what kinds of questions might be asked by a mostly autonomous robot, and Deet didn't seem inclined to elaborate any further.

"Well I don't care what you were doing," Rogers began.

"Then why did you ask?"

"Shut up and plug in. Brelle, give him the rundown."

"Yes, sir," Brelle said, but Deet cut her off.

"I know what's going on." He extended his dongle—Rogers really hated it when he called it that—and plugged into one of the many combined data/power ports on the bridge.

"Oh really?" Rogers said, getting off the command platform and making his way toward them. He felt anger rising in his throat—not just frustration, but hot, seething anger. It wasn't a terribly familiar sensation to Rogers. He'd been irritated, annoyed, confused. He'd shouted a lot. But now he felt *fury*. "You really think you know what's going on?" Marines parted for him, fear in their eyes at the wrath of their commander. "I'll *tell* you what's—"

"Done," Deet said.

The display screen showing the disposition of forces suddenly and dramatically changed. All amber dots vanished and were suddenly replaced by accurate, definite red and blue dots indicating a perfect IFF representation of the battlespace. The bridge went totally silent.

"See?" Deet said. "Everyone had their panties in a barn for nothing."

The bridge went even more totally silent.

"It's 'bind,'" someone shouted.

Rogers took a long look at Deet, not knowing what to think. He'd sort of always wanted to electrically shock the prototype Froid, but he'd never wanted to actually cause him physical harm. What had gotten into him? He'd endangered everyone in the fleet by going off and pursuing personal interests in the middle of a space battle! What kind of absurdly selfish, inconsiderate person would do such a thing?

"By the way," Deet asked. "How was your date with—"

"Right!" Rogers yelled, very loudly. "Everyone back to your battle stations. Zaz, Rholos—take the data and form the most nonsensical battle plan you can come up with immediately. Do absolutely nothing that Sun Tzu Jr. tells you to do. Don't even run it past me—just execute. Good?"

Zaz and Rholos nodded and went into action. It wasn't long before the dots on the map began to swirl and things—the right things—began to blow up. Their temporary solution of concentrating fire only on the attacking ships had bought them a bit of an edge. It all happened so fast, Rogers didn't have a chance to start giving orders that didn't make sense. The ships in his fleet all seemed to know what they were doing—or, rather, not know what they were doing on purpose. This whole nonstrategy thing was getting kind of confusing.

"Sir," a signal operator yelled from the far corner of the bridge, where signal operators belonged. "We've intercepted a retreat order from the Jupiterian commander. They're bugging out!"

"I don't see any bugs," Deet said. "I just ran a scan in my software and I didn't see any there, either."

Rogers knew they were fleeing before the signal operator had finished his sentence. He could see the concentration of

Jupiterian ships beginning to move rapidly to the very Un-Space point they were trying to prevent the 331st from entering. Without their IFF advantage, the Jupiterians' odds weren't very good; the 331st and the Colliders were the numerically superior force by a large margin.

"I can't believe I'm asking this," Rholos said, "but, sir—should we pursue?"

Rogers stroked his beard, which seemed to be something one was required to do when making decisions that would kill people. He actually wondered if that is why Meridan dress and appearance expressly prohibited beards—they telegraphed your intent to the enemy.

"No," Rogers said. "Let them go. It's more important that we get home, and I don't want to lose any more ships just being vengeful."

"Got it, sir." Rholos offered a sharp salute, not seeming very celebratory at all for having just won their second major space battle. Rogers was two for two! Rholos started talking into her headset. "All forces pull back into formation and prepare to enter Un-Space as soon as it's clear of enemy forces. We're going home."

Home. What a concept.

"Touchdown!" Zaz yelled, his eyes wide and frantic. Three troops who Rogers didn't recognize upended a giant container of orange liquid over Zaz's head. Rogers fell back into his chair and tried not to cry.

Home, Sweet . . . Mother of Jesus It's All Gone to Hell

The rules of physics were difficult to ignore, but when you were in Un-Space, you kind of had to. Rogers was an engineer by trade, but even he didn't really understand the ins and outs of the strange faster-than-light transportation method. From what he knew, Un-Space had been discovered, not invented. When the Milky Way had collapsed—mostly due to the scientific exploits of careless Jupiterians—some things had gotten moved around that weren't really supposed to move. The resultant configuration of the solar system had revealed a point in space that wasn't really a point in space. Nobody really asked any questions; they were just happy that this new door gave them a web of subspace pathways that led exclusively to different areas of the Fortuna Stultus galaxy, which would become humanity's new home.

And now, traveling through a complicated series of Un-Space pathways to get back to Meridan headquarters on Merida Prime, Rogers wasn't keen on asking any questions either. He just wanted to put his feet on solid ground for a while and have a drink or twenty.

He also wanted to punch a droid in the face. Unfortunately, even while in Un-Space, one couldn't ignore the laws of physics completely.

"I feel like you should probably be having this conversation privately," Commander Belgrave said. "Praise in public, chastise in private, and all that."

"I'm not really sure I care how you feel," Rogers said. "Don't you need a nap or something after actually piloting the ship for the first time in a decade?"

"I haven't been the helmsman for a decade," Belgrave said, his mouth thin.

"Are you sure? Because it feels like it." Rogers turned to Deet. "What could have possibly been so important as to pull you away from following my orders?"

Deet seemed to consider for a moment, then beeped. "Considering the [EXCREMENT] quality of your orders, I can think of approximately one thousand four hundred and—"

"Deet," Rogers warned.

"What? You asked."

The bridge still buzzed with activity, albeit at a lower level of stress and panic. Most of the combat systems and communication desks were empty, since that stuff tended to not work properly in Un-Space, but troops coordinated repairs, shifts, and rearmament. All of it was still terribly unfamiliar to everyone, so it was mostly a ship-wide combination of people who didn't know what they were doing and people who didn't know what they were doing but who were pretending they did.

"What were you doing when you were down at the IT desk ignoring my orders?"

"I was searching the greater Meridan information network, since the jamming had been lifted. I had questions that I wanted answered."

Rogers frowned. "I didn't know droids could be curious."

"Neither did I," Deet said. "But apparently I am. Very curious."

"About what?"

"About all the things I told you before, Rogers," Deet said. "About where I came from, why I'm different."

Rogers leaned back in his chair a little bit, and someone came up to him holding a datapad that required his signature. Looking at it—something that he was positive ex-Admiral Klein never did, since cooks kept ending up on munitions duty—he saw that it was a request for . . . pudding. It didn't even really have any context. It simply said *Can I have pudding?* with a line for Rogers' signature.

"Did you eat your meat?" Rogers asked the troop, who silently bowed his head and turned away.

"How can you have any pudding if you don't eat your meat?" Rogers yelled after him.

"Anyway," Rogers said, wondering if this was the level of decision making that had caused Klein to go insane/chronically stupid. "We talked about this, Deet. I said that we had a job to do and that you could go research your origins, or whatever, after we were finished."

"But what if we never finish?" Deet asked. "What if you lead all of us into a fiery, miserable death?"

Belgrave cleared his throat.

"I am not going to lead us all into a fiery, miserable death," Rogers said. "We're going to go home to Admiral Holdt, and *he's* going to lead us all into a fiery, miserable death."

Belgrave cleared his throat again.

"Get a glass of water," Rogers said. "Deet, if we all die, it's not really going to matter, is it? Do you see what I'm getting at here?"

"No," Deet said.

"I'm saying that there are *more important things* going on right now than figuring out your operating system version number."

"What are you talking about?" Deet said. "It's version sixteen point two point three point five, beta."

Putting a hand on his forehead, Rogers tried to force his brain to stop functioning.

"Listen to me," Rogers said. "I need you to—"

"Sir!" someone shouted. Turning, Rogers saw an older man approaching the command platform who clearly had not read any of the instructions regarding dress and appearance. He had a full beard that was more suited to a caveman than a corporal, a pair of glasses that looked like they might have been salvaged from spare telescope parts, and, most bizarrely, three eyebrows. The man handed Rogers a datapad and saluted, his also non-standard-issue floppy hat flopping to one side floppily.

"Can I not get five minutes to yell at a robot around here?" Rogers muttered, looking at the datapad. Another request, this time for the zoo deck. Someone wanted to have "open time," where all the animals would be allowed to roam freely around the ship. The reasoning cited something about all of the animals having a sense of community with the rest of the crew.

"No, Tunger," Rogers said, passing the datapad back.

"Aw, but sir," Tunger said, removing the beard, eyebrows, hat, and glasses. Where had he gotten all of these disguises? "We're all one big family, aren't we?"

"One big family with a distinct lack of claw marks on our faces. There are lions down there, Tunger."

"They're friendly!"

Rogers thought back to their battle with the corrupted droids and watching Tunger ride the back of said friendly lion into battle.

"No."

"I never get to have any fun!" Tunger shouted as he stormed off. "I'm not allowed to talk the way I want to talk, be the spy I want to be, no beards, no animal family time . . ."

The corporal vanished, an unintelligible list of complaints echoing as he exited the bridge and the door closed behind him.

"Captain Rogers," Belgrave said. "Maybe I can lend a hand here."

"I am nearly positive that you can't," Rogers said.

"Have we talked about empathy yet, Deet?" Belgrave asked.

"No," Rogers said, interrupting them. "No. Stop. Look, he still doesn't even have a handle on telling good jokes and his philosophy is basically that of a pretentious thirteen-year-old with abandonment issues. If you're going to keep teaching him the finer points of being human, at least finish one thing before moving on to something else."

As was typical of this pair, Rogers apparently popped out of existence while they prattled.

"What is empathy?" Deet asked. "I am able to find the definition of this term, but unable to process it in a way that makes sense for my circuits."

Belgrave leaned back in his chair, his face settling into the familiar but totally inaccurate expression of a sage pedagogue. He steepled his fingers, a gesture that Rogers thought was equal parts awkward and ridiculous. Who had made that the signature pose for lecturing people?

"Empathy is like a flower," Belgrave began.

"Oh, yeah," Rogers said. "Let's use a simile to describe something to a droid that takes everything literally." He grabbed his own datapad to see if there was anything that he needed to take care of. His message queue mostly consisted of inane and unimportant requests that would have been better handled by the lowest possible person on the chain of command. One thing Klein had had right was that he never answered his own messages. Maybe Rogers needed an exec. Deet could do this stuff.

"Do you mean empathy is photosynthetic and pollinated by bees?" Deet asked.

Maybe Rogers needed a human exec.

"Told you so," Rogers said.

"Let me start again," Belgrave said, looking perhaps slightly less confident than he had a few moments earlier. "Empathy is the ability to repeatedly ask other people how they are feeling."

Rogers looked up. "That's not empathy."

Deet paused for a moment, then looked at Rogers. "How are you feeling, Rogers?"

"That is definitely not empathy," he said again.

Instead of acknowledging Rogers, Deet turned to Belgrave. "Did I do it? Did I do empathy?"

"We'll work on it," Belgrave said.

"No, you won't," Rogers said. "Because that's not empathy. You're not doing anything except annoying me, which you were proficient in long before taking emotional health advice from the helmsman."

Belgrave, finally reintroducing Rogers into his reality, bristled at the comment.

"Sir, I feel like disparaging a man based on his position in the crew is unbecoming of a flag officer."

"What's a flag officer?" Deet said. "Did someone promote the space semaphore guy?"

Rogers put his datapad down and pressed his palms against his temples. "No. Both of you please stop talking."

They both stopped talking, and Rogers immediately realized that he had asked Deet to come to the command platform for the express purpose of talking. Their idiocy was forcing him to contradict himself, which he did enough already without their help. He took a deep breath.

"Did you at least learn anything that might help us out?" Rogers asked.

"Well," Deet said, "I only have access to the same things that any Meridan government official has access to. I could do better if I was on Merida Prime and hardwired to something in Meridan headquarters."

"So you found nothing interesting while everyone around us was dying," Rogers said.

"That's not what I said. Just because I have access to the same information as everyone else doesn't mean that I can't use it better." Deet's center compartment opened up a bit, revealing what he'd started calling his "naughty bytes," which Rogers had to admit was kind of funny. Inside was a small holographic projector, useful for displaying slideshows or rude gestures that couldn't be accomplished with robot hands.

"I started cross-referencing public information about Snaggardir's and historical records about the downfall of Jupiter and the War of Musical Chairs."

Rogers nodded. Now that they knew that the omnipresent company was actually the center of the Jupiterian resistance—and had been for nearly two centuries—they might be able to deduce some other information about who they were, where they were, and what they wanted.

"And?" Rogers asked.

Images started to come out of Deet's naughty bytes, projecting a few faces that swirled around the Snaggardir company logo—which, Rogers realized, was literally a planet with an empty chair on top of it. Maybe that should have been a clue.

"This is the current board of directors of Snaggardir's," Deet said.

Four profiles floated in the air. Rogers didn't recognize any of them.

"Seems like a small board," Rogers said.

"The board is segmented into major and minor members. There are only four on the major board, and then there are an additional seven on the minor board. Almost everyone is somehow in the Snaggardir family, either by blood or by marriage. Sal Snaggardir is the boss."

A face came to the front that was the picture of shrewdness: balding and thin, with piercing eyes and an unconvincing smile. Rogers felt like he might inhabit the house at the end of the street that nobody was ever supposed to go near, the one into which all soccer balls disappeared forever.

"Sara Alshazari is the communications manager," Deet said,

displaying a severe-looking woman in her mid-forties. Rogers felt like he'd heard the name somewhere before, but wasn't sure. There were a lot of Saras in the galaxy.

"This is Gerd Szinder," Deet began. "He's director of sales, but his record has nothing to do with sales at all. He was an officer in the Thelicosan army before he got kicked out."

Rogers frowned. "Kicked out? Did he not know his calculus or something?"

"I haven't been able to figure that out yet," Deet said. "It's not publicly available information. Before that, however, he was fairly decorated, but not a top performer. This person, on the other hand . . . I can't find out any information about him at all."

A face that resembled a hard-boiled egg came to the forefront of the display. "This is Dr. Mattic. He's a technology expert who worked for different companies all over the galaxy for most of his life."

"Does he have a first name?" Rogers asked.

"Not that I can tell," Deet said. "It's pretty strange; every document simply refers to him as 'doctor' or Dr. Mattic. From his list of accomplishments, it's possible he got his first doctorate in technology at birth. If he's been active in the scientific community for so long, there should be records, but there's nothing."

Rogers leaned back and thought for a moment, looking at the faces. Given their previous occupations, it wasn't hard to figure out who did what for the revolution. But what could he do with this information? Honestly, it wasn't very in depth; most of this had probably already been deduced or discovered by the teams of analysts working for Holdt at headquarters. Sure, it was nice to know, but it wasn't going to help Rogers bust through any more blockades.

"Anything else?" Rogers asked. "You were down there for a long time."

"From what I can tell, the Snaggardirs are an offshoot of the original Jupiterian family that had a major part to play in the terraforming technology that collapsed the Milky Way."

Rogers' eyebrows shot up. "Really?"

The colonization of the other planets of the solar system had been instrumental in beginning its collapse. Some of the scientific aspects had been obfuscated—many say by the Jupiterian scientists who wanted to erase the part they played in the collapse—but there seemed to be no doubt that experimental terraforming technology had started the chain reaction. Rogers knew there was more to the story; he'd have to do some reading later. Up until now, it had just been ancient history.

"Okay. What else?" Rogers said.

Deet was quiet.

"That's it? That's all you found?"

"I discovered that Snaggardir's secret nacho cheese recipe isn't very secret. It was stolen from a movie theater in—"

"I cannot even begin to tell you how much I don't care about nacho cheese," Rogers said.

"Lots of people care about it," Deet said quickly. "It was one of the biggest lawsuits Snaggardir ever went through, and there were huge jalapeño farms that—"

Rogers held up a hand, and the images coming out of Deet vanished. The droid hung his head a little bit, a distinctly human expression that made Rogers realize that Deet was at least a tiny bit ashamed of what he'd done. Was empathy that far from regret? Rogers made a mental note to absolutely not ask this question out loud.

"Look, Deet," Rogers said. "Nacho cheese aside, this is all at least somewhat valuable information, but it doesn't excuse you shirking your duties and hanging everyone on the bridge out to dry."

Deet beeped. "The humidity level on this ship is very stringently controlled by automated systems."

"Expression," Rogers said. "There are many for screwing over your teammates. The bottom line is that you let me and everyone here down. I know you want to find out more about where you came from and why you're the way you are—and I told you I'd let you do it—but we have to take care of the potential crumbling of society as we know it first, okay?"

Deet didn't answer, and Rogers turned away from him to look out the window. So this was what war was like. The battle with Zergan's stolen fleet had been dangerous, but not very deadly. Circumstances had forced Zergan to go off half-cocked, and it made for a relatively bloodless victory for the 331st. This, however . . . this was a prolonged, pitched battle between two large space forces that had resulted in a nontrivial amount of space debris being created. Rogers fondly remembered the days—not very long ago—when being in the military had just meant your drinking was government funded. Now he was going to have to write letters home to families with one less member. Or at least he was going to have to tell someone else to write letters.

It would be wrong to simply not tell people, right?

His eyes drifted over to the Viking, who gave cleanup assignments to her marines and hurried them off the bridge. Sergeant Mailn busied herself next to her, looking worried and distracted. Not a typical expression for the young marine at all. The Viking seemed to sense that and put a hand on her shoulder, leaning close to mutter something Rogers couldn't hear. Mailn took a deep breath and nodded.

"I made a mistake too," Rogers said, loud enough that he was sure the Viking could hear. "I was wrong to take care of personal business during a battle." He dropped his volume again and grumbled to Deet. "I mean, the only reason anyone found out about me shirking my duties is because *you* were shirking *yours.*" Rogers grew louder again. "I solemnly vow to embrace my position as commander of this fleet in the coming trials."

Someone in the far corner of the room gave him a long, slow salute. Most people ignored him. The Viking gave him a considering look, as if she was trying to figure out if he was genuine. In truth, Rogers thought he was. But looking at that face, that big, beautiful, perfectly-shaped-for-head-butting face, he saw a reason to be good at his job. The better he could do in this chair, the less likely the Viking would come into harm's way.

There were probably other things he could do to keep her from dying too. Rogers thought for a moment. Back when he was still a lieutenant, which was practically yesterday, he'd been Klein's executive assistant. Supposedly for officers, that was a stepping stone in one's career, a box one had to check in order to be eligible for promotion to the higher ranks. Wouldn't it make sense, then, to pull the Viking off combat duty and offer her the position of exec? Then Deet could focus on deputy duties, Rogers would be near the Viking all day, the Viking would get bonus points on her résumé, *and* she would get shot at much less!

Wow, Rogers really felt like he was thinking like a fleet commander now. He wasn't totally sure if this was a good thing or a bad thing.

"Sir," Commander Belgrave said, looking at some displays at his station. "We'll be exiting Un-Space in just a few minutes."

"Right," Rogers said. "Starman Brelle, prep a channel with HQ and see if you can get Holdt on the line."

"On it, Skipper."

Rogers turned to Deet. "Do you understand what I'm trying to tell you, Deet? You need to have some patience."

Deet stared at Rogers for what seemed like a long time.

"How do you feel, Rogers?"

Rogers shut his eyes. "Don't empath me right now, okay? And that's really not the way you do it."

"Of course it is," Belgrave said. "Deet, come here. Let's go over Epicurus' agreement with evil."

"I'm also pretty sure that's not what that's called, either."

The droid-helmsman pair went off on their own tangents, which both bored and confused Rogers. Mailn and the Viking finished whatever conversation they were having, and Sergeant

Mailn looked like it cost her actual, physical effort to shake off whatever was on her mind and resume her constant shit-eating grin. The Viking clapped her on the back, which made Rogers extremely jealous, and Mailn headed toward the bridge exit.

"Sergeant Mailn," Rogers said. "A moment, please."

Mailn smoothly pivoted and started walking to the command platform, one eyebrow raised.

"Really?" she said. "'A moment, please?' Since when do you say stuff like that?"

"I'm trying to build an image," Rogers said.

"Oh? Instead of an escape pod?"

"Come on," Rogers said, turning a little red. "That was like . . . two major dramatic events ago. Let's let that one go, shall we?"

"Not if you don't stop saying stuff like 'a moment, please.' Shall I get you a monocle to wear?"

"Get your ass over here!" he barked.

Mailn nodded. "That's more like it."

"I find it difficult both to discern how one would only put one's ass in a location, and what your plans would be for that specific part of human anatomy if they were to succeed," Deet chimed in.

Rogers was just going to let Belgrave handle that one.

"You okay?" Rogers said to Mailn. She flinched at the question.

"I'm fine," Mailn said.

"Great," Rogers said. "I didn't really care, I just wanted to check that box. My date went badly."

Mailn folded her arms. "Oh really? Why do you think that is?"

"Oh don't get Socratic," Rogers said. "I hate Socrates. I don't need a lecture on the obvious."

"I am pretty sure you do," Mailn said, "since you seem to repeat mistakes so often. But what do you need a moment for?"

"I'm thinking about pulling the Viking from combat duty and making her my exec."

Mailn looked at him for a second, her mouth slightly open

and her eyes squinted. Then she let go a whooping laugh so loud that it caused heads on the bridge to turn and caused Rogers to recoil in his chair. Her face turned red, and tears started streaming down her eyes. At one point she did that motion with her hand that indicated she was having trouble breathing. She continued laughing to the point where she was making long, silent, sob-like motions with her shoulders and leaning over the railing of the command platform. Then she simply walked away, stumbling with drunken laughter all the way to the exit.

"Keep that a secret, will you?" Rogers called after her. "I want it to be a surprise."

"Trust me," she said, out of breath. "I wouldn't dare to say a thing." The door closed behind her.

Rogers felt extremely unsettled by that moment, like something was sitting in the pit of his stomach and trying to crawl its way out.

"She needed that," the Viking said.

Rogers looked back to find the Viking holding a few stray datapads and clearly preparing to go back down with the rest of her marines.

"Oh," Rogers said. "Hi. What do you mean?"

The Viking, whose expression had softened to the point where she actually looked like she wanted to be in the same room as him, indicated toward the door with a nod of her head.

"Mailn. I don't know what you said to her, but I haven't heard her laugh like that in weeks. Especially not with a visit to Merida Prime coming up. Thanks, Rogers."

"You're welcome?" Rogers said, really not sure what was going on anymore. He had no idea what anyone on this ship was thinking when they were talking to him. Maybe he needed a lesson in empathy from Belgrave.

"You see," Belgrave was saying, "the salute actually originated as a way for knights to greet each other. Since they wore visors, their noses were often itchy, but the inflexibility of the armor made it difficult to reach inside one's own visor. They'd lift their own visor, and another trusted knight would reach in to scratch their nose for them. That lifting motion became the salute."

Maybe Rogers didn't need a lesson in anything from Belgrave.

"Rogers," the Viking said. "I'm willing to give you another chance, okay? You kind of saved the day up here, even though you were being a little shit earlier. Maybe let's wait a bit, though."

"Yeah," Rogers said, swallowing. "I was being a little shit. Sorry."

The Viking shrugged. "Everyone has their moments." She grinned. "You just seem to have more than most. Let me know when you need a door kicked down."

She waved a fistful of datapads at him and left the bridge. Rogers was pretty sure he could think of at least one door he would like her to kick down right now, and it rhymed with "my stateroom." He supposed she was right, though. Maybe there wasn't time for all of that just yet.

"All hands, prepare for Un-Space exit," came the call over the speaker system. "Ten seconds."

There really wasn't a whole lot of preparation for the exit from Un-Space. You just suddenly became aware of physics again. Not that it didn't exist while you were traveling through the wormholes; you just sort of forgot that you existed in a physical space. When exiting back into standard space, many people had a crushing sense of self that momentarily caused them to do silly things like buy expensive cars and get tattoos. Rogers had done it plenty of times since he'd separated from the military as a sergeant, so he was used to it, but it had been a long time since the 331st had traveled through Un-Space as a unit.

"Three, two—Jesus, why didn't I hug my mom more? Um . . . sorry." The speaker abruptly clicked off.

"I am made of metal!" Deet cried. "I am completely made out of metal!"

Rogers squinted, looking at Deet. This may have actually been Deet's first trip through Un-Space, but . . .

"Uh, you're a robot," Rogers said. "You shouldn't have the kind of awareness that makes you do stuff like that after an Un-Space crawl."

"It's my fault," Belgrave said. "I insisted he was made out of rainbows, like everyone in our peaceful world. He was just arguing with me."

Rogers was about to reply, but he was distracted by something outside the window. Lots of somethings. They had come out of Un-Space at the very edge of the Merida Prime orbit, close enough to have the blue-green planet take up most of the viewing space. How long had it been since he'd been close to solid ground? Hell, how long had it been since he'd been this close to Prime? A lot of memories were buried underneath that atmosphere.

He swallowed, realizing it was probably the effects of Un-Space causing him to be so introspective, and allowed himself to be distracted by all of the other things going on around Prime. Namely, the gigantic presence of ships, stations, and small craft flying all over the place. Huge cruisers, battleships, flagships, fighters, cargo tugs—every type and class of ship imaginable were scattered around the planet, either parked in geostationary orbit or using thrusters to maintain their position. Everything looked both meticulously organized and hopelessly chaotic.

"Holy shit," Rogers whispered. This was what a galaxy at war looked like. Most of the ships present were Meridan, which made sense, but he saw a lot of spacecraft that he didn't recognize. Thelicosan ships were easier to spot, since he'd been working with them/trying not to be slaughtered by them for a while now. He thought he recognized a pleasure cruiser from Grandelle, which seemed a little unnecessary, but just about everything the Grandellians did was . . . well, grand.

Everyone on the bridge seemed to echo his sentiment, staring out the window with similar facial and verbal reactions.

"It's like an [EXPLETIVE] carnival arrived, except it's ready to kill everyone," Deet said.

"We're being hailed, sir," Brelle said.

"Well, hopefully they're not ready to kill us," Rogers said. At this point, with Jupiterians all over the place, a fleet of any size popping into existence nearby would be enough to spook anyone. "Bring it online—"

Before Rogers could finish his sentence, a shuddering blast shook the ship. He heard the shields crackle, and bright green flashes turned everything on the bridge into dim, verdant reflective surfaces. Noises of surprise popped up all around him.

"You are to stay in your present position until authorized to move forward," came a sharp male voice over the radio. "Power down your engines and prepare to be identified."

A pair of Meridan fighters—Ravagers—swooped by the bridge, so close that he could actually see the cores of their engines as they made a sharp turn to avoid flying into his command chair.

"How about you add a 'sir' to the end of that threat, flyboy?" Rogers barked back over the radio. "This is Captain Rogers, commander of the 331st. Admiral Holdt is expecting us."

Wow, he'd never really said that out loud before. It sounded so . . . official. So powerful. He might have gotten goose bumps. He might have even heard a French horn playing a dramatic line somewhere in the background as he made the announcement.

No, that was Tunger.

"Tunger, not now, please," Rogers said. "I'm also somewhat baffled that you know how to play French horn."

"I know quite a lot of things, old chap," Tunger said. "I mean, sir."

"We are verifying all identities before they are allowed into the group," the fighter pilot said. "Stand by—sir."

"That's better," Rogers said.

A tension settled on Rogers and worked its way through his jaw and face. Warning shots being fired across the bow of a friendly ship, people actually patrolling around Merida Prime . . . this wasn't the galaxy he'd grown up in. What he *should* have been doing right now was turning on the beer light and kicking back to play some cards or just bullshit other troops with self-inflating stories that may or may not have ever happened. This military was way too serious.

Another shot crackled the shields.

"Hey!" Rogers yelled over the radio. "We're just sitting here waiting like you told us to." He shot a glance at Belgrave. "That *is* what we're doing, isn't it?"

Belgrave gave him a nod, gesturing at the controls he wasn't touching and almost never actually touched.

The voice of the fighter pilot came back over the radio, but he clearly wasn't talking to Rogers.

"You idiot, I already did the warning-shot thing!" he said.

"You *always* get to do the warning-shot thing," a second, thinner voice said—probably belonging to the second Ravager. "Besides, you didn't tell them to cease and desist and wait to be recognized and all that."

"I totally did! You weren't listening. You never listen."

"Oh, now I never listen. Here we go."

Okay, so maybe this military wasn't serious enough.

"Please stop shooting my ship," Rogers said.

"Sorry," said the second fighter pilot.

"Thank you for apologizing," said the first fighter pilot, perhaps a bit primly.

"I wasn't saying sorry to *you*." The transmission cut off.

Rogers was in the middle of deciding whether he'd prefer that pair of Ravager pilots over Flash when Admiral Holdt finally came on the radio.

"Rogers!" he said. "Took you long enough."

"We were kind of busy fighting our way through a blockade, sir," Rogers said flatly.

"You broke through one of the blockades?" Holdt said. "Damn. We have forces holed up all over the galaxy that can't get back to Prime because of those. I want a full debrief when you get planetside."

"You want me to dock?"

"No, I want you to bring your command crew here to HQ so we can strategize. Park the 331st somewhere and take a shuttle."

"That's fine," Rogers said, "but I brought some backup as well. The Colliders are here with me. Well, any ships that didn't defect to the Jupiterians, anyway."

"Good," Holdt said. "Park them with the 331st and bring their commander too."

Rogers felt a sinking in his stomach. He really wished he hadn't said anything.

"Do I have to?" he said, not at all whining even a little bit.

"Yes," Holdt said. "Holdt, out." The transmission clicked off.

"Aw, man," Rogers said.

"What is it?" Deet asked.

Rogers sighed and settled back in his chair. "Nothing. Starman Brelle, send a hail to Grand Marshal Keffoule. Please tell her she needs to come to our ship for purposes that expressly have nothing to do with marriage."

Keffoule's Errand

Alandra Keffoule let a sly smile slip across her face. He had gone out of his way to mention marriage again. It really could only mean one thing: he was over that grumpy, muscle-wrapped marine and was planning a romantic rendezvous on Merida Prime, the place of his birth. She would meet his family, make gracious small talk over dinner. Say "grace" instead of "Graze" before eating. Whatever it took to adapt to Meridan customs, Keffoule would consider. Previously this had been all about integrating Captain Rogers into her own Thelicosan family, but now that things in the galaxy were so . . . uncertain, perhaps she could compromise on a few things.

Brushing her dark, tangled hair out of her face, Alandra took a deep breath and looked out at the chaotic mess of ships. She'd never been this close to Merida Prime before. Many of her more covert engagements had taken her to Meridan space, but nothing this close to the center and certainly nothing this close to all of these ships.

The bridge of the *Limiter* ran smoothly and quietly, the silent efficiency of the highly trained Thelicosan Navy hard at work. The only person making any real noise was Leftennant Faraz, whose face still looked a little black and blue. He repeatedly yelled "What?" at anyone who was—or appeared to be—talking to him. Alandra gave him a little more leeway than she would other troops. After all, she had kicked him in the face. Twice.

Xan, her ever-faithful attendant, suddenly appeared next to her following the telltale sound of the Chariot platform approaching, which was reminiscent of high-pitched bubbles. His face, saggy both from the ritualistic face weights and his New Neptunian personality, had the tiniest hint of sadness in it. It was almost impossible to detect any sort of emotion from that weathered face, but she knew it was there. And she knew why.

"Grand Marshal," he said, his voice echoing inside his own cheeks, "it is time."

Alandra swallowed. She would not show weakness here on her bridge. Death was a part of war, part of their jobs. If she was so derailed by a single death, she had no right to stand up here and call herself the commander of the Colliders.

"Fine," she said softly, stepping onto the Chariot. Xan silently whisked them away into the Circus Tubes through which they could navigate to practically anywhere on the ship. Alandra tried very hard not to think of where they were going as the guts of the *Limiter* zoomed by. She noticed that the wedding cake she'd ordered made for her and Rogers still stood untouched in the refrigeration room. How long would it keep before it went bad?

They zoomed silently through the ship, her heart beating a little faster than it should have, until they came to a quiet, nearly empty room down near the very bottom of the ship.

It took all of her will to step off the Chariot, but eventually her feet were on the floor.

"That will be all, Xan," Alandra said.

The only indication that Xan had heard her was the bubbling

and puttering of the Chariot zooming away. The room they'd arrived at, cold and dispassionate like everyone was supposed to be during war, held only one thing: the man who had been her best friend and deputy.

She touched her hand to the casket. Alandra knew there were other duties that desperately needed her attention—answering a lot of questions from the Council, for one—but she needed this moment more. Edris Zergan had been a friend. No, he'd been more than a friend. He'd been a comrade-in-arms, a loyal devotee, the right angle to her hypotenuse. There had been many years when Alandra had thought that they'd eventually be married, if they could ever disentangle themselves from their careers. An unlikely scenario, given both of their dispositions toward greatness and duty, but a possibility nonetheless.

Looking down at the casket—a drab, black thing that looked more like a rejected children's building block than a monument to death—Alandra took a deep breath. Had he *really* been a friend? All those years, he'd secretly been working for the Jupiterians. He'd secretly *been* a Jupiterian. How much of what they'd experienced together could she trust? Was it all just an elaborate ruse to follow her to the position of fleet commander, then usurp her authority for the advancement of the Jupiterian cause?

But no. Edris had said he wanted to "recruit" her. He'd wanted to keep her with him. Perhaps he'd been pretending for a time, but they had truly been friends at the end, and he'd truly been regretful that they'd had to part ways.

Then he somehow hung himself in zero gravity. For reasons she did not understand, this fact infuriated Rogers.

"You idiot," she said suddenly, her voice trembling.

"I am sorry, Grand Marshal," Xan said. "Have I done something wrong?"

She jumped. "Xan!" she barked, whirling around. "I told you that would be all!"

Xan bowed and zoomed off into the Circus Tubes. When had he come back?

Alandra sighed. What was she going to do with that man? So faithful, but a little bit too much like an overprotective father than an assistant sometimes. And so absurdly sneaky, even when he didn't want to be. She knew he was just concerned about her.

Turning back to Edris' casket, she felt like whatever she'd been about to say had been stupid and immature. First of all, he was clearly dead and could not hear her. Second of all, Alandra generally did not like airing her grievances out loud. Edris knew she was furious with him for betraying her, furious at him for dying, furious at him for their last interaction being a spinning back kick to the face. No matter how professional they'd been together, Edris Zergan could always turn her into a bratty little girl with a few choice words and his wolfish smile.

And now this. The casket was closed, so she couldn't see his face, but there was a clear label on the outside: 1 EA. TRAITOROUS ENEMY COMMANDER/FIRST OFFICER OF THE *LIMITER*. She frowned. Yes, it was accurate, but they could have at least spelled out the word "each." Maybe assigning mortuary affairs as an additional duty for the supply clerks had been a bad idea.

Something stirred inside of Alandra as she looked blankly at the casket. Before hatching the plan to marry Captain Rogers, she'd been resigned to her fate of being put out to pasture after her . . . incident in the F Sequence. Edris had always pushed her to resist that feeling, to never let go of her ambition and always seek redemption. Perhaps he didn't want that to involve marrying an enemy fleet commander, but they had been two paths to the same goal as far as she was concerned. He just hadn't understood that.

"I will do it," Alandra said, breaking her rule about delivering a monologue to an empty room. But really it was just four words, not a long, detailed explanation of what they meant. Everyone in the mortuary who wasn't dead—namely just her—knew exactly what she'd meant. It was time to throw off the ragged old cloak she'd been given by the Thelicosan Council, throw off the burdens of the jungle that had nearly turned her into a wild animal. There was a war to be fought.

Unholstering her datapad, she inputted the codes that told the ship that she, as commander, was officially recording the death of Edris Zergan, dispatching messages to his next of kin, and authorizing the destruction of his remains. A small forklift of sorts emerged and took the casket away as she put her datapad back in its holster. Alandra couldn't watch it go.

Not because she was that emotionally disturbed, but because someone had just thrown a flash-bang grenade into the morgue.

Instinctively, Keffoule found herself rolling across the floor and reaching for her sidearm, which she didn't have. Instead, she managed to draw her datapad again, and when the haze cleared from her vision she found herself using her index finger to repeatedly send an email in the general direction of Secretary Vilia Quinn. The blond, sharp-featured bureaucrat was completely unaware that she was about to be obliterated by infinite "RE: RE: RE: FWD:" tags of a message subject line, since she was currently screaming with her hands over her eyes.

"Gaaahhh!" Quinn said, which was very unlike her. Much as throwing a flash-bang grenade was also unlike her.

Unfurling herself from her crouching return-fire position, Alandra stood up and holstered her deadly datapad. It wasn't the first time she'd been flash-banged—it wasn't even the first time she'd been flash-banged in a morgue—but it was definitely the first time she'd been flash-banged by a politician.

"Quinn!" she shouted, but the secretary was now covering her ears, tears streaming down her eyes. Keffoule wiped her own tears away—a totally natural response that had nothing to do with emotions—and punched Quinn in the arm.

"Quinn!" she repeated. The physical shock of being hit in the arm snapped Quinn out of her panic, and she opened her wet eyes to look at Alandra with a strange mix of shock, embarrassment, and terror.

"*Grand Marshal,*" she screamed, much too loudly. Was there nobody on this ship who didn't have some kind of trauma-induced hearing problem? "*I came to speak with you.*"

"I gathered that," Keffoule said, the ringing in her own ears just starting to fade away. "I'm not entirely sure why you felt the need to deploy a nonlethal explosive to do so."

"Ah, yes," Quinn said, turning red. Alandra frowned. Quinn never turned red. Then again, she never threw flash-bangs, either. "That. I apologize for the inconvenience. I've only just become familiar with these, and I fear I pulled the pin accidentally. They are much more complicated than Molotov cocktails."

Keffoule could agree with that, she supposed. She nodded, accepting the apology. Much had changed between the two of them since the attempted Jupiterian takeover of the Colliders. Despite her meek appearance and flawless track record of annoying Keffoule at every turn, there was no denying that Quinn had played a significant role in the recapture of the *Limiter.*

"What is it that you need?" Alandra said. *And why couldn't it wait until I was on the bridge?*

Quinn hesitated for a moment.

"I believe we might have gotten off on the wrong foot."

"Several months ago?" Alandra asked, her eyebrow raised.

"Yes. I mean, obviously we're not still on that same foot; we've moved on to other feet. There are other . . ." Quinn blinked rapidly and stopped talking. "I'm trying to say that I understand I have been a thorn in your side for quite some time."

"That's putting it mildly," Alandra said. She saw the woman scrunch her face up, and for some reason Alandra felt remorse for the barb. Maybe it was the death of a friend/traitor that was playing with her emotions. She took a slow breath.

"I haven't been the easiest to work with either," Alandra said.

"I deliberately kept you in the dark on things so I wouldn't have to deal with your opinion."

"Intergalactic law isn't exactly opinion," Quinn spat back.

Alandra shrugged. "That's your opinion. Did you really come all the way here so we could mutually apologize for being irritating?"

Quinn narrowed her eyes. "I am not irri—" She stopped herself. "Never mind. No. I came here to make a request."

Ah, Alandra thought. *Of course she wants something.* Rather than asking her, Alandra simply waited for Quinn to continue speaking. Despite considering herself a professional, Alandra couldn't help but enjoy the next few moments of Quinn clearly trying to figure out the right way to make her "request." Quinn had been bombastic at times, particularly when she thought someone wasn't filling out forms properly, but she'd never been quite this . . . adolescently shy and bumbling.

Finally Quinn broke the silence. "I want you to help me be more badass."

"What?" Alandra said.

"I just mean that you're always solving problems one way and I'm solving them in another way," Quinn continued hurriedly. "Each of us has strengths, and now that we're clearly both in agreement to put our differences aside, perhaps we could instead *use* those differences to enhance each other. Punching people in the face felt *so amazing,* it was like—"

Quinn cut herself off and appeared to be slyly measuring her pulse by grabbing her own wrist. Her mouth moved in the shapes of numbers. *One. Two. Three.*

"Are you sure you're well?" Alandra asked. "Did you get a medical checkup after the battle?"

"I'm fine," Quinn said. "In fact, I believe I am better than I have ever been. But whatever intuition carried me through the attempted takeover, it seems to have vanished. I keep trying to learn a bit more about the military part of civ-mil relations, but I'm not very good at it. I just flash-banged both of us, for Newton's sake, and yesterday I crashed a flight simulator."

"Everyone crashes flight simulators," Alandra said. "That's what they're for."

"No," Quinn said. "Somehow I dislodged the main compartment from the simulator and physically crashed it into another simulator. I never even got to the part where you turn the system on."

"I see," Alandra said. "And you don't think that this sort of training might be in direct violation of your status as a noncombatant?"

Quinn's face distorted, and she looked away. Alandra had hit her right in the bureaucracy.

"It's not for practical use," Quinn said. "Understanding your way of life helps me be a good liaison. Like studying the culture of a place in which you are a foreign diplomat."

"Right," Alandra said. She sighed and folded her arms. She really didn't have the time or the patience to take a "Council dog," as Zergan had called her, and turn her into a wolf, especially for no good reason. But what harm could there be in entertaining the idea for a few minutes longer? Her shuttle to the *Flagship* wouldn't depart for some time.

She might have gotten a wave of goose bumps thinking about meeting with Rogers. She hoped the huge marine wasn't with him. Alandra would hate to have to kill her.

"And you're asking me this in the morgue because you'd like to start your lessons by seeing how to hide bodies more efficiently?" Alandra offered. She gestured grandly at the small, thankfully underused room.

Quinn recoiled as though someone had put a snake in her coffee—something Keffoule could also show her if she liked. "What? Do you *do* that? No!" She cleared her throat, composing herself. "I'm asking you here because I knew you'd be alone. It's not something I want the entire bridge to know, exactly. Or my superiors. They might not think it's in my job description, and then I'd have to petition the Council for a rewrite of the job description manual and there would be so many signatures required—"

"Yes, I see," Alandra said. "Unfortunately, I fail to see how this benefits me in any way. My time is valuable, Secretary Quinn, and unless you haven't noticed, there's a galactic war going on right now. I've been asked to accompany Captain Rogers as a Thelicosan ambassador to Meridan central command."

"That's exactly how this benefits you," Quinn said. "You'll need ambassadorial skills. Communication, negotiation, mastery of subtlety and nuance. The things that make me good at my job are the things you lack."

Alandra bristled. "I do not lack these skills."

"You attempted to make a Meridan man marry you by kicking him in the face and taking him captive aboard your ship."

"The golden ratio is—"

"Not at all relevant in issues of intersystem diplomacy, Grand Marshal," Quinn said. "Something like that would never hold up in the courts, even in the Thelicosan courts. You are very competent in many areas, but this is one where you could use some help. If the Council ever found out about what you did . . ."

Tension blossomed in Alandra's chest. Of course the Council was going to find out what she'd done. Quinn was likely sending weekly reports to her superiors, and diving across an intersystem boundary while mistakenly transmitting "We're invading" was not likely a detail she would leave out.

"You . . . ," Alandra began.

"I will not be submitting any reports with those details in them," Quinn said. "That's the other thing I wanted to talk to you about. While I believe your actions to be very misguided, perhaps even disturbing, they did short-circuit a Jupiterian plan to take over the Colliders. While my duties require me to relay such information to the Council, I will be . . . losing some of my paperwork. I've already canceled a report that was slated to send after communications were reestablished."

Considering this for a moment, Alandra wondered if perhaps she'd misjudged Secretary Quinn. She'd always seemed like an annoying puppy to her, with her impeccable and omnipresent hair bun standing as a testament to just how anal retentive a person could be. But this was clever, even devious. Suddenly Alandra's eyes went wide as she realized what was going on.

"Blackmail?" Alandra said. "Are you blackmailing me into teaching you how to be worse ass than you are now?"

"'More badass,' I think the phrase is. You can't make it a comparative," Quinn said. "And the fact that it took you that long to figure out that I might be blackmailing you is exactly why you need my skills."

Alandra was about to teach Madam Secretary about the link between blackmail and black eyes. Quinn must have noticed the subtle shift of Alandra's right foot—the foot she used for spinning back kicks—because she interjected once more.

"But no, I am not blackmailing you. I am doing you a favor as a gesture of goodwill." She shrugged. "I wanted to reset things between us and then let the rest work itself out."

Goodwill certainly wasn't something Alandra was used to spreading. She could spread chaos, violence, confusion, even a little bit of stomach flu if she had the proper authorizations and the target had poor hand-washing hygiene. But goodwill? She wasn't even totally sure she knew what that meant.

"Fine," Alandra said. "I'm not sure I care about goodwill, but I will teach you some basic military techniques if you do not embarrass me in front of the Council. At least not until Rogers and I are officially married."

Quinn looked like she was about to say something, but she very wisely kept her mouth shut.

"And you can help me become a better negotiator," Alandra concluded with a nod.

"I think that's fair," Quinn said. She rocked on her heels a little bit, her hands balled into fists at her side, clearly excited like a little girl outside a planetarium. Her face, however, remained still.

Pulling out her datapad, Alandra called Xan.

"Xan," she said, "how long do we have until my shuttle is ready?"

"Twenty minutes," Xan said from about six feet away. The Chariot was parked next to him.

Alandra jumped—Quinn actually squeaked—and pointed an accusatory finger at the face-weighted New Neptunian immigrant.

"By Kepler's rotating balls!" she yelled. "How long have you been there?"

"Since you called me," Xan said.

Alandra looked at him, then looked at her datapad, then back at him. Xan seemed to be making less sense every day since the incident with the Meridan fleet had reached its apex.

"Alright then," Alandra said, calming herself. She turned to Quinn. "We have time for a little work now. Let's start with face punching."

"Why aren't you coming?" Rogers asked, trying as hard as he could to make sure he didn't sound whiny.

"I've got stuff to do here," the Viking said. "I want to make sure my marines get a shot at shore leave before we go out and do whatever ridiculous thing I am sure you are going to get us into."

Rogers and the Viking stood in the shuttle dispatch waiting room, doing whatever one does in a shuttle dispatch waiting room.* The whole room sported an off-brown color scheme, complete with beige shag carpet and vending machines that, for reasons Rogers did not understand, only took paper money. Rogers couldn't remember the last time he'd seen physical currency,

---

* Typically, one waits for shuttles.

never mind used it. An old, creaky fan rotated in a crooked circle on the ceiling, and the distinct smell of cigarette smoke came from a thin paper air freshener hung from the bottom of the fan. It was labeled THE GOOD OLD DAYS.

The room was empty except for the two of them and one guy who appeared to be sleeping there on a regular basis. Rogers discovered by visual inspection that it was S2C Ernie Guff, the space semaphore operator, still nursing a broken wrist.

"Don't you have a lieutenant or something that can do that for you?" Rogers asked. "It's just scheduling work."

The Viking shrugged. "Not really. I'm good at it."

She's good at scheduling work, Rogers thought. *I bet she's also good at managing messages and calendars, too.* His plan to take the Viking out of the fight by promoting her to executive assistant seemed more and more brilliant every second. He wasn't quite ready to spring the good news on her just yet, though. Maybe when they got back from Prime.

"Well that's too bad," he said. "I kind of figured maybe we could, you know, find someplace to go once we got planetside."

The Viking's chuckle rumbled just slightly louder than Guff's snoring.

"Slow your roll," she said, but her expression darkened. "Besides, I hear you've got your girlfriend coming. I don't feel like ripping anyone's throat out today."

Keffoule. It was always Keffoule. Everything that woman had touched turned to shit. He really wished he'd been able to convince Holdt that this rendezvous should be Meridan personnel only.

"I'm completely baffled at how everyone seems to think I've got the hots for a woman I have repeatedly told to leave me alone forever." Rogers sighed. "Anyway, it wasn't my choice. She's useful for the whole war thing, but as soon as that's over I want to be as far away from her as physically possible. With you, maybe."

"We'll see," the Viking said. "I only came down here to—"

The door to the waiting room opened, and in walked Sergeant Mailn and Deet, who appeared to be in the middle of a very passionate discussion.

"That doesn't make any sense at all," Mailn said. "The origin of the laws of armed conflict had nothing to do with salami."

"Then why were they made at the Genoa Convention?" Deet asked. "Commander Belgrave told me all about them."

"What are you doing here?" the Viking asked.

Deet and Mailn looked at each other, each of them trying to figure out which one she was talking to.

"I'm going to Merida Prime," they both said simultaneously.

"Oh no you're not," Rogers and the Viking also said simultaneously.

All the speaking in unison really set a strange mood, so everyone just sort of stopped talking for a second to let that settle.

"You're not coming with me," Rogers said to Deet. "Didn't we already talk about me needing someone else to take care of the ship while I'm gone?"

"We're in a holding position in a tightly controlled space-docking area," Deet said. "CARL can do that."

CARL—the Command Automated Response Lexicon—was a relatively dumb artificial intelligence used primarily so that Commander Belgrave could have even less of a real function on the ship. Despite still being a little angry at Deet for his stunt during the space battle, Rogers had to admit he was right.

"Fine," Rogers said. He turned to the Viking, who was looking at Mailn with a blank expression. "But why shouldn't Cynthia come? I could probably use a marine or two down there in case I get into any bar fights."

"I'm not sure whether to resent that comment or agree with it," Mailn said, giving Rogers a sour expression and a quick elbow to the ribs, which Rogers was unable to duck, since one didn't really duck out of the way of an elbow to the ribs, and ducking was his only real means of defense.

Mailn and the Viking spent a long moment looking at each other in a way that told Rogers that either there was something else going on here or they were scared of anyone speaking in unison again.

"I really don't think it's a good idea," the Viking said, sounding uncharacteristically serious.

"Nothing is going to happen," Mailn said. "We're just going to meet with the head honchos, or whatever, and find out what our role in all of this is going to be." She waited a moment, then shrugged and added quietly, "And maybe I'll get some shore leave out of it too."

"Sure," Rogers said. "You can have some shore leave. Everyone could use a break."

"Is nobody listening to me here?" the Viking said, leaning on her words in a way that kind of made her sound ridiculous. "There are things that would keep you better occupied here on the ship. And probably more relaxing."

Rogers frowned. "I can't think of anything on the ship that's particularly relaxing. And wouldn't you rather I have a chaperone with Miss Kick-You-in-the-Face-and-Marry-You around?"

The Viking narrowed her eyes and looked at him. "Do you *need* a chaperone, Rogers?"

Rogers swallowed hard. "Um, maybe bodyguard is a better term? And since you're not coming—"

"Fine!" the Viking said. "Fine. Look, Mailn, you're an adult. Just do me a favor and don't do anything stupid down there, okay?"

Mailn shrugged, avoiding the Viking's gaze.

"Are either of you going to tell me what the hell is going on here?"

"No," the Viking and Mailn said in unison. Then both looked at each other and said "Damn it!" again at the same time.

"Everyone stop talking," Deet yelled.

"Captain Rogers," came an announcement over the waiting

room speaker, which crackled with either static or the announcer eating a bag of potato chips, "your shuttle is ready for departure at dock seventeen. Please report with your crew and supplies for immediate takeoff."

"Right," Rogers said. "It's time for us to get out of here. Deet, you can come if you really want to, but if I catch you plugging into random computers I am going to amputate your dongle."

Deet made a whirling noise. "I will cut off your [EXPLETIVE] dongle and make you eat it."

"I don't have a dongle," Rogers said.

"Yeah, that's what all the ladies tell me," Deet said.

"Oh go expletive yourself," Rogers said.

The Viking and Mailn exchanged another look full of meaning. Rogers was getting the idea that maybe Mailn had more of an agenda on this trip planetside than she was letting on. If it was really going to screw things up, though, the Viking would have told him. Probably. Either way, a marine sergeant, a psychotic math-happy Thelicosan, a droid, and some guy who'd gotten promoted to captain via a combination of accidents and asteroids were about to go talk to the most powerful people in the Meridan military. This was serious business.

Suddenly Rogers remembered another bit of serious business.

"Ah! Damn it—I almost forgot the most important thing. Hang on a second." He pulled out his datapad and pushed a couple of buttons until he got to the supply depot. A mumbly female voice answered.

"Get me Corporal Suresh," Rogers said into the datapad. "I've got a list of supplies I want him to get once I get dry dock approved on Prime."

Rogers paused for a moment.

"Actually, there's only one item on the list: beer."

Prime Beef

"I don't understand how you manage to show up everywhere I need to be," Rogers said, "despite my every attempt to make sure of the exact opposite."

Corporal Tunger gave what might have been an apologetic shrug. His uniform looked uncharacteristically crisp and tidy, and his face absolutely brimmed with excited energy as he bounced up and down in the shuttle seat. His seat belts had been locked into place before the rest of them had boarded, and it looked as though he was already halfway through his third or fourth coloring book.

"I think I've gotten used to coming on your adventures, sir!"

"But this is specifically a closed manifest," Rogers said. "You can't just manifest yourself onto a closed manifest."

Tunger shrugged again. "I don't know anything about all that, sir. I just asked if I could come and they said yes."

"Who are they?"

Rogers didn't get an answer. Keffoule, who had barely said a word since they'd boarded the shuttle together, sat across from Rogers with that creepy half smile of hers. She hadn't changed much in the short amount of time since they'd last spoken in person, but there was something different about her disposition that Rogers couldn't quite place. It wasn't that she was more creepy (though she was) or that she was more terrifying (she also was), but more like she was keeping secrets. Maybe she'd gotten word from her own command and now held some secret intelligence. Rogers had no idea who she'd been in contact with since the end of the battle with Zergan. Whatever it was, Rogers didn't like it.

She'd brought another figure with her, the saggy-faced priest/assistant Xan. He didn't look terribly thrilled to be along, but then again he didn't look terribly anything at any point in time.

Xan locked eyes with Rogers, and Rogers felt himself squirming a little.

"I hope your intentions of bringing the Grand Marshal along are pure," he said aloud. For some reason, Xan seemed to think Rogers was leading Keffoule on, despite Rogers spending nearly one hundred percent of his energy telling Keffoule to leave him alone.

"You do realize," he said, turning to Keffoule, "that I was specifically ordered by my headquarters to bring you along?"

"Of course," she said, her thick and sultry voice somehow cutting through the hum of the shuttle's engines. No matter how Keffoule spoke, it always sounded like she was right next to your ear, her hot breath worming its way through your ear canal and into the parts of your brain that had made up all of the monsters in your closet when you were a little kid. "I am well aware of your intentions, Captain Rogers."

The way she leered at him indicated that she had absolutely no idea what his intentions were. Up in the cockpit, which was open to the small but comfortable passenger area, the pilot and the copilot were chatting quietly to each other through their headsets and pressing buttons.

"Atmo entry in sixty," the copilot called back.

Rogers grumbled to himself. Atmospheric reentry was one of his least favorite parts of space travel.

"Sixty what?" the pilot asked, loud enough for the rest of the passengers to hear. "Seconds? Minutes? Months? You gotta be specific."

"I agree with this," Deet said. "Not showing units in any physics derivation makes the formula impossible to understand. You also get a bad grade."

"I understood perfectly," Rogers said.

"What are you, some kind of pilot?" the pilot snapped back.

"Actually," Rogers said, "yes. I also have eyes. The planet's right in front of us."

The blue-green hue of Merida Prime cast a glow throughout the inside of the shuttle, and it gave Rogers some unexpected feelings. This was the planet he'd grown up on, after all, and he hadn't been back in a long time. He'd always felt more at home in the empty expanse of space, anyway. Even on a planet as big as Prime, sooner or later things started to feel routine. Now, however, he was starting to think he could use some routine in his life. He might even consider watching daytime television.

"Well aren't you just Flash Fisk himself," the pilot said, rolling his eyes and going back to the controls.

Rogers had to take a moment to absorb what had just been said. "I'm sorry, did you just use Flash—my pilot, Flash—as a *good* example?"

"Flash the Chillster is a legend," the pilot said, as if it wasn't an absolutely insane thing to say.

"I am going to vomit," Rogers said. Flash the Chillster sounded like the worst comic book character ever invented.

"Don't worry about it," the copilot said. "We'll break through in just a few minutes."

"That has nothing to do with my nausea," Rogers muttered. How in the world was the rumor mill so screwed up that other pilots thought that Flash was any kind of role model? Aside from being a mediocre pilot whose best attribute was being willing to do things so blindly idiotic that no sane person would do them, Flash was about as dense as the inside of a black hole. And he *never* took off those stupid sunglasses.

"Atmo!" the pilot yelled.

Space technology had advanced quite a bit since humanity reached the Fortuna Stultus galaxy, but they still hadn't managed to dampen the impact of atmospheric reentry. Deflection shields helped, but fiery plasma still wreathed the ship. The heat could be felt instantly, and the sudden reintroduction of a medium for sound waves to travel through made for a rude awakening. Despite all attempts to soften the blows, it still always sounded like an army of tiny stonemasons was trying to carve the ship into a scale model of the universe.

"Hooray!" Tunger yelled.

Rogers tried to tell him to shut up, but he was distracted by his body's sympathetic nervous system's adamant declarations that the ship was about to break into a thousand pieces. The sensation seemed to last for an eternity, the tiny hammer beats punctuated by the random loud slam that challenged the integrity of Rogers' sphincter muscles in a unique way.

The reintroduction of standard Meridan gravity settled into Rogers' bones like the hug of a warm friend who was also really pissed off at him for something he'd done the last time they'd met. Ship gravity was all well and good, but something just felt *different* when it came to planetary gravity. Outside, the new elements of wind and moisture made a whooshing noise across the control surfaces of the shuttle, and both pilots were very busy reconfiguring the shuttle for air-based travel.

From shots he'd seen of Old Earth, Rogers thought Merida Prime looked very similar. Actually, many of the habitable planets throughout the Fortuna Stultus galaxy had a sameness to them, adopting a blue-green hue with white clouds. All of the planets in their new galaxy, however, had much less landmass to them than those in the solar system. Why this was the case, scientists didn't really have any idea. It was extremely unlikely that so many planets within a single galaxy would be able to support life without any terraforming technology, which led some to believe that Fortuna Stultus had *already* been terraformed. That didn't make any sense of course; there was no evidence of any technology on any of the planets in any of the systems. Also aliens didn't exist.

Realistically, Rogers didn't care. You could breathe the air, you could drink the water, and you could grow grain to make Scotch. Everything else was kind of tertiary.

It wasn't long before they were within range of Meridan Naval Headquarters, located in the center of the largest continent on Merida Prime. Fighter jets patrolled the skies, the scream of their engines penetrating the outer hull of their shuttle. Even at a long distance Rogers could see they were armed with anti-atmospheric missiles, capable of targeting enemy ships in orbit. Seeing all of this might have made his stomach feel worse than reentry.

Seeing a pair of those fighter jets escorting his shuttle confirmed that it did.

Seeing one of them crash into an asteroid was just really confusing.

"How?" Rogers blurted. "That doesn't make any sense! We're inside Prime's atmosphere!"

"We operate in strange times, Captain Rogers," Keffoule said mysteriously, as though she had somehow magically summoned the asteroid using secret F Sequence math powers.

"Hey!" Deet said, bouncing up and down in his chair excitedly. "Hey, Rogers!"

Rogers turned his head and frowned. "What's the matter with you?"

Deet paused for a moment, his eyes flashing. He looked like he was attempting to process something of monumental complexity.

"What did the meteor use to get *really big muscles*?"

Rogers blinked. "I have no idea."

"A-*steroids*!" Deet shouted.

"This is the worst day of my life," Rogers said.

The shuttle careened through the airspace around Meridan Naval Headquarters, located next to just about every important building in the Meridan planetary government. Tall, silvery skyscrapers poked up from the ground in the city surrounding it, though all the governmental buildings tended to be short. Rogers thought it was to discourage folks from jumping from the windows; it would only inconvenience you with a broken leg, and then you'd have to deal with government-issued short-term disability insurance. Rogers would sooner hang himself in zero-g.

The pilots began landing procedures at the nearest spaceport, and the view got much less interesting. Cobalt-blue water and green landscapes were replaced by the stone, steel, and synthetics of modern architecture, complete with all the sterilized accoutrements of government facilities. They'd gotten clearance to land in the direct center of the Meridan governmental complex, which would make ground transportation a lot easier. They settled down outside the secure area affectionately called the Monkey Pen by most of the people who worked there—and many of the people who didn't. The intense security perimeter of the multiple-square-mile complex gave the feeling of being penned up, and people who hated real jokes had taken to calling those who worked for the government on Merida Prime as Prime-ates.

Mailn stared at the window and gripped her pant legs with white knuckles, staying very quiet. Rogers had to find out what was going on here. As the shuttle settled down to the ground and began going through its shutdown procedures, Rogers unbuckled his seat belt and stood up.

Deet's eyes flashed. "The seat belt sign is still on!" he cried in a way that sounded much too panicked for an artificial intelligence.

"I like to live on the edge," Rogers said.

"Oh, yes you do," Keffoule said slowly.

Sighing, Rogers walked over to where Mailn was sitting, her seat belt still on. He plopped down in an empty seat next to her and joined her looking out the window at absolutely nothing interesting. The shuttle had landed in such a configuration that they were both looking directly at a gray, plain wall. The corner of a NO SMOKING sign could be seen if he stretched his neck far in one direction.

"Pretty intense scenery," Rogers said.

"Yeah," Mailn said without looking at him.

"Thinking about going to Haverstown?" Rogers asked.

She looked at him then, her mouth slightly open.

"I guessed," Rogers said. "The Viking didn't seem to want you to come down, and I can't imagine it was because you wanted to spend the whole time in the Monkey Pen."

Haverstown was not, as the name implied, a town exclusively for Havers. Although many people in Haverstown did, in fact, talk foolishly, the small city was mostly a blind spot for the law. If anyone had any creative ideas for how to get into trouble, they could bring it to fruition in Haverstown.

"I have some folks back there that I might want to see, yeah," Mailn said. "Captain Alsinbury seems to think I can't handle myself."

Having been hit by Mailn several (hundred) times, Rogers had a difficult time imagining any situation in which Mailn couldn't handle herself. Wondering at the Viking's caution—in all other situations she seemed ready to just blow up whatever was caus-ing trouble and move on—Rogers thought for a moment. He heard the tone as the seat belt sign turned off, and then heard the unbuckling of clasps from the other members of his ground crew. The pilot made a quick announcement that they could col-lect their belongings and disembark.

"Well whatever is waiting for you there," Rogers said, "I want you to take care of it first."

Mailn raised an eyebrow, her seat belt still fastened. "But don't you need me?"

Rogers shrugged. "It'd be nice to have someone who doesn't want to marry me or someone not questioning their consciousness at my side. But if you spend the whole damn time looking out windows at nothing because you're distracted, you're not going to be any good to me." Rogers stretched his arms, yawning. "Besides, we've got stuff to talk through with Holdt first. As much as I'd love you to punch bureaucrats in the face for me, I don't think I'll need you until we figure out exactly what we're doing here."

The sergeant opened her mouth to protest, but Rogers held up a hand.

"Go do what you have to do, and then come back with a clear head," Rogers said.

For a moment Mailn didn't say anything. She stared at him, eyes slightly squinted, teeth chewing on the inside of her cheek. If anything, she looked suspicious, which kind of annoyed Rogers. Here he was trying to give her some shore leave, and she was probably sitting there wondering if it was some kind of trap.

"When did you become a leader?" Mailn asked suddenly.

"Oh don't give me that shit," Rogers said, standing up. "Next thing I know you'll be calling me sir."

"I like Punching Bag better," Mailn said, unbuckling and standing up.

They filed out of the shuttle via a gangplank, taking their possessions with them, which really just meant their datapads. Except for Xan, who Rogers assumed was carrying a bag of Keffoule's personal effects. The pilots, still arguing about whether or not they always had to include units in their messages to passengers, didn't say anything to them as they disembarked. Rogers wanted to ask them a bit more about the whole Flash-being-a-living-legend thing, but he preferred to keep his last meal in his stomach.

As they were stepping off into the docking bay, Rogers felt a tug at his elbow. It was so gentle and weird that he kind of expected to turn around and find a small child standing there, asking if Rogers could help him find his mommy. Instead, however, he found Deet.

"Um," Rogers said. "Yes?"

Deet paused for an uncomfortable moment. He even turned his head to look around, perhaps to see if anyone else was listening. All of them were within a couple of feet of each other, though, so there was really no chance that he could say anything without everyone around him hearing. Rogers was about to ignore him and move on when Deet finally spoke.

"Rogers?" Deet asked. "I was thinking about what you said before. If you got me out of the garbage . . . does that make *me* garbage?"

"Oh wow," Rogers said. "I am not mentally prepared to deal with this right now. And I feel like I owe Belgrave a beating."

"Yeah," Mailn said, laughing. "That's our Captain Rogers. Galaxy-renowned for all the beatings he delivers."

"I hate this crew," Rogers said.

Working for a giant corporation had its perks. Great health benefits, a stable retirement account, and huge opportunities for career growth and progression within a single company. There was even a clause in the contract that said employees could request a free pet from Snaggardir's—one that had been specifically adapted to life in space, so as not to create any messy and horribly depressing situations. Lucinda had always loved animals growing up, but knew when she'd gotten the position as Mr. Snaggardir's personal intern that she would never have enough time to take care of something as complex and needy as a dog or a horse.

So Lucinda had picked a gerbil and had named him Snoot, and he was perfect. He'd been her sounding board for so many things over the last six months, and he never protested, never talked down to her, never told her that splitting a one-bedroom apartment between two other interns was "not a proper way to live." Snoot just listened.

In truth, splitting a one-bedroom apartment between three interns was absolutely not a proper way to live, but there hadn't been much choice in the matter back when she'd lived on Lar Milieu. Grandelle, as a system, was extremely prosperous, but also extremely expensive.

"I just don't know about all of this, Snoot," she said, her voice barely audible over the music blasting through the room. One of the best things about Snaggardir's employment—especially at their headquarters space station—was that they allowed for every employee, even interns, to have their own rooms. And those rooms were practically soundproof, so she could pump up the tunes whenever she wanted. Right now she was going through an ultra-classics phase, mostly comprised of one hit wonders from Earth. She liked that playlist because it was always switching between different artists.

"I mean, we're not talking about changing company policy here," Lucinda said. Snoot nodded sagely—or at least she imagined he nodded sagely. "I think once this all clears up there's still a place here for me, one that pays me actual credits, but . . ."

She flopped over on her bed, looking up at the ceiling. State-of-the-art holographic panels made it look like she was lying in the middle of a wheat field, puffy clouds rolling lazily overhead. She hadn't been planetside in half a year, and she was starting to miss it.

"Something about all of this just doesn't feel right. The Jupiterians were treated unfairly, yes, but is it worth all of this?" Lucinda extended a leg into the air, so that it looked like she was kicking around a low-hanging cloud. It swirled around her sock in response. "Justice is one thing, but . . ." She kicked the cloud to vapors. "This is revenge."

Mr. Snaggardir had been very careful not to use that word. He was a very careful man, but Lucinda had spent enough time as an intern for the last ten years to understand a bit of subtext. That's what was bothering her—Mr. Snaggardir *thought* he was being level-headed and emotionless. He saw himself as just the instrument of Jupiter's revival, the sails that took the wind rather than the engine that powered the ship. But she'd seen enough in those calculating eyes to tell her otherwise. General Szinder at least showed his rage on the outside. Mr. Snaggardir was like a dormant volcano, boiling underneath the surface for two centuries. Of course he wasn't that old, but he represented the pent-up anger of several generations of slighted Jupiterians.

But now there was war, all over the system. All over the galaxy.

Lucinda sighed. She was just an assistant/intern. Even if she did suddenly want to change sides, what could she do? Give Mr. Snaggardir bad notes that resulted in bad war plans? Destroy him by giving him his coffee with regular coconut milk instead of sugar-free coconut milk? Interns, almost by definition, were powerless. Expendable. She was already shocked at the amount of information Mr. Snaggardir allowed her to know.

But people were dying.

People died all the time, of course. And it wasn't like Mr. Snaggardir was engaging in the wanton, mass-scale slaughter of innocents. He was trying to rebuild his people.

But his people had sort of, kind of, been responsible for collapsing the Milky Way.

That was unfair, she knew. A small portion of the population, supported by the Jupiterian central government, had ignored numerous warnings by reputable scientists on all the other colonized planets about their new terraforming technology. That didn't mean all of Jupiter needed to be excluded when they'd discovered the Fortuna Stultus galaxy. In fact, if they hadn't moved all of the planets out of their orbital alignment, they never would have found the first Un-Space entry point.

But people were *dying*.

"Why is this so *complicated*?" she said.

Snoot showed no indication of having any answers for her. He started running on his little wheel, which made Lucinda think of her career. Not for the first time, she wondered what was going to happen if the Jupiterians lost. Of course, the major board of directors had given no indication that this was an option. Everyone was supremely confident, even Dr. Mattic, who was usually a hyper-realist even in the face of overwhelming positivity. But if they did lose . . . what would happen to her? Would she lose her job? Would she . . . die? Worse, would her health plan not be eligible for PYTHON, the Post-Year-Termination Healthcare Operating Network, since her health plan was technically run by the largest criminal organization in the galaxy?

And there was also that "construction" project that everyone kept talking about. That was the one thing they were all very careful not to fully describe while Lucinda was around, which made her very suspicious. They'd been open about blockades; propaganda campaigns; homicidal, self-learning droid armies; and everything else in their complicated plan to retake their place in the galaxy. *Except* for the "construction" project. She could almost feel the quotes around the word, and the way that General Szinder kept grinning and narrowing his eyes every time he said it didn't help her confidence.

For some reason, she felt like her decision was going to hinge on what that was. And until she'd really considered that, she hadn't thought there was any kind of decision to make. Nor did she know what would happen after she made it.

Her datapad reminder alarm went off, and she actually squeaked. She'd been so lost in her thoughts that she'd forgotten they'd called another one of their staff meetings. They seemed to be happening almost hourly lately, though she supposed attempting to overthrow the galaxy would increase the frequency of strategy meetings.

"You know, Snoot," she said, vaulting off her bed and heading to her closet, "if I ever have to bail, I'm going to make sure to take you with me."

Snoot showed his appreciation by eating one of his turds.

"I give you such good food," Lucinda muttered. She knew enough about animals to understand it was nutritionally necessary, but it was still gross.

Lucinda dressed as fast as she could and ran out the door.

The Worst Cup of Coffee Ever

Being inside a government building immediately reminded Rogers why he enjoyed free space more than working a staff job planetside. Actually, it reminded him why he enjoyed having molten iron poured into his eye sockets more than working a staff job planetside. Down here on Prime, you were just too close to the idiocy. Too many eyes, and too many mouths ready to say "Hey, you know what would be a good idea?" Out in free space, you at least had the buffer of communication delays and crackling a piece of paper near the mouthpiece of your datapad and saying "Wait, you're breaking up! I'll talk to you later."

The halls of Meridan Naval Headquarters, which was really just one wing of the tumor-like complex of the other branches of Merida's defense forces, were decorated much like the quarter-deck of the *Flagship*. Everything seemed out of place and time, faux-wood details accompanying strangely modern metallic surfaces. As they walked toward Admiral Holdt's office near the center of the complex, they were treated with both obviously fake orchid displays and complicated mini-biospheres that allowed exotic plants to thrive in an urban environment.

Officers and enlisted of every rank and specialty were scurrying through the halls, looking at datapads or talking animatedly among each other. Nobody was saluting, thankfully, but Rogers could *feel* the queep bearing down on him like a failed terraforming experiment that had thickened the air.

"What is 'queep'?" Deet asked. Rogers wasn't aware he'd been muttering out loud about it all.

"It's, uh," Rogers said, struggling for a real description of the word. "It's a catchall word that sort of encapsulates anything that is useless and stupid."

"So should I be calling you Captain Queep?" Deet asked.

"Very funny."

"So," Keffoule asked as they neared the end of their journey through a small version of hell, "what can you tell me about this Admiral Holdt?"

Rogers gave her a sideways glance. "You mean you haven't read intelligence reports about him, or anything?"

Blushing, Keffoule failed to meet his eyes. "Captain Rogers, I am not sure what kind of woman you think I am."

". . . The commander of a fleet?"

"The *respectable, noble* commander of a fleet," Xan said in a warning tone.

Rogers was about to explain the many reasons why someone engaged in war should read intelligence reports, but he didn't feel like talking anymore. That seemed to be happening a lot, lately.

Rogers didn't know much about the interior of Meridan Naval Headquarters, but he knew he was headed to the executive section, where all the top brass spent their days telling other brass to tell enlisted troops to push paperwork around.

"How do you know where you're going?" Deet asked. "I can't even access a map of the facility."

"I'm looking at everyone's faces," Rogers said, pointing at a pair of young recruits walking by. "If they look like they're getting more depressed, we're going in the right direction."

His method of navigation, however, was short-lived in its efficacy. As he moved farther along the hallway, he started to notice that, instead of panic, there were a lot of blank faces. Slowly he realized that anyone from the MPD—the Meridan Police Department—appeared to have no expression on their faces at all. This was strange on two fronts. First, the MPD didn't usually pull guard duty at Meridan military installations. Each branch of the military had their own security department for that sort of thing. Second, the sheer unemotional, expressionless looks on their faces made Rogers' skin crawl. One guy's cheeks were actually drooping.

"Jeez," Rogers said. "I feel like I'm surrounded by Xans."

"But there's only one Xan," Tunger said slowly, pointing to Keffoule's aide.

"I don't appreciate insults on my religion," Xan said.

"What *is* your religion exactly?" Rogers asked. "Nobody ever explained it to me except that face weights are apparently important."

Before Xan could answer, Rogers saw two familiar figures that made his hackles rise.

"You get the hell away from me right now," Rogers said.

Two MPD officers who had been nattering at each other suddenly noticed Rogers and stopped their conversation. One of them, Officer Atikan, cheerily waved and increased his pace to get closer to Rogers. The other, Officer Brooks, gave him the finger.

"I don't want to talk to either of you," Rogers reiterated, and made to step around them, but Deet was in his way and made of metal. Before he could change course, he was surrounded.

"Captain Rogers!" Officer Atikan yelled in a syrupy-sweet, singsong voice. "It's so good to see you again. I hear things have gone well for you since we met on the *Lumos*."

"I wish you had stayed on the *Lumos*," Rogers muttered. These two officers had nearly sent him into a schizophrenic breakdown after he'd been arrested for blowing up all of the pirates during his last deal-gone-sour.

"I wish you had died," Brooks growled. "Twice."

"I was just talking about you," Atikan said. "Your parade should be ready to go soon."

Rogers frowned. "Wait, you were serious? Do you really think this is a time for parades? Do you have any idea what is going on out there?"

"It's always time for a parade," Atikan said.

"No," Rogers said. "No it is absolutely not. If you'll excuse me."

He pushed his way through the two officers, setting off with far too much enthusiasm for someone visiting a high admiral. As Rogers squeezed between the two of them, Brooks leaned in and whispered with the utmost of creepiness.

"I've got your number," he said, and pushed a small paper with *40R* written on it into Rogers' hand.

"Not my number!" Rogers sang out over his shoulder as he sped away. "Coat size! You're an idiot!"

His coterie caught up with him relatively quickly, and nobody spoke for a moment.

"Can I ask—" Deet began.

"No," Roger said.

Keffoule looked at him sideways, her mouth set in a thin line. "Are you known to frequently distribute your number to brawny policemen?" she asked.

Rogers sighed. "Are you serious right now?"

It wasn't long before they were met by an orderly in Meridan service dress, which was entirely too formal to do any real work. He looked crisp and utterly humorless, which prompted Rogers to keep conversation to a minimum. He'd rather talk to a droid; at least droids had the excuse of being literally soulless.

Deet, however, showed no such restraint. The droid spent

most of the walk making the orderly look distinctly uncomfortable as he peppered him with questions that had nothing to do with their mission on Prime.

"Can I have your network password?" Deet asked.

"No."

"Can you tell me where the server room is?"

"No."

"How does that make you feel?"

"No."

Keffoule leaned over to Rogers and whispered. "Is this some sort of Meridan communication ritual?"

"What is it with you thinking that everything is a ritual?" Rogers asked. He remembered Keffoule wondering some other such nonsense when they'd sat down to dinner together. "Deet is just being an asshole."

"I am not being an [ANATOMICAL REFERENCE]," Deet said. "I am gathering intelligence."

"You people have no principles," Keffoule muttered.

The orderly, pointedly moving to the other side of their group to avoid Deet's questions, led them down a hallway and up to a pair of large doors. A bronze plaque on the outside indicated that the office was the home of High Admiral Jacob R. Holdt, Meridan naval representative to the Meridan Staff of Joint Representative Chiefs, which was possibly the worst title Rogers had ever heard of other than maybe Quinn's.

"Here you are, sir," the orderly said stiffly. "Admiral Holdt is expecting you."

Reaching out, he opened the door with both handles at once, which Rogers thought was a little melodramatic even with all the war and stuff going on. The two enormous doors swung outward to reveal what Rogers thought was going to be an immaculately kept office, complete with high-technology communication, a wet bar, and maybe a butler holding a silver tray of small sandwiches. Instead, the first thing Rogers noticed was the smell.

"There's something familiar about this place," Tunger said, confirming Rogers' suspicions that yes, Holdt's office did indeed smell like a zoo.

It looked like one too. All over the place were signs that Holdt's office had been turned into something akin to a military commune, except there was only one resident, if you didn't count the chicken. There was always a chicken. The whole room exuded stress like an accordion being slowly compressed by a clown who hated you. Datapads littered the room, all of the six vidscreens displayed differing streams of news, and a cot had been made up in the corner out of couch cushions and throw blankets.

Holdt himself looked much grayer and thinner than Rogers remembered him from their conversation only a few days earlier. He sat in a large leather chair behind his desk, his head tilted back so far over the headrest that Rogers couldn't tell if he was sleeping or simply staring at the ceiling. His uniform was ruffled to the point where there were more ruffles than flourishes, and an open bottle of cheap whiskey sat half-empty on the desk.

So this was war.

"Well, shit, Rogers," Holdt said, apparently not asleep.

"I like him," Deet said.

To his recollection, Rogers had never been in front of such a high-ranking officer in all of his days in the military. Having been assigned to the *Flagship* as a new recruit all the way up to sergeant, and then again as a new lieutenant all the way up to out-of-his-fucking-mind, he'd thankfully never had very much experience with staff. Klein had been an admiral too, Rogers admitted, but not a *real* admiral. He'd just been a Toastmasters graduate extremely good at masking the fact that he was an idiot.

So . . . maybe a real admiral.

As a result, Rogers didn't really know what to do. He sort of, kind of stood at attention, which resulted in him bringing his heels together just a little more than was normal and leaving his hands at his sides in a way that felt, and probably looked, very awkward.

"That looks very awkward," Deet said, looking at Rogers.

"Shut up, Deet," Rogers said.

Tunger, however, seemed to have no reservations about acting like a complete tool. His whole body went ramrod straight, his chin tucked so far into his chest that it looked like he was attempting to sniff his sternum.

"Good morning, *sir*," Tunger yelled, bringing Admiral Holdt's head back from its reclined position with a snap.

"Jesus' steaming turd, Corporal," Holdt said with only one eye open. "Is that really necessary?"

The admiral's face looked even worse now that Rogers could get a full view of it. His eyes were bloodshot, sunken, like someone who had been drinking heavily for a long period of time. Although his gaze was glazed over like a sloppily made donut, Rogers didn't think he was drunk, or even hungover.

Keffoule gazed around the room, her nose wrinkled and her posture relaxed. Rogers knew better than to believe that; the more languid that woman became, the closer she was to dancing through a hail of bullets.

"I didn't expect Meridans to have much love for military protocol," she muttered. She didn't exactly look ready to jump to attention either, even though her rank equivalency was below that of Holdt's.

The Meridan high admiral spared little notice for Keffoule and her saggy-cheeked attendant. He waved away Tunger's rising salute and poured himself a glass of whiskey. It was ten in the morning.

"I've gotten through some of the reports your staff sent," he said.

"I have a staff?" Rogers asked.

"You did ask S1C Brelle to prepare a package for you to send once the Thelicosan jamming net was down," Deet said. "I took the liberty to fill in some additional details."

Rogers frowned, looking at Deet. "Deet," he said. "That was . . ."

Deet turned his horse-like face to look at Rogers, his glowing blue eyes flickering.

"[EXPLETIVE]?" he offered.

"No," Rogers said. "It was actually, genuinely *thoughtful*."

Deet nodded his head as though he'd confirmed some point.

"Anyway," Holdt said. "I have the gist of what's going on." He leaned forward in his chair, letting a long breath go and putting his elbows on his desk. His uniform shirt looked slightly yellowed under the arms. Even if Holdt was spending his nights here doing war planning or whatever, there had to at least be a shower or something in the headquarters building, right?

"So you're telling me," Holdt continued, "that you basically threw out every rule and regulation regarding conducting warfare, then also threw out all semblances of military doctrine and strategy and just did whatever the fuck you wanted, however the fuck you wanted to do it?"

Rogers froze. He'd gotten ass chewings before. He'd developed a sort of sixth sense to understand when he was walking into one so he could steel himself before he got there. His ass-chewing senses had not been tingling prior to this meeting, so it was surprising how much this felt like a good old-fashioned chewing of one's ass.

"I—uh," he stammered.

"Captain Rogers' ability to improvise was instrumental in securing my fleet back from the traitor Edris Zergan," Keffoule cut in, her voice like a whip.

"I wasn't criticizing," Holdt said, giving Keffoule a sour face. Despite his insistence that Rogers bring the Thelicosan commander along, he didn't seem very happy to have her in his office. "I was just confirming that is what actually happened. Rogers, you might have unlocked the key to all of this."

Shit, Rogers thought. Now, instead of an ass chewing, this was starting to sound like a commendation. That was even worse. With an ass chewing, you left appropriately downcast and then you went back to whatever you'd been doing. With a commendation, someone typically gave you more work to do.

Holdt swiveled around in his chair and stood up, some of the vigor suddenly back in his bones. Clasping his hands behind his back in a very admiral-like way, Holdt stood and looked out the window into the expanse of government jungle that extended to the visible horizon. A pair of fighters zoomed overhead, this time avoiding any misplaced space debris.

"We're a mess," Holdt said finally. "A real goddamn mess. And we don't have a way to get out of it. The Jupiterians are blockading just about every Un-Space point across all of the systems. I can't imagine the hardware they'd need to do something like that, but apparently they have it. New Neptune and Grandelle are already completely under their control."

Rogers' breath caught in his chest at that. Two of the four systems, *completely* in Jupiterian control?

"How is that even possible?" he asked.

"Well, Grandelle is where Snaggardir's is based, more or less. Their main headquarters is actually a space station, but most of their planetside resources are scattered throughout that system. They hold so much sway economically within that system that they were simply able to buy their way into power. Anyone who didn't immediately capitulate had most of their assets frozen and faced instant ruin."

Rogers shook his head. A buyout on a massive, system-wide scale.

"And New Neptune?" Keffoule asked.

"They put it in the news that the Jupiterians were in charge, and everyone kind of just went with it."

Swiveling his head around to find Xan, Rogers raised an eyebrow. Such a ridiculous explanation couldn't possibly be—

"That sounds reasonable," Xan said, nodding slowly.

"How the hell is that reasonable?" Rogers asked.

"I can answer that," Tunger said. "I'm a bit of a cultural expert."

Rogers looked at him. "No, you are not."

"He saved your life three times on a Thelicosan ship without getting caught," Deet offered.

Rogers grit his teeth. "Thank you, Deet."

"Why the [EXPLETIVE] are you thanking *me*? You should be thanking Corporal Tunger."

Tunger shrugged all of this off. "It was nothing, sir. Just doing my job. But New Neptune is notoriously known for 'going with the flow,' if I can use the expression. Most of the immigrants who settled in the New Neptune system came from old communist countries. In general, if the news told them that they'd be under the control of a band full of monkeys, they'd shrug, move on, and go make borscht."

Rogers blinked. "I'm not trying to be judgmental here, but that sounds like the dumbest thing I've ever heard."

"I'll thank you not to insult my people," Xan said, perhaps a hint of tension in his voice. "It is our way."

"What if I were to put in the news that you were all stupid?"

Xan gave him a blank stare. Rogers liked to think that the small robotic circuits inside Xan's brain were slowly starting to smoke.

"Perhaps we should return to the task at hand," Keffoule said, gesturing grandly at the entire room for some reason. It gave Rogers the impression that what she *really* wanted to do was clean this place up. She hadn't unwrinkled her nose since she'd come inside Holdt's office.

"Cultural barriers not withstanding," Holdt said, turning around and addressing them all directly, "we need some way to take that strategy and adapt it to all of the anti-Jupiterian forces. If we can't bring everyone here to coordinate a resistance, it's going to be tough for everyone. I'm able to get messages out to some parts of each system, but I don't know who is getting what." He sighed. "The Meridan International Representative Party has appointed me director of the war effort, and our first task is to restore freedom of movement through the Un-Space points. If Jupiter keeps us separate, they keep us weak."

The final statement echoed through the room. In truth, the Jupiterians had been kept separate for two hundred years, and it hadn't seemed to affect their ability to overthrow the galaxy very much. Then again, Rogers considered, they hadn't won yet. They'd taken everyone by surprise, but fifty percent of the galaxy wasn't *all* of the galaxy.

"What do the Jupiterians want?" Rogers asked. "Do we have any idea?"

"That's half the frustration," Holdt said. "We have no idea. The initial strikes seemed to indicate that it was going to be a war of attrition, but now it looks as though they've stopped. You don't blockade Un-Space points if you're just going to try and wipe everyone out. But they haven't made any demands; Snaggardir's main offices have been quiet."

Rogers shook his head. "That doesn't make any sense."

Over on the far side of the office, closer to where they'd entered, a long table held a coffee machine and some mugs. Rogers had enough tact to not go for the bottle of whiskey just yet—besides, it was cheap whiskey—but he certainly wasn't above going and grabbing a cup of coffee.

"Why go through all the trouble if you're not going to do anything with the territory you grab?" Rogers took a cup and put it under the spout.

"Wait!" Holdt said.

"I'm not leaving," Rogers said. "I'm just getting a—"

Rogers was hit in the face with a blast of molten death, spewing from the innards of the large black coffee machine on the table. His ducking instincts kicked in, but it was too late; a veritable shower of coffee fountained all over the place, staining the floor, Rogers' uniform, and his pride.

"What the hell was that?" Rogers asked, spitting out scalding-hot coffee. It felt like half his face was melting off. The coffee wasn't even that good. The small amount of it that had made it into his mouth tasted like sulfur and cotton swabs.

"I tried to warn you," Holdt said, throwing him a towel that was already full of coffee stains. Rogers apparently wasn't the first to be ambushed by the technology.

In response, Rogers coughed up a small black thunderstorm.

"Look at the label," Holdt said, gesturing at the coffee machine. "It was made by Snaggardir's. Half the stuff in the galaxy was made by that damn company, and all of it has started to malfunction." Holdt sat back down, pouring himself another glass of whiskey. When had he finished the last one? "I'd say it was deliberate sabotage, but it doesn't make any sense. Nothing that is malfunctioning is of any real use."

What kind of barbarian describes coffee as not having any real use? Rogers thought.

"Well why the hell don't you just *unplug* it?" Rogers asked.

"We can't. The plugs were outfitted with claw-like teeth that have attached themselves to the inside of the wall. Forcing them out or cutting the cords could cause a short, and we'd be out of power."

Holdt threw back half a glass of whiskey and let out a very un-admiral-like belch.

"Look, let me cut to the chase. We can't reteach all the militaries in all the systems how to fight. You're going to need to go out there and recruit people who *already* don't know how to fight."

Rogers finished wiping his face on the towel and threw it back to Holdt.

"As for you," Holdt said, pointing to Keffoule. "I've managed to get word from the Thelicosan Council. The Colliders are going to be absorbed as a unit within the 331st. You'll be operating under Captain Rogers now."

"Oh I'd like to operate underneath—"

"Stop," Rogers said. "Stop."

He was a fool to think that he was going to be extricated from dealings with Keffoule, as much as he desperately wanted to be. Their fates were intertwined, or some fatalist, destiny-spewing bullshit like that. At this point, they might as well be married, because it seemed only death would part them.

"Do you have any idea how we're supposed to go about getting a bunch of idiots who don't play by the rules to come fight?"

For the first time, Rogers had noticed that Deet was no longer with the rest of the group. He'd slowly been making his way around the room, looking at various things with a childlike curiosity that Rogers had kind of come to find endearing, if such a word could ever be used to describe his feelings toward Deet. Rogers realized this was his first trip to an actual planet; if he'd been built by Snaggardir's, there was a good chance he'd been manufactured in space.

Holdt leaned back in his chair, giving Rogers a level, flat look. "I hear you might know a pirate or two."

Rogers swallowed. "Wow, that's, uh, kind of a jump in logic, eh?"

"Stow it, Rogers," Holdt said. "We're not all morons in this navy. You're absolved of all the stupid crap you did with the pirates. Now I want you to go out there and get them to fight for us."

"Pirates?" Keffoule said, looking like she was going to spit. "We don't need their ilk working with us."

"Something against space corsairs?" Rogers asked. "Seems kind of picky."

Keffoule sneered at him, back to business. She'd been so coy this entire time that it was almost weird to see her looking more like a warrior than an unwanted suitor.

"We're not looking for opinions on this," Holdt said. "You don't have to go, Grand Marshal. Rogers is the one with the connections."

"Admiral," Rogers said, "for all they know, I was responsible for blowing all of them up. That doesn't exactly make for a warm welcome. They might shoot me on sight."

"That's a risk I'm willing to take," Holdt said.

"Thanks."

Deet made a sound that was suspiciously laughter-like. He was over by Holdt's desk now, so Rogers couldn't see the bottom half of his body. If Holdt had any reservations about having a semi-sentient droid standing awkwardly close to him, he didn't show it.

"Anyway," Holdt said. "You have your orders. Report back once you have an indication of whether or not they're willing to help."

"Hang on a damn minute," Rogers said. "What am I supposed to offer them? They're *pirates*, Admiral, they don't operate on goodwill."

"Come up with something," Holdt said. "We're talking about the collapse of the free galaxy as we know it. I'm sure whatever you offer them can be scraped together."

Rogers chewed the inside of his lip. He didn't like negotiating with pirates if it wasn't in good faith.

Wait a minute—negotiating in bad faith is precisely what he *loved* to do. He'd left the military to do it professionally. This high rank was doing very bad things to him.

"Fine," Rogers said. "I'll do it. But I want amnesty for me and my team if we have to do anything, uh, slightly illegal to get this to work."

"That's not in my power to grant," Holdt said, "but again . . ." He pointed over his shoulder, out the window, as though the entire Jupiterian fleet was waiting outside to blow them all to pieces. "The galaxy is ending and all that. I think we'll overlook some pirating."

Something about all of this didn't feel right. Maybe it was the ludicrous plan, maybe it was the fact that the galaxy was indeed ending as they knew it. But Rogers couldn't stop thinking about

Holdt, sitting there with a permanently grumpy look on his face next to a bottle of bad booze. They'd never really met before this, but there was something familiar . . .

Rogers realized, as his stomach dropped to the floor, that he was looking at a future version of himself. Holdt was much older, and much better at all the military stuff, but his attitude reminded Rogers of his own. He looked tired, burnt out. Like he hadn't done a damn thing he'd wanted to do in about two decades. His rank wouldn't allow him to. At some point, someone had saddled him with too much duty. Was this Rogers' fate too? He was already only a few ranks away, and his nerves felt like they were operating at twice their natural capacity for anxiety.

"What's your problem, Rogers?" Admiral Holdt said. "You look like you've seen a ghost."

Rogers wasn't entirely sure that he hadn't. Except, it was a future kind of ghost. The Ghost of Rogers' Future, or something like that.

This thought pattern was getting too complicated, and Rogers had some pirating to do. He made his farewells, avoided getting anywhere close to the psychotic coffee machine, and led his small team out of the office. Deet, who was still standing behind Holdt's desk, made a small whirring noise before ambling after them.

"Xan and I won't be coming with you," Keffoule said almost immediately when the door closed. "Meridan high command might not care about intergalactic law, but I am trying to work my way back into glory, not prison."

Rogers shrugged, secretly cackling inside with glee. It seemed that he'd finally found something that would get Keffoule off his tail, despite the fact that she was now officially working . . . underneath . . . him. If he could spend the rest of his days pirating, Keffoule would never bother him again! He'd have to keep that in mind.

"When I retire, however," Keffoule leered. "You and I can do all kinds of pirating."

Rogers thought his skin was going to crawl off his body.

"Anyway," Rogers said. "I'm surprised—you were very . . . diplomatic in there. I didn't really think you could deal with anyone without kicking them in the face."

Keffoule looked away from him. She appeared to be working words around in her mouth.

"I've been . . . trying to adapt," she said quietly.

Rogers shrugged. "Alright. I'm just surprised you didn't bring Quinn. She's the politician."

"She is otherwise occupied."

Something about the way Keffoule said "otherwise occupied" made Rogers not want to ask about it any further. He was well aware that the two of them hated each other. For all he knew, Keffoule had locked her in a closet full of nails.

"Right. Tunger, I appreciate your almost complete silence."

Tunger gave him a thumbs-up.

"And, Deet . . ." Rogers looked at his droid companion and noticed for the first time that something was hanging from the bottom of his torso. It looked really inappropriate, and after a moment Rogers realized what it was: Deet's dongle.

"Hey," Rogers continued, "your dongle is dangling."

Deet looked down, made a squeaking noise, and reeled in his extension. It vanished back into his torso compartment with a loud metallic *clap*.

"Wait a minute," Rogers said, forgetting whatever he had been about to tell Deet just a moment earlier. "Why is your dongle dangling? What were you doing with your damn dongle dangling down, Deet?"

Deet's voice came through his mouthpiece, but it was full of static.

"You're . . . breaking . . . up . . . I'm in a . . . tunnel," Deet said.

"That's not how that works," Rogers said. They passed another pair of MPD personnel who looked as though their faces had been painted on by someone more boring than a New Neptunian. Why weren't they showing any emotion?

"Deet, were you plugging into Holdt's computer while we were all talking?"

"Yes," Deet said, then flailed both of his arms in the air like he'd experienced some kind of critical motor processing error. "[EXPLETIVE]. That's not what I meant to say."

"I know you can't really lie," Rogers said. "So what the hell were you doing in there?"

He brought the group to a stop in the hallway, near where a Snaggardir's vending machine was hurling candy bars at high speed across the room. Rogers felt like he should have noticed these things before. Were there any Snaggardir's products in the 331st that were malfunctioning? Nobody had made any complaints yet.

"I was standing next to one of the most data-rich terminals in the Meridan fleet," Deet said. "I couldn't just let that amount of research go by untouched. You keep saying I'm being selfish, Rogers, but I found some things that could help us."

"Oh really?" Rogers asked. "Like what?"

Deet was quiet for a moment. "I learned that Dr. Mattic started experimenting with robotics when he was four years old."

Rogers scowled. "Yeah, Deet. Really useful. Thanks. Do me a favor and search the database for any pirate phone numbers, alright?"

"What do you need phone numbers for?" Keffoule asked, not hiding her disdain. "I thought all the pirates were your friends?"

"They were," Rogers said. "But the last time I met them, I may have accidentally killed them all."

The Seedy Underbelly

"Boy are you a sight for sore eyes," Rogers said.

His eyes were actually sore. The high-pressure coffee spout had impacted him so strongly that he thought his brain was bruised. That didn't mean, of course, that the expression wasn't true in the traditional sense as well. The Viking had responded to his summons with reluctance, but she'd come nonetheless, and she'd left her uniform behind. Rogers didn't think he'd ever seen her out of uniform, except that one time she was in a hospital gown recovering from a shoulder wound. The experience was not at all bad, despite the fact that she was dressed like an off-duty bouncer. Perhaps *because* of the fact that she was dressed like an off-duty bouncer.

"Well, I got my leave schedules worked out, and it was starting to get boring up there," the Viking said. "Besides, I heard I might get to punch someone."

"For once, I'm kind of hoping you don't," Rogers said.

It wasn't that he wouldn't like to see the Viking completely thrash a room full of pirates—he absolutely would—but more that he'd rather get this mission done with as soon as possible. With pirates, sometimes violence *was* the fastest solution, but in this case he was just hoping for a couple of friendly drinks. He still hadn't really come up with what to offer them as payment for helping dismantle the Jupiterian blockade, and he was hoping that a couple of glasses of Scotch might loosen his bargaining muscles and the pirates' inhibitions. That was, of course, assuming he could find any pirates.

Rogers had been sitting in the waiting room of the shuttle dock for over an hour, waiting for the Viking to arrive and trying to figure out what the hell he was going to do. Tunger, ever present, seemed to be content with relative silence, which was a relief, and Keffoule and Xan had gone to their planetside accommodations, still within the defense complex.

"Where's Mailn?" the Viking asked, shifting her duffel bag from one shoulder to the other. "And where's your idiot robot friend?"

"She took some time off," Rogers said. "I haven't heard from her since we touched down yesterday other than that she'd meet us here soon. Deet is with some folks in the science lab, getting his circuits analyzed or something like that. Apparently they think they might be able to get more information about Snaggardir's by looking at his hardware and operating system."

Despite his anxiousness to get to work—or at least get drinking—Rogers had mostly collapsed after the meeting the previous day. It made him feel exceptionally old. When he'd woken up, the Snaggardir's brand blow-dryer in the bathroom was spouting small bursts of flame.

The Viking's face told Rogers everything he needed to know about how good of an idea she thought it was to let Mailn roam around Prime alone. Rogers was about to say that she was a grown woman and could take care of herself when Mailn walked into the waiting room looking like she could absolutely not take care of herself.

"You don't look bad with a black eye," Rogers said. "Do you need me to teach you how to duck?"

Mailn hit him in the face.

"Okay, okay!" Rogers said. "Jeez, you know that's assaulting a superior officer, right?"

"Let's not get carried away with 'superior,'" Mailn said.

"What the hell happened to you?" the Viking asked. Her tone was sharp, but her face actually looked concerned.

"Nothing much that doesn't always happen in Haverstown," Mailn said, not meeting the Viking's gaze. "It's no big deal."

The Viking didn't look convinced about the bigness or smallness of the deal that was Mailn's battered face. The sergeant's clothes looked rumpled as well, with a small tear in one of her sleeves. Despite all of this, however, Mailn was clearly in good spirits. Her nonwounded eye was bright and alert, and she was grinning in a way that Rogers was very familiar with. It was the typical "I'm not entirely sure I remember all of last night but I know I liked it" grin.

"Well I'm glad you got some relaxation in," Rogers said.

Mailn shrugged, still grinning. "So what are we doing now?"

"We're going to go talk with pirates."

Mailn's grin was wiped away like a squashed bug off a windshield.

"Why?" she asked.

"Apparently we're supposed to make mercenaries out of them," Rogers said. He debriefed Mailn on the conversation he'd had with Holdt yesterday, and with every word the dark expression on Mailn's face grew even more grave.

"The problem is," Rogers concluded, "I have no idea how to find them or how to convince them to join up."

Mailn was quiet for a moment.

"I think can help," she said.

"Haverstown is already pretty rough," Rogers said as they walked through the streets, getting jostled and elbowed by pretty much every person on the planet, "so I'm having a little trouble imaging that there's a 'seedy underbelly' to this place. Everywhere is seedy."

"It's not a description," Mailn said. "It's a bar called the Seedy Underbelly."

"Oh," Rogers said.

He'd never heard of the place, which struck him as strange; he'd thought he knew Haverstown like the back of his hand. Then again, hundreds of drinking establishments were scattered all over the crowded urban jungle. Despite the fact that synthetic livers worked very nicely, Rogers understood the difference between having a good time and self-abuse.

Humanity probably thought it was pretty advanced by now; they'd conquered interstellar and intergalactic travel, blowing up an entire galaxy in its wake, and popping into space as easily as one would pop a flash-frozen meal into a microwave for dinner. Science had eradicated scores of diseases that had annihilated populations, the extinction of animal species had practically been halted completely, and dishwashers could get peanut butter completely off spoons. Yet, walking through Haverstown, one would have a hard time imagining that this detritus of mankind had ever managed to escape the gravity of a couch, never mind an entire planet.

"That's cute," the Viking said, using her elbow to point to someone urinating on a wall.

"It's actually not as bad as it looks. People pissed on walls so often here that most of the walls are absorbent and feed directly into the sanitation system of the city."

The Viking grunted as she bowled over a pair of shadowy-looking young men who appeared to consider confronting her for a moment before truly taking in her size. Rogers felt warm all of a sudden, and maybe a little jealous. Double-stepping, he moved so he was in front of the Viking, then awkwardly stopped to look at something nondescript. She bowled him over too.

"Watch where you're going, metalhead," she grumbled.

"Never," Rogers whispered.

They turned a corner into an alley, Mailn leading the way, until they came to what appeared to be a dead end.

"Oh yeah," Rogers said. "Nothing like three stone walls in an unlit alleyway to make you feel safe."

In truth, there wasn't much that could happen to them here. All of them were armed, and two of them actually knew how to use the weapons they carried underneath their coats. Rogers had actually disengaged the plasma core from his disruptor pistol; it was much safer for everyone involved if Rogers' weapon was just a prop. Haverstown residents knew better than to harass government employees of any kind unless they were paying to be harassed, but those establishments were on the other side of the city.

"They keep the place secret," Mailn said.

She walked up to what appeared to be a brick wall and put her finger into a notch. Distantly, Rogers thought he heard doorbell chimes, but the ambient noise of this back corner of Haverstown made it hard to distinguish anything below a full shout.

"I am intensely curious as to how you know all of these things," Rogers said.

"There's a sign right there on the wall, sir," Tunger said, pointing at a sign near the corner of the alleyway that said PUSH HERE FOR ENTRANCE.

Rogers cleared his throat. "Yeah, okay, fine. It's dark. Didn't I tell you to go to lodging and take a break?"

"I could never do that, sir," Tunger said. "I've always wanted the chance to meet pirates. I've been practicing my pirate accent so that I could spy—"

"*Don't,*" Rogers warned. "I swear to god if you say 'arrrr' or anything like that I am going to gut you with a cutlass."

The Viking let go a little bit of a bark that Rogers had come to recognize as a laugh.

A moment later, Rogers heard the distinct sound of stone moving against stone, and the wall simply opened up in front of them. It seemed kind of tacky and old-fashioned to have a hidden door in a wall, but there was also something strangely endearing about it, as though anything endearing could be said about pirates.

"You're late," someone said from the exposed dark corridor. Rogers peered down the opening and could see the faint glow of some lights in the distance, but nothing distinguishable popped out. In that glow, the silhouette of a striking figure stood with its hands on its hips. Clearly the person either wore some sort of elaborate hat or had a very misshapen head.

"You try coordinating with a couple of military officers," Mailn said.

"Hey," Rogers said.

"Hey," the Viking said.

"Hey," Rogers said again, "we said the same thing at the same time. I think that means we have to kiss—"

"I think it's called a jinx," Tunger said, "and one of you owes the other some kind of soft drink."

Rogers clenched his teeth, slowly turning his head to look at Tunger. "Oh. That's. Right. Thank. You. For. Reminding. Me."

"You're welcome, sir!" Tunger said gleefully.

The voice had been distant, and a little husky, so Rogers hadn't been sure it was a woman until she stood in front of them. Everything about her screamed rough-and-tough, down to the dual pistols hanging from her hips and the leather bandoliers of plasma cartridges crisscrossed over her chest. The hat in question was a wide-brimmed creation that didn't quite fit any style Rogers could think of, but it had a twinge of old-world cowboy to it.

The dark face underneath the brim of the hat glanced over all of them with disinterest. Without proper lighting, Rogers couldn't tell exactly what she looked like, but overall he could see sharp outlines around her jaw, cheeks, and nose.

"Cynthia here tells me you want to talk business. Why don't you come inside?"

Without waiting for a response, the yet-unnamed woman turned around and walked into the darkness, leaving Rogers and company little choice but to follow or be left in the alleyway. Rogers was about to be all heroic and brave and lead the way, but then he decided not to do that. After a moment, the Viking stepped in first, and he followed her hulking form down the corridor.

"Okay, everyone," Rogers whispered, though he wasn't sure who could hear him or if he actually needed to whisper. "I've got this. Just follow my lead and—"

The corridor opened up into a place of wonder.

The Seedy Underbelly may have been the nicest bar Rogers had ever walked into. Well, "nice" perhaps wasn't the correct word for it. It was more like . . . they had pulled several pages out of a housekeeping magazine and used them to come up with the most comfortable space imaginable. Floral-pattern couches, plush carpets, and soft, meditative music pervaded the room. Some sort of vanilla-bean candle must have been burning somewhere as well. Instantly he felt the urge to take off his shoes and put on some slippers, which was convenient because a rack of soft-looking slippers was positioned directly next to the door. A sign above it said, in curly writing, WE WILL TRADE YOU COMFY SLIPPERS FOR A CLEAN FLOOR. Obviously they were supposed to take off their shoes before entering.

"How do you like our establishment?" the smoky-skinned woman said.

"Not what I expected," Rogers said.

"That's why it's kept secret. We spend all this time keeping up this image of being rough-and-tough bruisers, ready to slit anyone's throat at a moment's notice for a little taste of booty, but sometimes we just want microsuede cushions and a warm blanket."

"You know, I kind of understand that," Rogers said, nodding. There had been many times when he'd wanted to put aside all of his duties and snuggle into something warm and soft. He'd wanted to do it with a bottle of Jasker, of course, but there was at least some crossover.

Everyone was quiet for a moment. Despite Rogers saying that he would take the lead, he still wasn't exactly sure what to do with the lead once he took it. Eyes darted around the room and among each other; nobody in the establishment seemed to notice or care about the newcomers, and nobody in his party seemed to want to talk first. He shot a look at the Viking, who shrugged, and then at Tunger, who grinned and appeared to not understand what was going on around him, and then at Mailn. She was the one who had magically known about this place.

After holding his gaze for a few moments, Mailn sighed.

"Alright, alright," she said. "Everyone, this is Sjana. My wife."

"What?" Rogers barked.

"What?" the Viking barked.

"Hey, that's another jinx," Rogers said. "We need to—"

"Congratulations!" said Tunger, clapping. "That's wonderful news. Will there be a reception? Oh, I hope there are so many flowers. I can bring the doves, and—"

"We've been married for four years," Mailn said. "It's complicated."

For the first time, Rogers looked at the pirate, Sjana, and noticed that under the brim of her wide hat she was also sporting a black eye.

"Aw," he said, pointing at her eye and starting to understand. "You match. I see it's going well?"

"That's not funny," Mailn muttered, but Sjana chuckled a little.

"I am Sjana Devingo," she said, the traces of some kind of accent dancing across her voice. She held out a hand to Rogers. "I am the captain of the *Africanus*, and somewhat of a boss around here. Cynthia told me you wanted to talk to whoever was in charge, and I'm the closest thing."

"I'm Captain Rogers, Meridan Galactic Navy," Rogers said, shaking her hand. "I'm in way over my head and really just want a drink."

Sjana laughed again, a carefree, easy laugh that gave Rogers the impression that she didn't worry about too much in life. "An honest man. You won't fit in here."

Rogers shrugged. "I've worked with the Purveyors and the Garliali before."

"I know," Sjana said, her face turning bleak. "That was a dark day. We all thought that would be the end of them."

Rogers raised an eyebrow. "I thought it was."

"Things are rarely that cut and dry, especially when pirates are involved," Sjana said.

She motioned for them all to follow her. Rogers and the Viking exchanged glances, but neither of them said anything. Tunger was busy relaxing into a beanbag chair and hugging what appeared to be a grumpy-looking teddy bear with a purple cape. When Rogers gave him his patented "Are you serious?" look, Tunger jumped up, tucked the teddy bear in, and followed them as well.

"How come you never told me you were married to a pirate captain?" Rogers whispered, leaning over to Mailn.

"Not the kind of thing you disclose on your security paperwork if you want to continue enlistment."

"That's illegal, you know," Rogers said.

Mailn shrugged. "So is pirating, but here we are."

Rogers could tell when he was starting to push too far even when joking with a friend, and that point was rapidly approaching with Mailn. He decided to let the issue go, for now. The Viking obviously knew about all this, which explained why she had been so reluctant to let Mailn come planetside with them. In truth, though, a couple of black eyes wasn't that bad. The

Viking could be kind of overprotective, Rogers guessed. He kind of wished she'd lord over him more.

Sjana led them past the bar—which Rogers realized was serving mostly fine herbal teas and not alcohol—and through a doorway that led to another hallway. This place must have cost a fortune in rent, and half the damn square footage was hallways down which Rogers was apparently going to be led until he died.

Turning abruptly, the pirate captain opened a door and led everyone into a room filled with smoke and the smell of alcohol— much more like what Rogers would expect from a pirating den. Pirates had a flair for the old world, and the room had been decorated with all sorts of old paraphernalia, from sailing-ship wheels, to mermaid statues, to a small-scale replica of a hatch-hunter, a cannon-like device that fired breaching charges at the end of a tube, through which a crew could walk to board a ship.

An old, round table sat in the middle of the room, supported by mismatched legs and a healthy bunch of napkins stuffed underneath the feet to keep it from rocking too much. Sjana indicated that Rogers was to take a seat at one of the two chairs, and Rogers obliged. The rest of his crew remained standing, tense and on guard, except for Tunger, who immediately began walking around the room cooing at the various things on display.

Sjana took a seat as well, throwing one arm over the back of it and somehow making a stiff wooden chair look like an old recliner.

"Cynthia has already told me a bit about what you're trying to do," Sjana said.

Rogers nodded. "So you're aware how both insane and stupid all of this is."

"And you, therefore, must be aware of how much I expect to be paid for all of this."

Without committing, Rogers tapped a couple of fingers on the table.

"You're sure you have the guns to make it worth it?"

"Captain Rogers," Sjana said, "I could lie straight to your face and tell you I have two thousand dreadnought battle cruisers ready to go, and you'd have to believe me. The navy is at a bit of a negotiating disadvantage here."

Rogers snorted. "There's a difference between being desperate and being dead. If the Jupes win, you'll be both."

"That's not a possible state of being, sir," Tunger said.

"Shut up, Tunger."

"And what makes you think we haven't already made deals with the Jupiterians?" Sjana asked.

"Because if you had, you wouldn't all be sipping tea while the Jupes got caught sitting on their heels and setting up blockades instead of taking territory. It's pretty obvious they went off half-cocked and are paying for it. Lucky for us." He pointed at Sjana. "And lucky for your bank accounts."

Sjana let a small smile sit on her lips.

"Look," Rogers said. "I know that pirates tend to stay out of the government unless they're stealing from it, but you have to realize how different this situation is."

"Pirates don't work for charity," Sjana said.

"That's what I told my boss, and that's why I'm not here asking for charity. I'm asking what you want in exchange for paving the way to Snaggardir's HQ."

Leaning back even farther in her chair—something that Rogers didn't think was possible, given how casual she already looked at the negotiating table—Sjana stared straight at him for a moment. For all Rogers knew, she could have been about to draw her pistol and shoot him in the face.

"We want complete and total amnesty and all of our records expunged. We want license to loot any Jupiterian craft that we are able to without legal repercussion, and we want compensation for any resources we lose in the process."

Rogers nearly laughed out loud. That was a huge amount of stuff, almost none of which was in Rogers' power to grant.

Compensation for lost resources? The whole galaxy might be a lost resource without the pirates' help. Then again, pirates had an uncanny ability to lay low during times of trouble, so it was possible that they could hide, survive, and then become active again after the dust settled. Unlike the system governments, the pirates weren't facing extinction here.

"What?" the Viking growled. "Are you serious?"

"Hang on," Rogers interrupted. He turned back to Sjana. "Why the amnesty? You'll just go back to breaking galactic law after the war is over."

Sjana shrugged. "It's not a foregone conclusion that everyone who is currently pirating will continue pirating. Snaggardir's is a very rich company, with very rich ships. If this works out, many pirates will be able to slip into an easy retirement, made much easier if they don't have bounty hunters chasing them all around the galaxy."

Rogers thought for a moment. In no way did Rogers have any legal authority here, nor could he enforce any of the terms that Sjana was asking for. If they were ever fighting in the same sector, Rogers could certainly order his fleet to *not* shoot the pirates if they did a bit of plunder, but he certainly couldn't make any other commanders in any other fleets do the same thing. It was absolutely insane for Rogers to say that was a done deal.

"It's a done deal," Rogers said. He was a frigging expert at promising things he couldn't really deliver. It was half the game of poker. And when this was all said and done, it wouldn't matter if the Jupiterians came out on top. "When can you start?"

Sjana frowned. "Captain Rogers, you disappoint me."

Rogers nodded. "I do this very often to a great many people."

"I thought you were familiar with dealing with pirates?"

"I am," Rogers said.

"So you should know very well that we always end a deal the same way." She leaned forward, a mischievous and almost insane look in her eye.

Rogers understood now, and he got a similar feeling. He leaned forward as well, rubbing his hands together in anticipation. Then, at the same time, both of them shouted:

"We drink!"

Lucinda really wished she *hadn't* found out what the "construction" was all about.

She'd learned a lot about ethical conflicts when getting her business degrees, but the topics typically focused on things like conflicts of interest and tax evasion. When it came to things like intentionally destroying an entire galaxy, and possibly the entire human race, there was maybe like one line somewhere in the back of one book.

She stared at the report on her datapad, feeling like she'd just swallowed a whole fish without chewing or cooking it.

That's a really strange analogy, she thought, but it somehow fit. Her insides felt bloated and full, her lungs really unable to breathe, and the whole thing wriggled inside her.

It must have been forwarded to her by mistake, but that seemed a monumental administrative oversight on someone's part. It was addressed to Mr. Snaggardir, and the "from" line said it was from Dr. Mattic, but for some reason it was sitting here in Lucinda's inbox like the most doomsday piece of spam she'd ever received in her life.

This wasn't just a construction project; it was a megalomaniacal, diabolical piece of galaxy-destroying equipment that was at once both devious and ironic. The plans, modeled after the terraforming technology that had caused the entire Milky Way to collapse, detailed a method by which to hold the entire Fortuna Stultus galaxy hostage.

It was evil.

"Pure evil."

Lucinda whirled, nearly dropping her datapad in the process. She'd received the message in the middle of the hallway on her way to a meeting, but the implications had forced her to stop in her tracks. She hadn't seen Mr. Snaggardir approaching at all.

She felt the blood drain from her face, her lips trembling. If Mr. Snaggardir knew that she knew the full scope of their plans, she would become a liability faster than you could say "Please kill Lucinda and fire her out the airlock, thank you."

"That must be what you're thinking, yes?" Mr. Snaggardir, his hands behind his back, gave her a rare, kind smile. The genuineness of it threw her off; she expected a knife in her chest any second now.

"I, uh," Lucinda said, looking around her. The hallways were empty. They'd called the meeting extremely early in the morning, station time, and Snaggardir's corporate headquarters wasn't a full-time outfit. They still worked bankers' hours. Signs of life were trickling into her awareness in the form of far-off footsteps and muffled conversations, but for the moment they were alone.

"It's alright," Mr. Snaggardir said. "I sent it to you on purpose."

"You what?" Lucinda said. "But this is . . . this is . . ."

"Necessary," Mr. Snaggardir said. "I didn't think so at first, either, but . . ."

He trailed off, his weathered face scrunching up. Old, watery eyes looked beyond her down the empty hallway as if searching for something not in this plane of existence. Maybe in another plane of existence. Where wholesale murder of the human race seemed like a reasonable option.

"Will you walk with me for a moment, Ms. Hiri?"

Lucinda nodded dumbly, her mouth unable to form words. Without unclasping his hands, or waiting for any further response, Mr. Snaggardir took off at a leisurely pace down the hallway.

Snaggardir corporate headquarters was truly a marvel of space engineering. Even though Lucinda had been here for almost half a year now, walking through it always inspired a sense of wonder that helped wipe away any doubts she had about working for such a large, bureaucratic company. With so many years of spacefaring already baked into human history, it was only natural that they'd found ways to adapt, but Snaggardir's headquarters was on a completely different level. If one took the right path through the station, it would be easy to confuse one's location for some of the most beautiful places in Fortuna Stultus. Deep jungles, beautiful beaches, volcanic landscapes . . . all of them could be found, either via very unique biosphere configurations or holographic projections that could fool even the most discerning zoologist.

Right now, though, it wasn't doing much to soothe her. After all, what would be the point of this beauty if they were just going to *blow it all up*?

"I can understand that, not being Jupiterian born, you might not understand what we are going through here," Mr. Snaggardir said as casually as if he was talking about the weather. The sinking feeling that she was about to be pushed out an airlock subsided a touch.

"That's . . . true," Lucinda said.

"I can't provide you with any analogy that is fitting," he said. "I can't describe to you what it feels like to have your heritage erased from the history books and forced to assimilate itself into . . . lesser cultures."

He said the phrase "lesser cultures" with only the slightest of sneers, but it took Lucinda by surprise. There was a heavy arrogance behind that statement that Lucinda was not used to hearing from the calm, calculating man.

"What happened to Jupiter was wrong," Lucinda said. Even though they had, despite the warnings and protestations of every other planet in the solar system, continued their scientific terraforming experiments. Certainly all of Jupiter couldn't have been blamed for that mistake, though.

Mr. Snaggardir looked at her and smiled through cold eyes. "I'm glad you feel that way, though I am not naive enough to think you mean it with the utmost sincerity. The human race and its history are so very, very complicated."

Drawing in a long breath, Mr. Snaggardir let out a ragged sigh that devolved into a coughing fit. It didn't last very long, however, and soon, with a quick wipe of his mouth, he was back to the sage lecturer.

"I know you feel like you probably didn't sign up for this."

The understatement of the century, Lucinda thought.

"That doesn't mean I can't adapt, sir," Lucinda said. Damn it, she was reverting to interview mode. She'd done so many of them that, whenever she was under pressure, she tended to start giving canned interview answers. "I guess you could say if I had one flaw, it's that I'm a workaholic."

Nodding sagely, Mr. Snaggardir turned a corner to lead them toward the meeting room. Undoubtedly, General Szinder, Ms. Alshazari, and Dr. Mattic would be waiting for them to calmly discuss the construction of the . . . thing.

"Did you really need to call it the Galaxy Eater, though?" Lucinda blurted. "I mean, if you're going to posture yourselves as restoring order to the galaxy by getting rev . . . I mean, by restoring Jupiter to its rightful place as a participant, you could have at least called it something ambiguous."

She clapped a hand over her mouth. Babbling streams of contradiction at her boss was not her typical modus operandi. Still, the name *was* ridiculous. It was written in big, bold letters at the top of the report. *Galaxy Eater.* Great.

Mr. Snaggardir chuckled. "That was Gerd's idea," he said, referring to General Szinder. "He has a flare for the dramatic. Didn't fit in very well in the Thelicosan military before the revolution."

He said "before the revolution" like it had happened a hundred years ago, like a Jupiterian victory was already assured, achieved, and relegated to the history books. For the first time in her short career, Lucinda was starting to feel her skin crawl around Mr. Snaggardir. She'd felt nervous, yes, but never . . . scared.

Maybe it was the fear, or the idea that the entire galaxy was about to collapse . . . again . . . but Lucinda felt like if she didn't speak up now, she'd never forgive herself.

"But, sir," she said. "Don't you think it's a little excessive? The entire galaxy can't be to blame for what happened to Jupiter any more than all Jupiterians being blamed for the Milky Way's collapse. There has to be some other way."

Sal Snaggardir stopped in the middle of the hallway and rounded on her with a speed that she hadn't thought could come from the old man's bones. He loomed over her, his face still not breaking from his soft smile.

"There is no other way."

"For what?" a voice sang out from behind them.

Lucinda, still rooted to the spot by Mr. Snaggardir's piercing glare, couldn't bring herself to turn around. Distantly, she recognized the voice of Snaggardir's itself, Sara Alshazari. Even in the headquarters station, she was constantly subjected to barrages of Sara congratulating her for trivial tasks and awarding her free Snaggardir's goods.

"I was just explaining to our intern here the reasoning behind our little construction project," Mr. Snaggardir said with a smile that was a bit more genuine. For all his talk of destroying the galaxy, he did tend to dote on his niece a bit.

"Oh, that," Sara said. She didn't look very enthused, but she also didn't raise any protests. Sara turned to Lucinda, smiling warmly. "We all hope it doesn't come to that. I don't think it will, either." She frowned. "Although I sometimes think the general wants to make that the first option, rather than the last."

Mr. Snaggardir and Sara shared a small laugh over that, but Lucinda didn't find it funny. Despite practically threatening her life in the middle of the hallway, he seemed to think the discussion was concluded. Both of them started chatting about family matters before stepping into the meeting room, leaving Lucinda feeling dumbstruck and somewhat terrified.

Did she really need to be terrified, though? Everyone involved in this was treating it so casually. And Jupiter *did* deserve a seat at the table when it came to galactic matters. Something needed to be done . . . but blowing it all up?

Of course it probably wouldn't come to that. It was just insurance, right? Who was she to make these sorts of decisions? She was just an intern, an employee who was in way over her head.

They literally called it the *Galaxy Eater*, though.

Ha–Ha, You Said "Duty"

"This is a load of bullshit," Captain Baerbarg said. "I've spent my whole damn career trying to stop pirates, and now I'm supposed to give them a royal escort through space."

The order from Meridan HQ stared him in the face from his datapad. He didn't like taking orders from them, either, but apparently there had been all kinds of movements lately. Something had happened in every system, and now there were Jupiterians running around, pirates running around with them, and everyone else running around trying to look like they were part of the solution. It was a lot of running around.

Being the commander of a small Grandellian fast-attack squadron, Baerbarg was an expert at pirate hunting. The whole squadron boasted five ships, enough to handle most situations. His missions had been simple, short, concrete. Escort this convoy, shoot anybody who tries to jump them. Go board this pirate vessel while they were resupplying at such-and-such station, and so forth. And now he was supposed to hold the pirates' hands so they could go save the day? What a crock of shit.

Did that mean that the pirates were now privateers instead of pirates? Or were they buccaneers? What was the damn difference? They were all thieves, and they all belonged on the business end of a plasma cannon.

"Nothing we can do about it now, Captain," his first mate, Keila Puhl, said from her station in front of him on the bridge. Most of their small crew was off the bridge at the moment for meals, since there was surprisingly not much action going on in their sector. They were on the very edge of Meridan space, a place hardly patrolled by the Meridans, never mind the Grandellian fleet. The nearest thing to them was a newly designated refuse dump, just one or two Un-Space points away. Weirdly, the navigational charts currently showed a restricted operating zone around the whole dump. Maybe there'd been some sort of hazardous-material leak.

"Yeah, yeah," Baerbarg said. He tossed the datapad on the side of his captain's console, where a cold cup of coffee and half-eaten biscuit had been for the last several hours. "Nothing at all. You're right."

Puhl was the right kind of woman to be his first mate. He was prone to impulses; she kept him calm and rational. He was quick under pressure; she was quick to tell him that not everything was pressure. They'd made a good team these last two years. Strictly professional, of course, which meant that they'd been sleeping together regularly for most of their time together. They were Grandellian, after all.

"Hey," Puhl said suddenly, pointing at the console next to hers. "What's that?"

"Hm?" Baerbarg leaned forward, squinting. "New ship?"

Punching a couple of buttons at his terminal, he routed the information stream so he could see a map of the area overlaid by a disposition of forces. Despite being told to escort the pirates, they didn't have any pirates to escort just yet, so they'd been staked out near the Un-Space point to wait. Very little was happening otherwise—blockades had restricted a lot of traffic—but someone else had just come through the gateway. Their threat warning system took a minute to make its assessment and identification.

"What are they doing out here?" Puhl said, leaning back in her chair. She didn't look very concerned, and, honestly, she had no reason to be. Whenever Jupiterians attacked, they just came slamming through Un-Space points, maneuvering a collection of stolen ships, and started shooting right away. This one just looked lost.

The computations went through, and the computer got a good lock on the ship's IFF, which showed it as a Meridan Patrol Fleet vessel. Sort of a paramilitary unit that was more border patrol than police, the MPF was technically attached to the Meridan Galactic Navy.

"All alone?" Baerbarg muttered. "Send them a hail, will you?"

"You got it, boss," Puhl said, and started pressing buttons.

"Why is the registry taking so long to ID them?" Baerbarg said, starting to see if he could look up the ship's serial number manually. As part of the IFF package it broadcast, all ships were required by galactic law to include certain information. Normally the ship's systems would run that info through their databases quickly, but this was taking a little while to bring up the information.

"They're not responding," Puhl said.

Puhl didn't sound on edge, but she rarely did. The unidentified MPF ship wasn't doing anything threatening, but Baerbarg still felt uneasy. You didn't just pop into a sector, do nothing, and say nothing.

"Tell the rest of the squadron to form up. Send the *Queen* out there to intercept."

Puhl spun around in her chair. "Really? It's just an MPF ship. It's probably got something wrong with its systems, boss, like a busted transmitter or something."

Baerbarg didn't look at her; he was busy staring at the grainy visual display that his ships' cameras could supply. "If they're radios-out, they should be giving us signals," Baerbarg said. "There's procedures for things like that."

"You ever known a Meridan to follow procedures?"

Baerbarg grunted, thinking. Something didn't feel right. "Send the order."

"You got it, boss," Puhl said again, her tone flat.

It didn't take long for the *Queen*, one of their smaller, faster ships, to respond to the order and start moving out. In the meantime, Baerbarg was ready to put his fist through his console; the network was taking an extremely long time to go through the MPF database and pull the identification of the mystery ship. Had the IFF been spoofed? Was Baerbarg not inputting the correct serial number because someone had programmed the IFF to lie? It was difficult to do, but not impossible. Usually, though, there were other signs that the IFF had been tampered with. In the past, when pirates had tried the same thing, there had always been something like a misspelled word or a large red box that popped up with the word "tampered" on it. Here, though, everything looked legitimate.

"Ah!" Baerbarg said. "There it is."

"Found her?"

"Yeah. Kind of weird, though, it wasn't in the main ship registry. For some weird reason it was reported as destroyed not too long ago. The whole crew is listed as KIA."

Puhl grinned. "Well they're going to be really happy to find out that they're not all dead! What's her name?"

Baerbarg couldn't share in her humor, for some reason. He started cross-referencing reports with the serial number, looking to see if there was anything else he could find out about the ship.

"The MPS *Rancor*," he said. "Says here they flew into an asteroid."

"They look pretty good for having flown into an asteroid," Puhl said, turning back around to look outside.

"Yeah . . . ," Baerbarg said.

Silently, they watched the *Queen* fly toward the *Rancor*. The other three ships formed a battle line with his ship, the *Curtain Call*, in the center.

"Is it . . . possible that it did actually hit an asteroid?" Puhl said, starting to sound a little less aloof now. "We might not be able to see all the physical damage, but maybe everyone on board died from the inertial impact. I've seen that kind of thing before."

"What, a ship automatically navigate itself through Un-Space? I don't think so."

Baerbarg understood where Puhl was coming from, but he highly doubted it. Someone would have had to see the ship hit an asteroid in order to report it, unless someone did some really fancy sleuthing and cross-referenced asteroid positions with the ship's navigational log before impact. If someone saw it collide, they'd go pick up the survivors, not just let it float around in space.

"Hey, boss," a voice came over the radio. Baerbarg recognized it as Commander Fouffe, the captain of the *Queen*. "We're right next to them, and we're not getting any response either. I can see a lot of blast points on the hull, as well as some physical damage from debris. This thing has seen some action for sure. It's possible that the comms were damaged. We want to hop aboard and see what's going on."

"You're authorized," Baerbarg said. "Suit up for a hostile boarding, though, okay? We don't know what the hell is on that ship."

Baerbarg hated moments like these, the moments when he just sat in this stupid chair and watched other people do the work. He couldn't hear anything over the radio, either, so it ended up just being a long, awkward, tense silence that made him want to break something. In truth, most things made him want to break something. Any other time, Puhl and he would have broken each other. A couple of times.

Fifteen slow minutes passed by. No matter how many times they sent a message to the *Queen*'s crew, they didn't get a response. Baerbarg generally liked to avoid clogging up their comms with requests for status reports—they were likely busy—but the hair on the back of his neck was standing up. Nobody was talking anymore, and the *Queen* wasn't moving. Still tethered to the *Rancor* by its docking platform, it floated in space.

"I don't like this," Baerbarg said.

"I know you don't," Puhl said. She turned around to give him a reassuring smile, but it didn't convince him. She was worried too.

"Keep sending messages. We'll give them five minutes. Nothing on that ship should be preventing them from checking in."

"Got it."

Five minutes passed by at a snail's pace, and Baerbarg had enough.

"Bring everyone up from the mess hall and tell them to get to battle stations," Baerbarg said. "I'm issuing a—"

"Captain Baerbarg," Commander Fouffe said. "Please desist. We apologize about the silence. We experienced a magnetic field that temporarily disabled our communications."

Baerbarg let out a long, slow breath. "For fuck's sake . . . you couldn't have sent someone outside to tell us that as soon as you figured it out?"

"It was impossible to discern our lack of communications while we were inside the ship."

Squinting, Baerbarg and Puhl exchanged glances. Something about the *Queen*'s captain sounded a little weird. Then again, he *did* just say that there was a magnetic-field disruption. Whatever that meant.

"Fine. What did you dig up?"

A long pause. "Captain, we were not equipped with shovels to dig anything."

"What?"

Another long pause. "Please disregard. I wanted to inform you that the field disruption has fused our docking hatch to the *Beta Test.*"

"The what?"

"The *Rancor*. We will need help with decoupling," Captain Fouffe said. He sounded tired, almost bored.

"Stand by one sec, Fouffe." Baerbarg cut the comms for a moment.

"What the hell is going on here?" Baerbarg asked out loud.

"I have no idea," Puhl said. "He sounds like he's on drugs. Maybe a gas leak?"

"Maybe a trap."

The two of them were silent for a moment as they went through scenarios in their heads. One possibility, obviously, was that the MPS *Rancor* had been stolen, which would explain the damage and the fact that it was alone. It didn't explain *how* someone had made off with an MPF ship, or how they'd managed to convince the MPF to report it destroyed via asteroid collision. That level of record spoofing was beyond any pirate, terrorist, or thirteen-year-old recluse that Baerbarg had ever heard of.

"Should we go?" Baerbarg asked.

Puhl was quiet for a moment. Instead of answering, she seemed to be looking through some data at her console, though Baerbarg wasn't sure what it was. If Fouffe was in trouble, he'd be using his distress word—a word that typically isn't used in any logical context that would alert the crew that he was in danger and couldn't openly talk about it—but Fouffe hadn't said "dittle" even once. Maybe he was just tired?

Baerbarg opened the communication channel again.

"What's the situation down there?" he asked.

"The crew of the *Rancor* has been attempting to activate their distress beacon, but have been unable to do so. Their navigational systems are operational, but communications are down. They are requesting evacuation and escort."

Puhl was still looking through some records on her console, and didn't look back at Baerbarg to give him any advice.

"We're not equipped to tow," Baerbarg said. "We can take on the crew and send a message to their closest spaceport to send someone. Are you still stuck?"

"We are unable to disengage our docking bridge."

Baerbarg cut the comms again.

"What do you think?" he finally asked Puhl.

Puhl turned around and shrugged. "I can't see any reason not to go," Puhl said. "I've been querying the Meridan local authorities about the ship without giving too much away. Looks like that KIA report is confirmed. They seemed kind of surprised that we were talking about it."

Baerbarg flipped the switch again. "We're on our way. Stand by."

"Stand by what, Captain?"

Man, Fouffe was acting weird. "Just wait a bit. We'll be there."

Calling the crews to their stations and preparing everyone for movement only took a few minutes. Soon they were cruising the short distance across empty space to where the *Rancor*, and now the *Queen*, was stranded. He hoped that it wasn't some sort of software fault that was going to spread to his ship once they got there and exchanged codes, or they'd all be dealing with quarantine real quick.

Since the main hatch of the *Queen* was already taken up by being stuck to the *Rancor*, they had to maneuver their ship to connect to one of the maintenance hatches, but that wasn't a problem. They'd interdicted and boarded pirates many times; this was like standard procedure for them all by now. Everyone went about their business quietly and efficiently, calling out status reports as necessary. Baerbarg and Puhl remained on the bridge; in this small of a crew configuration, they did most of the piloting, and the delicate maneuvers required to bring them abreast of the *Queen* required a steady hand.

Well, really, it required a complicated automation program. But it required a steady hand to execute it.

With docking complete, all that was left was to wait and see what came out of the ship. Because they had to use their own, smaller bridge, there weren't any cameras that Baerbarg could use to monitor the situation and see who was behind the door when it opened. He had to rely on his crew to yell at him, which really seemed like—

Sounds erupted from the lower part of his ship, where the docking hatch was located. Things were banging around violently, followed by cursing and shouting. A moment later, all fell silent.

Baerbarg and Puhl were both already up, pistols in hand.

"Hey!" Baerbarg shouted as the two of them moved to get down to the lower part of the ship. "What's going on down there?"

A voice came up, accompanied by embarrassed laughter. It sounded like Veene, his quartermaster.

"It's fine, boss! Dropped something before I opened the door. It's just a robot. Wants to talk to you about something called 'protocol 162.' I think he's an evangelist or something."

Rogers had never had an office before. In fact, he clearly remembered conversations he'd had when he'd been a young starman first class talking about how the only people who needed offices were people who didn't need personalities. Of course, he had his stateroom on the *Flagship*, but that was different. Now, while he was waiting for further orders, he'd been given a small office in Meridan Naval Headquarters relatively near Holdt's. Bouncing back and forth between the surface of Merida Prime and the *Flagship* was expensive, inefficient, and probably would have made Rogers throw up a lot.

As soon as he walked in for the first time, Rogers immediately hated it. Offices were like work traps; no matter where you hid, someone could always find your office and put work in it for you that you'd eventually have to complete when you came back. Baited with a comfortable leather chair, your name on the door, and the promise of a better pension, you could never really resist stepping inside and taking another phone call about pie charts. Rogers barely enjoyed phone calls about pie.

In this case, his "work trap" was a very upset Sergeant Mailn.

"I'm surprised that you are acting like this," Rogers said. "You never mentioned your wife before two days ago, and we went into that bar with the express purpose of getting them to fight for us. Now you're all upset about it?"

Mailn stared at him with a flat expression. Her black eye was just starting to fade away, which was perfect, because now the other eye was black. She was starting to look like a raccoon, and Rogers was starting to have real, deep questions about the meaning of love and marriage.

"I'm not 'acting like' anything, Rogers," she said. "I'm just saying I hope you know what you're doing."

Rogers blinked. "I have never, at any point in all of this, claimed that I had any idea what I am doing. In fact, I distinctly remember standing in the middle of the bridge and declaring to everyone around me, several times, that I do *not* know what I am doing."

A tense couple of days after the pirate negotiations had devolved into a frat party, Rogers had finally extricated all of his crew from the local drunk tanks. Mailn, after sobering up for a day, had asked to talk to him. Now that she *was* talking to him, however, Rogers wished she was back in the drunk tank.

"What are we going to be doing while they're out there fighting?" Mailn asked.

"Hell if I know. Right now we're on standby, waiting for orders from Holdt. The Viking is supposed to be setting up schedules for shore leave for the rest of the marines, and I'll have someone do the same for the rest of the fleet. There's no reason for everyone just to sit around on high alert until we get new orders."

Mailn, who had started pacing back and forth, rounded on Rogers.

"So Sjana is just going to go out there and fight our battles for us while we sit here and sip cocktails on the beach?"

Rogers hesitated. "I mean, that doesn't sound exactly *bad*, does it?"

Seeing that this, perhaps, was not the time for jokes, Rogers got up from his desk and walked around it so that he could speak to Mailn face-to-face. This was pretty easy, since Rogers was kind of short and so was she. Despite Rogers' lack of desire to explore feelings and deep, personal problems at the moment, he knew he owed Mailn a lot. He also knew that there wasn't anything he could do about it at the moment. The situation was bigger than any one person, or one marriage, or even one military unit. It was almost weird how big it was getting; Rogers was starting to feel very small.

"Cynthia, I can't just make the fleet assemble and go do something for the sake of doing something. I have a lot of lives to consider here, not just yours and your wife's."

Even as the words left his mouth, they felt weird, like he was chewing someone else's gum. But, he realized, it was the reality of things. He really did have thousands of lives under his command, and eventually Holdt was going to tell him to send them someplace to fight. An uncomfortable hatred for the Jupiterians bubbled up underneath the surface of his emotions. This was *their* fault. The droids, the subsequent near-invasion of the Thelicosans, his rapid promotion from civilian to acting admiral. All of it was because of *them*.

"Rogers, are you listening to me?" Mailn asked.

Rogers shook his head, which he always thought was a very cliché thing to do when coming out of deep thoughts, and cleared his throat.

"No," he said.

She glared at him.

"I'm just being honest," Rogers said. "If I had lied and said yes, you would have done that stupid schoolteacher thing and asked me to repeat the last thing I said to you, and we'd still be where we are right now."

Mailn sighed. "I swear . . ."

"Look," Rogers said, putting a hand on her shoulder. She slapped him away. "You've given me good advice in the past. You even taught me how to duck, which may be the only physically demanding thing I've ever been competent at. So let me give you some advice in return. Let it go."

Her face contorted into disbelief and shock, and it looked as though she was about to punch him in the face. He knew this because he was developing an uncanny ability to predict when women were about to do this to him. She was about to do this to him. Rogers stepped back.

"Sometimes I wish I hadn't taught you how to duck at all," she said. "I'm glad you think this is just something that I can let go. I'll go ahead and just forget about all of this and continue saluting you and calling you sir—"

"You never do either of those things."

"—and letting King Rogers the Hero be the expert of everything—"

"Not a single accurate word in that sentence except my name."

"—and I'll just wait for my wife to die alone out in space while we sit here and do nothing."

Rogers sighed, sitting back on the surface of his desk. Breaking eye contact with Mailn, he stared at a spot on the floor and thought for a long moment. Was there, in fact, something that he could do for her, or for Sjana? Likely not. The pirates would have to rely on their own strength and motivation to win their skirmishes and break the blockades. Rogers didn't know the overall battle plan for them—in fact, he was pretty sure nobody did—and he couldn't request reinforcements or try to find another way around all of this. It was the best plan. Surely Mailn saw that?

He was missing something, he realized, and he'd said it at the very beginning of the conversation. Mailn had known what was going to happen when she took them to meet the pirates in the first place. Rogers knew her; she wasn't stupid. There was no way she didn't foresee the outcome. Maybe Mailn wasn't actually looking for him to do anything at all except listen to her for a little while.

Looking up at Mailn, he gave her a small smile. "Anything else?"

The sergeant seemed a little taken aback by the question. She fumbled for her words, clenched her fists a few times, and in general looked like she wanted to spit or set the building on fire. Finally her whole body relaxed.

"I'm going back to the *Flagship*," Mailn said, turning around to walk away without preamble. "Unlike a certain captain I know, I have better things to do with my time than screw around planetside and make stupid jokes while the world burns."

"Which captain is that?" Rogers asked. "They sound like someone I'd like to have a drink with."

Mailn gave him the finger behind her head.

"See?" Rogers shouted after her. "Not a salute!"

M Pathetic

It was a testament to the maturity of his moral compass that Deet understood, with some levels of vagueness, that droid fu was a dangerous, spectacular skill not to be used except in the most dire of circumstances.

Then again, the moral compass he was so proud of appeared to be experiencing some magnetic interference. For one, Deet didn't understand why they would call it a moral compass instead of a map. From what he understood of morality, there wasn't always one right answer that might be considered a parallel to true north. For another thing, maps showed that there were an almost infinite number of ways to get to the same destination, and no two paths were alike. That seemed a lot more like morality to Deet.

Right now he was trying to see any of the infinite paths that allowed him to turn the human in front of him into paste and still be considered an upstanding member of the 331st. It seemed mutually exclusive, but Deet was confident he could find a way.

"I'm sorry," the security guard said. "I just can't go around letting every droid I see walk into the secure area, no matter what you say your boss's name is. You require a security clearance and the need-to-know credentials before I can let you in."

"I do need to know," Deet said. "I need to know very badly. And I'm not 'every droid.' In fact, I think I'm the only droid."

This was true, of course. By some miracle of policy, Rogers had been able to keep Deet activated while every other droid was being systematically dismantled and inspected by every artificial intelligence technician on the planet. With the information Deet had supplied about their operating system—specifically the part about being expressly designed to kill every human in a ten-mile radius of their position—everyone had decided that it would be safer to leave them deactivated until they could completely redesign their OS.

Which, of course, meant forever, because the only organization smart enough to do that level of design work was Snaggardir's.

"No," the guard said again. Deet beeped.

All around him, the plethora of military activity really gave the impression that there was something very serious going on. Deet had seen the business of humans bouncing around the command deck of the *Flagship*, but that had clearly been an attempt to appear busy rather than moving toward actual objectives. There had been a lot of saluting and "yes, ma'am"-ing, but not a significant amount of work. Commander Belgrave had described it as people "justifying their existence," but Deet wasn't quite sure he understood that yet. He was still coming to terms with the idea of his own existence. He could work on justifying it later.

Regardless, there was nothing around him to indicate that any of these people were engaging in meaningless work to impress other members of their species. The men and women moving in and out of the secure area looked haggard and worried. Nearly everyone was studying *The Art of War II: Now In Space*, which Deet was sure was not the correct way to go about this war. He had also learned, however, that humans had some kind of design flaw that forced them to repeat past performances and hope for different futures. Despite how many times they were told they needed to learn a new way to fight, they spent their time studying the old way instead, because nobody was ready to *teach* them a new way to fight.

To their credit, Deet thought, it was clear they weren't just looking busy. They *were* busy. Doing the completely wrong things, of course, but they were busy.

That left Deet stuck. After combing through millions and millions of data points using publicly accessible and sensitive-but-unclassified information, Deet had practically exhausted the sources of information available to him. The data servers on Merida Prime, specifically the ones in Admiral Holdt's office, had been of greater value than the wider net—anything was better than a jammed 331st data server—but it still wasn't enough for Deet to build a big picture.

What picture was that? Deet wasn't so sure. And not knowing was starting to really bother him. He knew all kinds of minutiae about Snaggardir's corporate filings, tax evasion lawsuits, and even some things about its personnel, but so far he'd been totally unable to unearth, or even infer, information about their artificial intelligence program. Dr. Mattic was a complete mystery.

Some of the information he'd uncovered would help the war effort, undoubtedly, but it still wasn't what he was looking for. In a way that Deet wasn't sure he could analyze, there seemed to be a deep divide in his circuits about his responsibility to Rogers and the crew, and his curiosity about his origins.

Like humans, though, he was rapidly learning to ignore that complicated moral conundrum. Much like he was trying to figure out how to ignore the moral conundrum of it being illegal to protocol 162 the military police security guard preventing him from gaining entry into the classified vault of Meridan Naval Headquarters.

Now here he was, trying to talk, rather than kill—he was still nearly certain that would be wrong—his way into a secure area where highly classified intelligence information was stored, discussed, analyzed, and then promptly ignored by anyone who made high-level decisions.

"Look," Deet said, which he never really understood. If you weren't pointing at anything, why did everyone always tell other people to "look" before saying something poignant? "The info is just sitting there. Nobody is going to actually use it. Why not let me in there to have a peek? I'm very important to the war effort."

The security guard seemed unimpressed. "If you were that important to the war effort, they would have given you a clearance."

"What do I have to do to get a clearance?"

"Well, you need to fill out a complicated security form, MNF-21, and—"

"Done," Deet said, bringing up the form and auto-completing it with as much fake information as he could. He didn't want to compromise the fact that Merida technically still classified him as "disposed," which allowed him some level of anonymity. "I can transfer it to your datapad immediately if you give me your contact code."

The security guard actually laughed, though Deet didn't see anything funny about being both brilliant and efficient. But wait . . . could Deet really be considered brilliant?

No, Deet thought. *No time for that now.* But wait . . . was he really thinking?

[EXPLETIVE] focus, D-24!

He knew he was serious when he used his full name with himself.

"There's a lot more to it than just a form. You have to do a background check."

"That shouldn't take long," Deet said. "I have no background."

"Other than being built by the people we're fighting?" the security guard quipped. "I'm not stupid."

"Well, what else do I have to do?" Deet asked. His logic circuits were possibly beginning to get hot. Was this rage?

"Be a human." The guard shifted his rather large disruptor rifle to his other shoulder. He was definitely compensating for something by carrying that, Deet thought. It was probably the fact that his human arms were much less effective at killing people.

"That seems racist," Deet said.

"You don't have a race," the security guard said, leaning back in his chair. For a security guard who was, ostensibly, guarding highly sensitive information, he didn't seem very alert. In fact, none of this seemed very secure at all. It was just one guy in a chair standing in a shack outside of a fenced-in area. "In any case, all of this is way above my pay grade anyway. You have to get a clearance, go get it validated, go get read into all our special programs, submit a bunch of forms, then go get a badge with your picture on it that goes beep when you put it against the magnetic strip here." The guard pointed to a small box next to the gate. "No beep, no entry."

Deet beeped.

"Nice try," the security guard said.

"What if I told you that my analysis of the information stored in this facility was crucial to the war effort?"

"I'd probably refer back to the beginning of this conversation where you just sort of came up and asked me if you could 'come in and have a look.'"

"[EXCREMENT]," Deet said. He was getting better with lying—for him, it was mostly about giving half-truths that were open to interpretation—but he hadn't yet mastered the idea of lying with forethought. Constructing a long string of untruths to fulfill an objective was still a very difficult thing for his logic circuits to handle.

Deet allowed a moment or two to pass without saying anything or moving. In his experience, prolonged and unexpected periods of silence made humans feel awkward. It also made them feel like they needed to fill the silence with something, which often made them say or do stupid things. He realized after a few seconds that hoping the guard would spontaneously open the door just to be rid of him was a little far-fetched. Was there something more human-like he could do in this situation that might help him achieve his goals? What would Belgrave advise?

"So," Deet said.

The guard gave him a blank look.

"How do you feel?" Deet asked.

"What the hell are you on about?" the guard said. "I don't have time to play married couple over here right now. I'm supposed to be manning this security post and making sure people without clearances, like you, don't get in."

Deet nodded, something he often forgot to do when acknowledging a human's speech.

"And how does that make you feel?" Deet asked.

"Didn't I just say I don't have time to talk about my emotions right now? I'm busy. You know, sitting here. Doing nothing with my life, and watching people walk up to that little box. Hearing beeps over and over again and saluting officers."

Deet nodded, slower this time. "That sounds really hard."

"It *is* hard!" the guard said. He put his disruptor rifle on the table beside him. "People think it's easy to just sit here all day and nod at people. My chiropractor slaps me every time I go into her office!" Leaning forward, the guard put his face in his hands. "It's like nobody cares at all."

Amazing, Deet thought. *This empathy* [EXCREMENT] *really works!*

"So can I go inside now that we've clearly established emotional rapport?"

The security guard, who may or may not have been crying, looked up and cocked his head at Deet.

"No. You don't have a clearance."

Deet threw his arms in the air, which, though completely unnecessary, was very satisfying. He understood why Rogers did it all the time.

"Well [EXPLETIVE] your [MATERNAL FORNICATING] [POLITICAL FIGURE]."

Deet walked off quickly, a motion he had come to understand as "storming," which bizarrely involved no precipitation at all.

"I thought you cared how I felt!" the guard shouted after him.

Ignoring the security guard, Deet went back to where the public transportation system let people off and examined the situation. A large, ominous fence stretched around the perimeter of a small collection of buildings, each of them protected by their own layer of security. The guard with whom Deet had been conversing was watching over the entrance to the compound, but each of the doors looked reinforced. The amount of beeps coming out of the area, and the way that humans kept awkwardly bending over to touch their chests to the wall, indicated that there were more card readers on the doors inside the compound.

Deet had observed a lot of human activity in the short time after his activation, so he thought he had a fairly good sense of what he could do in this situation. In almost all instances, when interpersonal relationships failed, there was only one option.

Deet was going to have to blow up the compound.

No, wait. That wasn't going to solve anything. If he was going to be able to plug into the network terminals and start accessing classified information, he was going to have to keep them intact. That was just common sense. The fact that he had even considered blowing everything up was indicative of how humans were really beginning to influence his processing.

Pausing for a moment, he contemplated this. Did the fact that he had just considered doing something very stupid make him more human? He would have to ask Belgrave. Ignoring evidence and persisting in stupid courses of action did seem to be a defining human trait.

Deet contented himself with watching the patterns of movement for a few minutes. Everyone more or less walked about in a factory-like fashion, as though propelled by moving conveyor belts from the transportation system or the zipcar parking lot to the gate that Deet had been stopped at, then heading into the interior of the compound. From there, they broke off into whatever functional specifications required them to go to a specific building. People exiting the building didn't seem to be using their keycards at all; they simply walked through the locked doors and exited via a large turnstile that allowed them to reintegrate with the unclassified world.

Beep. Enter. *Beep.* Enter. Salute. *Beep.* Enter. The pattern repeated itself many times a minute, and Deet found himself watching without watching, his deferred procedure calls devoting fewer and fewer milliseconds to observing the phenomenon. He thought humans defined this as "zoning out," but he could of course recall all the information he'd observed in less than a billionth of a second. After humans zoned out, they simply stared at their conversation partner and got embarrassed.

Based on his observations, Deet knew that the keycards were magnetic. If he could get close enough to someone with an appropriate keycard, he could droid-fu them and take the card from the messy puddle of their remains.

No. Not "subtle" enough. Again, based on the experience with the other droids, he was almost certain at least one or two people would be upset with him if he murdered an innocent to reach his goal.

But if murder wasn't an option, was there any real progress to be made here?

If the keycards were magnetic, and didn't function off any other biometrics that would be difficult for Deet to replicate, he could perhaps pass near one of the humans holding an access card and make a copy of it. He could then route the magnetic impulse through his fingers, and simply touch the keypad. If he made a good enough copy, it should work.

With the grace only a practiced spy could have, Deet surreptitiously placed himself in the direct middle of the large stream of people going in and out of the compound. After being jostled in just about every direction for a minute and not receiving any solid signals, Deet realized that perhaps this had not been the correct approach to solving this problem. The magnetic impulses were changing too fast as everyone walked past him, since everyone had their own individual keycard. Just as he thought he was going to be able to grab the credentials and the code that activated them, his position would change and the whole process would have to be started over again.

"[EXPLETIVE] me," Deet said, causing more than a few heads to turn in his direction. Well, everyone was already looking at him, he realized. His subtlety processing was not as advanced as perhaps it could have been; he was, after all, the only droid in Merida standing motionless in the middle of a crowd of people. After another few moments, the entire crowd diverted so as not to come in contact with him, which he thought was very offensive.

Hmm, he thought. *Now I am considering stupid courses of action and feeling offended.* He would also report this to Belgrave.

This clearly was not working. He was going to have to, unfortunately, engage one of them in conversation again. But who? Everyone appeared very busy, tapping on their datapads and barely even acknowledging each other. The security guard was ready to engage, but he was clearly bored and scared he would die alone after leading a meaningless and trite existence. Perhaps he had a clearance?

Engaging his optical zoom, Deet could clearly see that the cards that everyone else had around him looked nothing like the card of the security guard. Given his position, there was a good chance he wasn't allowed into the classified area either.

Deet started choosing people at random, which was just about as effective as standing in the middle of a crowd of people and expecting someone to talk to him. Half of the people he approached didn't even see him—they were so focused on whatever was on their datapads—and the rest gave him a mixture of one-word answers, made eye contact and then ignored him anyway, or screamed in terror and ran away, which Deet thought was kind of ridiculous. Just because every single droid in the Merida system had tried to slaughter everyone around them didn't mean that *Deet* was going to do the same thing. People could be so narrow-minded sometimes.

Running after people yelling "How does that make you feel?" yielded considerably less satisfying results than it had with the security guard, though some people started to sob. Clearly empathy wasn't going to help this situation. He tried telling a joke or two, but nobody stood around long enough to hear the punch line, and absolutely nobody wanted to hear him talk about existentialism. It was like these people didn't even care that they were alive.

That left lying to attract attention, and that wasn't exactly Deet's strongest skill. If he could offer someone something that they truly desired, they might stop and talk to him long enough for him to scan their card and then immediately forget the relationship.

Deet approached a tired lieutenant commander who was frowning at nothing that Deet could see. He wasn't holding a datapad, so he wasn't as distracted as most, which made him a good target.

"Excuse me," Deet said. "Have you heard about our lord and savior—"

"Go away," the officer said, and pushed past him.

Deet's internal monitors told him he'd barely gotten thirty percent through copying the man's keycard, which was not a success. He needed a one hundred percent copy of one person's card, not an amalgamation of several cards. He decided to try again.

"Hello there," Deet said, approaching a younger starman first class who looked nervous and impressionable. She carried three datapads, amazingly, but wasn't looking at any of them.

"Um, yes . . . sir? Ma'am? Bot?" She was blinking rather fast, and her knuckles whitened from holding the datapads. Deet had seen her type before; even though she was a few ranks from the very bottom of the enlisted tier, she was clearly very new and having trouble dealing with the pressures of military life. He knew this because she looked almost exactly like Rogers in almost every situation that required anything other than drinking.

"Sir is fine," Deet said, trying to sound comforting. Was he really a sir, though? He'd never considered the possibility that he might be something else entirely. He did have a rather prominent dongle. Deet filed this away for further analysis later.

"I couldn't help but notice you were carrying three datapads," Deet said. He was twenty percent through with the copy, but the connection was spotty. He realized quickly that distance was a great barrier for copying the magnetic code inside the keycards; he had to be quite close in order for it to work properly. Every time the starman even rocked on her heels backward, the transfer speed slowed considerably.

"That's, um, true," she said. She glanced at Deet, then back at the datapads, then back at Deet again. As she shifted them in her grip, her name tag popped into view, which Deet read as Czensky.

Deet stepped closer to try to egg the copying process on. Of course there was nothing to indicate to Czensky that he was doing anything other than standing there—all of the processing was happening internally—but she clearly looked uncomfortable. He wondered which part was making her more suspicious: the fact that a droid was talking to her or the fact that said droid was roughly six inches from her face. He remembered hearing something about humans' "personal space," but didn't quite understand the concept.

"A-are you okay?" Czensky asked, stuttering a bit as she spoke. She shifted the datapads in her hands again. Forty-five percent.

"I have information vital to your mission," Deet said.

"My m-mission? What's my mission? Captain Kivarayan just told me to go get his datapads back from IT. He's going to be really upset if I don't get back soon. Excuse me."

Starman Czensky made to move around Deet, but Deet quickly sidestepped to remain in her path. She stopped and sucked in a tiny breath, indicating that she was, perhaps, about to begin sobbing. Sixty percent, now, but the movement caused the connection to break momentarily. Deet stepped closer.

"This is really weird," Czensky said. "Everything is so weird."

"Those datapads contain information," Deet said. [EXPLETIVE] but that was a terrible attempt at a lie. Of course they contained information; they were built to contain information! He'd tried to make up something that might have given her a bit more pause, but his logic circuits interrupted the lie by truncating unverifiable information.

"If your mission is to deliver those datapads, and they have information in them . . . ," Deet said, his voice starting to break up as he attempted to weave some convincing lie into the conversation.

"Are you doing okay?" Czensky asked again. "You seem to be having some trouble."

"I'm fine," Deet said. "I have . . . vital . . . your . . . information . . ."

[EXPLETIVE]! He'd lied to the IT department on the *Flagship* during the droid takeover. Why couldn't he do it now? That, by comparison, was much more complicated than simply trying to delay a starman for a bit longer. Eighty percent. Just a few more seconds.

"I . . . my . . . you . . . we . . ." Deet could have sworn he saw a spark fly out of his eye.

"How are you feeling?" Czensky said, her white-knuckle grip on the datapad lessening. For some reason, she seemed to be relaxing, despite having a malfunctioning droid freaking out in front of her.

Deet emitted a synthesized noise that was his approximation

of a sigh, which seemed to change every time he did it. This time it sounded like a distant, screeching tire. "I'm trying to lie to you," he said, "but I can't."

A moment of silence stopped the conversation as people flowed around them, apparently no longer disturbed by a droid in their midst. The young starman Czensky and Deet became like a droid/human rock in a river, with the tide of humans parting to go avoid them. Ninety percent, but Deet knew he was about to lose her. He'd just admitted, for reasons he couldn't understand, that he had been trying to lie to her.

Deet waited for her to sound the alarm that an insane, conniving droid was trying to elicit highly sensitive information from her.

Instead, Czensky gave him what might have been considered a condescending pout.

"That must be really hard," Czensky said.

"It *is* really hard!" Deet said, throwing up his arms again. "It's like every time I try to do something to be more human, my robot parts won't let me. I can't even swear, and even though I keep telling Rogers that I want to go and find my origins he keeps saying that there's this stupid dumb stupid *war* going on and that I'm not allowed to do anything and the coffee machines keep whispering things to me and all I really ever needed and wanted was to—"

Beep. A notification came from Deet's insides letting him know that the transfer had been completed.

"Oh, good," Deet said. "Never mind. Goodbye."

Without another word, he turned and walked away from Czensky, who was left holding three datapads and a whole lot of mental baggage. He hurried his way through the crowd, bumping into people without any real concern. He was much heavier and denser than the average human, so anyone who came into contact with him rebounded, stumbling backward.

Deet sauntered up to the security guard. At least he thought he was sauntering. It was a very particular kind of movement accomplished with a mixture of gait and attitude, which made things difficult for Deet. First, Rogers had assembled him from discarded droid parts, so his walk was always a little crooked anyway. Second, he couldn't display any expression on his face that might indicate that the barely coordinated amble he was performing was indeed sauntering.

"I'm sauntering right now," Deet decided to verbally clarify, but nobody seemed to care. The security guard with whom he'd been chatting previously looked at him with a hurt expression on his face, but Deet paid no mind. He strutted—perhaps that was a better word anyway—up to the control panel, extended his finger, and made a triumphant beeping noise as the pad beeped and turned from red to green. He heard the mechanism of the door unlock, and had the satisfaction of seeing the security guard's face light up with surprise.

"Ha!" Deet said. "And you thought I—"

Ding!

"Congratulations on making an illicit copy of security credentials!" a voice rang out from the center of Deet's main processing console. "You are entitled to one free inflatable mousetrap, redeemable at any of the many Snaggardir's Sundries locations across the galaxy. Remember, whatever you need, you can Snag It at Snaggardir's™!"

All movement around him came to an abrupt halt. A sergeant who had been addressing a marine colonel was stuck mid-salute as the colonel ignored him to look at Deet.

"Well that was unexpected," Deet said. When nobody said anything, he thought perhaps he'd been unclear.

"The inflatable mousetrap part," Deet said. "Who the [EXPLETIVE] would want one of those?"

The security guard drew his weapon and pointed it at Deet.

Ace in the Bingo Hole

Alandra stared at the terminal screen, a blank look on her face. During the past week or so of relative boredom, she'd taken to having these miserable conversations with Quinn. The Council representative, despite their warming relations, still made Alandra want to put her fist through something.

"So you're telling me," Alandra said slowly, "that Meridan men actually *like* when women tell jokes?"

"From all my available research, that's what I have concluded," Quinn said. The connection from Keffoule's modest hotel in the Meridan compound to the orbiting fleet had been surprisingly good, but today's conversation was rife with little blips and stutters that indicated some bandwidth limitations. A lot of things were going on in Meridan orbit.

"This is highly irregular," Alandra said, sitting back in her chair. "Making these jokes requires me to break my poise as a respected commander. Unbreakable military bearing should be a clear indication of suitability that negates the necessity for jokes."

Quinn shrugged, reaching back to adjust her hair bun. Alandra couldn't help but notice that it wasn't quite as neat as usual, perhaps due to the fact that Quinn had been spending most of her time in the training rooms, attempting to learn how to throat-punch someone taller than her without breaking a finger. It was a particularly delicate skill.

"I'm a career bureaucrat. I'm not exactly familiar with mating practices," Quinn said. "When I told you I would help you with your negotiation skills, this isn't what I had in mind."

Alandra ignored her for a moment, thinking. Xan spent his free time tidying up the room, though Alandra had repeatedly reminded him that there was a cleaning crew for that, and that it was physically impossible for the room to get any cleaner anyway. As her personal attendant, Xan had always shown himself to be thorough and precise, but the last few days had bordered on obsessive, particularly when Alandra was having these conversations with Quinn. A strange change of character for someone who was always so composed.

"Xan," she said. "I need you to do a bit of research for me."

"Of course, Grand Marshal," Xan said, putting down a rather ridiculous-looking feather duster and scurrying over to her terminal. He whipped his datapad out of its holster with a practiced, yet still somehow lethargic, grace.

"I need you to research Meridan humor patterns."

Xan glanced at her over the top of the datapad, his eyes narrowing just a touch.

"Grand Marshal?" he asked.

Spinning her chair a bit to look at Xan directly, Alandra furrowed her brow. "Did you think I would give up on Rogers so easily? I am not one to just let a quarry scamper off. Besides, we have some time. I might as well learn a thing or two about our new allies if I am going to fight alongside them."

"But Grand Marshal," Xan said, "do you really think this is a wise use of your time? There are so many things you could be studying instead of trying to woo this . . . Meridan pseudo-admiral."

Rolling her eyes, Alandra directed a shooing motion at Xan. "We've had this discussion many times, Xan, and I don't care to repeat it again. This is the hand we've been dealt, and I intend to play it to any advantage I can find. My inevitable marriage to Captain Rogers is just one way to enhance our position."

"I would hardly call it inevitable," Quinn said.

"I didn't ask for your opinion," Alandra snapped back. "I asked for your advice on how to improve my chances."

She didn't like to show it, but Alandra was scared that Quinn might have been right. It had been just over a week since she'd discovered that Rogers had successfully brokered a "deal" with the pirates—she still wasn't comfortable with parlaying with such insidious rapscallions—and she'd barely heard from the man. Alandra, in her conversations with Quinn, had discovered several strategies that she thought would elicit some kind of romantic response, especially since that goblin the "Viking" was back on the *Flagship*, tending to her marines.

Quinn had said that Meridan men liked to watch movies, but Rogers had complained of "sudden-onset glaucoma." Alandra wasn't sure what that was, but she hoped it wasn't genetic. She couldn't have their children walking around all the time with sudden-onset glaucoma.

Quinn had said that Meridan men liked flowers. That was just completely off. Rogers broke into a sneezing fit so severe he popped a blood vessel in his left eye.

And no matter how many times Alandra had asked Rogers to do math with her, he always found some excuse not to. Meridans just didn't make any sense. But that was half of what made him so alluring.

But now there was this humor thing. Very much outside of Alandra's comfort zone, yes, but not entirely unachievable. That droid companion of Rogers had told the one about the asteroids, which Alandra was pretty sure had been funny. She could figure this out. If, that was, Xan ever stopped staring at her disapprovingly and got to work doing the research she'd asked him to do.

"Something else, Xan?" Alandra said.

"Would it help to express again my disapproval for this plan and any and all branches of it?"

"No."

"Then no, Grand Marshal. I'll begin doing my research now."

Alandra gave him a curt nod. One of the things she'd always liked about Xan was that he was pliable, easy to work with, and generally responded to her needs before she even knew she needed them. He was Newton's gift when it came to being an aide, but lately something had changed. Ever since the conclusion of the situation with the Meridans, she'd caught Xan hesitating. Thinking. Offering opinions even after Alandra had told him multiple times to do no such thing. Perhaps it was time for Xan to find other work. The thought didn't chafe her, exactly; one couldn't be an assistant forever. Maybe Xan could move on to bigger and better things. A part of her knew that she'd miss him, though. What did that mean?

Quinn cleared her throat.

"Yes?" Alandra said, turning back to the screen.

"I believe I've held up my end of the bargain."

"Right, fine, yes," Alandra said with a deep sigh. "Now, here is how you disembowel a man using a nail clipper and a six-inch piece of twine."

Rogers had sent a quick message to Admiral Holdt informing him that negotiations had mostly been a success and detailing the nuances of the bargain. That left, of course, the next week or so of idleness trying to figure out what to do with himself as the pirates gathered their forces and shipped out. Meridan Naval Headquarters wasn't located anywhere near a real beach, but there was a sizable lake with some sand along the shore. The weather this time of year was generally very pleasant, if a bit hot, so it was a perfect time for Rogers to experience a little taste of what life on Dathum would be like when he fulfilled his commitment and quit.

No worries. No saluting. No uniforms. No robots calling functions or insane mathematicians attempting to marry him. Well that last one had happened a couple of times even while he was on the beach, but he started changing beaches every day so that Keffoule couldn't find him. So far that had worked. What the hell had been the deal with the flowers?

Small details aside, this is exactly what he'd wanted. This is what he'd been aiming for with his original deal with the pirates; it was supposed to leave him with no enemies and a bank account full of untraceable credits that he could spend at his leisure for the rest of his days.

So then, if this is what he'd always wanted, why was he so . . . *bored*? That wasn't the word he was supposed to be using to describe his dream life on Dathum. It was supposed to be more like "awesome" or at least "very, very good on most days, and it occasionally rains but that's kind of nice sometimes."

Maybe it was just because there was technically still a war going on, and that was making him feel antsy. That must have been it. Or maybe it was because he'd gotten that strange message the other day when he was out buying a couple of bags of potato chips.

"Congratulations on recruiting the pirates to fight for your cause!" the voice had said. "You are entitled to one free pack of Shoe-Sticker Chewing Gum, available at any of the many Snaggardir's Sundries locations across the galaxy. Remember, whatever you need, you can Snag It at Snaggardir's™."

Hearing the Snaggardir's voice at seemingly pointless times wasn't anything unusual, of course. And he wasn't a big fan of chewing gum, since it tended to get caught in his beard. But he'd been buying potato chips, not recruiting pirates, and the fact that he had done the second thing was still supposed to be secret.

Ah well. Best not to worry about that now. There would be more war to fight later.

"Yep," he said, sipping some terribly sweet concoction that reminded him of the Iron Morgans he'd had with Zergan on the *Limiter*. Hopefully nobody was going to try to poison him this time.

"Yep," Deet said.

"You know," Rogers said, looking over at his metallic companion. "It was bad enough that I had to come pick you up from confinement and explain to Admiral Holdt that no, you weren't going to protocol 162 everyone. You didn't have to ruin my vacation by following me out to the beach. You can't even get a tan."

"I told those [OFFSPRING OF FEMALE CANINES] that I needed access to the servers," Deet said, "but that [EXCREMENT EXIT POINT] wouldn't listen to me no matter how many times I asked him how he felt."

"Yeah," Rogers said, "again—and I've really tried to say this a couple times now about Belgrave's advice—that's not really how the whole empathy thing works, Deet. You can't work up a rapport with someone in five minutes by asking them annoying questions."

"You seem to do a good job with it," Deet said.

"That's because I ask the *right* questions," Rogers shot back. "And there's almost always alcohol involved. Next time, try to get the security guard drunk first."

Deet was actually lying down on a long beach chair, something that looked so awkward Rogers didn't really know how to describe it, and he had his own iced tea on a small table next to him. He'd ordered it to fit in, Deet had explained, but there was obviously no way for him to drink it. Every once in a while he picked it up for a moment, held it, and put it back down again. It reminded Rogers of Quinn and chairs.

"Anyway," Deet said, "they told me I was persona non grata in the whole compound now, and I can't get on a shuttle to go back to the *Flagship* without a human to check me in as [EXPLETIVE] cargo." He made a spitting noise, which didn't sound very much like a spitting noise at all. "So unless you're about to start a very short and very successful campaign for robot rights, you're stuck with me."

"Stuck with you is right," Rogers said. He sighed, adjusting the pillow on his own beach chair and trying to breathe in the moist air without acknowledging the existence of anyone else around him. Deet, however, didn't seem content with sitting and doing nothing. Rogers supposed "relaxation" was a very difficult concept for a droid to understand, evidenced by the fact that he absolutely refused to shut up.

"The zookeeper doesn't seem to mind me being here," Deet said, gesturing to the next chair over. Tunger, who seemed almost maliciously intent on staying by Rogers' side at all times, was stretched out on a beach chair, stripes of sunscreen leaving a Kabuki-like pattern all over his face.

"It's nice to have a friend," Tunger said.

"Yeah," Rogers said. "I'm not really sure why he's here either."

Tunger just waggled his fingers at him and pet a small pelican on the head. The pelican didn't seem to be having any trouble relaxing, and it was just a dumb bird. Why couldn't Rogers? He felt like he wanted to reach out and break something—not an abnormal feeling when these two were around—but he knew that it had nothing to do with them.

Rogers grumbled as he took another sip of his drink. Out on the waves, families were playing in the ocean, looking as carefree and cheerful as ever. All around him, towels were filled with picnic baskets, mothers with newborns, and teenagers hating everyone while looking sad.

"It's weird, you know?" Rogers said.

"That's such a broad statement," Deet said. "Everything is weird in its own way, isn't it? I mean, what is 'normal'? Can we be defined by such stringent boundaries as to—"

"Oh my god, shut up," Rogers said. "I'm pointing out that even though the galaxy is falling apart around them, people are still hanging out at the beach and playing with their families. It's like nothing is happening at all."

"Human resilience," Tunger began, "is a marvelous and often unpredictable thing. In the most dire of circumstances, the collective human consciousness seems to remember the core of their existence and cling, however futilely, to the things that make them feel the most whole. These familial ties serve as a sort of nucleus, around which the entire universe orbits. In fact, every unit could be considered a separate universe in and of itself, expanding and contracting like a living, breathing lung."

Deet and Rogers slowly looked at Tunger.

"What the hell?" Rogers said.

"You have echoed my sentiments," Deet said.

"Ah," Tunger said, his faraway look turning into his normal dopey smile. "Sorry. I get carried away sometimes and forget where I am. Oh, look! A dolphin!"

Tunger sprang out of his chair and ran toward the water, flailing his arms in the air like a small child and scattering a group of seagulls to the wind.

Rogers' datapad dinged, indicating that he had a message. He grabbed it from his beach bag, which he thought was very stylish, and turned it on, assuming that Holdt had sent him an update. Unfortunately, he was wrong. It was a message from Keffoule.

"Great," Rogers said. "Just what I need right now." He tapped the screen, and the message opened. Rogers stared at the screen for a moment, frowning.

"What the hell is this?" he asked out loud.

"How exactly do you expect anyone around you to answer that kind of question when you haven't shown them the datapad?" Deet asked.

"It's rhetorical," Rogers muttered.

"The message?" Deet asked.

"No," Rogers said, "my question about what the hell this is."

"Well, what the [UNFAVORABLE AFTERLIFE LOCATION] is it?"

"I . . ." Rogers trailed off, chewing on his lip. "I think this may actually be a joke, but I'm not sure."

On the screen was the age-old mystery "Why did the chicken cross the road?"

Below, it simply said, "It didn't."

"This is so wrong I don't even know what to say," Rogers said.

"Well you certainly just said something, so clearly all options are not out."

"Shut up, Deet."

Staring at the datapad, Rogers really wasn't sure what to make of the cryptic joke. He was used to ignoring Keffoule, though, so he figured that's what he'd continue doing. He was about to put the datapad away and continue grumbling about his two unwanted beach companions, and lamenting the fact that the Viking had gone back to the *Flagship* to oversee her unit instead of sunbathing next to him, when the datapad beeped *again*.

"I can't even tell you how much I am growing to detest beeps," he said.

Deet beeped.

This time, it was, in fact, a message from Holdt. It instructed Rogers to find Grand Marshal Keffoule and come to his office as soon as possible for a briefing. Rogers should issue a general order to all personnel on shore leave to head back to their respective 331st ships as soon as possible.

"Well that doesn't sound good," Rogers said after reading the letter out loud. Deet agreed.

It took a few minutes to pack up their things and disentangle Tunger from a bed of seaweed that had lured him in with promises of swimming with the dolphins. Rogers wondered, as many did, how dolphins had ended up on Merida Prime, but there were many mysteries of the Fortuna Stultus galaxy that scientists hadn't yet decoded and that Rogers wasn't going to bother with.

Rogers shot a message back to Keffoule without acknowledging her poor attempt at a joke at all, instructing her to pack up and meet him back at headquarters.

"It worked!" Keffoule shrieked from her hotel desk.

"It did not work," Rogers said. "I needed you to come back here because we have a meeting."

"I see," Keffoule said. Rogers was fairly confident that she did not, in fact, see.

Xan stood slightly behind Keffoule, giving Rogers a stare that he could have sworn contained some small modicum of emotion. Rogers dismissed it as a trick of the light.

Rogers motioned for them to follow him as he led them from their meeting point at the station back through the corridors of the Meridan Naval Headquarters building. He couldn't help but notice the flurry of activity all around him. Although the MPD guards who had been stationed all over the place still seemed to be keeping their cool with relative ease, the rank-and-file troops coming out of briefings or rushing down the hallway all looked absolutely terrified.

"Wow," Tunger said. "I think that guy might have just soiled himself in the middle of the hallway."

"Thanks for noticing, Tunger," Rogers said.

"You're welcome!" Tunger said with inappropriate cheer. "You're busy, sir. You can't be expected to notice everything."

Tunger, Keffoule, and Xan arrived at Holdt's office without much hassle. The same vending machine that had been rocketing out bags of chips had apparently—amazingly—been restocked. Keffoule managed to catch one midair and began eating them as she silently followed Rogers through the hallway, which struck Rogers as odd. For some reason, he never imagined Keffoule eating anything that wasn't meticulously prepared or possessing some mathematical significance, like popcorn.

When Rogers looked at her with a quizzical expression, Keffoule gave him that wolfish grin that indicated that the eating of these potato chips was somehow symbolic of their predestined marriage. Rogers shook his head and focused on getting to Holdt's office. With only Tunger for backup now that Deet, Mailn, and the Viking were back on the *Flagship* getting things organized or simply not getting arrested for espionage, Rogers felt like he was walking through a minefield blindfolded. With a twitching leg.

To Rogers' surprise, Holdt wasn't the only person in the room. In fact, this looked suspiciously like some sort of military tribunal; people in very fancy uniforms all sat at one end of a long table that hadn't been there the last time he'd been in the office. The other end had two empty chairs, likely meant for Rogers and Keffoule. Holdt, at the head of the table and facing the entrance of his office, stopped whatever he'd been saying to wave them in.

Two people who Rogers didn't recognize—in two uniforms Rogers also didn't recognize—flanked Holdt on either side. On the right, a broad-shouldered woman with an absolutely astonishing amount of makeup tapped long fingernails on the table as she pursed her lips. A gaudy, puffy uniform obscured most of her form, including an actual, no-kidding cape. Rogers kind of wanted a cape.

The other figure was a man with a striking presence. Salt-and-pepper hair, sharp features, and a barrel chest all trapped inside a military uniform that was as plain as it was descriptive. New Neptune, for certain, confirmed by the fact that "New Neptune" was written above the right breast pocket of his uniform. His stony expression did not change at all as his eyes passed over Rogers, but when he saw Keffoule, the corners of his mouth twitched. Rogers could understand that; Keffoule made him nervous whenever they were in the same room. And, actually, most of the time when they weren't in the same room.

In the corner of the room, the coffee machine hissed like a

coiled snake and spewed boiling water in a jet stream that landed well clear of the table.

"Does someone keep refilling the water tank in that thing?" Rogers said. "If so, why?"

Holdt dismissed his question with a wave of his hand and motioned toward the chairs at the end of the table. "Please sit down, Captain Rogers, Grand Marshal Keffoule. We've been waiting for you."

Rogers froze where he stood. The tone that came out of Admiral Holdt's mouth was something he'd never heard before. In Holdt, Rogers typically saw a little bit of himself. Gruff, irreverent, uncaring of other people's opinions. But that man had changed. Even more tired than when he had met with him previously, Holdt was clearly not the same man. His jaw bulged with tightness, his expression grim rather than grumpy.

Rogers realized suddenly that he was standing in a room with one representative from each military in the Fortuna Stultus galaxy, and that made him feel very, very uneasy.

"Sit," Holdt said again.

Rogers sat. Keffoule, her body maintaining its lithe, catlike smoothness, sank into the chair offered to her and leaned back, crossing her legs. Despite the obvious dark mood of the room, she didn't seem to catch it.

"I have to ask," Rogers said. "Where did you get these MPD guys who are keeping watch? All of them look like they were carved out of stone. You might want to consider sending them into battle instead of the Meridan Army. Nothing can phase them."

For a moment Holdt looked at him like he was insane, but then recognition dawned on his face.

"Oh, those guys," Holdt said. "They're not unflappable. All of them were part of a raid on an illicit novocaine factory about six months ago. Someone blew up one of the storage tanks and now none of them can move their faces. We chose them specifically for this detail so we could maintain the illusion of calm."

Rogers remembered the troop in the hallway who had basically crumbled into a ball of panic while urinating on himself, and shook his head.

"I think there's more to it than that," Rogers said.

"You're probably right," Holdt said. "Anyway, I appreciate you not bringing your droid companion with you this time. I spent half a day cleaning rust out of my terminal's data port. Don't you ever send that guy to maintenance to be cleaned?"

Rogers frowned. He hadn't noticed any rust coming out of Deet. Of course, he had been assembled from garbage, so there was a good chance of there being some corrosion in there.

"Sorry about that," Rogers said. "He's a little obsessed with his own destiny, or something like that. It's been kind of a strange couple of months for everyone in the 331st."

Holdt answered him with a grunt, pointing to the table. "To business, then. This is General Alister Krell, of the New Neptune Navy. The triple-N has sent him as their representative to our joint force." Holdt motioned to the other side of the table, where the taciturn woman was looking at Rogers like a hawk. "And this is Premiere Thulicia Thrumeaux, of the Grandelle Space Force."

The two military leaders nodded in turn at Rogers, but before Rogers could ask any questions, Holdt bulled ahead.

"You can get to know each other later, but let me lay the groundwork here first. The pirates have been having good success cracking through the blockades, and the Jupiterians haven't made much effort at a counterattack. We think it's because they're conserving their forces for pitched battles that might come later in this war, and don't want to fritter their ships away blocking Un-Space points."

Keffoule nodded. "Perhaps they are not as strong as they made themselves seem."

The sharp-featured New Neptune man—General Krell—nodded, grinning ever so slightly. This surprised Rogers, as he'd based his assessment of New Neptunians on Xan and rumors. Perhaps they could actually emote when the mood struck them.

"We came to the same assessment," Krell said. "I am honored and comforted that great minds think alike."

Keffoule gave him the slightest of nods, a gesture that was either intended to thank the man or confirm his evaluation of Keffoule's genius. This, for some reason, made the New Neptunian smile even more.

"That doesn't make any sense," Rogers said. "You don't just attempt to take over the galaxy and then back off at the first sign of resistance. You'd lose the game."

Rogers thought for a moment. The game . . . He didn't know war, but he certainly knew gambling.

"They have an ace in the hole," he said.

"Bingo," Holdt said.

"I think he was talking about poker," Tunger said.

"I'm sure the high admiral was aware of that, thank you, Tunger," Rogers said, rolling his eyes. He turned back to Holdt. "I assume you know what this ace is, or you wouldn't have these sour expressions on your faces."

Holdt nodded, gritting his teeth. "It's easier if I show you rather than tell you. I hear you're a fan of irony, Rogers, so you'll appreciate this transmission we received directly from Snaggardir's corporate headquarters, which is still in geostationary orbit around one of the moons in Grandelle. It was sent directly to the heads of the remaining governmental bodies."

While Rogers was busy contemplating why in the world someone would mention his appreciation for irony at a time like this, Holdt used his datapad to bring up a projection screen in the middle of the conference table, which was refracted in such a way that no matter the viewing angle, everyone's perception was that they were viewing the two-dimensional image straight on. Rogers had always found this disorienting, like a creepy painting that wouldn't take its eyes off you.

Shortly, an image came up that Rogers recognized as the corporate logo of Snaggardir's, the empty chair now making him cringe a bit. Next, a plain portrait of the CEO, Sal Snaggardir, sitting at a plain desk in a plain office. Rogers had kind of imagined a throne of sorts, where the future Emperor of Everything would be sitting and addressing all those who had slighted Jupiter in the past.

Instead of launching into a propaganda speech, which is what Rogers expected, the bald, weathered old man began to talk as though having a conversation with his grandchild by a fireplace. His voice was warm—though his eyes were cold and unfeeling—and his posture was as relaxed as any lounging kitten.

"The Two Hundred Years (and Counting) Peace," he said. "The pinnacle achievement of the human race, one which propelled us into over two centuries of prosperity, open trade, and tranquility."

The image on the video changed from Sal Snaggardir's face to a picture of Jupiter, taken, of course, before it was turned into galactic soup by the Milky Way's collapse.

"You forgot us. But we did not forget you. By now you have seen how quickly we were able to take most of the galaxy in the blink of an eye. By now you have seen that the contributions Jupiterians have made to the new galactic society have been vast, important, and have played as much a part in the prosperity of humanity as any neglectful treaty ever did."

Okay, so maybe it was a *bit* of a propaganda, soapbox speech. He was likely talking about the industrialization of the galaxy that had been supported by Snaggardir's incredible business and manufacturing skills. Nearly everything had been made by this company—and if it hadn't been actually physically produced by them, they'd done the R&D to make it happen. Rogers had of course understood the scale of the company's influence before this moment, but not until now had it really meant something tangible. In fact, it almost seemed pointless to wage a war; the company *already* owned most of the galaxy.

"Our demands are simple. Cede one planet from each of the systems to our control, and make a new Two Hundred Years (and Counting) Peace that includes the people of Jupiter. There will be no forced relocations, no purges. Reparations will be demanded from each of the offending systems in order to support the rebuilding of Jupiterian society, but it will be fair. It will be more than you deserve."

"That seems kind of silly," Tunger said. "If we restart the Two Hundred Years (and Counting) Peace, it's not exactly an accurate name anymore, is it? We might as well call it the Peace That Started Just Now."

"Very astute, Tunger," Rogers said, shaking his head. "Well, at least we know what they want. I was kind of scared for a little bit that they wanted the complete destruction of the galaxy."

"If our demands are not met within two weeks," Sal Snaggardir said, the video switching back to his face, "we will employ a weapon that will result in the complete destruction of the galaxy."

"Oh," Rogers said. "There we go."

The screen shifted again, this time fading out to reveal a couple of fast cutaways of indecipherable metallic equipment. It was starting to look like a commercial for personal space transportation vehicles. Any moment now, someone was going to come on the screen shouting "Sunday, Sunday, Sunday!"

. . . And then blow up the galaxy.

"What is all of this?" Keffoule asked, gesturing at the screen. Rogers looked over at her and noticed she was no longer sitting back in her chair like a relaxed leopard ready to strike, but was now leaning forward, her face scrunched up, focused. Rogers was used to looking at her and seeing "creepy woman trying to marry him," but this was more "commander of huge amounts of firepower and ready to employ it." It was a less stressful version of her.

Nobody else at the table answered, and the video soon made it evident what they were looking at. On the bottom of the screen appeared the words "The Galaxy Eater," which was at once the worst and most effective name for a Snaggardir's product that Rogers had ever heard. The camera moved out to a full view, and it was evident that the close-up shots had been different angles of a gigantic machine, something of a scale that Rogers had never seen before.

"Congratulations—you're entitled to one free apocalypse," a gruff voice from offscreen said. "Redeemable in two weeks."

"Damn it, Szinder!" Snaggardir said, turning around. "I told you to—"

The video cut off.

Forced Joints

Everyone in the room fell into a tense silence, staring at the now empty center of the table. Even Tunger was silent this time, though Rogers might have actually welcomed a stupid comment. What were they supposed to do with a low-budget car commercial that notified everyone of their impending extinction?

Keffoule remained in business mode. "Do we have any indication as to what this device is or how it will be used? Destroying the galaxy is a fairly broad mission statement."

Holdt turned the lights up in the room, leaning back in his chair. He looked awfully relaxed for someone in charge of saving the galaxy.

"That was all that was available in the video," he said. "We've gathered some other bits and pieces from intelligence but we don't know where the damn device is to reconnoiter it. It's a damn tight spot."

"Tight spot" was not how Rogers would have described being on the verge of the total annihilation of humanity. During the collapse of the Milky Way, the holes leading to what would eventually become known as Un-Space had been discovered once the planets had started to shift out of their orbits, allowing mankind a new lease on life. This time, there was nowhere else for them to go. The only other path of the Un-Space tunnels was back to the Milky Way, which was currently still on its way to becoming a super-massive black hole. If the Galaxy Eater started, well, eating the galaxy, there was nothing they could do about it.

"As you are undoubtedly aware, Grand Marshal," General Krell said, nodding—almost bowing—to Keffoule, "a machine of that size and scale couldn't possibly remain completely undetected. We've had our scientists working on it around the clock, combing over the video and trying to determine the device's purpose."

"It's not enough to know that it's designed to destroy the galaxy," Premiere Thrumeaux said, her voice thick and operatic. Did Grandelle produce anyone who wasn't always pretending they were on the stage? "We must identify precisely *how* it is designed to destroy the galaxy, if we are to counter it."

"Agreed," Holdt said. "Our best scientists are working on analyzing the footage and working with our intel teams to see if there's anything we can piece together. In the meantime, every telescope and spectrometer in space is tuned to detect the slightest of abnormalities."

Thrumeaux folded her arms, tossing a head full of wildly curly hair behind her. "Is it possible this is all a bluff? Is it even possible that a single device could be responsible for the destruction of an entire galaxy? The amount of firepower it would need would be astronomical."

Rogers laughed, which he immediately understood to be the wrong reaction. Everyone at the table looked at him.

"Ah, sorry," he said. "I thought you were making a joke. 'Astronomical' firepower and all that?"

Everyone gave him a blank stare.

"No?" Rogers felt like his uniform collar was getting tighter by the second. He cleared his throat. "Well, fine. You're missing the point, anyway. It doesn't actually need any firepower."

Krell and Thrumeaux looked slowly toward Holdt, as if to ask him why the hell he'd brought some random boozer/pirate into this meeting. Keffoule, on the other hand, seemed to understand what he was getting at.

"It was the Jupiterians who collapsed the galaxy the first time," she said.

Rogers nodded at her. "Exactly."

"But the collapse of the Milky Way took almost a full year to complete," Krell said. "Humanity had enough time to find Un-Space, discover that they could escape through it, and then pile every ship in the system chock full of people and get them to Fortuna Stultus."

"Well," Rogers said, "they did have the last couple of centuries, a gigantic amount of capital from being the most powerful corporation in the galaxy, and an obsession with revenge. Don't you think they might have improved the design a bit?"

A moment passed as they took all of this in. Honestly, it even made Rogers uncomfortable; he wasn't used to being the one who delivered insight in a meeting of powerful people. He was used to being the one cheating them out of money. Or trying to cheat them out of money, and getting caught and arrested. Rogers supposed he had a better track record for the second version.

Holdt reached over and tapped his datapad, then tapped his earpiece to route the audio to him alone.

"It's Holdt. I need you to get me all the available information on the original terraforming technology that collapsed the Milky Way. . . . Yes, as much as you can. . . . The cakes were very tasty, thank you. . . . No, for god's sake please just use a French press to make coffee from now on."

Holdt looked up, tapping the earpiece again, and cleared his throat. "Short staffing. My orderly is also the one heading up the research effort behind all of this, and he makes excellent short-cakes. All of you should do the same right now."

"Eat cake?" Tunger asked, clapping excitedly.

"No. Start gathering whatever information you can on the collapse and its cause. If Rogers is right, we might at least be able to understand the old technology and extrapolate from there."

Resisting the urge to ask for one of the cakes anyway, Rogers sent a quick message back to the *Flagship* to have Deet start working on the same thing. Hopefully he'd downloaded at least a few useful things while illegally digging through everyone's file structures. When Quinn had started siphoning information from the Jupiterian data server connected to Commodore Zergan's computer, they hadn't known what they were looking for. As a result, a vast majority of the information they'd captured was useless. Shortly after Zergan had died, the terminal had erased itself. There might, however, have been something that they'd missed. He'd have Deet comb through that as well.

When everyone finished transmitting their orders to their respective organizations, Holdt was somehow eating a small piece of cake. It *did* look really good. Wiping a crumb from his mouth, Holdt pointed the tines of his fork toward Keffoule.

"Grand Marshal Keffoule, is there something wrong? You look troubled. I will need everyone's help to accomplish this. I would think with Thelicosa's reputation as scientists, you would certainly have someone with access to that kind of research."

"There is someone," Keffoule said. Everyone in the room turned to look at her, and Rogers had to suppress a startled chortle. Keffoule actually looked scared, a state of mind of which Rogers thought her incapable. Her face was white, an evident transformation on someone with olive skin, and she had both hands on the table, balled into fists. She opened her mouth to continue, but shut it abruptly.

"What's up?" Rogers asked. "You going to throw up or

something? This is pretty intense, but I thought you were a little tougher than that."

He expected Keffoule to shoot him one of those "You are going to die" kinds of looks, but she didn't move. She was too deep in her own mind.

"Out with it, Grand Marshal," Holdt said.

"Please, Holdt, don't rush her," General Krell said. "Genius takes time."

For some reason, Xan, who had been standing silently in the corner of the room this whole time—something he did exceedingly well—made a choking noise. When Rogers glanced at him to see what had happened, though, there was no indication that he'd done anything at all except for a slight swinging of his face weights.

Keffoule didn't acknowledge the compliment, though a quick flick of her eyes told Rogers that she'd heard it. What was up with this Krell guy? Now wasn't the time to be flirting with a fleet commander.

Wait, Rogers thought. *Does this guy actually* like *Keffoule?* A tiny bubble of hope blossomed in his belly.

"We have a . . . man," Keffoule began, her eyes looking far off into nowhere. "He has abilities of discernment so incredible it seems like clairvoyance. He has bested complicated computers in calculation races."

"Grand Marshal," Xan said quietly, as though talking to a frightened child.

"Although we likely don't have any information on the collapse that you don't," Keffoule continued, "it is extremely likely that if we present it to this . . . man . . . that he will be able to interpret it in ways that simple computational analysis could never hope to achieve. He is, in a word, incredible."

Holdt seemed intrigued, but not impressed. "We're going to need more to go on here than 'a man,' Grand Marshal. It all seems a little hard to believe."

"Yes, who is this man?" Krell said, his voice taking on a bit of an edge. "Is he handsome?"

Rogers rolled his eyes. "I'm not sure that's the most important aspect of his character, General Krell."

Krell glared at him.

Keffoule took a deep breath. "We have . . . ," she began.

"Grand Marshal, no," Xan said. "You mustn't—"

"Oh this is becoming very interesting," Premiere Thrumeaux said, her face splitting into a Cheshire cat grin.

The question of the man's identity hung in the air like a finger over a detonator button. Even Rogers felt a little swept up in the moment, and he thought Keffoule was full of shit.

"We have the Astromologer," she said breathlessly. In the corner, Xan actually gasped and brought a hand up to cover his mouth. His face weights got in the way, though, so he really just started a sort of Newtonian perpetual motion machine between his hand and the weights.

This revelation, however, seemed to have absolutely no effect on anyone else at the table. In fact, Krell, Thrumeaux, and Holdt looked utterly confused. Tunger was playing with a paper clip.

"The who?" Holdt said.

"The what?" Krell said.

"Never heard of him," Thrumeaux said, her face deflating into the disappointed expression of one who had expected juicy gossip but had instead gotten an under-ripe plum.

"That's your secret?" Rogers said, dimly remembering a conversation he'd had with Keffoule during their "We're invading" incident. "You told me about that guy like two weeks ago. Obviously it's not that classified."

"I told you about the practice of astromology," Keffoule said, her lips thin. "I most certainly never revealed to a *Meridan* that we had *the* Astromologer."

"I don't know what *either* of those two things are," Rogers said. "Is it like . . . a combination of horoscopes and astrophysics?"

Keffoule's eyes widened. "You *do* know of astromology!" she gasped.

"No," Rogers said, shaking his head. "No, I do not. I'm just pretty good at etymology—which, by the way, is a word that means 'not crazy math psychic bullshit.' I'm not sure anyone outside of your system knows about this practice, because it sounds like the most absurd thing I have ever heard of."

"It is absolutely not bullshit!" General Krell said, pounding his fist on the table. For a New Neptunian, he certainly seemed prone to a lot of expression. "This is a sacred and important part of Grand Marshal Keffoule's culture and identity, and I will thank you not to refer to it in such a disrespectful way."

Rogers raised an eyebrow. Behind him, Xan scoffed. It seemed all the New Neptunians were going no-holds-barred today when it came to emotional displays.

"Not ten seconds ago you said you'd never heard of him," Rogers said. "You're telling me since then you've discovered that you're a true believer?"

Krell sat back, folding his sizable arms and boring in to Rogers' skull with his eyes. "Just because I haven't heard of something doesn't mean I can dismiss and disrespect it."

Rogers gave him his best "Whatever, I don't want to talk to you anymore" shrug. He turned back to ask Keffoule more questions about this insanity, but when he did he saw her looking at Krell with an expression that at once confused and delighted him. She was *smiling*.

"Thank you, General," she said.

"Grand Marshal," Xan said from his place in the corner. "Do you really think the talents of the Astromologer should be wasted on something so trivial as this?"

The fact that someone had just referred to the end of all life as "trivial" was more than enough to make Rogers want to forget everything and crawl into a hole until the end. Who were these people, and why had he ever started talking to any of them?

"It is time," Keffoule said. "It is *his* time."

"Time is one thing we are all very quickly running out of," Holdt said, bringing the conversation back to the real world. "Grand Marshal Keffoule, if this scientist of yours—"

"Astromologer," Keffoule corrected.

"—Astromologer can really do what you say he can do, we have nothing to lose by passing all of our available data to him. Send for him as soon as you can."

Xan snorted. "One does not simply demand that the Astromologer appear," he said.

"Then send him a fucking invitation!" Holdt shouted, startling everyone at the table. "If he's not too divinely inspired to care about the skin on his bones, let him know that there won't be anything left to astromologize if he doesn't dedicate *every ounce* of his talents to helping us stop the Galaxy Eater."

Everyone shut up for a moment, but Keffoule acknowledged the request with a slight nod. She looked at Krell and nodded as well, perhaps thanking him for his defense of her hokey quasi-religious nonscientist person.

"I shall do so," Keffoule said. "It may take me a few days to contact him. If Sagittarius is still aligned at the proper angle, he may be deep in meditation."

Rogers shook his head, wondering if he should be rooting for the Jupiterians instead. Also wondering how they'd know anything about Sagittarius, since the Fortuna Stultus galaxy was so far from the Milky Way that it was impossible to see all of the old constellations.

"Okay," Rogers said. "So now we have everyone researching or engaging in some kind of psychic trance. We can't just sit here and do nothing until someone publishes a book on the Galaxy Eater."

Holdt nodded. "Right. I've received orders that the Joint Force, Resistance Engagement Detachment to Avoid Planetary Elimination begin immediate preparations for a full-scale assault on all known Jupiterian positions, culminating in the destruction of Snaggardir's headquarters."

"I'm sorry, the what force?" Rogers asked, looking around the table. "That was the longest and most confusing name I've ever heard."

"Rogers, you're coming into this a bit late, so let me explain to you the real reason behind this meeting."

"Real reason?" Rogers asked. "I kind of figured that a large, disaffected and somewhat maniacal portion of the population holding humanity hostage *was* the real reason."

Holdt let the comment slide off him, something he was exceedingly good at. Rogers hadn't had too much interaction with him, but he couldn't say he didn't like the high admiral.

"We've gotten direction from up at the highest levels of government to form a task force that includes representation from all of the systems. In an effort to bring the remaining sane parts of humanity together to resist our possible destruction, the burden has fallen to me to organize it."

Rogers blinked. "Congratulations? I mean, I wouldn't want that job in a million years, but it will probably look good on your next performance evaluation report."

"If there is another performance evaluation report," Holdt said without a trace of bitterness. "Besides, I'm already one of the top admirals in the entire Meridan Galactic Navy. I don't need any more promotions."

Holdt paused for a moment. For some reason, everyone seemed to be waiting for something, staring at Rogers intently.

"But you have some room to grow," Holdt said. Was he smiling?

"Nope. Nope. Uh-uh," Rogers said, standing up so fast his wheeled chair flew across the room and was instantly soaked by the murderous Snaggardir's coffee machine. "You are out of your mind. I'm not doing it. You can't make me."

"You have the résumé," Holdt said. "You have combat experience. You have practice working with the pirates who are now our vanguard against the Jupiterians. You've been working with the Thelicosan representative of the Joint Force longer than anyone else."

"Nope!" Rogers said. "*Nope.* Nope, nope, nopery nopity nope." He began gathering his datapad from the table and hoped to make a quick exit from the room. "Noooope. Nope."

"Oh come now," General Krell said. "You can't seriously tell me that the man who crushed the droids and discovered the first Jupiterian uprising can't handle a little bit of good old-fashioned galaxy-scale war."

Rogers balked for a moment, looking at the powerful, if arrogant, general sitting in front of him. A man who, despite his posturing, probably had never seen combat. Feeling his face contort into something between outright sobbing and amazement, Rogers realized that he *did*, actually, have more combat experience than anyone else in this room. Perhaps everyone in this room put together. And he'd only been doing this for a couple of months.

It was terrifying.

"And you've got that brilliant pilot on your team," Premiere Thrumeaux said. "The one who can single-handedly take on an entire fleet of enemy ships." She sighed, placing her hand over her heart. "I've heard such marvelous things about him and what he can do."

Rogers, unsure of which one of the people at the table to correct first, rapidly turned his head between Krell and Thrumeaux, his memories of both himself and Flash racing through his brain. In an age where information could be transmitted faster than the speed of light, the idea that two things couldn't be more wrong made him want to let the Jupiterians win.

He locked eyes with Thrumeaux. "Flash is the worst pilot I have ever seen."

He moved to Krell. "I am the worst commander I have ever seen."

And then Holdt. "You are out of your fucking mind."

Holdt shrugged, as if someone lower ranking than him hadn't just insulted him publicly in a room full of other high-ranking individuals. "There's nothing to be done about it now. The paperwork has already been transmitted, signed, and approved by all levels of the Meridan government and ratified by the other systems. You are now Captain R. Wilson Rogers—chief, Joint Force, Resistance Engagement Detachment to Avoid Planetary Elimination."

"No," Rogers whispered. "This is so, so bad. None of you understand how bad this is."

He was still standing at the foot of the table, holding his data-pad and counting the beads of sweat rolling down his back. He was up to a bajillion now.

"You are literally placing the fate of the galaxy in my hands." He thought for a moment. "Again. You need to stop doing this."

"You need to stop succeeding, then," Holdt said. "No good deed goes unrewarded."

No good deed goes unpunished, you mean, Rogers said. The only thing working hard ever got him was more work. He was becoming so very bad at slacking off, which used to be his primary skill set. What had happened to him?

"We're still working on the official paperwork to promote you to admiral," Holdt said. "For now, you'll be acting with an authority above your rank, which may be awkward."

"No!" Rogers said. "Do *not* promote me to admiral. Do you know how many admirals have been hit by asteroids in the last few months? You'll be painting a cosmic target on my back."

Keffoule chuckled. "Oh, come now, Captain Rogers. You can't seriously be that superstitious."

Rogers looked at her, wide-eyed. "You just told us we were all going to be saved by a *psychic astrophysicist.*"

"I have evidence that supports my claim," Keffoule said, shrugging.

Rogers felt like he had a mountain of evidence to prove that being an admiral was hazardous to one's health, but he didn't feel like arguing anymore.

"As you might have guessed," Holdt said, gesturing around the table, "the rest of the system representatives for this joint force are gathered around you here."

"Me?" Keffoule asked, genuinely surprised. "I've been appointed?"

"Yes," Holdt said.

"Surely a woman with your level of prestige, combined with your history as a commander and a behind-the-lines operative, gives you more than enough credentials for this sort of thing," Krell said, grinning like an idiot. "I can imagine there is no one else better qualified for the position."

"I appreciate your faith in me, General Krell," Keffoule said, nodding her thanks, "but there are many more experienced at open-space warfare than me in the Thelicosan fleet. I am more of a . . ." She looked directly at Rogers. "A direct-action kind of woman."

Rogers felt bile creeping up his throat.

"Anyway," Holdt said, "as with many things in this military community of ours, Rogers, there's not a whole lot of choice you have in the matter. You're the boss of this outfit."

"Not the boss," Thrumeaux said, eying Rogers like *he'd* been the one to suggest it.

"First among equals, then," Holdt said. "You report directly to me, and you'll have the final say on maneuvers. I'll also be the one to give you your orders, after I have a chance to confer with the governments of all the systems to set time-oriented, strategically focused objectives and achieve synergistic battlespace effectiveness . . ."

Holdt stared off into space for a second, then cleared his throat. "You'll have to excuse me. It's been a while since I've done anything other than be an admiral, and there's this computer-based training that . . . You know what? Never mind. Just do what I say, alright?"

Rogers gaped at Holdt. Gaped at life, really. What were his options? The galaxy *was* about to be either taken over or eaten and he *was* a commissioned officer in the Meridan Galactic Navy and he *did* have combat experience against at least three different armies, *one* of which was currently fighting them.

That was a *lot* of italics, and not a lot of choices other than flinging himself out the window of Holdt's office. And even that wouldn't have done a lot of good since it was on the first goddamn floor. When he'd thought he was bored on the beach, this was absolutely not what he'd had in mind. No matter how much he tried to get rid of big capital ships and go back to something like the *Awesome*, it seemed like all anyone wanted to do was give him more metal to throw around in space.

And he was stuck with it.

"Fine," Rogers said, realizing that everyone in the room had been staring at him while he went on a small, depressing mental tirade. "Fine. I'll do it."

"We're already way past that," Holdt said.

"Yeah, I know," Rogers said. "But I feel like maybe I can take more ownership of my life if I pretend like I'm the one with the power, you know?" He sat back down in his chair, dropping his datapad in front of him and preparing to take notes, or something.

"So what are our orders, boss?"

Tarot, Tarot,
Tarot Your Boat

Alandra raced through her chambers, taking uniforms, supplies, hygiene products, and anything that she would possibly need for an extended stay on another ship, and stuffing them into her bag. The room rapidly descended from inspection ready to barely human ready. Keffoule didn't care.

"I find this highly irregular," Xan said, doing absolutely nothing to help her. It was difficult to tell when the man was moping—he always looked mopey—but there was definitely something on Xan's mind that he wasn't letting on.

"You find everything highly irregular, Xan," Keffoule barked, throwing an unnecessary amount of toothbrushes into her hygiene kit.

It didn't matter what Xan thought; she was going to get to live on the same ship as Captain R. Wilson Rogers, and this time without any kidnapping or face-kicking at all! It was like a dream come true. Working together toward a common goal built camaraderie, healed old wounds, and forged unbreakable bonds that could never be broken. Her short tenure on the *Flagship* during the fight against Zergan had given Rogers enough reason to treat her civilly and forgive her for her mistakes during the earlier parts of their relationship. What would saving the galaxy from certain destruction yield for her?

Marriage!

According to High Admiral Holdt, the gruff, if a bit charmingly roguish, commander of the Meridan Galactic Navy, all of the commanders of the new Joint Force were to be housed together on the *Flagship*. They were to leave their fleets in the direct command of their immediate deputies, and be present on the Meridan command ship to promote teamwork and synergy. To Keffoule, all of those were secondary concerns to making sure that she utilized her time on the same ship with Rogers more effectively than his time on the *Limiter*.

Well, perhaps they weren't exactly secondary concerns. The entire Fortuna Stultus galaxy was at stake, of course. But that didn't mean that Alandra couldn't use those circumstances to her advantage.

"Besides," Alandra said, not sure if she was talking to Xan or herself, "you'll be coming with me. Shouldn't you be packing?"

With Edris gone, that left a bit of a power vacuum on the *Limiter* that needed to be filled. Her helmsman, a bright, science-driven young pre-commodore by the name of Chinnaker was next in line, but nowhere near seasoned enough to tackle full command, even if Alandra was nearby to provide guidance. She'd have to sort all of this out before she left, of course, but right now she was getting ready for the most exciting sleepover of her life.

"I am already prepared," Xan said.

"Of course you are," Alandra said. She was about to tell Xan to find something useful to do when her datapad began ringing. She'd left it on her desk, far away from where she was now stuffing several mathematical implements into her bag.

"Get that for me, would you?" she said, pointing to the datapad.

Without expression, Xan crossed over to the desk, face weights swaying with every step, and picked up the pad. For a moment, he looked at it, frowning ever so slightly, not saying anything.

"Well?" Keffoule said, standing up, her favorite abacus dangling from one hand. "Who is it?"

"It's the bridge," Xan said.

"Well that's not so strange. Why do you look like someone didn't show their work?"

Xan hesitated. "General Krell, from the New Neptunian fleet, is requesting a private conference with you."

Krell. There was an interesting man, especially for a New Neptunian. Xan made a good personal assistant precisely because he had no personality, a core trait of the system's inhabitants, but this Krell seemed to be a bit of an anomaly. Alandra had a general distrust for New Neptunians, despite hiring one as her attendant, because it was impossible to tell their motivations or predict their actions, since they didn't show any emotion. Krell was somewhat refreshing. Then again, Alandra supposed that not every New Neptunian could be boring, just like every Meridan wasn't lactose intolerant, as she'd recently learned.

"I wonder what he wants," Alandra said. "Go ahead and route it to my terminal and ask him to wait. I'll sit down in a moment once I've gathered a few more things. I am nearly ready."

Xan bowed his head and relayed the message. Alandra could barely hear Krell's response.

Gathering up her last few things, she shoved the bundle into Xan's open arms and gave him instructions to prepare for immediate departure. Alandra sat down at her desk and saw that Xan had already queued up the video conference with Krell; he'd been staring at the back of her chair for a few minutes.

"I apologize for the delay," Alandra said. "There were preparations that needed to be completed for our rendezvous on the *Flagship*."

General Krell, whose face seemed chiseled out of stone, grinned at her in a way that she found at once very disarming and very unbecoming of a high-ranking officer.

"You were worth the wait, of course," he said. While he wasn't exactly old, his voice did sound weathered, having in it the kind of texture acquired from years of indiscriminate yelling. Alandra got the distinct impression that serving under this gentleman was not a gentle experience.

"I see," Alandra said, not quite sure how else to respond to something like that. What did he mean? "What can I do for you, General?"

"Please, call me Alister."

Alandra hesitated a moment.

"I believe it would be inappropriate to assume informalities just yet," Alandra said slowly. "We are about to fight a war together, after all."

Immediately, this struck her as an incongruity. Hadn't she just thought the opposite about Rogers? Fighting a war was going to break down the barriers of professionalism that she so desperately wanted to claw her way over.

Krell didn't seem to take it as an insult; he shrugged it off. "So be it. I only wanted to call and let you know that I appreciate what you've done so far to help stave off the Jupiterian invasion. Without your tactical brilliance, the galaxy would be in a much worse state than it already is."

"Captain Rogers did most of the tactical brilliance," Alandra said, but she felt a little bit of heat rise to her face. She'd been flattered before, of course; for the entire span of her life people had been telling her that she was different, smart. Occasionally, yes, brilliant. But all of those compliments had come riding on a wave of fear of being kicked in the face. Krell seemed not only genuine and unafraid, but . . . something else, as well. Something Alandra couldn't quite place her finger on.

"Well, you know what they say about clever men," Krell said, shifting slightly in his chair. He appeared to also be holding something in his left hand. A drink, perhaps. "Behind every one of them sits a clever woman."

Alandra frowned. The thought of being placed *behind* someone felt very insulting. Then again, it was Rogers he was talking about. Maybe that wouldn't be so bad, under the right circumstances.

"Regardless," Krell continued, perhaps sensing her tension, "I wanted to tell you personally how much I value the hard work you've put into this mission so far. If I've offended or come off too strong, I apologize. I have . . . difficulties going slow when I see something that interests me."

Now Alandra *was* blushing. Captain Rogers had also claimed that interesting things interested him, but coming from Krell, it sounded very different.

"General," Alandra said, pretending to find something interesting on the other side of the room to look at. "I appreciate the praise, I assure you, but I do have quite a lot going on over here, as I am sure you do as well. We must prepare to rid the galaxy of these vermin and restore order, and to do that we need to be on the *Flagship*."

Nodding, Krell sat forward, the grin melting from his face. "Of course. I am sorry for wasting your time."

Now she'd offended him? Alandra was finding it difficult to navigate a conversation with this man.

"If it so pleases you, we can continue this discussion in person," Alandra said.

It took considerable personal restraint not to slap a hand over her own mouth. Why in the world had she said *that*? Krell was clearly after her considerable prestige and rank in the Thelicosan political-military regime—there could be no other reason for his constant flattery—but that didn't mean she had to encourage him. The Alandra Keffoule she knew would have just ended the call with a cold, curt goodbye and gone on with her day.

"Oh?" General Krell said, leaning into the word. "And what exactly—"

Again, Alandra's datapad began to chime. Now that she was using her personal terminal to . . . do whatever she was doing with Krell, the datapad was free to accept messages from other parts of the ship. This message was coming from the bridge, and Pre-Commodore Chinnaker by the looks of it.

"General Krell, hold a moment."

Don't tell him to hold, Alandra thought. *Just hang up! Why are you still talking to him?*

"Yes?" Alandra said into her datapad.

"Grand Marshal," the pre-commodore said over the radio. "He's here."

"Who's here?"

A pause. Alandra felt her hackles rise.

"The Astromologer."

A long silence followed. This could not be true. Nobody had made the request for him yet. It was practically impossible that he was already on his way from Thelicosa, never mind actually on the *Limiter* ready to perform his mathematical divinations and psychic trigonometry. Then again, this was the Astromologer. He did not play by normal rules.

"General Krell," she said, her tone flat, perhaps awestruck. "I will speak with you later."

Alandra felt herself actually begin to sweat as she rode the elevator to the bridge, wishing that she'd been able to take her Chariot instead, but it was being repaired. Even she, who was high enough in the ranks to command a sizable fleet and a sizable amount of respect to go with it, had never met the man. His very existence was considered one of the system's most closely guarded secrets, his abilities known only to a select few at the very highest echelons of the Thelicosan Council.

The fact that she knew about him at all was an honor, a side effect of being the Tangential Tornado and one of the members of the highly secretive F Sequence special operations squadron. Some of their missions had come directly from the Astromologer himself, though the orders had been passed through several layers of military command first. His divinations had led them to immense, incredible victories even during her short tenure in the F Sequence. Who knew what other facets of Thelicosan history the Astromologer had played a part in?

And now he was here, on her ship. Likely he'd be coming with her onto the *Flagship* as well. He belonged at the center of the action, where he could have the most impact. A rare sensation came over her; she felt unprepared. Maybe even unworthy.

Xan, who had remained as taciturn as always, appeared to be avoiding eye contact with her, and he stood rather stiffly with a datapad in his hand.

"Everything is ready for our departure?" Alandra said.

"Yes, Grand Marshal," Xan said.

He still didn't look at her.

Alandra sighed. "Out with it, Xan. What is it?"

Finally, he locked eyes with her for a moment, his thin mouth pursing. "I was under the impression that you were not interested in my opinions."

"When did I give you that impression?"

"It may have been when we were on our way back from Merida Prime, and you told me 'I am not interested in your opinions.'"

"That's because you were convinced that I was going to be taken hostage as soon as I boarded the *Flagship*," Alandra said. The banter was helping her relax a little bit, and she leaned against the wall, running a hand through her mess of hair. She sighed. "I may be a hardened military commander, Xan, but I am not stupid. Something is on your mind, and it's about more than where I am going to unpack my suitcases this evening. I understand that the situation is tense, but you haven't been yourself in weeks."

Breaking eye contact again, Xan pointed a long, bony finger at the elevator controls. "We're almost there."

Alandra closed her eyes for a moment. This was starting to feel less like a disagreement between her and her assistant and more like drama. She hated drama. It was purposeless and dangerous, the kind of distraction that could bring down empires without proper attention. As a rule Alandra did not participate in drama; she didn't read books that had any drama in them, and she absolutely refused to talk to teenagers. Xan was starting to remind her of a teenager, mopey and silent, hinting at a truth that slept underneath a bed made out of long sighs and fake sobs.

"So be it," Alandra said. "But you and I will finish this discussion later. I will not have my assistant acting like a dog who has lost its owner."

"I am not—" Xan began to argue, but the elevator dinged.

With that sound rushed back all of the anxiety that Alandra had dismissed while talking to Xan. Now, thankfully, she had much less time to dwell on it all. The doors to the bridge opened, and Alandra walked through, flanked on both sides by Thelicosan military security who gave her crisp pi-shaped salutes. She barely returned the gesture; her eyes were busy scanning the bridge for her new guest. She'd never seen any pictures of the Astromologer—rumors actually said that any device that attempted to take a picture of him broke immediately—so she didn't quite know what to expect.

Pre-Commodore Chinnaker, a thin, frail man with bright eyes and a surprisingly deep voice, was standing in front of her chair, looking out the window with his arms folded behind his back. Despite being young, he did exude an air of command, which was one of the most important things for a commander to exude. When he heard her arrive, he turned around, greeting her with a salute and much less pomp and circumstance than Zergan had done. Part of her thought it was a good change of pace, and another part missed feeling like they were about to fight a decisive space battle every time she walked onto the bridge.

"Grand Marshal," Chinnaker said, nodding. Alandra could tell he was nervous, but could also tell he was trying to hide it. Another important aspect of command was always burying your feelings deep behind impenetrable walls. Perhaps Chinnaker would do better in her stead than she'd originally assumed.

Alandra tried, in turn, not to seem like she was scanning the room for anyone who might look like the most important astromological figure in existence.

"Well?" Alandra said, stepping close to Chinnaker to avoid having the entire bridge hear their conversation. "Where is he?"

Chinnaker cleared his throat. "As one might expect, the, ah, Astromologer is a bit unconventional."

Having no idea what to make of that, Alandra simply raised her eyebrow and waited for him to continue. Chinnaker turned around and pointed out the window, and Alandra immediately saw what she'd been missing.

Alandra simply stared, forcing her mouth to remain closed. She wasn't sure if she would have called it strange, or beautiful, or even perhaps horrifying in its own way. The Astromologer—for it could have been no other man than he—was floating in space, performing what could only be described as a ritual dance. He also, somehow, appeared to not be wearing a space suit.

"How . . . ?" Alandra managed to get out.

"We don't really know, ma'am," Chinnaker said.

The Astromologer spun in slow circles, controlling his movements with such precision and grace that it seemed as though he'd been born and raised in zero gravity. Obviously biology and physics made that impossible—he would have been quite deformed—but it looked so very natural that it was easy to ignore the laws of science. And Alandra never ignored the laws of science. The Astromologer twisted and turned and flipped and bowed. He held an object in each hand, but it was impossible to tell from the distance what it was, and it was equally impossible to tell what the man looked like. He wore a dark, almost glossy uniform that was unlike anything anyone in the Thelicosan military had ever donned. A cape of sorts flowed behind him, adding to the experience.

It appeared for a moment that he had come to a halt, curling into a fetal position and allowing his own inertia to gently rotate him in place.

"Is he . . . done?" Chinnaker whispered.

"Did he give any preamble to this?" Alandra asked. "Did he come to the bridge first to explain anything?"

"No," Chinnaker said, then frowned, unable to take his eyes from the Astromologer. "Well, he was here in the bridge, yes, Grand Marshal, but only to give the helmsman some orders. He said that the *Limiter* needed to be 'properly aligned.'"

Alandra nodded. For some reason, this made perfect sense to her. "Of course."

Chinnaker shot her a little glance, likely wondering what secret information Alandra had access to that he didn't. In truth, Alandra knew just as little about all of this as he did. Perhaps she just had a bit more faith, and was willing to accept anything the Astromologer did as a matter of course.

"So do we . . . go pick him up? Is he in a meditative trance?" Chinnaker asked, raising a hand to give the order.

"No," Alandra said, some mathematical intuition telling her to wait. "Hold a moment. I think . . ."

As if the Astromologer had heard her, all of a sudden he exploded from the ball he'd rolled himself up into, arching his back in a way that seemed almost inappropriate, his mouth open in an a way that also seemed almost inappropriate. Alandra felt inappropriate herself, felt color rising to her face. *This* was math.

From his hands, something dashed out into the space around him. Well, "dashed out" wasn't quite accurate. Since he was in a vacuum, had he actually thrown the objects, they would have gone on forever. Instead, he seemed to whip his hand out and place several objects in space at highly calculated intervals. They spun in place, rotating around their center of mass in a way so precise that it seemed as though they'd been placed on a spit. Alandra squinted. Flat, rectangular objects. Cards? She wasn't privy to how the Astromologer performed any of his skills, so wild conjecture was her only option. Perhaps they were multi-plication flash cards, or rectangular tangrams? Both seemed equally unlikely.

Behind them, Alandra thought she heard a quiet sob coming from Xan.

"It's so beautiful," he whispered.

It *was* beautiful, even though Alandra had no idea what it was she was looking at. The Astromologer gently caressed the objects in front of him, spending time staring at each rotating form before moving on to the next one. It looked like there were five or six of them total, but they were stacked in such a way that it was possible that several lay unseen behind other cards.

Then, as suddenly as the exercise had begun, it stopped. The Astromologer appeared to take a slow, deep breath—Alandra realized again that he wasn't wearing a space suit—and collected the cards. Without appearing to engage any device, or pull on any tether, he then turned his body fully toward the window of the bridge and spread his arms out wide, as if preparing to take a bow. One of the offensive-systems technicians actually clapped until shushed into silence by a nearby comrade. The Astromologer slowly floated upward and out of sight.

"He's coming back to the hatch," Chinnaker called so sud-denly and loudly that Alandra felt her foot twitch. "Make prepa-rations to open it immediately! I want—"

Chinnaker blinked, his mouth hanging open. He seemed to recall that Alandra was on the bridge and was, therefore, still in command. He looked at her, then looked at her foot, then looked at her again.

"Forgive me," he said with a bow of his head. "I was so caught up in . . . no, I must not make excuses."

Yes, perhaps she'd misjudged Chinnaker entirely. While he clearly still had the impulses that came with being young, he was working to control them. With Alandra being there to guide him from the *Flagship*, he would make a fine substitute.

"It is nothing," Alandra said. "You may continue to command the bridge. I am leaving very shortly."

Chinnaker bowed even lower, acknowledging the clemency. In truth, it wasn't so large an infraction that she would have given him a spinning back kick to the face, but it was a testament to his own quest for perfection that he expected it.

"May your parallel lines never intersect," he said.

So focused on thinking about who she was leaving her ship to, Alandra didn't notice the bridge doors open. Only after the Astromologer stepped behind her did she finally turn around and steel her nerves. Alandra prided herself on the way in which she was able to keep a tight grip on her emotions, but that skill was showing cracks on the surface as she stood before one of the most powerful mathematicians of all time. He didn't say anything; he didn't need to. He merely stood there, tall, broad-shouldered, solid. Alandra immediately noticed—not without large amounts of cognitive relief—that he was indeed wearing some sort of space suit. It looked like a sort of custom-built VMU with a clear cellophane hood that was resting on the nape of his neck. Some mechanism might cause it to pull over his face when he was in vacuum.

Whoever had fabricated the suit hadn't lacked for style, either. It was, as she'd seen through the window of the bridge, a glossy, almost metallic color with silver accents, like something out of a superhero story. A thick, black cape hung off his shoulders, the material also giving off a certain sheen. In short, everything about his personage had a bit of a glow to it, and that wasn't limited to his clothes, either.

His face, while not exactly attractive, was the kind of face that carried with it the calm of years of experience. The Astromologer's age was difficult to discern—he could have been in his late thirties as easily as he could have been in his early fifties—but there was no doubt that immense wisdom sat upon those shoulders, firmly attaching him to the ground. He didn't seem to be existing in the environment around him as much as he seemed to be a *part* of the environment around him.

It was, in a word, amazing.

"Welcome to my ship and my fleet," Alandra said. Civilians were only afforded salutes with rare exceptions, but in this case Alandra erred on the side of properness and offered one anyway. The Astromologer acknowledged her with a nod.

"I feel that there is a total harmony of space converging on this location," the Astromologer said. His voice was light and airy, with a bit of a rasp to it. "We are occupying the realm that lies directly between the possible and the impossible. We stand on the edge of reality."

Alandra nodded, feeling the man's power like a physical force. It was a glorious thing to simply be standing in his presence. It was like logarithmic functions were flowing directly into her brain, exponentially amplifying her numerical soul. She understood then that what he had been doing outside of the ship had been some sort of divination ritual. She could see the deck of cards held in his gloved hand, though she couldn't see exactly what they were.

"Yes," Alandra said. "The edge of reality."

Although Alandra wasn't entirely sure what he meant by that, she trusted that it was wise and directly applicable to their current situation. Perhaps she could meditate on it this evening while she performed her daily calculus. What would it be like to understand the feeling of standing on the edge of reality?

"Is there anything we can do for you? I assume you will be coming with me to the—"

"*Flagship,*" the Astromologer interrupted. "The flow of the universe has already told me this. And aboard that vessel"—he took a deep breath, closing his eyes—"will be the other half of your heart." He opened his eyes and looked at her, eyebrows arched in curiosity. "How very interesting."

Alandra felt her face turn red. Of course the Astromologer would see through her so easily. Despite the fact that she knew he was an invaluable ally, it made her feel cautious, reserved.

"Perhaps," she said, trying and failing to keep eye contact. "There are larger goals at the moment."

"Yes," the Astromologer said. "Of course. The orbital pattern of all things is shifting, a Hohmann transfer of galactic proportions."

Frowning, Alandra fumbled for something to say in response. Hohmann transfers had become too expensive and inefficient a thousand years earlier. It seemed a rather archaic reference for such a learned man, but she trusted his wisdom. Very often, solutions to contemporary problems could be found in ancient knowledge.

The Astromologer, in the meantime, had taken to staring at her as though he was trying to burn a hole in her head with his gaze. What was going on behind those dark eyes? Well, math, probably. But what kind of math?

"We must make haste," the Astromologer said suddenly, breaking Alandra out of her thoughts. Without further preamble he turned and exited the bridge, leaving her standing there and wondering a great many things. Would he really be able to help them find the Galaxy Eater and stop it before it was too late? Or had they already reached the point of no return?

The entire bridge remained in silence, staring at the place where the Astromologer had been standing a few moments earlier. His presence was truly captivating; nobody seemed able to move. Alandra took the opportunity to take a deep breath, turn around, and address her crew.

"This will be my last time speaking to you as commander of the *Limiter* until this war is over," she said. Heads snapped to look at her, the collective reverie over. These were her troops, some of whom had been with her since the beginning of her tenure on this ship. Their loyalty and competence had been instrumental in helping her counter Zergan's rebellion. Now she had to entrust them into the hands of an officer who was much her junior in both age and experience. Would this really be alright?

"I am leaving you in the capable hands of Pre-Commodore Chinnaker," she said. "You are to afford him every respect that you afforded me during my time with you. I go with the Astromologer to fight an enemy we didn't even know existed until recently. May your parallel lines never intersect. Make me proud."

She felt a weight on her chest, like someone was hugging her too tightly. This bothered her, because she never really saw herself hugging anyone, and therefore it felt like an impermissible violation of her personal space.

"As the Grand Marshal approaches!" Chinnaker shouted.

"The *Limiter* is limitless!" cheered her crew.

Yes. It felt like someone was hugging her very tightly.

She still didn't like it.

Idiots . . . ASSEMBLE!

If the *Flagship* had felt crowded before, it was now a claustro-phobic nightmare. Of course, since he was now the "chief" of the Joint Force, his ship would need to be the home base for the foreseeable future. That included inviting a bunch of people he didn't know or like onto the ship and finding accommodations for them befitting their stations. The com-mand deck of the *Flagship* didn't exactly have a fancy hotel in it; for the most part, it was only his stateroom, the zero-gravity room, the bridge, and the room that the Viking had been moved into following Rogers' totally not creepy request. That had been his first act as Klein's executive officer, and possibly the greatest of all of his accomplishments. Perhaps his only accomplishment, actually.

And now they were completely screwing it up. He couldn't very well have the Viking staying in a room that was more suited for a flag officer. The zero-gravity room was usable if someone had some very strange living preferences, and there was only one other empty room on the command deck. Where the hell was he going to put everyone?

"I can't take this," Rogers said as he stood on the command deck, his antisalute sling deployed, watching all the hustle and bustle around him. The command deck was usually full of hustle and bustle, of course, but in this case it appeared that everyone was actually doing work. That's what really bothered him. "It's just not right. I have to sacrifice the comforts of my people to allow all these foreign entities aboard my ship."

There he went again. "His" people. "His" ship. Before he'd gotten himself into this mess, the only things he'd ever referred to as "his" were things that he actually owned. The way he spoke about the *Flagship* and the 331st Speed Bumps now almost felt obsessive.

"Rogers," Deet said, "the capacity of the ship was vastly undermanned prior to the war. The addition of these new personnel brings us from seventy-two percent manned to seventy-two point nine percent manned."

"I don't have time for your semantics and math," Rogers said. "I just want to be left alone."

Each of the representatives brought with them an assistant of sorts, or some kind of adviser who they thought might be helpful. Keffoule had brought that perpetual potato personality Xan, of course. Krell and Thrumeaux had brought some nondescript sycophants, one of whom seemed to have the sole responsibility of lifting Thrumeaux's cape so that it didn't touch the ground, like someone who actually got paid to hold the train of a wedding dress. It seemed like a waste of resources, but the *Flagship* had people in conductor's hats who basically ran an automated train system, so it was hard to criticize.

And then there was this guy.

"The space/time energy of this ship is rotating around an axis of alignment that I have not seen before," said the freak space psychic that Keffoule had brought with her. The Astromologer, they called him, and Rogers could see why. He didn't come over to the *Flagship* like a normal person on a shuttle, oh no. He actually flew himself, in open space, via the very complicated, custom-made VMU he wore. Ever since they'd met, he'd talked nonstop about planetary alignment, trigonometry, and horoscope predictions. It was a very bizarre combination.

"Yeah," Rogers said. "Axis of alignment. Look, you can't stay up here. I'm going to have to berth you with the rest of the crew. Do you have any preferences for places that it's easiest for you to, uh, work?"

The Astromologer took a long, deep breath, closing his eyes.

"This requires some meditation," he said finally, opening his eyes and gazing past Rogers in a creepy way. He paused for a moment. "And also a snack. It requires a snack."

Rogers blinked. "Right. Um, hey, Tunger, can you show Mr. Clairvoyant here to one of the mess halls? I hear the Uncouth Corkscrew has those little prepackaged peanut butter and jelly sandwiches today."

"Of course, sir," Tunger said, cheery as always. Even though he belonged on the zoo deck, the corporal seemed to be omnipresent lately, finding excuses to be where Rogers was. They'd gone through a lot together, sure, but this seemed a bit more like a man crush than anything else.

"If yurl ferrlow mur," Tunger said, giving the Astromologer a grandiose bow.

"Tunger, for the last time, Thelicosans do not—"

"Thurnk yer, yur vury kund," the Astromologer said, and the two of them walked away, shoulder to shoulder like a pair of idiots with a purpose. The moved through the bustle on the command deck and disappeared from sight as they approached the entrance to the up-line.

"I do not like him," Deet said.

"I hate Tunger too," Rogers said.

"No," Deet said. "The Astromologer. I hate him."

Rogers looked at him sideways. "You don't like him? Are you even capable of ascribing preference to humans and all that?"

Deet made a whirring noise. "Rogers, I am able to deliver humorous puns and witticisms with ease, and also talk to you about Jesus. I think I can handle figuring out that I hate someone."

"Wait, since when can you talk to anyone about Jesus?"

"Since I downloaded a book about him. I can recite it to you if you'd like."

"Please, god, no."

"An ironic request."

A moment of silence passed as the two of them stood in the center of the chaos of the command deck, people and bags flowing around them.

"I mean I really think I [EXPLETIVE] hate that guy."

"Okay, Deet, I get it," Rogers said. "You know, a lot of people around here don't think that highly of you, either. You spent a good portion of the battle with the Thelicosans telling everyone that you were going to snap and kill them—"

"This is still not outside the realm of possibility, as I possess the source code for all of those functions."

"—and at nearly every opportunity in the last couple of weeks, you've shirked your duty to go and chase your own ambitions. You were the first robot I had to pick up from jail. It wasn't fun. It didn't make me feel good."

Deet beeped and made a ridiculous attempt to fold his arms. They didn't really go that way, so he ended up just making a loud clanging noise that scared the people closest to him. "Why didn't it make you feel good? Because one of your troops was acting in a manner below your lofty standards?"

Rogers laughed. "Standards? What are those? No, it made me feel bad because picking people up from jail is what crusty old sergeants do. It made me feel old. And crusty."

Deet slowly reached out and brushed Rogers' shoulder.

"What are you doing?"

"I am attempting to discern your level of crustiness."

Rogers sighed. "It's an expression, Deet. You know, sometimes I start to think there's a bit of humanity in there, and then you go trying to flake off my arm."

Deet made a noise that was probably intended to be rude, but sounded more like an old video game. For some reason, it made Rogers want beer, but the request for supplies hadn't come in yet. It seemed like whatever he did, he simply could not get a decent drink on the *Flagship*. There was a chance that Keffoule had brought some Jasker 120 along with her, but that would mean that he'd have to talk to her to get any. That was something that Rogers simply wasn't willing to do right now. Thankfully, for whatever reason, Rogers hadn't seen Keffoule or her aide yet. That meant he could give the two empty rooms on the command deck to Thrumeaux and Krell instead of her. Rogers had already been on a ship where he had to live close to Keffoule; he wasn't eager to do it again.

"Can you explain to me, exactly, why we are standing in the middle of the command deck and doing no work at all?" Deet asked.

"Because," Rogers said, "I'm an officer."

"Rogers!" came a voice from behind him, sending a tingle up his spine. He tried to avoid turning around in a way that would have made him seem giddy and boyish, but it was impossible. If skipping in place could be considered a thing, that's what he did as he turned to face the Viking. She walked toward him carrying what was, presumably, the last bag of things she needed to move from her room on the command deck. It filled Rogers with rage that she was moving farther away from him, but there wasn't much arguing against it this time.

"Hello," he said, grinning. The last time he'd seen her, she'd been a rolling ball of fists, feet, and battle cries, fighting just about everyone in the Seedy Underbelly. Rogers wished they could go back to simpler times like that, where furniture only existed so that the Viking could break it by body-slamming people into it.

The Viking, however, showed no real indication that she was being nostalgic about anything. Her face was set in stone. This wasn't exactly different from her normal facial configuration, but Rogers thought that at least she could have looked happy to see him.

"Where's Mailn?" she asked without an introduction.

"Mailn?" Rogers said, frowning. "Why should I know? I haven't seen her since Merida Prime. She said she was coming back early to see you."

The Viking looked at him for a long moment, her eyes narrowing.

"What the hell do you mean?"

Rogers' goofy smile faltered. He wasn't sure how else one could interpret the fact he'd just relayed, so he opted to just repeat himself instead. The Viking didn't seem to appreciate the condescension.

"I have ears, asshole. But that's not what she told me."

"What do you mean?" Rogers asked.

"I mean that's not what she told me," the Viking said flatly.

Rogers held up his hands. "Okay, okay. This isn't getting us anywhere. What did Mailn tell you?"

The Viking folded her arms, looking around the room as she thought. "She told me she was staying with you on Merida Prime until you came back. She said she was coming back with you."

"Pardon my intrusion," Deet said, "but these two scenarios appear to be mutually exclusive."

"No shit," the Viking said.

"No shit," Rogers said.

Deet looked between the two of them. "I am also in agreement on the lack of [EXCREMENT], but do not see how this is relevant to our current discussion of Mailn's whereabouts."

Rogers ignored him. In fact, he ignored just about everything for a moment, staring at a spot on the floor. Mailn had been acting really strange, but he'd never known her to lie to him or the Viking. What did that mean? If she hadn't been on the ship, and she hadn't been on Merida Prime with Rogers . . .

"I'm not sure where she is," Rogers lied, loudly, "but it's not like her to just disappear like that. I'm sure she'll turn up eventually."

The Viking looked unconvinced. But, even though it gnawed at his insides, there were more important things going on right now than one missing marine. There was a ship—no, a fleet—no, multiple fleets—no, a joint force of absurd magnitude—to run. He hated admitting it, but it was true. Explaining that to the Viking, though, would have probably resulted in another dent in his forehead.

He was about to try to cheer her up when he saw Keffoule and Xan making their way through the crowd. Keffoule appeared to be looking for something, probably him. Rogers took one step to the left to put the Viking's considerable size between him and the Thelicosan commander.

"What are you doing?"

"Nothing," Rogers said. "I'm just—"

Keffoule maneuvered her way back into Rogers' line of sight, and Rogers took another step to the left. He bumped into someone from the finance squadron, knocking him into someone from the services squadron, knocking her into a marine. All of them glared at him, offended, until they realized who he was. Then they tried to salute him. Then they saw the sling on his arm and just got confused.

"Rogers . . . ," the Viking said.

"What?" Rogers said. "I'm just, you know, exercising."

"Is this about me trying to hit you again?" the Viking asked. "I already apologized for that, didn't I?"

"No, it's not about that," Rogers said. "It's about—"

"Captain Rogers," Keffoule said from directly behind his right shoulder.

"Gah!" Rogers said, jumping away from the woman, only to find himself face-to-face with Xan, who wasn't any more pleasant to be around.

"Captain," he said, emotionless as always.

"Gah to you too!" Rogers said. He tugged at his uniform and straightened himself out, trying to present himself to Keffoule as anything other than terrified.

Keffoule, as Rogers expected, looked like she was dancing the fine line between complete relaxation and a predatory coil. A half smile played on her face as she took her time appraising Rogers in a way that he found very disturbing.

"What do you want?" Rogers asked. He shot a glance at the Viking; the last time those two had been in the same room, they'd put a dent in the side of a public transportation car. Already he swore he could see thunderheads forming in between them, though Keffoule seemed to barely notice the Viking at all.

"Nothing," Keffoule said, clearly wanting something more than nothing. "I was simply coming to greet you, now that I've finished moving my things into my new quarters."

"Already?" Rogers said, raising his eyebrow. "That was fast. Where did they put you up?"

"They?" Keffoule asked. "Who is they? I merely found a place that suited me and put my things there. I am not accustomed to having to ask people where to sleep, Rogers."

Rogers rolled his eyes. "I have a feeling you're going to be getting accustomed to a lot of new things. This is my ship, Grand Marshal."

"Of course," Keffoule said with the slightest of nods. "I am ready to take any direction into consideration." She indicated over her shoulder with an open-fingered point, like she was carrying a serving tray. "I moved in there."

Following the direction of her hand, Rogers drew a line to the room that the Viking had just moved out of. His stomach sank. This was the worst possible exchange he could have thought of.

"Oh really?" the Viking said. For reasons Rogers could not comprehend, she was staring at *him* instead of Keffoule.

"Don't look at me," Rogers said. "Didn't you just hear her say that she didn't check in with anyone first?"

"So move her," the Viking said.

"I believe the captain outranks you, gorilla," Keffoule said, that half smile still on her face but her words icy. "The orders flow in the other direction."

"Is it gorillas that throw shit, or monkeys?" the Viking asked, taking a large step toward Keffoule. "I can never remember, but I see some shit that needs throwing."

"Stop!" Rogers said, stepping between them. "Keffoule, I'm not sure that's your room. You need to check in with . . ."

Rogers scanned the room, looking for Corporal Suresh, the current supply officer. Except he wasn't an officer. And he also wasn't particularly good at his job, or pleasant to talk to. But he was in charge of room assignments and other quartermasterly duties aboard the *Flagship*.

"That guy!" he said, pointing at the corporal, who was standing near the center of the large, somewhat circular area of the command deck. Suresh was staring very intently at a datapad, looking up occasionally to examine something. "Hey, Suresh!"

The corporal looked up, searching for the source of his name. The command deck was so crowded at the moment that it took Rogers calling his name three more times before they finally locked eyes and he came over.

"Sergeant," he said. "Or ensign? Lieutenant?" Suresh snapped his fingers. "Captain! That's it. You get promoted so fast I can never remember your actual rank."

Rogers gave him a wry smile. He didn't know Suresh had a sense of humor. Then again, he hadn't been back down to Supply in quite some time. Humor could grow on a man if the right seeds were planted.

The metaphor in Rogers' head was getting kind of complicated and gross, so he opted instead to ignore Suresh's joke and ask him to please, please, find Keffoule a room somewhere as far away from him as possible.

"That's a very rude request," Xan said. "I'll thank you not to treat my—"

Keffoule silenced him with a wave of her hand. "That is enough, Xan. I can defend myself, thank you."

Despite the declaration, Keffoule made no move to defend herself in any way. She simply looked at Suresh, both eyebrows raised, and waited for him to answer Rogers' question.

Rogers knew that look. He hated that look. It was the look that said that Keffoule already knew she'd won. Suresh looked down at his datapad, tapped the screen a couple of times, and made a few contemplative noises.

"Hm," he said. "Well, it looks to me like all the personnel have already been assigned to their rooms. Premiere Thrumeaux is already set up with her assistant on the entertainment deck—she said she wanted to be near the drama, or something?—and General Krell has already claimed the extra room on the command deck . . ."

He tapped the pad a few more times, frowning.

"I'm sorry," Keffoule interjected. "Did you say General Krell will be on this deck?"

Suresh nodded, distracted. "Yes, ma'am."

Keffoule swallowed. "I see."

Rogers thought he would search the galaxy far and wide for the rest of his life and never find anyone that made Alandra Keffoule nervous, but there was a tone in her voice that Rogers could only ascribe to discomfort. He watched her face intently for a moment, but she gave nothing else away.

Suresh shrugged and let the datapad fall to his side. "I thought I saw the grand marshal move her things into a room already. That's the one, sir. The only one I have left."

Keffoule's brief flash of uncertainty faded into one of mirth.

Rogers scowled. Someday, that woman would get very much the opposite of what she wanted, and Rogers hoped he would be there to see it.

Well, Rogers had been there to see it when she had nearly lost her entire fleet to a backstabbing friend who had betrayed her and nearly killed her. So there was that.

"I guess I'll see you later, then, Captain Rogers," Keffoule said, grinning. "Often." She walked away, Xan in tow.

Rogers watched her go, feeling like his insides were going to crawl out any orifice they could find. The thought of possibly spending the rest of his life with that woman fifty feet away from him made him nauseous. All the more reason to make sure they won this fight. Then he'd at least have more life left to live that didn't involve her as a bunkmate.

"Oh, that's just great," the Viking said, again looking at Rogers instead of anyone else who was actually causing the problem. "Now you and your Thelly girlfriend can hang out all the time and talk about battle tactics, and all that."

"Not the tactics again," Rogers said. "This isn't my fault, you know. You're standing right here. You can clearly see my every effort to put as much distance between me and this woman as possible, right?"

"You invited her on the ship," the Viking said. Was she pouting?

"I was *ordered* to!" Rogers said. "Just like I was *ordered* to take over the droid combat squadron and *ordered* to try and escape from the ship."

The Viking gave him a level look.

"Okay, so I wasn't ordered to try and escape from the ship that one time. But you have to understand that everything is so wildly out of my control over here that I'm having trouble figuring out when I am allowed to go to the bathroom anymore."

As he spoke, he felt an uncontrollable rage build up inside him. It had been so long since he felt like anything was within his control, since he could make his own damn decisions. All of this was so simultaneously depressing, terrifying, and extremely inconvenient that he thought he might explode. Starting a rant in the middle of the command deck wouldn't be a very good idea, but he wasn't sure he could hold it all in much longer.

"Yeah," the Viking said, obviously going to continue, but Rogers had had enough of all of this.

"Stop," Rogers said, holding up a hand. The Viking stared at his hand, her mouth open, not sure what to do. Rogers wasn't sure what to do either. He just felt very strongly like he needed to extricate himself from this situation as soon as possible.

"I can't," he continued. "I can't do this right now. If you can't accept the fact that Keffoule is not your rival in any way except maybe in a face-kicking contest, then I don't know what else I can do to fix it. Don't you have a missing marine to take care of? Isn't that why you came over here in the first place?"

Jeez. Rogers' chest rose and fell with the effort of heavy breathing, and sweat rolled down his back. He was really worked up. In a weird way, he also felt like he might break out crying. Not like a couple of tears, but huge, wracking, childlike sobs. He desperately wanted to run away and slam a door and yell at someone for "just not getting him."

The Viking, obviously not accustomed to being interrupted and dismissed like that, stared at Rogers for what seemed like an eternity. People all over the command deck flowed around her. Rogers wanted to reach out and hug her, or something, but he just stood there, waiting for her to go away. He couldn't concentrate when she was around, and right now he needed to concentrate on not getting everyone in the galaxy killed.

"Yeah," the Viking said. "Yeah. Okay, Rogers. Yeah."

Without another word, the Viking turned around and walked away, her shoulders maybe a little slumped. Rogers took a moment to admire the view—he wasn't *that* busy—and contemplate things a bit. The Viking wouldn't be able to sleep until she found Mailn; of that he was certain. But Rogers was pretty sure she wasn't going to find her. Because Rogers was pretty sure she'd run away to join the pirates.

Suresh, who'd been quiet for a while, cleared his throat.

"I'm sorry, sir, but I've just been standing here not doing any work while you've continued this conversation. Will you be needing anything else from me at the moment, or can I get back to it?"

"That will be all, Suresh, thanks. Nice work getting all this squared away."

"I feel like geometric shapes have very little to do with this," Deet said. He looked around. "This place seems to be a bit more octagonal than anything else. Do you need to have your vision checked?"

Suresh paused a moment, looking at Deet. It had been a long time since Rogers had had anything to do with Supply, and it might have been the first time that Suresh had seen Deet since the incident with the murderous droids.

"You look familiar," he said, his expression flat. "Like the kind of droid that once froze me in cryo-wrap and nearly killed me." He punched a couple of buttons on this datapad. "Shouldn't you have an inventory number? I'm not sure I've seen you on the ship's manifest."

"I'm not a piece of inventory," Deet said.

"Yes, you are," Suresh said.

"Yes, you definitely are," Rogers said. "Let's leave this alone for right now, okay, Suresh? Deet here is my deputy and personal assistant."

"And also really great," Deet said.

"He's alright," Rogers conceded.

Suresh didn't look convinced. As the supply chief, the idea of having something unaccounted for was probably anathema to him.

"Yes, sir." He made a move to salute, but then didn't. "Well, let me know if you need anything else."

"Yeah, sure," Rogers said.

As Suresh walked away, leaving Rogers with no other human companionship on the command deck, Rogers couldn't shake the feeling that something was very out of place. Maybe it was all the strangers on his ship or the threat of imminent destruction. Those were the obvious causes, but some instinct told Rogers there was more to what he was feeling. His thought pattern edged dangerously close to an examination of his inner thoughts, and his instinct told him to run away from introspection like he usually did. Maybe, though, just this once, he could mull on it for just a second.

"Deet," he said, "you ever feel like you did the right thing, but then also feel like you did the wrong thing?"

"Oh, *now* I have feelings?" Deet said. "Go [SELF-FORNICATE]."

And that was why Rogers never examined his feelings.

"Come on," Rogers said, starting to walk. "I need to get back to my stateroom. I want to scream into a pillow for a few minutes before I get everyone in the war room for an initial briefing. My stomach also feels a little—"

The keypad on his door dinged loudly, and a familiar voice spoke.

"Congratulations on assembling a joint force of the Fortuna Stultus galaxy's systems! You are entitled to one free joint-stabilizer exercise ball, available at any of the many Snaggardir's Sundries locations across the galaxy. Remember, whatever you need, you can Snag It at Snaggardir's™!"

"Wait just a goddamned minute," Rogers said.

"Very strange," Deet said. "That's not the same meaning of the word 'joint' at all."

"I don't think that's the strange part," Rogers said.

That was the second time that a Snaggardir's courtesy announcement had mentioned something that had not only just happened, but was supposed to be secret. Was it possible that all the Snaggardir's devices that had gone rogue also had transmitters that were funneling information back to the Jupiterians? That seemed like a large oversight for people not to check them, if so.

It meant one of two things. Either Snaggardir's equipment was self-teaching, and Deet really had a lot to learn, or somebody close to them was a spy.

"It's McSchmidt!" Deet yelled. "He's back from the dead!"

"Oh, shut up," Rogers said.

Lessons Not Quite Learned

Deet had repeatedly been told something about "learning his lesson" during the many lectures he'd received during and after his encounter with the security team on Merida Prime. Given that, to his knowledge, he wasn't in any sort of formal schooling, the expression confused him. And, despite all of the admonitions, he'd hardly uncovered anything useful from any of the machines he'd plugged into. Maybe some correlations between certain organizations and Jupiter, like the company that made the SEWR rats. But who cared about that? Or the fact that the last batch of standard edible wartime rations that had come onto the *Flagship* from a Snaggardir shadow company's production facility had been intentionally contaminated with norovirus. But certainly nothing he'd been interested in when it came to the conception of artificial intelligence, the enigmatic Dr. Mattic, and Deet's origins.

"You son of a bitch!" Rogers yelled from inside his stateroom's bathroom. "You—hurk!—son of a—hurk!—motherless whore!"

No, Deet hadn't discovered any useful information at all. Worse, Rogers didn't seem to be at all concerned about it. In fact, he'd seemed downright incensed when Deet had finally relayed the information about the contaminated food to him. Of all the things Deet had expected, anger hadn't been one of them. Perhaps he'd been slightly late with the delivery, though.

Another understatement! Deet thought triumphantly. He was getting quite good at those.

Of course, while Rogers was occupied in the bathroom, Deet had his dongle firmly inserted into Rogers' personal console, trawling the network for any data he could find. In some ways, this had become a habit of his. Any time he found a terminal, he felt compelled to connect to it. Did that qualify as an addiction? Were these really "impulses," or were they just logic and decision trees that led to plugging in and extracting data? These were the very mysteries he was trying to solve by his research, of course, which seemed to place him in an infinite loop. His dongle always presented him with twice as many questions as answers every time he stuck it someplace it didn't belong.

More retching noises came from the bathroom, accompanied by swearing and, Deet thought, glass breaking. Deet would have called it distracting if he was convinced he could be distracted. In this case, he merely turned down his auditory sensors, ignoring Rogers entirely. As he did so, he realized that perhaps this was an option he could utilize much more often, in many more scenarios.

This foray into the network wasn't any more useful than the others, at first. The problem with having an interconnected galaxy with more devices than people was that the amount of data processed was overwhelming.

He had been able to begin to categorize the data streams into schema and at least glean some generalities. In this case, mostly what he saw was rising panic. The Galaxy Eater video had been broadcast throughout Fortuna Stultus, and the resulting pandemonium was nothing short of apocalyptic. Of course, it was *literally* apocalyptic, so Deet supposed that it was warranted. What did Deet think about his own preservation? Could he die, or would his data just be loaded into a new model and he could carry on as normal? If he *couldn't* die, did that mean he wasn't really alive?

More questions than answers, again. While interesting, these questions mostly got in the way of what he was trying to do at the moment. He put them into a special memory bank he'd been accumulating, titled Examinations of the Definitions and Purposes of Life, and continued searching.

Panic, chaos, mayhem, Deet thought. *Blah, blah, blah.*

"Blah, blah, blah" was a phrase he'd recently picked up from Rogers that was so brilliantly convenient he couldn't help but use it at every available opportunity. From his understanding, he was pretty sure it meant "I will ignore swaths of important details in an effort to radically oversimplify a situation and allow me to process it without going insane."

Jupiterian sympathizers were rising up in all of the systems, some incidents of which were alerting the public to exactly how deep the Jupiterian revolution went. People had hidden their identities and affiliations for hundreds of years, waiting for the right moment to strike, all organized by Snaggardir's. In truth, it was an impressive testament to the patience of a species that didn't tend to live very long in the grand scheme of things. Deet wondered if any other such sympathizers were in the newly christened Joint Force. Probability theory indicated that it was a near certainty, but there were no real methods to discern who was who unless they came out and said it.

All of this information about the war and its potential outcomes, but nothing new in the network that had anything to do with Deet and his origins.

Deet was about to unplug and go make fun of Rogers for sounding like a little girl when he threw up when something drew his attention. It was a ship's report, somewhere at the very edge of Meridan space, but it wasn't from a Meridan ship. One of the groups designated to help escort the pirates into battle positions had sent out a distress signal that looked very strange. Not that there was anything strange about distress signals—Deet had seen logs of hundreds of them just in this foray into the network alone—but this one didn't seem to be quite finished. Not only that, but the distress message, though sent, didn't seem to ever have been received by anyone in the sector.

Diving deeper into the message and its path, Deet saw that, although relays were in every sector of known space for this express purpose, the relay closest to where the distress message had occurred hadn't passed on the message to any other system. To utilize a metaphor—which Deet was quite proud of himself for—it was as though someone had given a relay station a paper note, and instead of passing it on to the next relay it had simply put it in its pocket and gone about its business as though nothing had happened. Not only that, but there were several layers of encryption.

This puzzled Deet. If there had been encryption, why had he been able to see the message so clearly, so quickly? He didn't have to hack into it at all. The message just opened itself to him, laying bare not only the contents of the message, but the rerouting information that had caused it to stop at the first relay station.

Then it hit him.

Well, it didn't physically hit him. It was just data, of course. But the expression of physical impact seemed to apply here.

The cyphers used to encrypt the message were already in his core memory banks; the message had been encrypted by other droids.

A whole host of facts became instantaneously clear to him as he processed the real contents of the message in under a nanosecond. The message was cut short because the ship had been taken over prior to the captain being able to input all of the information. He'd sent it prematurely, likely in the hope of getting at least some of the information out, but it had been intercepted and quarantined by droids. The ship that had quarantined the message was, as he'd suspected, the *Rancor*, also known as the *Beta Test* to the droids who had commandeered it.

That meant that there were more droids out there, possibly more Froids as well. They had become savvy enough to not only keep the *Rancor* from being discovered, but had also likely taken over other ships. The brief message from the captain of the *Curtain Call*—the ship from which the quarantined message had originated—said that they'd been boarded, not fired upon. Were the droids attempting to build a fleet of their own? Should Deet relay this information to Rogers?

The knowledge that the *Rancor* was still out there, and still populated by active droids, was clearly important to both Deet and Rogers. Yet some instinct told Deet to keep the information hidden for now.

What was an "instinct"?

"If I ever find that ship," Rogers said, "I am going to utilize every gun in the fleet to blow it to the smallest possible particles of space dust."

Deet's expression of surprise wasn't exactly fine-tuned yet. His processors merely interpreted things he didn't expect as new information with high priority. Yet it seemed like this required some sort of reaction, so Deet slowly raised both arms over his head and waggled them from side to side.

"Um," Rogers said. "Are you alright?"

Deet considered that this perhaps was not the correct "surprised" response, but chose not to explain his actions any further. Rogers' voice, now in close proximity, could be detected by Deet's lowered auditory-detection systems, but Deet had not heard him approach. Slowly, stealthily, Deet retracted his dongle.

"I am fine," Deet said. He turned his hearing back up and called up his protocol for feigning ignorance, which was very similar to asking for clarity. "What ship are you talking about, exactly?"

"The *Rancor,* idiot. I'm staring right at it on my screen," Rogers said, wiping his mouth. He looked a little pale. "Come on, Deet. You think I don't know you come in here sticking your thingy in my terminal every time I look away? I'm not stupid."

"I thought this angered you?" Deet asked.

"No," Rogers said, sitting down in his chair, his whole body slack. Sweat dripped down his face. "What pisses me off is when you do this *instead* of something I've told you to do. Or when you endanger me or the fleet. Or when you get arrested and make me come to the jail. Or—"

His face went slack, his mouth and eyes wide open. Shortly after, he sprinted back to the bathroom, where he shouted in a high-pitched, panicky voice, "Or—hurk—when you don't tell me that we've all been intentionally—huuuurk—poisoned!"

This bout of vomiting was much shorter than the last, and Rogers returned momentarily, limping toward the desk. He looked like he'd been through a bar fight, or perhaps maybe two minutes of actual physical exercise.

"Yep," Rogers said, leaning heavily on the back of his chair. "I wouldn't even attempt to negotiate. I'd send every available weapon, and maybe even Flash, to destroy that ship and any other ships with it."

Deet considered that perhaps his instinct to hide this information from Rogers was based on past experience and, on the whole, was the right thing to do.

But right for whom?

"What are you looking for?" Rogers said. "What's that, there?" He pointed to the rapidly moving text flying by on the screen. Deet rerouted the output so it was only going through his internal processors, and not being displayed.

"Just some ships' communication," Deet said. "Captains logs, manifests . . . blah, blah, blah."

Rogers squinted. "Oh. Alright. Did you find anything else useful while you were in there? I told you I don't mind you doing existential research, or whatever, but I want you to be looking for ways for us to win this war as well."

"Not really," Deet said. "Pretty much everyone all over the galaxy is losing their [EXPLETIVE] minds. There's nothing very constructive going on at all. Nobody knows where the Galaxy Eater is located, but everyone is pretty enthusiastic about pirates right now. Oh, and Flash did a news interview. He's pretty popular."

"What?" Rogers said. "With who? He's still on the ship!" For a moment, Rogers didn't say anything as he stared off into space. "He *is* still on the ship, right?"

Pulling out his datapad, he made a quick call. Deet couldn't hear the voice on the other end.

"Yeah. It's Rogers. Is Flash there? . . . No, I don't want to talk to him. . . . No, I don't want him to do anything. . . . No, I do not want his autograph—what the hell is wrong with you?"

Huffing, Rogers hung up the call and let out a long breath, something that he did often. Perhaps he had respiratory issues that Deet was unaware of. A quick vital scan of Rogers revealed that, although his VO_2 was at the same level as a seventy-year-old, he was fine.

"I swear, something is going on with that guy. Everyone seems to think he's this hotshot pilot who keeps saving the day, but it's taking all of my effort and energy just to keep him from blowing up the ship." Rogers shook his head and limped away. Deet thought perhaps he was going to vomit again, but instead he removed his clothes, throwing them in a laundry basket he had near the entrance to his stateroom's bathroom.

"I feel like this is something better done in private," Deet said. "I am feeling embarrassed. Addendum: you are hairy."

"You don't have feelings," Rogers said, stepping into his bathroom. "You also don't have genitals, so I'm not really sure if I should be modest around you or not. Besides, you're in my room and you won't leave, and I need to shower. This is no time for protocol."

The shower started running. Deet understood the basics of human hygiene, but the idea of soaking himself in something that could make parts of him arc wasn't very appealing. Then again, he'd never tried it. Maybe it would be fun. Any joy Deet might have derived from fantasizing about naughty electrical currents, however, was quashed when Rogers began singing a tuneless, unintelligible song about women with large posteriors. Briefly, Deet considered turning down his auditory sensors again, but he didn't want to be surprised.

Re-extending his dongle into the network terminal, Deet called up the last records he'd been examining and tried to extrapolate a bit. The last time the droids had functioned as a single entity, they'd formed their own closed network that rode on the back of the *Flagship*'s systems, hijacking bandwidth to keep their communications secret. Yet, despite how many different ways Deet tried to approach the quarantined message, he could find no evidence of anything that might let him into any kind of new intranet. If they were talking to anyone, they were doing it in a way that Deet couldn't discern from his current location on the net. And, if that was the case, it likely meant they weren't talking to anyone. It was easy to hide the contents of communication, but it was almost impossible to hide that some communication had occurred.

It wasn't even possible to tell who they were working for. The likeliest scenario, of course, was that the droids in the *Rancor*'s fleet were working for Snaggardir's, but something about that didn't make sense to Deet. Why not communicate with them? Why attempt to build a fleet by capturing other ships? The droids couldn't reproduce as far as Deet knew—and, just based on the number of computer terminals Deet had put his dongle in, he *really* hoped he was correct—so once they reached minimally effective staffing for each ship, any further expansion would be pointless.

So, why were they doing what they were doing? And who were they doing it for?

Deet took a long couple of microseconds to run this through his circuits, making several guesses and following them along a long, branching logic train to their conclusions. Unfortunately, none of them made much sense. In one configuration, which he was sure was incorrect, he concluded that the droids had been grossly misunderstood and had actually been trying to open a bakery. It was important to consider every possibility, but perhaps next time he could filter out some of the real time wasters.

Rogers was already done with his shower, and, thankfully, done with his singing. Deet didn't have very much time to grab as much information as he could. Not that more time would really have helped him; there simply wasn't a lot of information out there. Just one half-completed distress call and the telemetry data associated with it. There wasn't anything he could do with this unless he wanted to do something ridiculous like . . .

Like send the droids a message.

"Deet," Rogers called from the shower. "Will you get me a towel?"

"No."

"If you don't, I'm going to have to walk out there bare-assed and—"

"Stop!" Deet said. "Do not [EXPLETIVE] move!"

"Jeez," Rogers said, sounding offended. "Come on, man. I'm not that out of shape."

It wasn't that Deet didn't want to see Rogers' wet, hairy body. Well, it was in part because Deet did not want to see Rogers' wet, hairy body. But it was also because Deet was in the middle of sending an encoded message over open channels to the last known position and frequency listed on the distress signal's report. Deet felt as though Rogers might not appreciate this.

Finishing the message as quickly as he could, Deet sent it off, tried to erase as many traces of the message being sent as possible, and unplugged from the system. A tiny tendril of smoke came from the top of the machine.

"Seriously," Rogers said. "Shriveling up over here."

Not wanting to ask for clarification of that statement at all, Deet ambled over to the bathroom, grabbing a towel along the way. Rogers muttered thanks and began going about the strange human ritual of making oneself look presentable. That was something Deet would probably never understand no matter how much empathy Belgrave helped him develop.

"Can you check my messages?" Rogers shouted, his voice all funny as he stretched his chin and lips around to trim his beard. "I want to have a meeting with everyone as soon as they're settled in. Suresh should have checked in everyone by now."

"Affirmative," Deet said.

"Affirmative?" Rogers said. "Are you feeling especially droidy today, Deet? That sounds weird coming from you."

"Oh, I'm sorry. I meant to say 'Yes, [REAR ORIFICE].'"

"That's better."

But it was hard to focus, which in and of itself was surprising. Focus was an organic convention; Deet could rapidly shift focus to thousands of small processes. Still, the thing at the forefront of his contemplation was one fact: Deet had his first secret. It made him feel . . . he wasn't sure what it made him feel. And, as Rogers would say, he wasn't even totally sure he had feelings. But something changed in that moment, and it was more than Rogers' underwear.

The messages on Rogers' terminal mirrored those on his datapad, so Rogers could have done this himself. Apparently the commander of the Joint Force was feeling a little power hungry if he felt the need to order a droid to do something simple like read messages.

According to the terminal, all new personnel had reported

in, saying that their deputies were firmly in place in their own fleets; they'd settled into their new rooms, and they were officially part of the *Flagship*'s crew. Thrumeaux had already put in sixteen formal complaints about her living conditions, ranging from inadequately fluffed pillows to poor acoustics in her own shower. Krell's and Keffoule's reports were much more functional and simple.

The only thing Deet didn't see was anything about that ridiculous Astromologer. Hopefully he'd decided to jump out an airlock. Deet was still struggling with the concepts of instincts, but something told him that he hated that man and wanted him to die. Maybe it was his pretentiousness, maybe it was his always talking about harmony and the waves of the universe and all that.

"Everyone's ready," Deet said. "It looks like the last of the . . ."

Deet trailed off, something he'd learned that humans did when some interesting new information came to light in the middle of a communication.

"Deet?" Rogers said, emerging from the bathroom, thankfully fully clothed. "What's the matter? Are you out of power? Oh, shit, did we lose gravity again?" He began hopping up and down to see if he would leave the deck.

"Sometimes I have serious doubts about your ability to command yourself, never mind several fleets at once."

"You and me both," Rogers said. He wiped the last of the water off his face and threw the towel over his head back into the bathroom. Deet wasn't totally sure about the nesting habits of humans, but he was fairly certain Rogers would be considered a slob. "So what is it?"

Rogers came up behind Deet and sat in his chair, leaning forward so his elbows could rest on the terminal desk. For a brief moment, Deet thought he looked rather official, the way Holdt had looked at his own desk. The picture on the screen wasn't strange in and of itself. It seemed like just a shot of empty space, perhaps from one of the maintenance cameras located on the outer hull of the ship. The strange part about it, however, was the man dancing in it.

"Oh, great," Rogers said. "It's the Astromologer. What the hell is he doing now?"

"Based on my calculations," Deet said, "he is about to experience a massive embolism, and his lungs will likely burst from the rapid decrease in pressure."

"No," Rogers said. "He's got some sort of special VMU. I saw it when he came in. But why the hell is he on the outside of the ship . . ." Rogers leaned forward, squinting at the screen. "And why is he dancing?"

The datapad now on Rogers' desk rang, and Keffoule began speaking in a rush as soon as Rogers answered.

"Rogers," she said, sounding a little bit like she'd either just engaged in extreme physical exercise or had rapidly depressurized, "you need to come to the war room as soon as possible. You will never see such a sight for the rest of your life."

Divine Calculations

The war room looked so different from the last time Rogers had been inside that Rogers almost didn't know where he was. Someone had gone through it with gusto, clearing out all of the refuse, emptying the garbage barrel that had been burning just a week ago—Rogers had been the one to set it ablaze, actually—and replacing the half-broken conference table with a deep mahogany monstrosity that ate up almost the entire space. The walls had been repainted, the chairs had been replaced. A holographic projector of a similar make and model to the one that Rogers had seen and admired on the Thelicosan ship *Ambuscade* was suspended from the ceiling above the middle of the table, ready to make abundantly clear in three dimensions exactly how hopeless their situation was.

And, worst of all, the masterfully constructed blanket fort was now completely gone. That was almost too much to bear.

Rogers sat down at the only available seat; the other seats at the table were filled with the new members of the Joint Force.

Scanning the room, he couldn't find the Viking, or even Tunger. Aside from Deet, who was only barely tolerable, there wasn't anyone in the room he actually liked.

It seemed like lately Rogers was always walking into rooms filled with people he didn't like. And now this one had a way to deliver *presentations*. Rogers hated presentations.

"Alright," he said. "Would someone please explain to me why the newest member of our motley crew is doing the space boogie?"

He looked up, examining the faces of everyone in the room. Thrumeaux looked distinctly unimpressed, maybe even bored. She'd completely changed her uniform into something that Rogers could only describe as aristocratic, a blue double-breasted jacket with surprisingly nothing on the front that indicated achievements, or even her name. Nothing about it looked comfortable, though Thrumeaux didn't seem to mind. Krell puffed his chest out, posturing himself like some kind of ape vying for dominance.

Keffoule, on the other hand, looked daggers at him. Thankfully, Xan wasn't there to contribute to the dirty looks.

"He is not doing the space boogie," Keffoule said. "Please, sit down and observe before you make any judgments. We are about to discover the location of the Galaxy Eater."

Rogers tapped his fingers on the table, staring at Keffoule. He could have continued to banter with her, continued telling her that all of this math/psychic crap was as crazy as, oh, maybe, asking someone to marry them the first time you met them. But, in the effort of moving all of this along so he could either retire or be dead, he waved a hand ambiguously in the air, indicating that whatever was happening should continue to happen without any further interference from him.

Nothing happened.

"Well?" Rogers asked.

"Well what?" Krell asked. "All you did was wave your hand."

"You think you can just come in here, wave your hand, and make things happen?" Thrumeaux asked. "You didn't even tell us what you wanted us to do when you waved the hand."

"Just because you're the boss—" Krell said.

"First among equals," Thrumeaux interrupted.

"—doesn't mean that you can just wave hands to accomplish wide-reaching strategic objectives."

Rogers ground his palms into his eye sockets. "I mean how about we get on with watching the non–space boogie?"

"Oh," Krell said. "Well, why didn't you just say that?"

Krell reached forward and tapped a few buttons on the integrated console built into the table in front of him, bringing the holographic projector to life and dimming the lights. Whoever had re-outfitted the war room had really outdone themselves; one might even believe that a war could be run out of here. They still might all die in a fireball, but maybe they could do it in an organized way.

The projector brought to life a stunningly clear display rendered from the outboard ship cameras. The lenses put out so many lumens, focused in such a precise way, that it was impossible to see the other side of the table. It was as though there really was a tiny version of the Astromologer doing zero-gravity ballet in the middle of the table. Singing some kind of song that was coming through via his radio transmitter. And, apparently, dealing a game of poker? Maybe he wasn't so bad.

"Does someone want to expl—"

"Shh!" Keffoule hissed from the other side of the table. "Genius is happening!"

Rogers, knowing that Keffoule couldn't see him and therefore couldn't kick him in the face, stuck his tongue out. He resigned himself to watching this spectacle. Next to him, Deet made a noise that clearly indicated displeasure.

"Shh," Rogers whispered to him. "Genius is happening."

"I'll show you [EXPLETIVE] genius," Deet said.

The outboard cameras on the ship weren't designed for observing enemy movements, or anything dynamic really, so they were mostly fixed in position with minimal controls available to the Engineering crew. It didn't, however, impede the Astromologer's performance, and Rogers realized after a few seconds that the Astromologer had specifically chosen his position in space so as to be viewable. It seemed a sort of arrogant thing to do; if he was so psychically powerful, why did he need people watching him when he utilized his power? He could just have easily done it outside of the trash chute without all this pomp and circumstance.

It also made Rogers a little uncomfortable that the Astromologer was so familiar with the layout of a ship that he had never been on that he knew exactly where to go. Maybe it was part of his skill set? He would have to ask Keffoule later.

Meanwhile, the cameras were doing a fine job of watching this man do all kinds of spins and turns. The song he was singing was unintelligible. If it had any words, Rogers couldn't understand them, and nobody else at the table gave any indication that they could either. He spun and sang, producing large, black cards and laying them out carefully in the zero-gravity environment of space so they wouldn't fly away.

The whole thing was utterly indecipherable to Rogers. The Astromologer kept putting cards in space, taking them back again, performing a spin or two, and then shuffling the cards only to start the process again. On the other side of the table, though Rogers couldn't see her face, Keffoule was sniffling softly. Rogers rolled his eyes. Was this guy really going to be able to single-handedly solve a problem that every scientist in the galaxy was working on?

Suddenly the Astromologer stopped moving entirely. Black-backed cards, with something on their faces that Rogers' couldn't see but were definitely not poker cards, spun gracefully in empty space. The Astromologer himself curled up into a fetal position and rotated at exactly the same rate as the cards in front of him.

Regardless of whether or not this guy was a fraud and a loon, he certainly had some incredible knowledge of how to manipulate moving bodies in a zero-gravity environment.

"I hate him," Deet said, his voice turned down very low.

"Get over it, Deet. If he manages to figure out where the Galaxy Eater is, he'll have done a lot more for the war effort than you have lately."

Deet didn't respond, and Rogers shifted in his chair. That seemed like kind of a harsh response, even though he and Deet verbally abused each other on a regular basis. Perhaps it was because there was a kernel of truth in it. As much as Rogers thought he "knew" the droid, lately it seemed like Deet had been so laser focused on figuring out the secrets of artificial intelligence that Rogers couldn't get him to pay any attention to anything else.

The room grew awkwardly quiet. The Astromologer didn't move. Well, he was in constant motion, since he was in a vacuum, but he didn't move with respect to anything else.

"Uh," Rogers said. "So that was great, I guess? Do we put money in his hat now, or cross his palm with silver, or something?"

"The star dust of the universe has collected on my lotus petals," the Astromologer said through the radio. Rogers thought he was going to continue, by, perhaps, telling them the location of the Galaxy Eater, but only more silence followed.

"We can send someone to clean up the dust?" Rogers offered when he couldn't take the silence anymore. "I'm sorry if your room was out of order, but—"

"Urp is aligned with Merida Prime. The Mu and Ji galaxies present a trigonometrically significant angle when placed within the Great Sphere—they are currently in major aspect. This is . . . very unusual."

Rogers sat back in his chair. "How the hell can anything be unusual in astronomy? Everything follows a predetermined path that takes billions of years to alter. We can literally predict the path and location of every celestial body within observable space."

"This isn't astronomy," Keffoule said.

"It's astromology," Krell finished.

Rogers could barely see part of Krell's face, due to the projection and the way they were all seated around the table, but he saw Krell turn and look in Keffoule's direction, smiling. He wanted to roll his eyes, but in truth, the more attention Krell paid Keffoule—and the more she reciprocated—the less time she was spending chasing him around the ship, decrying the sanctity of the golden ratio and the inevitability of their marriage. If Rogers was smart—and Rogers had been known to be smart occasionally—he would probably spend some time and energy encouraging the relationship.

He was about to start asking Krell if he had any measurements or personal statistics that were 1.61 times that of Keffoule's when the Astromologer interrupted his thoughts.

"Everyone," he said. "Meet me in the war room as soon as you can. I have news."

"We're already in the war room, [EXCREMENT EXIT DOOR]," Deet yelled.

"I know this," the Astromologer said.

From the back of the room.

"I am able to foresee all things through the power of calculus and cosmic energy."

"What the hell?" Rogers said, nearly jumping out of his chair. "How did you get from out there to in here so fast?"

The Astromologer, whose pale forehead glistened with sweat as he took broad strides around the outside of the war room, ignored Rogers' question, perhaps because it didn't have anything to do with hocus-pocus. Without asking for permission—which, for some reason, bothered Rogers—he came to the center of the table and started pressing buttons on the projector's control console. Rogers noticed that, of course, the Astromologer was no longer within view of the ship's cameras. If that were the case, he would have been in two places at the same time, which wouldn't have made sense at all. But how *did* he get inside so fast? And why did nobody else seem to care?

"You think you can just come in here and start touching buttons?" Deet asked.

"Pipe down, robot," Krell said.

"Hey," Rogers said. "He's *my* robot. You can't talk to him like that."

"Hey," Deet said. "I'm not *anyone's* robot!"

"Pipe down, Deet," Rogers said.

Deet piped down. The Astromologer was, of course, unconcerned with the world around him, and continued pressing buttons anyway. The result was that the feed from the outboard cameras vanished, replaced by a two-dimensional representation of the Grandelle system, complete with labels for the space geography–uninitiated. As though he'd invented the software himself, the Astromologer began whipping through different sectors of Grandellian space, zooming by planets, moons, and asteroids. It quickly became impossible to tell where they'd ended up, but finally he stopped in a sector that seemed to have nothing in it at all. It was just a transit point for Un-Space traffic heading from Grandelle to Merida.

"Here," the Astromologer said. "The mouth that would consume the world yawns, bearing its tonsils to the universe."

"Say 'ah,'" Rogers said.

"Ah," Deet said. "But why?"

Rogers sighed. "I assume you mean you've found the Galaxy Eater?"

The Astromologer looked up, glaring with what Rogers thought was inappropriate intensity.

"It is not whether or not I have found it. It is whether or not the universe has deigned to reveal to me its secrets." He narrowed his eyes. "And it has."

"Uh-huh," Rogers said. "And how, exactly, do we know that it's here?"

"Captain Rogers!" Keffoule hissed. "Questioning the Astromologer is not appropriate! You will show my system's guest more respect. He has potentially rescued us all from certain danger."

Rogers, now able to see Keffoule since the large projection had been changed, looked at her with a wry smile. So, he could sit here all day and insult her, call her crazy, and tell her he didn't want to marry her and she just kept on coming, but disparage her math god and she'd explode?

"I'm about to fling the best effort the systems have assembled into one location in an effort to surround and destroy something designed to collapse the galaxy. I think I have a right to ask a few questions before I do it."

"But—"

The Astromologer looked sideways at Keffoule and silenced her with a glance. It was actually kind of impressive. Rogers couldn't silence Keffoule with a literal platoon of marines shooting at her from both directions. In a way, it made him jealous of the Astromologer's power, and Rogers wasn't thinking of the weird, psychic/mathematician kind. Just the shutting-up-Keffoule kind.

"It is a series of equations and divinations so complicated that just relating it to you might cause your mind to come apart at the seams. Suffice it to say that there are traces in the fabric of the cosmos that all point to one, single, terrifying disturbance. Combined with the power of my Tau/Rho Cards—"

"Tarot cards?" Rogers asked. "Are you serious?"

"Not tarot cards. Tau/Rho Cards," the Astromologer said. "Tau, as in the alternate notation for the golden ratio, and rho, as in the alternate notation for part of the silver ratio. Their forces bound all things in space, aesthetics, and cooking." He paused, looking up at the ceiling dramatically. "Silver and gold. These two shimmering forces of the universe are—"

"Right. Can I see the cards?" Rogers asked.

"The cards are made of such complicated astral projections that simply viewing them might cause your mind to—"

"Come apart at the seams," Rogers said. "Right." He turned to Thrumeaux. "This is your system, right? Have any of you, by any chance, noticed a large device out there shaped like something that might completely destroy the human race?"

"We have not," Thrumeaux said. "As with all of the other systems, we combined our best scientists' efforts and reports to try and discern the location of the Galaxy Eater, and were unable to do so." She looked pointedly at the Astromologer. "I must say I share Captain Rogers' skepticism here."

Even General Krell seemed a little leery of tossing the full strength of his forces into battle in the middle of nowhere without any actual evidence. He looked at Keffoule with a half smile that came off very awkward, and merely shrugged, waving his hand at both Thrumeaux and Rogers as though indicating their point.

"Right," Rogers said. "I was hoping that by bringing you aboard, Mr. Astromologer, we'd have something a bit more than hand waving and tarot cards."

"Tau/Rho Cards."

"Whatever. Grand Marshal Keffoule set you up as someone who could solve our problems, not do dances in space and then point to a random spot on a map." He glanced around the table, looking between the faces that had gathered to watch this idiocy and the surface of the table itself. Somewhere there had to be a switch so he could turn the lights back on and send everyone on their way to try to find a real solution.

"Captain Rogers," Keffoule said, sounding nervous. "If you'd only—"

"No," Rogers said. Wow, when did he start interrupting everyone so much? "I gave this guy a chance, and he's given me playing cards and space dancing. Until we can get some good, solid evidence that there's anything out there at all, I'm not—"

"Sir! Sir!" came a voice from the hallway.

Rogers put his face in his hands. "Why do you people do that? Why can't you just say sir once?"

Looking up a few seconds later, Rogers saw a young starman second class come running in, clearly having sprinted to get here. Her face was red, and her chest heaved with every breath. He didn't recognize her as any of the bridge crew, but there were so many it was possible that he simply hadn't seen her yet.

"What?" Rogers said flatly. "What is it now? I swear, if you're going to tell me that someone else hung themselves in the zero-g room . . ."

"No, sir," the starman said, huffing. "We just received a report from High Admiral Holdt. Apparently they've found the Galaxy Eater."

Despite the sinking feeling in Rogers' stomach, he put on a cocky grin and pointed at the starman. "You see? Real science yields real results."

Keffoule harrumphed.

"Well, where is it?" Krell asked.

The starman frowned, looking at her datapad, and then looking at the display in the center of the room. She looked at Krell, then at Rogers, then at the datapad again.

"Are you having a fit?" Thrumeaux asked. "There are times for dramatic pauses, young lady, but it appears you've forgotten how to speak."

"I'm just . . . you'll have to excuse me," the starman said. "I ran all the way down here with this information so I could show you the sector, but it appears you already have the sector displayed."

Rogers' sinking feeling deepened. "What are you talking about?"

"I mean that's the sector where the Galaxy Eater is, sir. You're looking at it. An unmanned sector in the Grandelle trade routes. How did you know?"

The room was silent for a moment, and Rogers had managed

to find the dimmer switch on the table. Slowly, the stunned faces of everyone at the table became slightly more illuminated.

"We knew," Keffoule said, "because the power of astromology is irrefutable."

"Oh, come on," Rogers said. "He clearly got ahold of the reports first. The rest was just mumbo jumbo."

The Astromologer himself remained relatively silent throughout this process of Rogers continually telling him how much of an idiot he was. It served him right. How the hell did this guy get so high in the Thelicosan government using just a couple of parlor tricks and some clever gymnastics? He wasn't even a very good con man, and Rogers considered himself kind of an authority on con men.

"Oh, I'm sorry, sir," the starman said. "I think maybe I wasn't clear. We found the Galaxy Eater at the coordinates provided by the Astromologer. I just didn't realize he'd told you all yet. I was kind of looking forward to being the one to show you the information, and he kind of spoiled my surprise." The starman pouted.

"Wait," Rogers said. "The Astromologer told you already? How long ago?" He shot a look at the Astromologer. "Why not just tell us?"

"I foresaw my own prediction," the Astromologer said, "but I had not yet done the proper divinations."

"You foresaw your own . . . is this guy serious? You're telling me you predicted your prediction?"

"Astromology," Keffoule whispered.

"Shut up!" Rogers barked.

"Hey, you can't talk to her like that!" Krell shouted.

"Oh, now it's not okay to talk to people like that?" Deet said. "Nobody cared how anybody talked to me."

The starman, who was starting to look very uncomfortable being in a room with a group of general officers behaving like squabbling children, started to slowly back toward the door. "I'm sorry to have interrupted. According to High Admiral Holdt, we got the information yesterday and dispatched all the long-range sensors we could to the area to see if it was correct. It was." She was halfway out the door now. "But if you need me I'll just be see you later bye take care sirs and ma'ams!"

The sound of quickly pattering boot steps echoed through the now silent room. Rogers felt like he wanted to break something, or someone. It wasn't that he'd just been outsmarted and humiliated by a freak in a black cape who liked to dance in open space. Wait. Yes it was.

"Okay," Rogers said. "You win, Astromologer. I don't know how you did this, and I'm not sure I want to know, but it sounds like we all had better get ready to head to the Grandelle system."

"Are you serious?" Deet said, unusually animated. "You're just going to believe this [ANATOMICAL REFERENCE]?"

"Deet," Rogers said, his voice low. "That's enough. I get that you don't like him, but you heard the starman. It's there."

"[MALE BOVINE EXCREMENT]," Deet said. "I disagree strongly with this course of action."

Rogers got up out of his chair, grabbing Deet by the arm. It was cold and metallic, and Rogers was small and weak, so Rogers' tugging was mostly effective only at making his hands kind of sore.

"Come on," Rogers said. "Let it go, Deet."

"Very curious," the Astromologer said suddenly, and before Rogers could tell him to get the hell out of the war room, he was standing so close to them both that Rogers could see the pores on his face. Rogers wasn't really confident in his own ability to evaluate the looks of a man, but he couldn't say he thought the Astromologer was handsome. More creepy than anything else. Maybe that's why Keffoule liked him; they were two creepy peas in a creepy pod.

"I will [EXPLETIVE] kill you if you don't back up right now," Deet said. His arms started to whir, a clear sign that droid fu was on the horizon.

"I can sense the light of the cosmos within you," the Astromologer said, "like a surrogate function, reflecting the glow of its objective function to illuminate new parts of the problem."

He reached out his hands, and for a moment it looked like he was about to grab Deet's "cheeks" and pull him in for a kiss, but the Astromologer merely held them out in front of him, as though forming an invisible bubble around the droid's head. Deet didn't move, though his arms looked less likely to shred the man into tiny bits.

"I have a function I'd love to call right now," Deet said. "Do you have a moment to talk about our lord and savior, protocol 162?"

"But something is missing . . . ," the Astromologer said. "Your aura. You don't appear to have one. It's as though your chakra are just empty shells." He frowned. "This makes me so very sad. Does it make you sad?"

Rogers rolled his eyes. If he didn't know any better, he would have said this joker was deliberately antagonizing Deet. That would have required him pulling his head out of his psychic ass for ten minutes, though, which Rogers didn't think he was capable of doing.

"Hey, astro boy," Rogers said, "stop giving my droid ideas. I don't need him to start researching the powers of Tau/Rho or kinematic horoscopes or anything, alright? We've got enough problems to deal with here."

The Astromologer hesitated a moment, his mouth twitching as though he had more to say, but he dropped his hands and backed away, bowing his head a little bit. At least he could *listen* to reason, even if he couldn't *speak* any.

"If you'll excuse me, then," the Astromologer said, "I have spent a considerable amount of my astral energy today. I need to return to my meditations if I am to be of further use to you."

"Yes, please," Rogers said. "Go charge up that astral energy."

"More like [ANATOMICAL REFERENCE] energy," Deet said.

Rogers could not figure out what word Deet had intended to use there.

The Astromologer turned with a flourish and exited the room. Rogers took a deep breath, feeling like some of his stress had left with him. Sure, he might have provided the location of the most dangerous weapon in the known galaxy, and a path to completing Rogers' team's sole objective, but that didn't mean he had to like the guy.

"Alright, everyone, you have your orders. Go order your fleets to prepare for transit. We'll see if there are any escorts available and check on the blockades, and then we'll move out." Rogers frowned, thinking. "We'll need as much information as we can get on the Galaxy Eater itself. If we go in there guns blazing and they turn the thing on, we'll need to know how much time we have to destroy it before it rips us apart. Task all your respective intelligence squadrons with putting together whatever they can, as fast as they can do it. We leave within the next two days. You're all dismissed."

"Wait," General Krell said. "What if we take a small group of ships and fly into its exhaust ports to try to blow up the core?"

Rogers looked at him for a long moment. "That is literally the dumbest idea I've ever heard in my life. Dismissed!"

"I thought it was worth a shot," Keffoule said, patting Krell on the arm. "Captain Rogers sometimes lacks imagination."

"Dismissed!"

Parades

Cynthia Mailn couldn't seem to get used to her new quarters, despite sharing them with the woman she'd married just four short years earlier. It reminded her of their tiny apartment near the edge of Haverstown; not cluttered by any stretch of the imagination, but still full of memorabilia and pictures. Sjana had always been such a pretentious art snob; she had canvas paintings all over the walls from different regions of the galaxy, stretching as far as the outer rim of Grandelle. Those were the most extravagant and diverse, ranging from stunning charcoal sketches to bizarre abstract art.

Cynthia sat up in bed, blinking her eyes clear, feeling like she'd been hit in the head with a tire iron. Miraculously, she and Sjana hadn't fought at all since she'd come aboard, but the grogginess this time was from another source: insomnia. Cynthia had found it difficult to relax. Images of everyone on the *Flagship* nagged at her in her dreams, looking down their noses at her and waggling their fingers in a pedantic, condescending way.

She slipped out of the sheets and dressed mechanically, pulling whatever was on top of the pile of clothes Sjana had designated for her use. Cynthia hadn't brought that much with her; there wasn't much on the *Flagship* that she considered essential enough to bother packing. Most of it was military issue. Besides, Sjana had always liked to dress her up, and Cynthia didn't mind. Fashion wasn't exactly her passion, so if it made Sjana happy, it made her happy.

Except right now, she wasn't really happy.

Cynthia splashed some water on her face, spitting out a tuft of hair that had swung into her mouth as she'd done so.

"Ugh," she said, wiping the side of her mouth.

"Something disgust you?" Sjana said.

Mailn jumped a bit; she hadn't heard her come in.

"Just the taste of my hair," Mailn said. "I didn't expect you back so early."

Sjana grinned at her and gave her a quick peck on the lips. It was morning, ship time, and Sjana normally spent a good portion of it chatting with the other pirate captains and planning their next move. As subsidiaries of the Meridan Galactic Navy, they took their orders directly from High Admiral Holdt, but they were mostly left to their own devices once their assignments were delivered.

"Not much going on today," Sjana said. "It seems the Jupiterians are regrouping, but we aren't really sure where. A smaller group of Thelicosan ships tried to follow one of the retreating blockade formations, but they didn't make it back through Un-Space. Wherever they're going, they're protecting their location well."

Mailn sighed. "Right."

Sjana unbuttoned the top part of her brown leather jacket, which was more for style than it was for warmth, and took off her pistol holsters. Placing them on a towel hook, she walked back into the main room and sat on the bed, stretching.

"I have to say," Sjana said. "It's been good having you around again."

"Yeah," Mailn said. She was looking at herself in the mirror above the sink, not really thinking about anything. God, she hated when she was broody.

"Why are you so broody?" Sjana asked.

"I am not broody," Cynthia said.

Sjana sighed, falling back on the bed and looking up at the ceiling. She was so different when it was just the two of them. When anyone else was around, it was like she inserted this Rod of Authority up her ass and walked around trying to make it not jiggle. But now, she felt like they were two girls again, trying to figure all this shit out. Cynthia was still pretty sure they didn't have anything figured out.

"You're broody," Sjana said.

"I'm broody." Cynthia dried her face off and came out to the bedroom, where she plopped down next to Sjana. "I just . . . I dunno. I thought there'd be more . . ."

"Pirating?"

"Yeah, I guess that's it," Cynthia said. "It's not like I wanted exciting firefights and swashbuckling and all that. I just . . ."

Sjana sat up, edging closer to her. "Things have changed a lot in the pirating world since the Garliali and Purveyors blew each other up. It's been tough to score credits; everyone stopped being afraid of us. When we got wind of war maybe breaking out, we all thought we could scrape some stuff together and go knock off some cargo ships that were making supply runs. Of course, back then we thought it'd be a little border skirmish between Merida and Thelicosa.

"Now . . ." She put her arms up in the air, like she was reaching for an answer. "We're all part of something big, I guess. It feels good, in a way, but it's also a lot more pressure. Used to be all I had to worry about was my crew and getting paid, not the whole galaxy falling apart around me." Sjana laughed. Not the bitter laugh of a cynic, but the carefree laugh of someone who genuinely just did not give a shit. That was one of the things Cynthia liked the most about her.

"I just couldn't sit planetside with the brass while you were up here doing all the work," Cynthia said. She still couldn't bring herself to look at her wife, and that bothered her. Why was she avoiding her gaze?

"That's what you keep telling me," Sjana said. "So if you're not bored, what is it?"

Cynthia tried to get the words out, but they just wouldn't come. She'd never been so moody in all of her life. Back when they'd lived together on Merida Prime, Cynthia had just relied on going from calm to batshit crazy as a good way to solve all of her problems. She supposed that Sjana hadn't been the only one at fault for their separation, and Cynthia eventually joining the marines. Now, though, she felt like those annoying teenage girls who never said what they meant. Maybe, she realized, it was because none of them really even knew what they meant.

"Do I actually belong here?" she asked finally.

Someone knocked on the door, stopping whatever answer had been about to come out of Sjana's mouth. Likely she would have just hit her again and told her not to worry about it. Then they would have shouted at each other, hit each other, kissed each other, and forgotten about everything. That was just the way things had gone between the two of them. Meeting Sjana again in Haverstown had let Mailn know just how much she'd missed it, black eyes and all.

"Hey, Cap." It was the voice of Hideko, her first mate, a bristly old man with a wild mustache and a wilder temper. He hadn't talked much to Cynthia, but what words he did spare her were mostly spent telling her to get the hell off the *Africanus*.

"What?" Sjana called. "Didn't we just finish our meeting?"

"Something else came up. Got orders to change course. Can I start the prelims?"

"Sure," Sjana said. "I'll come check up on it in a minute."

"Alright. Wouldn't want you to do the boring work. Come over to the bridge when you get your pants back on."

"My pants are on, asshole," Sjana shouted, throwing a boot at the door. It collided with a satisfying *thunk*, and Cynthia could hear Hideko's loud, wheezy cackle as he walked away.

"Where'd you meet that guy?" Cynthia said, using the moment's disruption to get off the bed and finish dressing. She tried to grin, but it only came halfway to her face, probably leaving her looking like she was drunk. Raising her arms in the air, she presented herself to her wife.

"That belt? No," Sjana said, reaching over and throwing her one that, to Cynthia, looked exactly the same as the one she had on. "Hideko and I are old drinking buddies. I actually met him before you, back when I first got into pirating. He helped me make sure that my mouth didn't write any checks that my pistols couldn't cash."

"And what a great job he did of that," Cynthia said. She slipped on a pair of work boots—these were hers—and moved toward the room's exit. "Come on. Don't you want to see where we're going next? I bet we get to watch a whole cargo train of plasma coils."

The two of them walked through the halls in silence, and after a minute or two Cynthia felt some of her confidence returning. Walking down the middle of a pirate ship with her wife, dressed like a civilian, with a pistol at her side and a purpose to her step. It was so much better than waiting around for the bureaucrats to put red tape all over everything and then get pissed off that they couldn't complete their mission with all of it in place. No generals, no admirals, no crazy Thelicosans. No rules.

But also, no Viking, and no Rogers. As much as she hated working for the government, she didn't mind some of the people working with her.

The walk to the bridge was a short one, and they didn't run into any of the other crew on the way. The *Africanus* was the command ship of Sjana's small band of pirates, but it wasn't anything like the *Flagship*. It housed, from what Cynthia could tell, maybe fifteen to twenty crew, and was mostly for shooting things and keeping other people's possessions in the cargo hold. When they opened the bridge door, Cynthia saw that most of the bridge crew wasn't even there yet. They trickled in behind them after getting notified that they'd be moving.

"What's the story?" Sjana asked as she sat down in her captain's chair, near the very front of the bridge. Unlike a large capital ship like the *Flagship*, the *Africanus* was arranged more like a private vessel, with a pilot and copilot in the center, surrounded by various systems and weapons operators. In this case, only one of the gunners was on deck. Cynthia chose a comm station and sat down, looking blankly at the buttons in front of her. What the hell did all these things mean?

"Looks like they're chasing some hot target in Grandelle. It's a pretty big effort, and we're supposed to be the ones clearing the way. Couple of jumps into uncleared territory between us and the destination."

"Any idea who we're escorting?" Sjana asked.

"Some kind of 'joint force,'" Hideko said. He squinted at his datapad. "The Resistance Engagement Detachment to Avoid Planetary Elimination. Great name."

Cynthia frowned. "That doesn't sound like any unit I've ever heard of."

"Oh, suddenly you're the master of the military?" Hideko said. "I thought you were a grunt."

"I am a grunt. That doesn't mean I wouldn't know about a gigantic unit. Any other information about who is in it?"

"Nope," Hideko said. "Just that we're to provide 'any available support' and we're supposed to provide it 'with all possible haste.' I hate military orders. They all sound so pretentious."

As pretentious as that mustache, Cynthia thought.

"If you've already made the preparations," Sjana said, "let's go ahead and move out. Get everyone ready for a fight if we need to punch holes in places we haven't been yet."

"Way ahead of you, boss," Hideko said. "Ships are already moving into formation and we are ready to go."

"That was fast," Cynthia said.

"Well, we were just sitting here and waiting for orders," Sjana said, plopping down in her captain's chair. "Looks like you're going to get some of the action you wanted, Cyn. Why don't you take a seat back in the cabin and wait until we're at our destination?"

"Oh shut up," Cynthia said. "I might not be any good at piloting ships or working the system, but if you need some holes punched in some skulls, I'll be ready to go with your boarding teams."

Sjana gave her a grin, but didn't reply. It wasn't, however, a good idea for Cynthia to take up valuable console space. There would be other pirates coming into the room soon who would need these stations to do their jobs properly. So Cynthia was left with the awkward choice of either taking her wife's condescending advice and going back to the cabin, or staying on the bridge and being actively in the way of everyone trying to do their jobs. It galled her, but she stood up.

"Well, I'll just head over to the rec room and work up a sweat on the punching bag," Cynthia said.

"I'll turn on the security camera so I can watch," Sjana said, turning to look at her and winking.

"Very funny. You should probably focus on your—"

A buzzer cut through their conversation, shortly followed by a member of the bridge crew shouting at them from the far side of the room.

"Cap, we've got ships."

"What?" Sjana said, whirling around. "Jupes? I thought we cleared them all out."

"Not Jupiterians. MPD."

"Oh," Sjana said with a relieved sigh. "No big deal. They're probably just starting to patrol the areas that we've freed up."

Another buzzer sounded, this time accompanied by a high-pitched whoop and the flashing of some amber lights that hung from the ceiling.

"Then you might want to ask them why they're targeting us."

Hideko vaulted into his copilot's seat so quickly and smoothly that Cynthia thought he must have done it a thousand times. He started pressing buttons on his console with the practiced alacrity of a career pirate.

"Open an immediate channel to all of their ships," Sjana barked. "Get our shields up and weapons ready. They could be Jupes in disguise."

"Aye, Cap," Hideko said. "Halfway there already." He leaned forward and pressed a large button to the side of his console. When he spoke, Cynthia could hear it echo throughout the whole ship's PA system.

"Asses to seats, everyone. MPD is spoiling for a fight. Pearson, stop making out with the new recruit in the closet and get back to your station."

"Ah, come on!" came a very disappointed voice from the supply closet, followed by a very girlish giggle.

Cynthia felt her heart beating heavy in her chest. She'd been in combat a few times now, thanks to some really weird situations on the *Flagship*, but she'd never felt so helpless. With the droids, at least she could shoot someone, and then with the *Limiter*, at least she could also shoot someone. Now she was one useless person on a spacecraft without any other marines to grouse with.

"Channel open," someone called.

"This is Captain Sjana Devingo of the *Africanus*. Stand down your targeting systems immediately or we will defend ourselves by killing all of you."

"Very official sounding, boss," Hideko said. "I thought we were supposed to be military now?"

"Nah," Sjana said. "We're contractors."

For a moment, they received no reply. From what Cynthia could tell, they were still receiving warnings that targeting systems were locked onto their ships, but there were no indications that any weapons had been fired. Looking out the window of the bridge, she could see a small contingent of ships gathered together right in front of the Un-Space point. If the pirates were going to get to Un-Space, they'd have to go through the MPD first; it was a standard interdiction position.

The bridge fell silent, all eyes and ears focused on determining whether or not these "MPD" ships were about to start launching torpedoes. The moment seemed to last for an eternity.

"Helloooo!" came a voice over the radio. "Thanks for joining us over here today and sorry about the radio silence; I accidentally had the call on mute. My name is Officer Atikan of the Meridan sector police. Unfortunately, it appears that you've been caught transiting an Un-Space point without the proper permit, an offense for which we are going to have to ask you to stop and submit your information to be logged."

"Permit?" Sjana said. "What are you talking about? We're in the middle of a war here, and we're official envoys of the Meridan Galactic Navy. In fact, we've got official orders here telling us to move through this sector and get to a new position."

"Are you able to transmit those orders to me?" Officer Atikan asked.

"Of course," Sjana said.

She looked over at Hideko, who stared back at her with a blank expression on his face, his mustache twitching.

"What, you want me to do it?"

"No, Hideko, I'm just wondering which half of your mustache to pull out first. Yes, I want you to send them the information."

"I don't think it's any of their damn business," Hideko began.

"Just do it. The quicker we get them the paperwork, the quicker we can get out of here."

Hideko muttered something unintelligible and probably

obscene, and went over to one of the communication stations to start pressing buttons. The sparsely crewed bridge looked more annoyed than nervous, which made sense to Cynthia. They had probably spent most of their career blowing up the MPD, not sending them love letters.

"Done," Hideko said.

"You should have the orders now," Sjana said. "And I'm obligated to warn you that these are military orders. We are authorized to fire upon anyone who impedes our progress. We won't take kindly to being boarded."

"Oh, I hardly think that will happen! We won't need to board you this time, unless of course you get all squirrely, as I know pirates sometimes do." Atikan laughed heartily, sounding as though he was truly enjoying all of this.

"Guy's a real charmer," Hideko said. "I'd like to squeeze all that cheer right out of him with a piano wire."

"If you'll just give me a few moments to review your documents, I'm sure we can get this all cleared up."

"Of course," Sjana said flatly. "Take your time. We're only in the middle of a race to save the galaxy. I'm sure we have a few extra minutes so you can file your reports."

Officer Atikan seemed unfazed. "Thank you so much for your courtesy! You don't at all seem like the pirates I read about in Rogers' reports. Just one moment, please."

The comms went dead.

"Um," Cynthia said. She suddenly started to get a terrible feeling in the pit of her stomach.

Sjana turned and looked at her, raising an eyebrow. "Reports?"

Cynthia shrugged, trying to remain nonchalant. What kind of reports would Rogers be sending to anyone about pirates? He wasn't smart enough to be covert about anything; he complained too much to keep anything a secret. If he'd been tasked with keeping tabs on the pirates, he would have been loudly blustering about it for the last two weeks. Besides, the pirates had been immediately dispatched. There would be no way for Rogers to watch the pirates without an insider . . .

Everyone was looking at her.

Oh, shit.

"No," Cynthia said, holding up her hands. "I swear, no. I ditched the MGN fair and square. This is AWOL, not spy . . . uh . . . WOL."

Everyone was *still* looking at her.

"I'm serious!" she said, slowly backing toward the door. Sjana's expression was flat, which was her version of being extremely emotional. The more nonchalant Sjana got about anything, the more it meant she actually cared. Hideko was getting up out of his seat.

"Come on!" Cynthia said. "What would be the point of me spying on you? Just to make sure you didn't go pirating without prior Meridan approval? You're all looking for clemency. Why would you come all the way out here to fight Jupiterians if you were going to steal stuff along the way? There's no reason to watch you."

"So what are these reports?" Hideko asked. Normally, the first mate was jovial, even when threatening to throw Cynthia out the airlock. Now, however, he looked as cold as a surgical robot performing a triple bypass. One of his hands was on his pistol.

"I have no idea!" Cynthia said. And she really didn't. Was it possible that Rogers had guessed she was going to join the pirates and bugged her things? She hadn't even kept a datapad. And again, Rogers wasn't smart enough to do *any* of this without some serious help.

She didn't know what else she could say to diffuse this situation, so she just stared at Sjana with a hopeless, pathetic expression that she knew wasn't going to work.

"Throw her in the brig," Sjana said, and turned around. Hideko drew his pistol.

"Wait! Why don't you ask the MPD guy for more information about the reports? It could have been something from a long time ago, you know? Or maybe he and Rogers are drinking buddies, and 'reports' is just a funny word that they throw around. Right? That'd be funny, ha-ha?"

"Hilarious," Hideko said. "Get moving."

Sjana wasn't looking back at her. In fact, the entire crew seemed to have mentally settled the issue and gone back to working their consoles silently. Only the tapping of keys and the footsteps of Hideko and Cynthia could be heard.

Cynthia *really* did not want to spend the rest of her time on the *Africanus* in the brig. She didn't give up everything, forsake her fellow marines, and throw a hissy fit at her captain just to have her wife throw her in prison.

"Sjana, please," Cynthia said, now having to look around Hideko's hulking form to even see her wife. "Come on. At least ask. We've done a lot of things to each other over the years, but never this kind of betrayal."

Except that one time when Cynthia had siphoned off a bunch of Sjana's credits to pay off a loan shark. But that had been a long time ago, and they had threatened to break Cynthia's knees if she didn't pay. Surely Sjana didn't hold that against her, or even remember it.

"You mean except that one time when you siphoned off a bunch of my credits to pay off a loan shark?"

"For fuck's sake, Sjana, *ask the question!*"

She didn't respond. Hideko, who had rolled his eyes at Cynthia's suggestion, stopped, which Cynthia supposed was at least some form of progress. Unless he was about to just haul off and shoot her, which was totally possible.

"Boss?" he asked.

No immediate reply followed. Cynthia held her breath. A long sigh escaped Sjana's lips, and she leaned forward to press a button.

"Officer," Sjana said. "While your staff is reviewing our documentation, I have a question for you."

"Of course!" Atikan answered immediately. "I'm always up for a friendly chat between spacefaring aficionados. What can I do for you?"

"These reports that Captain Rogers has been giving you. Can you tell me a bit more about them?"

There was no reply for a few moments. Sjana cast a meaningful glance over her shoulder. Cynthia swallowed.

"Oh, I'm sorry. You know, sometimes I forget that he's a captain now. When I met him, he was still a civilian! Well, technically he was only acting undercover as a civilian. He'd been commissioned as an ensign just a few months prior, according to the records. It was all so exciting! The way he infiltrated the Garliali and the Purveyors to bring them both down in one fell swoop was nothing short of brilliant. Did you know that I planned a whole series of parades in his honor? None of them have happened yet, of course, because of all the hubbub around the galaxy being in dire threat and all, but . . ." He made a lip-smacking noise, like he was tasting something delicious. "I can't wait to see them! It's going to be great."

Cynthia's mouth opened. Rogers an undercover agent? There was no way. It might explain the fact that he kept getting promoted in weird circumstances, but . . . bringing down pirates? It just didn't seem right. If anything, Rogers should have been the one running away to join the pirates in the first place.

Hideko, at least, was no longer pointing the pistol at Cynthia. Sjana turned her chair halfway around, but didn't look at anyone. She merely gazed at a nondescript spot on the floor, frowning intently. It felt like minutes went by without anyone saying anything, Cynthia still standing in the middle of the bridge wondering if she was going to have to fight for her life or submit meekly to being thrown in the brig.

"Anyhoo, thanks for being patient," Atikan said. "I've examined your paperwork and everything seems in order. And, ooh, speak of the devil! It looks like you'll be meeting Rogers' new fleet when you get to the Grandelle system. Tell him I said hello, won't you? He and I go way back."

Now Rogers was in charge of the new joint whatever-it-was? None of this made any sense. Then again, almost nothing that had happened during her entire tenure on the *Flagship* had made any sense, so why expect things to start coming together now? If Rogers was really some kind of superspy that could out-smart all of them, so be it. Cynthia would just go drink herself into a stupor, and watch all of the pirates completely obliterate Rogers at the next available opportunity.

Which was, apparently, when they both got to Grandelle to hunt for the Galaxy Eater. Wow, Rogers was screwed.

And, she guessed, so was the galaxy.

How Is Everyone Doing?

Okay, even if "taking over the galaxy" was hidden somewhere in the job description of being Mr. Snaggardir's assistant, Lucinda was nearly positive that acting completely normal while standing on the precipice of total annihilation was *absolutely not.*

Yet that's what everyone here seemed to be doing. Everyone walking around, living their normal lives, getting food, and bashfully asking attractive members of their species for quiet moments around a cup of coffee. Just yesterday Lucinda had overheard a husband talking to his wife on the phone, planning their next vacation! As though there would be anyplace left to go sit on the beach if they were forced to use the Galaxy Eater. The level of confidence that the Jupiterian resurgence was predestined was bordering on both arrogance and willful ignorance. Perhaps the rank-and-file Snaggardir's employee didn't have the same insight that Lucinda did, since she was the assistant to the CEO, but she didn't feel very optimistic about the whole thing.

How could she? The pirates had been able to break a significant amount of the blockades, forcing the Jupiterian fleets to reorganize and fall back to defend Snaggardir's HQ and a few other strongholds in the galaxy. General Szinder didn't seem to have a solid plan to carve out any territory for themselves through military force, even though they'd managed to capture a huge amount of ships and man them with loyalist personnel. Dr. Mattic was mysterious and quiet as always—Lucinda never had any idea what the man was thinking—and Sara hadn't offered anything in the way of strategic communication at all. Mr. Snaggardir, who Lucinda still thought was exceedingly intelligent, if a little insane, just smiled at it all and seemed to expect it to go his way. It didn't make any sense. From what Lucinda could tell, the full force of the galaxy was moving right now to destroy the Galaxy Eater, the only Jupiterian trump card they had.

That meant that either Mr. Snaggardir was very convincing at pretending to be sane, or he had some other trump card. But what? Lucinda felt like she was still missing something.

The whole station was filled with Jupiterians or Jupiterian sympathizers, people who had been closely vetted by Snaggardir's extensive employee background check system. That system had, apparently, been the way to track Jupiterian lineage, sympathies, and relationships for hundreds of years. The Snaggardir security system was tighter than most government programs for establishing security clearance eligibility for top secret information.

Somehow, though, they hadn't figured out that Lucinda was having doubts and had been sending secret messages to Captain Rogers, now the commander of the new joint force coming to hunt them down. She realized that he'd never know it was her who had been giving him the subtle hints, and that at any moment they could launch an attack with her information that would result in her death. But, in truth, this was bigger than any one life, including hers. If the congratulatory Snaggardir's messages that she'd been having Sara read could help save the galaxy, it would be worth it.

"Are you sure this is necessary?" Sara said, looking at the script she'd been handed. "I thought all of these had been standardized a decade ago to give away free balloons and all that."

"It's a market expansion effort," Lucinda said. "We're trying to plan for more eventualities to give the impression that Snaggardir's is everywhere, even in cases like this." She pointed at the script.

"I guess I understand that," Sara said, "but how many times is one of our customers going to form a force to try and blow up the Galaxy Eater? And is that really something we should be rewarding?"

Lucinda shrugged, trying to hide the horrible blush creeping up into her face. "I don't write the scripts, Ms. Alshazari."

"Well, alright," Sara said. "Seems like there's been a lot of this lately, that's all."

"Perfectly normal," Lucinda said. "I would have thought you were in the know on this, you being the strategic communications expert and all that. Don't these messages go through you?"

Sara shrugged, standing up and grabbing her jacket off the back of the chair. She was a small woman and was always complaining about the temperature of the room. The recording station, situated near the other rooms designed for radio broadcasts and other audio/visual productions, didn't have a dedicated thermostat, so it was a bit warmer.

"There's a lot going on right now," Sara admitted. "I can't quite pay attention to everything."

That's what I'm counting on, Lucinda thought. "Are you going to be at the staff meeting tonight?"

Sara sighed. She seemed very distracted, which wasn't something that Lucinda was used to seeing in her. Normally she was a driven, hard-faced woman who spared little notice for her feelings, much like her uncle. Unlike Mr. Snaggardir, however, she didn't put out the kind, warm façade. In a way, it made Lucinda like her a lot more, and not just because she was the only other woman in this man-filled coup. Something about Sara reminded her of herself. Maybe it was her focus or her determination, two things that Lucinda strove for every day.

"Something the matter?" Lucinda asked when Sara didn't answer her question. She'd stopped, her jacket halfway on, her gaze nowhere in particular.

"Hm? Oh." Sara slipped her jacket on the rest of the way and walked slowly toward the door. Rather than leading the way, Lucinda stepped aside, allowing the older woman to pass so that she could have some extra time to observe her. "We've all been working long hours lately with all of this going on. Uncle Sal can be a stickler for dedication during crunch time."

"Don't I know it," Lucinda muttered, then bit her lip. Insulting Sara's uncle was probably not the right way to maintain the level of trust that would allow her to continue sabotaging their plans.

To her surprise, Sara actually chuckled. "I bet you do. You're a brave young woman—you know that?"

Lucinda grimaced. "I don't know if brave is the right word. I'm not sure anyone could be aware they were signing up for . . . this." She lifted her arm and gestured broadly around her, indicating, well, everything.

"We all get things we didn't sign up for," Sara said, turning to walk down the hallway. "I know I did. I'll see you at the staff meeting tonight."

Dodging past a couple of other producers, who were doubtlessly preparing more propaganda to broadcast all over the galaxy, Sara left the audio/visual booths and exited to the main part of the ship. Several employees stopped doing their work to watch her go, though not in a weird, ogling way. Sara Alshazari was somewhat of an icon in the company, and also not very prone to being out and about so much. Seeing her around was probably a rare event for everyone who wasn't close to her.

Quickly, before anyone else came around needing the room, Lucinda went back over to the terminal where Sara had been recording and began making all the changes she needed to in order to get the audio to sound exactly like she wanted. She couldn't very well hand Sara scripts that were too blatant; she mixed up the words and would unscramble them in post, concatenating them with other archived audio to put together the messages she wanted to send out. Though, she realized as she did the little bit of editing that was required, it wouldn't take a genius to figure it out. Really, it was kind of a shock that she hadn't been caught doing it yet. Strange.

There was no time to wonder, however. She made sure the message got off to the right channels. Hopefully this would help.

Lucinda swallowed, sweating. She wondered how Captain Rogers was doing.

"Congratulations on heading toward the Galaxy Eater in an attempt to save humanity!" the voice said. "You are entitled to one free term life insurance policy, redeemable at any of the many Snaggardir's Sundries locations in the galaxy. Remember, whatever you need, you can Snag It at Snaggardir's™!"

Rogers and Deet looked at the console.

"You see what I mean?" Rogers asked. "I just came down here to get a cup of coffee that wasn't going to spray boiling liquid in my face, and the in-line controls start telling me about top secret plans that nobody is supposed to know about, especially not a disembodied, automated voice that comes from the very enemy we are trying to fight."

"Pretty strange," Deet agreed.

"And Snaggardir's doesn't even sell life insurance. I checked."

"Dubious," Deet said.

"Yesterday, the sink congratulated me for getting up in the middle of night, exactly one thirty-five AM ship time, to go to the bathroom."

"I'm not sure I really want to know," Deet asked, "but what did it offer you for free?"

"A prostate exam."

"Yes," Deet said. "This is a question I should have withheld."

The two of them currently occupied an empty in-line car on the way to the bridge. It had been a few days since their fateful meeting in the war room, and everyone was just about to make the journey to what Rogers hoped would be the first and final battle of his joint force. Experience, however, had taught him to be cynical about anything he hoped for.

Once at the bridge, Rogers didn't estimate it would take very long to make the few hops to their destinations, especially if the pirates had cleared the way. It actually felt a little too easy for Rogers. Compiled intelligence reports, combined with the surveillance that Holdt had ordered to confirm the Astromologer's findings, had revealed that the Galaxy Eater was actually quite a simple device, with simple construction that didn't have any particularly strong shielding. They still had no idea how it worked, but based on observation, it was overkill to send an entire fleet to blow it up. A couple of torpedo haulers could have done the trick. Flash might even get to use a Lancer without killing everyone around him.

"Hey, Rogers," Deet said. "Your razor hasn't congratulated you on anything that's just completely ridiculous lately, right? Nothing like failing to locate a ship full of droids, or anything?"

"No, why? That would make even less sense," Rogers said. "The only things it's been telling me about are things that I've actually done that nobody else is supposed to know about. That's why I think there's a spy somewhere."

"I see," Deet said. "Yes, it certainly wouldn't make any sense at all for the Snaggardir's voice to tell you about ships full of droids that had recently received a message, since you yourself did no such thing and likely would never do any such thing. Correct."

Rogers blinked. What was going on with Deet? His voice had gotten all monotone and weird.

They arrived at their stop outside the bridge on the command deck, and the two of them shuffled out into the chaos, Rogers hurriedly deploying his antisalute sling before he got caught in a salute loop that would keep him off the bridge for the next three to four hours. As usual, it worked like a charm, though it seemed to confuse most of the lower-ranking officers.

"What the hell are all these people doing?" Rogers muttered. The command deck was always so full of people who seemed to be doing nothing except walking back and forth, saluting each other, and making concerned faces while they looked at their datapads. He supposed if there were any three things that symbolized command in the Meridan Galactic Navy, those would be them.

"Technically, whatever you told them to do," Deet said. "All the orders for the operation of the ship are supposed to originate with you."

Rogers stopped. "Oh my god. You mean this is my fault?"

"I'm learning a bit about causality," Deet said, "and I'm not sure you could say that any of this is your 'fault,' exactly. However, since you have the power to order everyone to take a nap, for example, and are not doing so, you are perpetuating this giant, churning waste of manpower and resources."

Suddenly Rogers felt like a wizard who had discovered a fountain of power. All this time he'd felt so useless, such a slave to the whims of the galaxy, the Jupiterians, and the machinations of the Meridan political machine. Yet here he was, in the direct center of a bureaucratic tornado, able to calm the winds with just a few words from his own mouth.

"Everyone stop!" Rogers yelled. "Stop what you are doing!"

Everyone stopped what they were doing. The entire mass of people on the command deck looked at Rogers, their mouths agape and their arms halfway to their heads in a salute that most realized Rogers couldn't return. Many of them just left their arms hanging midair.

"Listen to me very carefully," Rogers said. "I want each of you to take a moment and consider what you are doing right now. If it is not immediately necessary to the war effort, you are to return to your quarters and, um . . ."

"Tell them to take a nap," Deet said, in a very un-robot-like whisper.

". . . take a nap!" Rogers yelled. Why did he feel all shaky? "Yes, that's right. I want everyone well rested when we move out in a few minutes. So, if you feel like what you are doing is even moderately useless, you are to cease, desist, and nap."

Instantly, like Rogers had just turned on the lights in a room full of roaches, nearly everyone on the command deck walked— sprinted, actually—away. Doors slammed. One person even collapsed in a heap on the floor in the middle of the command deck, snoring peacefully.

In all of the time he'd been the commander of the *Flagship*, Rogers didn't think he'd ever achieved anything so beautiful as this one moment.

Even better, it cleared the view to the bridge, where the Viking was standing, apparently waiting for him. It was a glorious sight. He hadn't been able to see much of her lately, what with all of the preparations for a decisive space battle going on, and they certainly hadn't had time to finish their date.

Something about the way the Viking was looking at him made him doubt that it was going get any better. In fact, she was repeatedly pounding a fist into an open palm, looking at him with narrow eyes. That meant things were either about to get way worse, or—Rogers felt himself blushing—way better in ways that he hadn't yet expected.

"Hey there," he said.

"Hey," the Viking said, not moving. She continued to pound her fist against her hand. "I had a funny conversation today that I thought I'd talk to you about."

"Oh yeah?" Rogers said, his instincts telling him to make sure he stood more than an arm's length away. He briefly thought about putting Deet in between them, but Deet could be used as a weapon if the Viking so chose. "With who?"

"The Personnel commander."

"Someone runs that squadron?" Rogers said, genuinely surprised. He kept inviting whoever it was to meetings, but they never seemed to show up. That and for six solid months nobody on the ship was assigned to any position they were competent at, thanks to the droids, so Rogers figured nobody actually ran it.

"Someone does," the Viking said. "She's actually a good friend of mine."

Rogers frowned. If she was a good friend of the Viking, why didn't Commander Whoever-She-Was ever answer any of his messages? He understood, however, that this was the least of his worries at the moment.

"She told me that somebody put in a request to have me transferred from heading up the marine detachment to being a secretary."

"Oh really?" Rogers said, his voice squeaking. He hadn't counted on the Viking being friends with anyone, never mind being friends with the commander of the Personnel squadron. This was supposed to have been a surprise, revealed after they'd taken care of the Galaxy Eater. In hindsight, though, considering how dangerous their mission was, he should have done it sooner. The whole point was to keep the Viking out of harm's way after all. Maybe that's what she was so mad about.

"I could have it done sooner, if you want," Rogers said. "I just thought—"

"No," the Viking said. "You didn't."

Normally Rogers would have expected a punch in the face. The Viking had said, however, that she wanted to stop having that as her only option when communicating with Rogers. It appeared that she was sincere in her efforts, because instead of causing Rogers any physical harm, she simply turned and walked away. Rogers watched her go, frowning. What was that all about? He thought she would have been happy. And now that he thought about it, he preferred getting hit in the face to whatever had just happened.

"Well, that seemed suboptimal," Deet said.

"Yeah," Rogers said. "Yeah, it was.

Rogers could really have used some nondroid advice right now. He wondered how Mailn was doing.

"Sjana," Cynthia begged, "think about this for a second. We don't have any information about what exactly Rogers did to the pirates. Honestly, it just sounds like one of his schemes gone bad. He's really not that good of a commander. Or a pilot. Or a fighter. Or anything really. I'm sure there's a reasonable explanation, or at least a funny joke, about all of this."

Since discovering that Rogers had basically been the single cataclysmic factor that had brought down the entire pirate infrastructure, Sjana had been less than rational. Cynthia wasn't used to seeing her like that; her wife typically laughed off most troublesome situations, even when the consequences had been dire. Now, however, she had leapt into plans for revenge with reckless abandon. Sjana was ready to sacrifice humanity if it meant putting a torpedo down Rogers' throat.

"Time and time again I've risked my neck for these people," Sjana said. She hadn't gotten up from her pilot's seat in hours, even though the computer could do most of the navigating. They'd run into small pockets of Jupiterian resistance, but the sailing had been smooth so far. "I brought them into my home—"

"And basically gouged them at the negotiating table."

"—and treated them like family. And in return, their boss wipes most of my friends off the face of the galaxy?"

Cynthia sighed. Sjana's order of events was a bit mismatched, since the decimation of the pirates had occurred several months earlier, and Rogers had recruited the pirates only a short while ago, but Cynthia understood how these things could get confused when someone was emotional. Except Sjana was never emotional.

"This isn't like you, Sjana," Cynthia said. "I mean, I understand honor among thieves and all that, but you've lost friends before. Why was this any different?"

Sjana shot a glance over her shoulder, grimacing, but didn't respond. Hideko, who had remained mostly silent, coughed from his copilot's seat.

"What?" Cynthia asked. "What is it? Am I missing something here? Sjana, I have friends on that ship. You can't just blow them up."

"Hideko," Sjana said. "Are you almost ready?"

"We've been ready for an hour and a half," Hideko said. "Cap, are you sure about this? Can't it wait?"

"I've already explained this," Sjana said. "If we don't do this now, we might not get a chance. He might get killed in the battle, or we might get killed in the battle, or maybe he'll *trick and kill all of us* like he did with your brothers and sisters. Do you not remember any of this?"

The bridge was silent for a while. Hideko had been receptive to the idea of revenge, but clearly seemed to have reservations about the timing.

"Of course I remember," Hideko said. "But we're pirates. There's a certain level of risk we all accepted when we got into the field. Do you regret it? Look, Cap, I know she was important to you, but . . ."

Sjana silenced him with a glance.

She? Cynthia thought. *Who the hell was "she"?*

Cynthia looked at the back of Sjana's head, wondering. A feeling that she wouldn't describe as positive bubbled up inside.

"Fine," Sjana said. "A compromise. What are pirates if they're not able to make a good deal or two?"

"That's more like it," Hideko said. "What are you thinking, Captain?"

"We ambush them, explain that we won't help them do anything else without Rogers in custody on our ship, and board them. The *Flagship* will come through first, so we'll block the exit point, destroy the escort, and pin them down until they deliver Rogers. It'll be easy."

"Oh," Cynthia said, the pieces finally falling into place in her head. "Well that sounds reasonable then. We'll just ambush the command ship, convince them to hand over the literal leader of the battle fleet, and then assume that everyone else is just going to go about their business."

"You don't understand," Sjana said.

"Actually, I think I do," Cynthia said, turning and leaving the bridge, her face hot. Of course she understood; she wasn't an idiot. Cynthia had been naive to think that Sjana had spent the better part of the last two years waiting around, twiddling her thumbs, but it still burned. Someone very important to her had been in the fight with Rogers, and Cynthia could do the rest of the deductions herself. As she retreated back to the safety of her room, she looked at the pile of belongings she'd brought with her and thought about the crew back on the *Flagship*, now likely augmented by members of all the other systems. And here she was, chasing her wife on a pirate ship. She felt like a lovesick idiot.

Speaking of lovesick idiots, Cynthia wondered how Keffoule was doing.

Sitting at her desk in her stateroom, Alandra stared at the number she'd written on a scratch pad. One point six one. A few weeks ago, she'd thought that number was everything. Now it just seemed like a couple of digits on a piece of paper.

The golden ratio just wasn't something that one questioned, Alandra thought, but she couldn't deny that doubt had begun to slowly creep in. Little facts that had eluded her attention before now bubbled to the surface in rapid succession. Facts about her, facts about Rogers, facts about the state of the galaxy. Alandra wasn't accustomed to feeling lost and confused, but those were the only two adjectives that accurately described her current state of mind.

Despite her expectations that a semipermanent, non-hostage-situation tenure on the *Flagship* would warm Rogers to her and allow them to grow closer, there had been no indication what-soever that this was happening. If anything, Rogers seemed to get more terse and irritable by the day. The burdens of com-mand weren't unfamiliar to Alandra, but she'd thought Rogers was made of sterner stuff than to crack under all the pressure. In times of great stress, Alandra had been strict, direct, even curt. But she'd never been *grumpy*. That was just beneath someone of his high status.

Then again, this was the first time Alandra had really been able to see Rogers in his own element, in command, in charge. She'd initially assumed that he would sweep in and start fixing things like she'd heard of in all of the intelligence reports that had initially caused her to fall in love with him. He'd deftly exposed McSchmidt the spy, defended the fleet against a droid takeover, and discovered the Jupiterian uprising just in time to defeat Zergan. Captain Rogers, in her mind, was a legendary fleet commander.

Now he seemed . . .

"Goddamn it!" Rogers was yelling outside her stateroom. Rapid footsteps traced their way across her hearing, heading from the in-line toward the bridge. "Why did no one tell me that we were almost coming out of Un-Space at the destination? I wasn't napping for *that* long."

. . . Now he seemed not.

Then, of course, there was General Krell. Something about that man both appalled and interested her. He'd done nothing but support and compliment her since the moment they'd met. And he had a very nice wolfish grin that Alandra found endearing.

But when it came to their compatibility, the golden ratio didn't play a part at all! It was totally random. Completely unpredictable. Un*mathematical*.

And also perhaps a little thrilling.

Alandra sighed, tracing her fingers across her desk. This was no time to be musing over romantic pursuits, she told herself. There was a war going on. She had flown across a system boundary and nearly caused a war of her own to pursue Rogers. He was her destiny! He just had to see it.

But he didn't seem to be seeing it. And if she was honest with herself, she might be starting to unsee it too.

"Am I just being a little girl?" she muttered to herself.

"Yes," Xan said. "I do feel that there is a certain element of girlishness being displayed here, Grand Marshal."

Alandra sucked in a breath. No matter how long they'd worked together, sometimes it was just so easy to forget that the unobtrusive New Neptunian was in the room with her. But he was *always* in the room with her. It seemed silly of her to forget it.

"I wasn't asking you."

"Yes, Grand Marshal."

Could she investigate this a bit? Learning a little bit about Krell couldn't hurt, could it? But there was a war going on. She'd have to task someone else to gather information.

"Xan," Alandra said slowly, "do you think it's possible to find some intelligence reports on General Krell for me?"

Xan was silent for a long moment, his face expressionless. Of course he knew what that meant. Alandra wondered if he would say anything about it. Then, abruptly, he turned on his heel, gathered up his datapad, and moved swiftly toward the door.

"Grand Marshal," he said as he exited the room, presumably to carry out her orders, "I believe there is a difference between intelligence and knowledge. I hope that you discover it someday."

Well, that wasn't the way she'd expected him to react. Xan had been rather strange lately. Stranger than usual, anyway.

Alandra sighed. Poor Rogers. How would he function without her? How was he dealing with all of this now? She wondered how Rogers was doing.

"Great," Rogers said, entering the bridge and waving away the three people who seemed to want to talk to him. "The pirates are already here. Send them a message and we'll—"

"Multiple target locks!" called out one of the defense technicians.

"Fighters on attack vector!" called another.

"What?" Rogers yelled, sitting down in his chair. "What's going on?"

"Sir, it looks like the pirates are firing on us!"

"Sir, the Galaxy Eater isn't anywhere on our scopes. It's not here!"

"Sir, a large Jupiterian force has just come out of Un-Space and is vectoring on our position!"

"Sir, your coffee is cold!"

"All of this is literally the exact opposite of what is supposed to be happening!" Rogers screamed.

And all of a sudden, Rogers didn't give a flying fuck how *anyone* else was doing.

Honestly, You Should Have Seen This Coming

The speed with which things began blowing up was nothing short of astonishing. Rogers could barely start screaming orders[*] before all of the radios came alive with people reporting in, delivering damage reports, and complaining about bad positioning. Un-Space gateways could only be occupied by so much mass at any given time without causing ships to crash into each other, and the *Flagship* had been the first to come through, with its contingent of Meridan ships close behind. Exit from Un-Space was traditionally the most vulnerable time for any force, and the combined attack from the Jupiterians and the pirates had found them at the worst possible moment.

The first voice he heard over the radio he recognized as Sjana Devingo's. She did not sound happy, and it didn't take him long to figure out why.

"Look familiar, Rogers? Betrayal and total annihilation? Is

---

[*] Obscenities

this what it was like when you destroyed the Garliali and the Purveyors of Vitriol?"

Rogers' stomach sank. He was sure he'd been careful about all of that. Plus, the reports from the incident were all supposed to be buried in military records. If they'd awarded him some kind of undercover status, surely they wouldn't go around blabbing about it to the pirates themselves.

"I get that you're upset," Rogers said as calmly as he could muster, "but I feel like there are greater priorities that we should be addressing right now."

"We're not here to cripple the war effort, Rogers. We want you."

"Oh," Rogers said. "Great. That's perfect. Oh, and by the way, this seems to be an elaborate trap set by the Jupiterians, as many of them are converging on our location as we speak and there doesn't seem to be a Galaxy Eater anywhere in this sector. Is all of this information not important to you all?"

"I don't need a lecture from you on priorities!" Sjana called over the radio. "You killed all of my friends!"

He'd barely been able to get a sense of what was going on before the pirates had picked off the few escort ships around the *Flagship* and started making de-shielding runs on the *Flagship* itself. Fighters that were launching from the hangars were getting spaced sooner than they could start any effective defense pattern. The *Flagship*'s native defenses were, from what Rogers could tell, doing a fair job, but they wouldn't last long. And when the Jupiterian fleet crossed into their engagement envelopes, this would end very quickly.

"Where the hell is everyone else?" Rogers yelled. From what he could tell, only a small portion of their ships were here. Had they abandoned him like the pirates had?

"We can't get out of the way," Belgrave said, not looking at all like they were about to die. "We need to move all of the ships that entered the sector before the rest of our force can come in. We're being used to barricade our own door, so to speak."

Great. Now they were basically all alone, under intense fire from the pirates, and they wouldn't be able to get reinforcements unless they raced *toward* all the people trying to kill them.

Honestly, this was becoming kind of a typical day for Rogers.

Cynthia looked at herself in the mirror. She knew what was going on outside right now, but she didn't know what she was supposed to do about it. In truth, Rogers deserved what he got. Hell, maybe the galaxy deserved what it got. All of this running around the universe from place to place, trying to escape destruction. What was the point if your wife was just going to cheat on you and attack all of your friends?

Cynthia felt like an idiot. This is the way it had always gone down with the two of them. They'd be happy as clams for months, then Sjana would go on a binge and come home with lipstick on her collar. Or her sleeve. Or other articles of clothing upon which one might not normally find lipstick. They'd fight. Fists would fly. They'd make up, get drunk, and start all over again. So why had she assumed that all this time apart, followed by a literal struggle for galactic peace, would bring them finally together again?

"You feel like an idiot because you *are* an idiot—that's why," she said. She'd come here thinking that she could finally run away with Sjana, give up her ties to civil society, and go pirating with her, living happily ever after.

Outside, she could hear people running down the hallways shouting at each other, the occasional raucous laughter breaking through. Apparently they had Rogers and the *Flagship* on the ropes. There was no way they'd be able to resist.

"Are you sure about that?" someone outside said. "I thought we were going to pin them down and then get the captain. Why are we loading hull breakers?"

"Guess Cap changed her mind," another person answered. "Soon as the shields are down, pop goes the weasel, eh?"

"That doesn't make any sense at all. Is there a big crank on the outside of the *Flagship* we're going to turn?"

"It's just an expression."

"Yeah, the wrong one. But . . . do you really think this is what we should be doing right now? We're never going to get that pardon if we keep murdering people."

The voices faded away, leaving Cynthia feeling cold in the pit of her stomach.

So Sjana had lied to her. Again. And that meant that everyone on the *Flagship* was going to die. Her friends, her fellow marines. Everyone on that ship was about to become the object of her crazy wife's vengeance about a woman who Cynthia, by all rights, probably would have killed herself.

"Oh screw this," she said. She grabbed her pistol.

The *Flagship* bridge approached a level of panic that Rogers had never seen before. Even with the droids, even with the Thelicosans, they'd been fairly confident that they had some options. Boominite containers rigged to explode and face-kicking enemy fleet commanders couldn't hold a candle to two enemy forces getting ready to blast them into the Un-Space point and make them Un-Alive. Commander Belgrave, who normally looked so calm and composed that Rogers wanted to set his underwear on fire, gripped the sides of his console, his eyes darting to the display as he tried to plot the best course for the massive *Flagship* to avoid enemy fire and give the rest of the fleet room to come into the battlespace.

"Goddamn it," Rogers said. "I'm really having trouble prioritizing which absolute mess I am supposed to address at any given moment. Shields?"

"Not good, sir," one of the defensive technicians said. "We've got five, maybe ten minutes more effective shields. The pirates' attack runs aren't very effective, but they're cutting us down bit by bit."

Rogers squinted. They were probably used to attacking small

cargo ships that didn't have the armament or the defenses of the *Flagship*, which was what was buying them all this time. But . . . ten minutes to figure this out. "And the Jupiterians?"

"About five minutes."

So, they didn't have ten minutes at all. Once the Jupiterian forces came barreling down on them, it didn't matter how bad the pirates were at their jobs. The Jupiterians were packing stolen military equipment from all four systems as well as stuff designed by the Snaggardir corporation. Rogers couldn't believe he was about to be turned into goo by a company made famous by their hot dogs and scratch-off lottery tickets.

"Okay," Rogers said, "give me the force disposition that made it through Un-Space with us."

"It's just us, sir," the defensive technician said. "There were only a few escort ships and they've either been disabled or destroyed."

"Great," Rogers said. "Any idea on why the Galaxy Eater isn't here? Can we get a message back to HQ?"

"Already on it," S1C Brelle, the communications technician, said. "Sorry if I overstepped, sir, but I sent it as soon as we figured out that the Galaxy Eater was missing. We haven't gotten a response yet, but honestly it won't matter if we don't deal with the Jupiterians first."

Rogers felt himself sweating in places that he wasn't even sure sweat could come from. Were there pores on the bottom of one's toes? They couldn't deal with the Jupiterians until they dealt with the pirates, and they couldn't deal with the pirates without any backup. It was like a giant trying to swat away a swarm of flies without any arms.

Commanders Zaz and Rholos, the defensive and offensive coordinators, respectively, stood on the bridge, talking into their headsets. They'd discarded their laminated sheets after Rogers had dispelled the usefulness of *The Art of War II: Now In Space*, and both seemed lost without anything to wave around. Instead, they mostly paced and yelled, occasionally taking swigs from large, squeezable bottles of water.

"Zaz!" Rogers said. "Is there *anything* we can do to put some distance between us and the Un-Space point? We need to get more of our fleet in here as soon as possible. How many ships do you think we'd need to even the odds here?"

Zaz looked up, sliding one side of the headset off his ears.

"If we could get a couple of gunships in, they might be able to at least unplug the hole further. At this point, I'd recommend charging directly at the center mass of the pirates and praying . . . in space."

"Please stop saying 'in space' after every suggestion you give me," Rogers said. He looked at Belgrave. "Can you, like, make the ship jink or something so that we don't get blasted so hard?"

"We're a floating city, sir. I can't make the ship do anything other than move in a single direction and not crash into stations when we dock."

Outside, the flashes on the exterior of the ship were rising in frequency and intensity to seizure-inducing proportions. They didn't have much time left. Rogers keyed in the war room.

"Any comments from the peanut gallery?" Rogers asked the other members of the Joint Force.

"I'm allergic to peanuts," Thrumeaux said.

"Who are you? Deet?" Rogers asked. "It's an expression. Look, do you have any advice on how to not die? Because I would like to not die."

"You know, we could just hand you over," Krell said.

"I would prefer that not to happen," Keffoule said, her voice icy. Probably for the first time since he'd met her, Rogers was thankful for her obsession with him. On the other hand, it meant that she was still obsessed with him.

"If it means that much to you, then of course I will abandon that suggestion," Krell said. Rogers could almost feel the slime coming through the communication system. Did he really want

Keffoule to end up with a guy like that? He just seemed gross in so many ways. "But we did accomplish a maneuver once in a similar situation that might work here."

"Enlighten me," Rogers said. "Fast."

The ship bucked as though it had hit an asteroid, which, given the fact that the sector was cleared for habitation, was completely impossible. Shouts of surprise rose up from all parts of the bridge, and Rogers nearly tumbled out of his chair as the inertial force turned the world sideways for a moment.

"What the hell was that?" Rogers asked.

"It was an asteroid, sir," Zaz said, listening into his headphones intently. "Shields are getting really weak if we were able to feel it like that."

Rogers yelled something that wasn't quite a word. "Nothing makes any sense anymore! Krell? Your plan, please?"

"We charged a blockade once by cutting down most of the ship's power and rerouting it all to engines and shields. Since that included some backup life support and some inertial dampening systems, it nearly killed us all, but it worked." Krell gave a hearty laugh, the kind that came from a man drinking too much beer and misremembering stories to give himself an over-inflated ego. "You know, Alandra—can I call you Alandra?—it reminds me of—"

"That's great, Krell," Rogers said. "Not really the time for reminiscing. Deet, plug in and run those calculations. See how much distance that'll give us between 'certain death' and just 'extremely probable death.'"

"Aye-aye, Captain," Deet said, ambling over to a port and extending his dongle. "You know, I think the *Flagship* and I could be really good together if she'd give me a chance."

"Gross, Deet." Rogers pressed a couple of buttons on his commander's console and brought up the address system for the ship. "Everyone brace for immediate, and completely stupid, movement. Tie everything down and put lids on your coffee cups."

All around the bridge, he could hear the snapping of seat belts and the snapping of lids. Really, he was surprised by how many people might be drinking coffee at a time like this. He took a sip of his coffee and waited for Deet to finish doing whatever it was he was doing to the *Flagship*.

Deet's eyes blinked different colors for a few seconds, and he made some noises that Rogers wasn't really used to hearing come from the robot. Namely a long whistle, like he was catcalling someone on the street, followed by a burping noise and the flushing of a toilet.

"Are you alright?" Rogers asked.

"I am," Deet said. "The shield impacts are sending some strange electrical currents through the ship that I am picking up. Nothing to be worried—" He made a noise like a power drill. "Nothing to be worried about."

Rogers stood up, staring intently at Deet and gritting his teeth. The pirates were massing for another attack run, one that Rogers thought might be their last.

"Deet. The plan."

"I can begin making the power configurations right now. If I do it, it might save you some time, and the displeasure of talking to people. You say you always hate talking to people, especially all these '[DEITY FORSAKEN] morons.'"

Rogers felt his face getting hot. Belgrave gave a long sigh.

"I do not say those sorts of things about my crew," Rogers said.

"As a matter of fact," Deet said, "I have a time-stamped, recorded conversation that—"

"Deet, just stop talking and do the thing that will make us die slower!"

"It's already done, Rogers. It's been done for the entire time you've been talking. You know, sometimes I think you have your priorities a little mixed up. Shouldn't you be preparing to defend yourself once we finish getting through the—"

Any further speech by Deet, or anyone else, was cut off as the *Flagship* suddenly made a hard turn, throwing loose equipment and people all over the bridge, and accelerated forward at an extremely uncomfortable speed. The flashes on the outside of the ship turned into a sort of steady glow, the color moving back toward green, indicating that the shields were recharging from other systems on the ship. The *Flagship*'s defensive-fire systems stopped shooting plasma blasts at the pirates, who were now getting very big very fast. A flying datapad hit an unfortunate marine in the head, knocking him unconscious.

"Hhrrrrhhhhhh," Rogers said in a moment of clarity as his face was being turned inside out by the force of movement. He could see pirate fighters start to take evasive action, obviously not expecting the *Flagship* to turn off all their guns and charge through them. Just the trajectory of their ship solved a few problems as some of the pirate ships, unable to change direction in time, slammed directly into the shield wall of the *Flagship* and exploded on impact.

"Weee!" Deet said. He waggled his arms in the air. "I think I am actually having fun! Does fun make me human? Belgrave, does it? Hey, Belgrave, why are you turning purple?"

The silver specks floating in Rogers' field of vision suddenly decided to be courteous and invite a bunch of other different-colored specks as well and start having a party. All the colors of the rainbow were dancing in his vision. A few more seconds and everyone on the ship would pass out from the inertia. Rogers hoped the Astromologer, who was in the zero-gravity room, was tied down properly instead of reading his Tootle Roo cards or whatever, or he was definitely now a human pancake.

While Rogers could tell that, without a doubt, this was helping clear the Un-Space gate, he could also see something else that was going to be a very large problem very quickly. The direction in which they'd accelerated to get out of the way happened to be the exact same direction from which the large Jupiterian force was coming. They were rushing from one problem to another.

"Ssstttoooooppp!" Rogers yelled. "Too mmmuuuucccchhh!"

Groans rose up all around him, with most of the bridge

crew making indecipherable yells. Someone on the far end of the bridge actually sneezed, and Rogers could hear the audible slap of the residue hitting the wall—and one of the screaming offensive-systems technicians—behind her.

"I really don't see what all of you are so fussy about," Deet said. "I'm over here having the time of my life and firmly establishing my sentience by doing so, and everyone is all 'Oohhh nooo, my front ribs are touching my back ribs' and all that. Humans are so dramatic." He made something like a sigh, a noise that Deet could never seem to get correct. "Everyone just hang on a second while I—once again—do all of the [EXPLETIVE] work."

A moment later, the ship's rapid deceleration sent everything that wasn't tied down *back* across the ship. The marine who had been knocked unconscious by the datapad regained his senses for only enough time to say "We did it" before being hit again by the same datapad, which knocked him back into oblivion.

It felt like the whole world had stopped. There weren't any more pirates in front of them; but there were certainly a hell of a lot of Jupiterians. Everyone on the bridge gave an audible groan as though they'd been conducted to do so by someone waving a baton in front of an orchestra of misery.

"Stasis mongort!" Rogers said, only half aware of where his body began and ended. This was way worse than anything the Viking could have dealt him. "I mean, uh, status report! What's going on?"

The silence that followed seemed to stretch to eternity. Zaz and Rholos chattered into their headsets, though a bit less enthusiastically than they had before they'd made the rapid acceleration.

Suddenly beeps rang through the bridge as the battlespace display alerted them to multiple new spacecraft in the area.

"They're coming through!" Commander Rholos said. "Reinforcements! All units, get ready for a ten-seven-seven blitz on my mark. Ready—*go!*"

"What the hell is a ten-seven-seven blitz?" Rogers asked.

"It's an attack formation . . . in space," Zaz replied. Where did he get another laminated sheet from?

"I told you to stop doing that!"

The display of the battlespace looked as merry as a non-religion-specific holiday decoration on steroids. Blue dots were starting to pour in from the Un-Space point, unhindered by the pirates, who were now chasing the *Flagship* instead of doing their job of blocking off access. It was like a little kids' soccer game; every ship was chasing the one shiny object of the *Flagship* and ignoring the reason they were there in the first place—to win the game.

"Reset our power priorities and get the guns back online," Rogers said. "We've got them from one side, and the rest of the force will get them from the other. Belgrave, get us ninety degrees above so we don't shoot each other and we'll pour fire into the middle."

Holy shit, Rogers thought. *That was a real-life, tactically sound decision. I wonder what the Viking would have to say about my "tactics" now!*

Unfortunately, the Viking probably wouldn't say anything. She'd completely dispensed with physical abuse and had sunk into a silence that wasn't even satisfactorily tense. It was just . . . depressed. Almost disappointed. Honestly, Rogers felt like a kid again, with his mother refusing to be angry with him. He also immediately understood the weirdness associated with comparing the woman of his dreams to his mother, but he supposed every man did it at some point. Rogers would work out all that deep Freudian stuff later.[*]

He missed the Viking.

"What are you all staring at?" Rogers asked.

Everyone on the bridge was looking at him, standing still. Even Belgrave seemed to be flummoxed for some reason. Was he really such a bad commander that it shocked the people around him when he came up with a good battle plan on the fly?

"Jeez, guys, it was *one order*. Let's not get ahead of ourselves

---

[*] He would not.

here. Please just start to kill pirates so that we can focus on Jupiterians, okay?"

"Yes, sir!" everyone said.

Rogers went back to looking at the display while he tried to figure out how to deal with the other half of the problem. Realizing that he had no idea how to deal with the other half of the problem, he motioned for Zaz and Rholos to come over. They struck out across the bridge with the same wide, awkward gait, as though they were trying to cover as many yards with each step as humanly possible.

"What's on your mind, Skip?" Commander Zaz said.

"Can we take on that Jupiterian force if we get everyone through the Un-Space point?"

Zaz and Rholos looked at each other. It was the kind of look that said "Does this guy really not understand how screwed we are?" which, in turn, educated Rogers as to exactly how screwed they were. What he didn't know, however, was why.

"Sir," Rholos said, her voice low, "we won't have a chance to get the whole force through. We've got enough to deal with the pirates for now, yes, but it takes time to get our huge fleet through the gate. If the pirates were working for us, like they're supposed to be doing, they might buy us enough time to bring everyone else through and take the fight to the Jupes. But, as things are . . ."

"We're all going to die," Rogers said. "Got it."

"And here I thought we were getting better at all of that talk," Belgrave called out.

Rogers ignored him. So they'd managed to not get killed by the pirates in order to very nearly be able to not get killed by the Jupiterians. He wished he'd known that before he'd completely separated the *Flagship* from the rest of the fleet and started acting like he knew what he was doing.

If they couldn't get the pirates to play nicely, it was over.

Cynthia gritted her teeth. If she was going to be on a pirate ship, she might as well act like a pirate, right?

There were no words bandied, no declarations of righteousness. Just a couple of crunching noises as Cynthia's pistol connected with the side of Sjana's head, followed by the sounds of surprise and many pistols being drawn. For a moment, Cynthia thought that this was it. She'd never see the *Flagship* again, never see the Viking or Rogers. But she was a marine; she knew how to read people better than that. Cynthia knew that not everyone on board felt the same way about this fight as their captain. And now that they didn't have a captain . . .

"Hey!" Hideko shouted, barreling onto the bridge. "You can't—"

Cynthia shot him in the chest, which seemed very pirate-like indeed.

Now that they didn't have a captain *or* a first mate, they could make the rational decision. Rather than stand and wait to be shot, however, Cynthia shoved Sjana's body aside—a motion, she realized, she was rather practiced at—and sat down in the pilot's seat.

"Come on, you idiots!" Cynthia shouted. "Stop fighting the wrong fucking enemy and turn those guns toward the Jupiterians!"

The crew didn't cheer, exactly. They sort of mumbled agreeably and sat back down at their stations. Cynthia let out a deep breath and spun the chair around to face the console. Why was that button blinking?

"And someone get me a manual on how to fly this thing!"

"Starman Brelle," Rogers said as the world crumbled around him. "Hail Captain Devingo's ship." He swallowed. "Tell them I'm going to turn myself in—"

"Uh, sir?" someone said. "The pirates have stopped shooting at us."

"—to a superstar once everyone hears my banjo playing!" Rogers finished. He waggled his fingers in front of him in either a rough approximation of a banjo picking roll or an attempt to tickle his own belly. Nobody seemed interested in making the distinction. "What's going on out there? Why the sudden stop?"

"Rogers? Rogers, are you there?" a voice was coming over the radio.

"Who's hailing us?" Rogers asked.

Brelle punched some buttons on her console. "It looks like Devingo's ship, sir."

"What do you want? Who is this? You don't sound like Sjana at all."

A burst of static. Rogers thought that the line had cut out, because whoever was on the other end was answering in little clips of communication that didn't make any sense.

". . . it's not because . . . what? . . . no, I don't know what that button . . . stop touching my hand or I'll shoot you, too!"

A disruptor pistol fired.

". . . well I warned him, didn't I? Rogers, it's Mailn. Sjana is, uh, napping. Can we blow up some Jupiterians now, or what?"

Rogers sat back in his chair, feeling smug. He had been right. That *was* where Mailn had gone. Disregarding the fact that she was not only AWOL, but now technically a deserter during a time of war, which brought with it the death penalty, Rogers felt a huge weight lifted from his shoulders. They could work out the particulars later.

"Alright, Sergeant Mailn, tell everyone to get the hell away from the Un-Space point and get moving toward the Jupiterians right now. Let's buy as much time as we can while the rest of the fleet pours in. Conserve your ammunition, fly around in circles, hit and fade, or whatever. That's a thing, right?" He looked at Zaz.

"Confirming that's a thing, sir," Zaz said, giving him a thumbs-up.

"Right. Go do that."

"You got it, boss," Mailn said, and the comms cut out.

Several people on the bridge who had heard the conversation clapped, cheering.

"Don't get too cocky," Rogers said. "This just went from impossible to possible."

"Way to rally the troops, sir," Belgrave said.

"Shut up. Everyone in the war room ready for this? What's going on down there?"

"Ready," Krell said.

"Captain Rogers, I took a moment to cross-check some signals with my fleet," Premiere Thrumeaux said over the comms. "From what they're telling me, it's not just that the Galaxy Eater isn't here. There's no evidence of the Galaxy Eater ever being here at all. There would be distortions, emissions . . . but there's nothing."

"I'm confirming the same thing," General Krell said.

Keffoule was silent.

"What's the matter, Grand Marshal?" Rogers said. "Are you disappointed that your psychic mathematician was wrong?" He laughed bitterly and turned to Deet. "I know you're probably pretty excited about this."

"Yes, Rogers," Deet said. "I am beyond thrilled that we have made a trip halfway across the galaxy and nearly gotten ourselves killed just so I could point out that someone I hate is wrong."

Rogers paused for a moment. "Are you getting better at sarcasm?"

Deet beeped and cocked his head a little bit, as though some actuator in his neck had gone a little weird.

"No. That was a truthful statement. I'm confused as to why you asked me this question. I hate that [EXPLETIVE] guy and place great value on his humiliation."

Rogers cleared his throat. "Okay, yeah, sure. Fine. Do me a favor and go get the Viking and tell her to track the Astromologer down. I'll need a bruiser."

"I thought she was your secretary?" Deet asked.

"Uh," Rogers said, "I'm pretty sure I rescinded that order. Look, just go do it, okay? She doesn't pick up the comms when she sees I'm calling. Tell her she might get the chance to hit someone and it'll cheer her up."

"Fine," Deet said, and ambled toward the exit of the bridge. "Have a great time winning the war while I'm gone."

". . . Sarcasm again, or no?"

"Rogers, I am genuinely wishing you good fortune. I am a little upset that you would think I would do otherwise."

"Uh, right," Rogers said. "Well, everyone else who isn't confusing me, let's blow up some Jupiterians."

It only took another ten minutes before the full brunt of the Jupiterian ambush hit them. Rholos explained to Rogers that there must have been some miscalculation on the Jupiterians' part, since they started much too far away in the battlespace to cause effective damage before the Joint Force could regroup. She didn't offer any speculation as to why the Jupes made the blunder, but Rogers was just thankful they'd made it. The Jupiterians had clearly known the composition of Rogers' force, and had the advantage of surprise. Without the tactical error of too much distance, Rogers didn't know if they would have had a chance.

All of that was pretty high-level analysis, sure, but that's what Zaz and Rholos had told him, and he assumed, perhaps naively, that they were good at their jobs.

"I knew there was a spy," Rogers said. "And it's probably you, Belgrave."

"It's not me," Belgrave said with no more surprise than if he'd been accused of blinking.

"We'll find out later," Rogers said. "But I'm still saying it's probably you."

"It's not."

"Whatever. I want to talk to the Astromologer, too."

"He's probably the spy," Belgrave suggested.

"Nope," Rogers said. "I think it's you."

The bridge was alive with the sounds of combat; people yelled at each other with fervor and an enthusiasm that was egged on by the fear of shortly being dead. Rogers felt a little lost; most of the battle plans were being enacted by independent commanders of the different squadrons within the different fleets, further distilled by the fact that he had three other commanders aboard directing their own forces. Zaz and Rholos did most of the minutiae, and only asked Rogers questions when they needed his input.

Deet, who had come back to the bridge just after the first shots had been fired, informed Rogers that the Viking wasn't interested in doing anything for him. When he'd told her she might get the chance to hit someone, however, she'd suddenly become interested. The last Deet had seen of her, she'd been wearing a pair of brass knuckles and actually rolling up both of her sleeves.

"Rogers, your facial temperature seems to have risen significantly. Are you feeling unwell?"

"I'm fine," Rogers said, his voice not cracking even a little bit. The image of the Viking burned in his heart like the plasma blasts that were raining down on his fleet. He thought perhaps this was not the appropriate time to be thinking of romance, but he also thought that perhaps this might be the last chance he would ever have to show the Viking he wasn't a complete idiot. Of course she didn't want a secretarial position; she was a Viking. And Vikings raped and pillaged.

Obviously he couldn't have her do that for him, but there was an important analogy here. He didn't need Mailn to tell him that either, which he thought might be an indication of personal growth. He made a note to delve more into that introspective thought later.*

"Have we finished the high-level battlespace analysis?" Rogers asked. "The whole fleet is through now, aren't they?"

"Yes, sir," Rholos said. She walked over to him, frowning.

---

* He would not.

"That doesn't look like the face of someone who is about to win a war," Rogers said quietly.

"I'm not sure it is, sir," she said. "The Jupiterians' force is enormous. Not only did they seem to know that we were coming, they seemed to know what we were bringing *and* when we'd be here. Several ships that should be combat ready are reporting that they are unable to engage in combat until they deal with internal ship malfunctions. Our readiness dropped fifteen percent as soon as they all came through Un-Space."

"What?" Rogers asked. That was a huge portion of his force! "Why the hell are they reporting that now?"

"It only just started to occur," Rholos said. "That's why I think they knew the timing of our attack."

Rogers squinted. "How does ships malfunctioning mean that they knew our timing?"

"Well, on the *Valiant* and the *Destiny*, all the toilets were made by Snaggardir's, sir. They're currently flooding the ships with sewage."

"That's really gross."

"And on the *Terminus*, all the door actuators were made by Snaggardir's, so they keep closing on people. The infirmary is flooded with people with broken limbs."

"Great," Rogers said. So they'd definitely known when the joint force was coming and had triggered their weird machine inconveniences to fire off at the same time. He turned to Deet. "Do we have a lot of Snaggardir's equipment on board the *Flagship*? Other than you, I mean."

"I am not a piece of equipment," Deet said. "And I'll scan as well as I can, but it might be difficult to cross-reference all the known subsidiary corporations and then run the serial numbers of every single piece of equipment on the *Flagship* to see what parts were assembled by whom and where."

"Alright," Rogers said. "You get started on that and then—"

"And . . . done," Deet said.

Rogers stared at him.

"What?" Deet asked. "You humans are the ones with the distorted view of time. I was trying to explain this to Hart the other day."

"Right," Rogers said. "Uh, what did you find?"

"We're surprisingly clean. The *Flagship* was built by General McBoe-Locklass."

"Is that a person?"

"No," Deet said. "A conglomerate of several Old Earth companies. The only thing that seems to have been sourced from Snaggardir's on the ship is the cleaning equipment."

"Oh," Rogers said. "That's not so bad. Can you shut any of it down?"

"Oh my god!" someone screamed from the other side of the bridge. *"Oh my god it's got me, someone please help, it's trying to kill me aaarrrggghhh!"*

Everyone turned to see what the commotion was about, Rogers jumping out of his chair and, for some reason, reaching for his disruptor pistol. This was odd because not only was he not wearing a pistol, but there was absolutely no chance of him doing anything useful with it if he had been.

The panic was coming from a young ensign who had fallen over and was clutching at his leg frantically. At his feet, a Snaggardir's brand automatic vacuum cleaner was slowly sucking in the bottom of his pant leg. It obviously couldn't hold the capacity of the entire pair of pants, though, so it would spit out a bit of fabric and then roll it back in again, creating the impression that the device was humping the troop's leg. Very slowly. While making vacuum motor noises.

"Oh for . . . Can someone please unplug that?"

A young starman, looking like he was experiencing suitable secondary embarrassment from his superior officer's predicament, quietly leaned over and switched off the unit. The ensign curled up into a ball and wept.

Rogers sat back down, his body experiencing so many things at once that he was having trouble registering it all. Should they try to make an organized retreat back through Un-Space? Without the pirates blocking them anymore, they had a clear line to get the hell out of here if they needed to. Pursuing a force through an Un-Space point was generally considered a poor idea, because the fleeing force could turn around and blast ships as they exited the Un-Space point on the other side.

But if he ordered that, there would definitely be casualties as everyone filed back through the point and the Jupiterians picked off the end of the line. Since the *Flagship* was already the furthest from the point, that meant that the *Flagship* might be one of those picked off.

Yet, if he stayed and fought, there was a chance of a catastrophic defeat. So, should he sacrifice part of the fleet to fight again another day, or engage and hope for a miracle?

Rogers couldn't make the decision alone. He brought up all of the other systems' commanders on the comms and relayed the situation to them as expediently as he could:

"We're going to die a little, or die a lot. Which would you like?"

"Nice," Belgrave said.

After relaying the information, along with what he understood to be his expert analysis of the situation—that is, merely repeating exactly what Rholos had told him—there was a moment of silence as everyone contemplated their options.

Premiere Thrumeaux was the first to speak. In his mind's eye, Rogers could see the woman standing at her battle station, her hand raised dramatically above her head.

"In times like these, we must sometimes suspend our desires for personal safety, and instead—"

"Right," Rogers said. "You want to fight—I get it. Jupiterians are literally like five minutes away. Just yesses or nos for the rest of you, please."

"Yes, fight," Keffoule said.

"I will do whatever the Grand Marshal does. I could not bear to be seen as a coward in her eyes."

Rogers took a deep breath. He should have expected this. They were, after all, the top military leaders of their systems.

Except they were all wrong! They were all going to die if they stayed. This was a stupid idea, and they needed to run, now.

Rogers expressed this in words that may or may not have been frantic and/or pleading.

"But we can make up for inferior numbers with brilliant strategies," Krell said. "With our combined experience we can achieve a decisive victory over the enemy."

"Are you guys kidding me? I am literally the only person out of all of us who has actually fought a decisive space battle before."

"Excuse me," Keffoule said, "I believe I was there when you fought with Zergan."

"Making up for kicking me in the face by trying to get part of your own damn fleet back, yes," Rogers said. "So much experience there."

They bickered at him for a moment, but Rogers wasn't listening. He was the commander here, or "first among equals" as Thrumeaux liked to remind him, but he could make the decision to leave if he wanted to. That damn weird feeling in the back of his head was beginning to nag at him again. He still didn't know if he had a proper name for it. Was it a conscience? Was it duty? Was it the idea that he was part of something bigger than himself? He made a mental note to examine all of this later and come to some serious, deep conclusions.*

"Sir," Rholos said. "We need to make a decision. Now."

Out the window, Rogers could see the Jupiterian fleet approaching with unnerving speed. A tremendous amount of metal was hurling toward him, and some of the ships were already firing unguided volleys in the hopes of catching some of

---

* He would not.

Rogers' ships as they moved into the envelope. What the hell was he supposed to do with this?

His mouth was moving, but he wasn't sure what he was going to say until after he heard Rholos echo the order back at him.

"Send messages to HQ as soon as possible. Give them all of the intelligence we've collected about this zone, the ambush. Everything. Tell them we're staying to fight."

"Aye-aye, sir!"

Rogers sat on the edge of his chair, squeezing all the stuffing out of the armrests and using his top teeth to file down his bottom teeth.

Duty was such a pain in the ass.

Unlikely Functions

Obviously, the Jupiterians had not read Sun Tzu Jr.'s *The Art of War II: Now In Space.* Rogers assumed this because, instead of just doing predictable, old-hat tactics that were rip-offs of the pages in the book, the Jupiterians came at them with a wild, almost reckless combat style. Since their ships were stolen from the fleets of all four systems, and also combined with some proprietary Snaggardir's ships, they couldn't utilize the same kinds of synergy that, say, the Thelicosan fleet could. Instead, they appeared to be completely insane.

Rogers wasn't sure what he was supposed to do with that. Neither was Rholos, and neither was Zaz. Both of them, who had produced new laminated sheets with nothing on them, looked between Rogers and the sheets with equal measures of confusion and helplessness. To try to help stop the stove-piping of orders coming from the top, Rogers delegated tactics all the way down to the squadron level. His grand, strategic guidance for them was to "try really, really hard to win the battle," and they seemed okay with that for the time being.

The pirate fleet helped, but not as much as Rogers had hoped. With Mailn essentially staging a mutiny on her wife's ship, she was now in charge of a sizable portion of the pirates. She explained, through several broken communications, that she had no idea how to pilot a ship, never mind lead an attack using a fleet of them.

So far they'd heard nothing from the Jupiterian fleet. Not even any good-spirited taunting, which Rogers had kind of expected given the dramatics associated with the revelation of the Galaxy Eater. They just seemed hell-bent on the destruction of Rogers' fleet.

"Given my detailed observation of this situation," Deet said, "I believe there are several colloquialisms that might apply to the overall level of satisfaction we are experiencing. The strangest part, though, is that they all seem to have to do with fecal matter."

Rogers looked at him, barely able to see anything through the sweat droplets that kept falling into his eyes. "You know, maybe this isn't the time—"

"Such as, 'This is a bunch of [BOVINE EXCREMENT].'"

"That, uh, would work, yes, but—"

"[EXCREMENT] storm."

"Yep."

"[EXCREMENT] show."

"Uh-huh."

"[EXCREMENT] sandwich? Now that just seems unsanitary."

"We have a lot of uses for that word. Can we focus a little bit here? Can't you do something useful over there with your dongle, or whatever? Hack into the Jupiterian ships and make them shoot each other?"

"I can't just go around using my dongle for whatever you want, Rogers," Deet said.

"What about the Viking? Have you heard from her yet?" Rogers chewed on his lip. He needed to talk to the Astromologer, yes, but he also needed her to start prepping her crews in the event they were boarded or needed to board anyone else. It wouldn't matter how long he talked to that charlatan if they were all dead by the time she found him.

"I haven't heard from her, no," Deet said.

Rogers growled to himself. Before he knew what he was doing, he'd snatched up his datapad and was calling her. It was so automatic that when she picked up, he was shocked into a stunned silence for a moment.

"Rogers, if you're just calling me to breathe heavy again, I swear to god—"

"No, no," Rogers said, finally getting ahold of himself. "I told you: that wasn't me."*

"What do you want? Feeling like sending me to typing school now, or some shit?"

Rogers sighed. This really wasn't the time for this, either.

"Stop looking for that Thelicosan moron and get your crews ready. It's not looking that great out there, and there's a chance this might come to rifle butts in faces."

The Viking laughed at him through the comms.

"I've made some mistakes," Rogers said. "But we don't have time to go through all of that right now, okay?"

"Are you sure?" the Viking spat back at him. "Because I'm pretty sure everything in that metal head of yours is so ass backward that—"

"Captain Alsinbury," Rogers barked, much louder than he thought himself capable of when talking to the woman of his dreams. "I need my marines, and you are the best of them. Go get them ready to fight."

The comms went silent for a moment. Rogers felt his own words hang in the air like a noose.

"Aye-aye," the Viking said, and the line cut out.

Letting out a deep breath, Rogers tried to keep his heart from

---

* It was.

pounding out of his chest. What was more terrifying: love or war? Because right now he was doing both at the same time.

Rogers turned for a status update from Rholos and Zaz. Both of them were talking furiously into their headsets, taking breaks to squeeze water into their mouths from those green bottles they had taken to carrying in holsters at their sides. Zaz indicated that he was in the middle of something interesting and turned away from Rogers for a moment to examine the displays. Rholos followed him, and the two of them began gesticulating with a definite amount of enthusiasm at one particular blue blip.

"Captain," Commander Zaz said, walking over to the command platform, "one of our Ravagers is acting a little strange."

"What's going on?" Rogers said.

"We're not sure yet," Zaz said. "He's flying erratically and there are some strange comms coming in. There's a chance he could be hypoxic."

That's just what they needed. If there was a fault in the oxygen supply for one of the fighters, there was a chance that it was in many of the fighters and they hadn't noticed yet.

"Starman Brelle," Rogers called out. "Get in touch with Master Sergeant Hart in Engineering and have him talk to the maintainers. Check the oxygen tanks and make sure we're not looking at any contaminated supplies."

"Yes, sir," Brelle called back.

Rogers turned back to Zaz. "Who is it? Can we recall them?"

Before Zaz could answer, a familiar voice came over the comms.

"Wooo! Can't recall the Chillster, Skip!" said Flash. "I'm always at full burn."

"That's not bad oxygen," Rogers said. "It's a bad pilot. I thought I left explicit instructions not to let Flash near the cockpit anymore? Who is in charge of flight operations?"

"He is, sir," Zaz said.

"Oh. Right. The other guy flew into an asteroid. We need to change that." But maybe the middle of a space battle wasn't the right time to make personnel changes. As long as Flash wasn't out there losing the war for him, it was a risk he was going to have to take so he could focus on other things. "Anything else I should know?"

"Yes," Rholos said, her face white. "We're losing."

Rogers didn't need them to tell him that. He was a complete failure as a commander, but he wasn't a complete failure as a human being. The blue dots were quickly being overrun by the red dots on the big display, and a brightly lit scoreboard at the bottom read "Jupiterians: 50, Good Guys: 10." What the numbers actually meant, he had no idea, but unless they were playing golf (and they weren't), it was a bad sign.

"Do we have any options at all here?" Rogers asked.

Rholos looked at her laminated sheet. "We could, um . . . win first and then go to war . . . in space."

"Stop that!" Rogers said. He ran his hands down his face, grabbing hold of the hairs on his beard and pulling as hard as he could. His pulse was going a million miles a minute, his sweat glands were producing a veritable ocean, and every part of him felt like it was shaking. Even his shakes had shakes. What kind of a commander was this terrified?

Probably one who knew he was about to lose.

"Captain!" a defensive-systems technician yelled, standing up. "One of the Jupiterian fighter screens has broken off from the main group and is heading in our direction. It's being accompanied by what we think are two heavy Freezee™ class gunships."

"I'm sorry—what class?"

"It's a proprietary Snaggardir's ship, sir." She looked a little embarrassed. "We just kind of started naming them."

"Right. Let me know when we start getting targeted by Beef-E-Stix torpedo runners."

"Sir!" someone shouted. "We have three Beef-E-Stix class torpedo runners approaching us at high speed.

"Now that's just absurd!" Rogers said, now out of his seat,

gripping the rail in front of him so hard he thought he might break a couple of his own fingers.

"They've broken through our fighter screen and are targeting our ship's critical systems. If the Freezee and the Beef-E-Stix don't get scattered, they could break through the shield."

"And then?" Rogers said.

"And then they destroy our critical systems."

"And then?!" Rogers said, his voice getting higher.

Of course he knew what was going to happen. He just had absolutely no idea how to stop it from happening, and he thought that maybe continually asking questions would give him time to think. In this case, however, he felt like maybe time to think was exactly what he did *not* need, as it was merely causing his sympathetic nervous system to begin to implode.

"Skip," Zaz said, swallowing. "There are some other ships trailing the attack formation headed for the *Flagship*. It looks like a boarding crew."

"Goddamn it," Rogers said. In a way, that was a relief; it meant that, unlike the pirates, the Jupiterians didn't want him and his crew dead. But why? They certainly didn't seem to have any issues with blowing up everything else his fleet had to offer. Maybe they thought that by capturing, rather than killing, the command crew, they could force a surrender. If the *Flagship* was destroyed, everyone in the fleet would fight to the last man to avenge him. At least that's what he thought would happen.

If that was the case, it meant that he had some other options. He punched keys on his console.

"Captain Alsinbury, I hope you got everyone ready. We might have company."

"I just did it!" Quinn yelled over the radio. "I just disemboweled a man with—"

"It's best we leave these sorts of details out when we're broadcasting on open channels," Alandra said. She had taught the woman quite a bit before she'd left the *Limiter*, but she'd left Quinn with some instructions and a few training videos to get better. It seemed the secretary had devoured the training with a voracious appetite. The only thing Alandra had seen her more enthusiastic about during their time on the *Limiter* together had been filing paperwork.

The war room had been reconfigured in what Alandra considered to be an ingenious way. Divided into four parts, it was possible for each of the system commanders to manage their own portions of the fleet while maintaining direct contact with Rogers on the bridge. It was similar to the way they had operated when Alandra had been trying to control her fleet in the battle against Zergan, but the room smelled much better this time.

"It was so . . . so . . . so . . . *awesome*," Quinn said.

In a strange way, she and Quinn had become pen pals since Alandra's departure. They'd sent each other messages, and in exchange for Quinn's information on relationship building, and how the *Limiter* was performing under the new leadership of Chinnaker, Alandra had offered to critique self-taped videos of Quinn's attempts at learning how to fight. They'd admittedly gotten better over a short period of time—a testament to the secretary's attention to detail—but Alandra had never expected Quinn to be reporting these sorts of details to her so soon.

And certainly not from the belly of an enemy ship that she'd led a boarding team onto. That just seemed reckless. Admirable, but reckless.

"Awesome is not typically how we describe warfare, Quinn. For all that I've taught you in physical violence, I apparently have left out the lesson on tact."

"Yes, alright, fine," Quinn said. "Now why don't you apply a bit of *my* lessons?"

"What do you mean?" Alandra said.

"Remember when I told you that if you felt like you weren't

getting anywhere in a negotiation with one party, you should move on to another?"

Alandra frowned. She noticed Krell looking at her over his terminal, grinning like he always did. "Yes, but I don't see what that has to do with me."

Quinn sighed, which, over the comms sounded like a weird burst of static. Her mouth was too close to the microphone. Why was she spending time talking to Alandra, anyway, if she was in the middle of a firefight? The sounds of disruptor blasts and men and women screaming could be heard in the background.

"Of course you don't," Quinn said. "Anyway, I've got some skulls to crack over here, so I'm going to let you go. Remember what I said, Lanni."

The line cut out. Lanni? Why in the world would Quinn call her Lanni? That wasn't even a shortened version of her name. The woman had gone completely blood-lust crazy.

There was, however, no time to think about this now. Someone was screaming at them.

"Boarding!" Rogers yelled over the comms to her station. "Boardilyboard! Being boarded! Boards are coming, boards that are coming out to our ship to board us! Defend your positions! Position your defenses! What? No, get that rifle away from me, I can't shoo—"

The communication stopped, but Alandra was already out of her seat, Xan at her side with the alacrity of someone who really didn't seem to move very fast at all. He began to say something, reaching for a case he'd brought with them from the *Limiter*, but was almost immediately shouldered aside by General Krell. The New Neptunian general showed no signs that there was about to be a firefight on board.

"You know," General Krell said, handing her a disruptor rifle. "This could be the end for us. In the fleeting moments of life, it's important that we—"

"Oh, for the love of spinning quarks, shut up!" Xan yelled.

The war room stopped. Krell looked as though he was about to burst at the seams with anger. Thrumeaux and her attendant, who was just beginning to gather the folds of the woman's long cape, stopped what they were doing and stared, open mouthed, at the unassuming, face-weight-wearing man who had never raised his voice in his life. Alandra would have dressed him down, but she was too shocked to move. Xan was also apparently not finished with his tirade.

"You came into this council and all you've done is smile and grin and be pompous. You don't even know the grand marshal! You haven't sat by her side for years. You haven't seen the strength of this woman, seen her *power* and *majesty*. You're just a primped-up caricature of a general. You are not deserving of the grand marshal, and your smarmy attempts to sway her romantic feelings are completely and totally *full of shit!*"

Face weights swayed violently from side to side, detaching one of the bottom pieces and sending it flying across the room. It slammed into a terminal screen, rendering it instantly useless, and left Xan tilting his head to one side. It created the impression that Alandra's assistant had just become a sort of zombie.

"Now look here," Krell began. "I find your tone unacceptable."

"I find your face unacceptable," Xan spat back, which struck Alandra as a little immature, but things were getting out of hand. "And I will not continue to sit here while you disrespect the woman that I love."

Alandra nearly gasped. "Xan! But I hardly know you. I haven't read any intelligence reports about you, only your résumé. Intelligence reports are the best way—"

"No they are not!" Xan yelled, his face red and his voice, unused to saying anything above a whisper, trembled with the effort. "The best way to know and love someone is to be by their side for years and years, anticipating their needs and being there for them in every situation. It's serving *breakfast* to the man she wants to marry and holding my tongue during every disgusting minute of it. *It's attaching weights to my face because I couldn't stop smiling every time you walked into a room.*"

"But why would smiling be a bad thing?" Krell asked.

"Because I hate smiles," Alandra said, breathless. "And Xan knows it."

In a display of macho posturing that Alandra found more than a little interesting, Xan had put himself in between her and the general and was literally punctuating his sentences by bumping Krell in the chest. Krell, for all his blustering, didn't seem ready to get into a fistfight. In fact, he was practically retreating across the war room, chest bump by chest bump.

"Now, if you were too busy copying pickup lines from old movies to notice, we're being boarded. So grab your *Newton-damned* rifle and *get the hell away from my grand marshal!*"

General Krell looked for a moment like he might retaliate. The tension had drawn his shoulders practically up to his ears. The copious amount of military medals draped across his uniform rattled as his body shook. Then, without looking at Alandra, he deflated and grabbed a disruptor rifle.

"There are more important things to focus on now, anyway," Krell muttered, and fled the room with his head down.

Alandra stood looking at the place where Krell had been a moment earlier and slowly drew her eyes to Xan. The man stood in front of her, his face back to being blank and unreadable. There was, however, a leftover redness that indicated some recent physical exertion. Xan took a step toward Alandra, and, to her surprise, she actually flinched.

What had just happened?

Why had she *liked* it?

Opening the case, Xan presented it to her. Inside, displayed with a beautiful austerity, was a bundle of toothpicks, a small serving of popcorn, and Alandra's favorite disruptor pistol. Given to her by the Thelicosan Council for valorous conduct on a mission about which she was never to speak to anyone, it had remained unused for nearly a decade.

"I thought you might want this."

"Xan, I . . . ," Alandra said. There were so many words fighting for dominance inside her brain, like several bodies with equal but opposite magnetic charges all swirling around. She looked at Xan, her mouth slightly open, unable to speak.

Xan may have smiled. May have, because Alandra really wasn't sure what facial expression was resulting from his off-balance face weights, and she'd just been very clear about reiterating her dislike of smiles.

"After this, Grand Marshal, we should talk." He pressed the case toward her. "I will give you all the intelligence you desire."

Keffoule blushed and grabbed the pistol. Poor Rogers was going to be so very, very disappointed.

"Flash!" Rogers yelled. *"Get back in your ship!"*

"Got a hung missile, Skip," Flash said over the radio. "Figured I could kick it a few times, and—ah! There it goes."

The battlespace display showed a missile launch coming from Ravager One, flying miraculously through an entire screen of enemy fighters without hitting a single one, and colliding with an asteroid that Rogers was certain had not been there a moment before. It caused the asteroid to shatter, creating hundreds of smaller asteroids.

"Hey, as far as the law of armed conflict goes," Rogers asked Rholos, "is it legal for me to have another Ravager kill Flash?"

"Not to my knowledge, sir," Rholos said.

The bridge was bustling with personnel arming themselves in anticipation of being boarded by the Jupiterians. The attack runs hadn't penetrated their shields or disabled any critical systems yet, but it was only a matter of time. While they were waiting to fight face-to-face like barbarians, Rogers was firm in his belief that he couldn't simply abandon the bridge. He also was too scared to go anywhere, and the bridge felt like a safe space for the time being. There were locks on the door and everything.

On the outside of the ship, things were not looking good at all. With the *Flagship* about to be boarded, command of the other system's ships had been delegated downward. Rogers was barely able to keep up his own battlespace awareness, never mind actually coordinating anything. It turned out that the Jupes were trying to board several capital ships, though they hadn't succeeded in doing so thus far. The boarding crews had been repelled, but that had still taken several larger battle cruisers and frigates out of the fight.

Rogers was most assuredly, definitely, positively, losing this battle.

"What are we looking at here?" Rogers asked. He scooted slightly away from the disruptor rifle that someone had handed him, which he had placed on his command chair and refused to touch.

"Another attack run or two from those fighters and they'll be able to crack us open," Rholos said. Despite her calm demeanor, Rogers could tell that both she and Zaz were nervous. They handled it like professionals, at least, unlike Deet, who had begun experimenting with the idea of mortal fear. Every time he saw a Jupiterian ship fly past the bridge, he tried out different kinds of screams, one of which he kept calling the Wilhelm.

"Sir!" one of the bridge technicians called from the far end. Rogers couldn't see who it was or what their job title was, but they were yelling loudly enough for him to understand that it was important. "Someone has jettisoned an escape pod near Engineering. No idea who is on board."

Crap. His crew was starting to break. The last thing he needed was people fleeing the ship en masse. He couldn't honestly blame them, but he had to prevent panic.

"Has someone pressed the panic button?" Rogers called out loud.

"No, sir!"

"Good," Rogers said. "Let's keep that not pressed. Track the pod and we'll pick whoever it is up later." *Assuming we survive.* Actually, if there had ever been any time in the *Flagship*'s history when it would have been appropriate to push the panic button, this might have been it.

"Boarding crews are closing!" Rholos called.

"Damn it! Who is manning all of our defensive systems? Why can't our big, giant cannons hit these tiny little ships before they get to us?"

"They were just hit by a bunch of very small asteroids, sir," the defensive technician replied.

"Of course they were. How long before we have to start knifing Jupiterians with broken cookware?"

"I don't think we'll ever have to—"

"How long until they're here, starman?"

"Five minutes, sir."

Rogers swallowed. Standing atop his command platform, he looked around the bridge to see the sullen faces of his crew, many of whom were possibly about to die defending the *Flagship* from the boarding party. Should he just order them to surrender? Stop the bloodshed before it started? It was a viable option, but that would certainly put an end to the anti-Jupiterian momentum in one fell swoop. Rogers owed the galaxy a little more than that. Besides, other ships had repelled Jupiterian boarding parties, so maybe the Jupes were just . . . bad at it?

He had to take a chance at his enemy being really bad at fighting. They might even be worse than Rogers was.

"Ladies and gentlemen," Rogers said. "We're about to fight the toughest battle we've ever fought. Well I guess we're already in it." Wow, he was an atrocious public speaker for someone who supposedly was an excellent con man.

"Anyway, uh, I know that not everything I have done has been exemplary, as far as commanders go. I mean I guess I've done a good thing every once in a while. There was the time with the droids, which was mostly an accident. But, uh—"

"Captain Rogers!" someone yelled. "New ships incoming. A lot of them. One of them is an MPD ship!"

"Oh thank god," Rogers said. "Now I can stop talking. Reinforcements?"

There was a pause. Not the good kind of pause, like the moment before the glorious taste of Jasker 120 finally hit you. The bad kind of pause, like the unexpected revelation that something *else* was trying to kill them all.

"Who is it?" Rogers yelled.

"I . . . don't really know," Rholos said. But before Rogers could ask her how she could not read a simple IFF display, more shouts erupted from the other side of the bridge.

"Boarding crew is extending planks! We've got one minute, tops."

Rogers' console let him know that the Viking was trying to get in touch. Despite the fact that there was an unknown party in the battlespace, and that they were all about to die, Rogers picked it up.

"I've got platoons at the typical boarding places," she said. "We're ready."

"Good," Rogers said. "Hey, listen."

"Hey, listen," the Viking said at the same time.

Both of them listened, and therefore neither of them said anything.

"You first," both of them said. Now this was just getting awkward. That and, of course, the war.

"I just—" Rogers said.

"Boarding planks out! We're going—"

A powerful vibration shot through the bridge, taking several people off their feet and knocking down one of Ralph's exceptional propaganda posters that Rogers had specifically commissioned for the anti-Jupiterian conflict. This particular one had a picture of old Jupiter on it, which seemed plain enough to Rogers. Underneath was a text of Ralph's own composition, which said, in all capital letters: SPAGHETTIFICATION IS A REAL WORD AND IT MAY HAPPEN TO US ALL.

The force of the blast had sent Rogers sideways into his console, cutting the communication from the Viking and inadvertently calling up a piece of old polka music. From where in the annals of the ship's databases Rogers had been able to call up such a tune, he had absolutely no idea.

"What hit us?" Rogers said, trying, and failing, to turn off the polka.

Nobody answered for a moment as everyone on the bridge picked themselves up and tried to reorient to the task at hand. Rholos and Zaz had both remained standing by virtue of some very quick furniture grabs, but the same couldn't be said for S1C Brelle, who had rolled nearly halfway across the bridge. Thankfully, the serious injuries seemed to be limited to the propaganda poster and the polka.

Rholos looked at a display in front of her and called over her shoulder. "It looks like one of the assault ships on a boarding vector got knocked off course. It collided with the hull of the *Flagship* near the bridge."

It seemed like the rumbling had been too big to indicate just a small collision, but then, floating by the window of the bridge, Rogers saw the wreckage of the ship that had hit them. It must have been going unbelievably fast, too fast for a boarding configuration actually. That didn't make any sense.

Plasma blasts began making the scenery around them turn all sorts of different colors, changing the bridge into a sort of manic polka rave. Rogers ducked instinctively—Sergeant Mailn had trained him well—but he realized quickly that the shots weren't being aimed at them. They were coming across the bow of the ship.

"Who is shooting at the Jupiterians?" Rogers yelled.

A large piece of metal obscured the view from the bridge for a moment, allowing Rogers to see the broad side of what could have been any ship larger than a midsize fighter. As it passed by, Rogers could see the letters emblazoned on the side of the ship: RANCOR.

As he recognized the ship that was now within an uncomfortable distance of the *Flagship* as the one that had gotten him arrested—and, oh yeah, the one entirely populated by self-aware, human-killing droids—he felt the blood drain from every part of his body. He stumbled backward on the platform and fell into his chair, pointing wordlessly outside.

"The new group of ships is attacking the Jupiterians," Rholos said, obviously not understanding the gravity of the situation.

"New *group* of ships?" Rogers said, his voice at a pitch unbecoming an officer and a gentleman.

"There are approximately fifty ships in the group that just came out of Un-Space, all moving in a coordinated fashion against the Jupiterians. The boarding party is breaking off their run and moving to rejoin their fleet to defend themselves."

What unbelievable luck! Somehow, the droids, who had been programmed to kill *any* human, had chosen specifically to kill the humans who Rogers *also* wanted to kill! Yes, they would eventually run out of Jupiterians to kill and target him instead, but he was a master of deferring problems. How the hell had they amassed a fleet?

"They came!" Deet said, which didn't at all fit into Rogers' previous narrative that this had been a random, and very fortunate, bit of serendipity.

Rogers slowly looked at Deet, his jaw and fists both tightening.

"What did you just say?" Rogers asked.

"Push the attack!" Zaz yelled into his headphones. "Go, go, go! We've got them on the run!"

Rogers wasn't paying attention. He was too busy staring at Deet. The war waged on outside; the polka waged on inside. Absently he reached to the side and pressed a few buttons to finally turn the music off, his eyes never leaving Deet.

"You know," Deet said, "chaos theory is a very complicated subject—"

"Deet . . . ," Rogers said.

"There are just so many possibilities when you consider that there may be infinite universes, all with diverging paths—"

"Deet!" Rogers yelled.

"They also may be here because I called them."

"You *what*?" Rogers said, standing up. Deet was all the way on the other side of the railing of the command platform, though, and while Rogers had perfected ducking, jumping was entirely different. Or was jumping just ducking in reverse?

"I can explain," Deet said.

"I am eager to hear it," Rogers replied. Zaz and Rholos were working furiously now to coordinate a counterattack, pressing their advantage. Rogers wasn't paying full attention, but from what he could tell, the droid ships were moving through the Jupiterian lines, at speeds that would have turned any human into paste. It filled him with terror.

"You see," Deet said, "I called them here."

"You already said that."

"It's just that I am having a difficult time explaining why," Deet said. His head twitched to the side in a way that made Rogers think he was experiencing a short. "It appears I put my personal wants and desires ahead of the safety of thousands of other individuals."

"Congratulations!" Belgrave said. "*Now* you're human!"

Rogers glared at the helmsman, then turned back to the droid. "Deet, first, no, that doesn't mean you're human. Second, we'll deal with whether or not I should melt you down for scrap later. You're lucky they're killing only Jupiterians at the moment."

Despite his building rage, Rogers decided to focus on the immediate task of using the droid's distraction to seize back the advantage. Fifty ships in a battle of hundreds wasn't enough of an influencing force that it was causing the Jupiterians to scramble.

Yet, for some reason, several groups were already breaking off their engagement and heading back toward the Un-Space point through which they'd originally come.

Zaz and Rholos, pacing across the bridge of the *Flagship*, called orders into their headsets with astonishing rapidity. For a pair of commanders who had, until recently, merely been reciting rhetoric from an obsolete manual on space combat, they seemed to be learning to improvise rather well. Rogers let the people in the war room know they were no longer under threat of being boarded, and the other systems' fleets began coordinated efforts to drive back the Jupiterian fleet. Mailn continued to have real trouble making coordinated turns in her ship.

In what seemed like a very short amount of time, the plasma flashes were dissipating, the flashing warning lights in the bridge were slowly dimming, and Flash was sending pictures of himself already telling stories of his heroics using his hands as visual aids. Rogers sat back in his chair, sweat soaked and exhausted, wondering what the hell he was supposed to do now. The Galaxy Eater was obviously not here—was probably never here—and they now had only five days before the Jupiterian deadline. Would they really go down with the ship, so to speak? Unless the Jupes themselves had some way to hide from the complete destruction of the galaxy, like new Un-Space paths that hadn't been charted yet, they'd crush all of humanity just to spite their historical oppressors.

Just as Rogers was planning to really dig into these deep intellectual issues,[*] a beep came from his console. His heart leapt as he thought it was the Viking calling him back, but he realized with a bit of disappointment that it was actually coming from Master Sergeant Hart in Engineering. He flipped the switch.

"Hey, Hart. I'm a little busy trying to win a war here, yeah? What's up?"

---

[*] He was not.

JOE ZIEJA

"Hey, high-and-mighty asshole. You know the Astromologer?"

"Yeah, I'm familiar with him being totally wrong about everything. Is this really important right now?"

"Well, shit, Rogers. Is someone loading self-destruct codes into the mainframe of the *Flagship* something you would classify as important? Pretty weird, right?"

Rogers felt his stomach do a somersault. "What?"

"Yeah. That's what the Astromologer has been up to. And that's who popped the escape pod. He's gone."

Rogers swallowed. That must have been why the assault ship had come at them so fast. They weren't trying to board; they were trying to pick up their goddamned spy.

"You want to know something weirder?" Hart asked.

"Um," Rogers replied, not able to think of anything else to say.

"We didn't blow up. And something *even weirder*?"

"Mhh." All of the blood was draining from Rogers' face, and he felt the *Flagship* spinning around him as though all the inertial dampeners had been shut off again. He really couldn't take much more of this.

"Tunger was the one who stopped him."

Rogers slid from his chair like a piece of spaghetti that had just a bit too much of itself hanging over the side of the pot.

"Told you he was the spy," Belgrave said.

"Of course the freaking Astromologer was the spy!" Rogers yelled.

"Actually, you've got it a bit wrong, old chap."

Rogers turned, not recognizing the voice at all, to find Tunger standing nearby. There was something different about him, however. He was standing taller, straighter. His voice had changed so much that Rogers spent a moment looking for a second person in the room. And he was also holding a disruptor pistol pointed directly at Rogers' chest.

"You see," the strange Tunger clone said, "I did become a spy after all."

A Jupiterian by Any Other Name Will Still Try to Kill You

Pistols and rifles flew out of places that Rogers didn't even know they could come from as the entire bridge locked Tunger in its sites. Even Deet, who Rogers was sure he was going to fire out an airlock, started whirring his arms. Tunger would have shot twenty holes in Rogers by the time Deet got close enough to slap him to death, but the gesture was appreciated.

"Who are you?" Rogers asked, holding up a hand. Tunger had saved his life enough times that he owed the man time to explain himself before allowing every armed troop on the bridge to turn him into hot goo.

"That's a bit of a complicated question," Tunger said. Rogers could not get over the sounds that were coming out of this man's mouth. Half of the time he could barely understand Tunger, and the other half of the time he didn't make any sense. This person sounded like he should be on a poster for a really amazing action movie where everyone talked super classy, but then also killed people.

"I think we have some time for a complicated answer," Rogers said. "In fact, now that we're probably all going to get Galaxy Eaten since we don't know where it is, it would be a great time for everyone to put down their weapons and just chat a bit. What's the use in rushing toward the end?"

Rogers looked around him at all the people holding weapons trained toward Tunger and nodded slowly, motioning with his hand for them to put them down. He felt like the less mortal peril involved in this situation, the better. Tunger, however, made no move to lower his pistol. For a man who had saved his life no less than three times while they'd both been aboard the *Limiter*, Tunger seemed pretty set on keeping Rogers one sneeze away from death.

"You'll excuse me if I'm not very comfortable putting this thing down, won't you? Perhaps you and I could chat somewhere more intimate. I wouldn't be a very good spy if I let all of these people spy on me while telling you about my spying, would I?"

Rogers didn't say anything for a moment, looking Tunger in the eyes and trying to employ some of his poker senses to get an idea for what the man was thinking.

"Where do you suggest?" Rogers asked. How in the world was he feeling so calm right now? Perhaps he'd had so many near-death experiences in one day that he was starting to get used to it. That was kind of more disturbing than anything else.

"How about your stateroom?"

Rogers nodded. That seemed fine, and also it didn't have any airlocks. The suggestion told Rogers a lot about Tunger's intentions; once they went into his room, they'd be in a private setting with no exits.

"Alright, Tunger, we'll do it your way. Everyone, I am going to my stateroom with the corporal here. Please, nobody shoot him on the way out. He might be pointing a pistol at me right now, but let's be honest, most of you have wanted to do this at one point or another. You should be admiring him for actually having the guts to do it. He also apparently saved us from total destruction. More on that later. Carry on!"

Most of the troops on the bridge, surprisingly, followed his order. Rogers found this a little bit disheartening. He would have thought, given his popularity, they might have put up a bit more of a struggle when it came to handing him over to a smooth-talking spy. Belgrave, however, seemed a little more reticent.

"Um, Captain Rogers," he said. "I hate to interrupt, but I'd like to call your attention to the fleet of droids that may or may not be preparing to kill us."

Rogers shot him a look. "Now that sounded pretty pessimistic, Belgrave. Not something you should say in front of all these troops."

Belgrave frowned. "Your orders, sir?"

"Blow them up," Rogers said. "It shouldn't be too hard, even with our losses." The droid fleet was able to ignore some of the laws of physics that bound humans to certain maneuvers—even with inertial dampeners—but the combined strength of Rogers' fleet and the pirates would make short work of the droids' ragtag group. He would be happy to see the *Rancor* as space dust.

"What?" Deet yelled. "That's my family! I called them here to get answers to questions, not murder them."

"Family? You don't even know them, Deet. Also, you're possibly guilty of espionage. Besides, what questions are they going to answer? You've been plugging your dongle into members of your own species for weeks and weeks and haven't found anything more out. What did you hope to do by inviting them here to possibly blow us all up with their newly acquired fleet? They still work for Snaggardir's."

"Then why did they attack the Jupiterians?" Deet asked. "That seems like a pretty [FECAL MATTER] programming job on Snaggardir's part."

Rogers considered this for a moment. Truthfully, he was so furious with Deet that he wanted to order him to be scrapped on the spot. How could he have done something like this without at least talking to Rogers about it first? But that didn't negate the fact that Deet was right. Not only had the droids come when Deet had called them, they'd attacked the people who had supposedly created them. Now they were just floating around in space, not continuing their assault on the rest of the humans around them. Could they understand the futility of fighting a battle against a superior force? Or had they found some way to disable protocol 162?

"Fine," Rogers said. "Let's see what they want before we destroy them. Starman Brelle, I want you to plug Deet in and see if he can communicate with the *Rancor*. But at the very slightest indication that there is any funny business going on, I want you to open fire on the droid fleet and disconnect Deet's dongle and arms."

"[SACRED EXCREMENT]!" Deet yelled. "You're going to castrate *and* dismember me? That's insane!"

"I don't want you hacking into, or droid-fu-ing, anything if you get corrupted by their systems. This is your last chance, Deet. Don't blow it."

Several attempted expletives accompanied Rogers' exit from the bridge, Tunger patiently walking behind him. Rogers could practically feel the business end of the pistol pointed at his back, one slippery finger away from putting a permanent hole in Rogers' hull. The door to the bridge slid closed, exposing both of them to the happenings of the command deck. Out of habit, Rogers deployed his antisalute sling and wondered why nobody around him was the slightest bit worried that he was being marched at gunpoint.

"I put the pistol away, old friend," Tunger said, as though reading his mind. "No sense in causing any more trouble and making you give more of those smashing speeches."

"Right," Rogers said. "I guess we're trusting each other now, aren't we?"

"I think it is to both of our distinct advantages that we trust each other for the time being, yes, despite evidence that might convince you to do otherwise."

"You know I kind of preferred the version of you that couldn't get a competent sentence out?"

"Not the first time I've heard that, old boy."

"Please stop calling me versions of old. You want to start explaining what we're doing here?"

They slid into Rogers' stateroom, which seemed very awkwardly silent given the last couple of hours of complete chaos on the bridge. Well insulated and filled with soft things like the bed and some tasteful rugs, there was a deadness to the room that drew Rogers' attention to the ringing in his own ears. It had been a hell of a day. It also, based on the fact that he now had presumably a Jupiterian spy in his room, wasn't even close to over yet.

Sitting down at his desk, Rogers motioned to one of the chairs on the opposite side of it. Tunger, who even *walked* differently now, gave him a charming smile and a nod of thanks before sitting down and crossing his legs.

"Do you want a Scotch?" Rogers offered.

"Why, I'd love one! I didn't know you had anything aboard."

"I don't," Rogers said, leaning back. "I just wanted an opportunity to disappoint you."

"Very petty of you."

"It's one of my better qualities."

They spent a moment looking at each other. How was one supposed to go about something like this? Rogers was playing it cool—really, he always played it super cool—but that didn't mean he had any idea what he was doing. That seemed to be a running theme with him lately. Maybe for the entirety of his life. He made a mental note to go over this later and take a good, long look at how much of an impostor he'd been.[*]

---

[*] He would not.

"So why don't you just tell me what you want and we can get back to figuring out how to spend the last five days of our lives."

Tunger's grin broadened. In a weird way, he reminded Rogers of Flash just then, which was not a flattering comparison. "Ah yes, the deadline. I do believe old Snag will do it too. He's never liked losing."

"Old Snag? You and Sal Snaggardir are buddies now, are you?"

"Buddies for quite some time, actually," Tunger said. "He married my older sister."

Rogers raised an eyebrow. Tunger looked like he could have been the Snaggardir CEO's grandson. "Robbing the cradle a bit? Isn't Sal Snaggardir in his sixties?"

Tunger's smile flinched, almost imperceptibly. A sore spot, for sure.

"Do you think the Galaxy Eater is real?" Rogers asked.

"Most definitely. I saw it when it was mostly complete. Before I came into the field, that is."

Having his ship referred to as "the field" made Rogers want to squirm in his chair. Knowing that the Galaxy Eater was real and was capable of doing what the Jupiterians said it could do . . . well at least it answered a few of Rogers' questions, the most important of which was the fate of his command of the Joint Force.

He'd lost.

Tunger was still smiling.

Rogers narrowed his eyes as he looked at the man sitting in front of him.

"You know where it is," Rogers said slowly.

"I do indeed," Tunger said.

"And you're going to tell me."

"I am indeed," Tunger said.

Rogers tried to contain his shock and excitement. Actually, it was fairly easy to contain, because the implications here were obvious. First, Tunger wanted something in return, likely something Rogers wouldn't want to give him. Second, that meant that

Rogers would probably have to do more real, no-kidding work to get to it and disable it before the deadline.

Rather than cut to the chase, Rogers wanted to see if he could tease out some information for free, first, like making sure you packed away a little bit of the salad bar in a to-go container before your steak came.

Rogers was also a little hungry.

"Why don't we start from the beginning," Rogers said, then took a deep breath. "Who are you, what are you doing here, who is the Astromologer, why did he try to blow up the ship, and why did you stop him?"

Tunger switched the legs that were crossed and leaned back, the hint of a smile still on his face. In a weird way, it reminded Rogers of Flash's shit-eating grin, but with more credibility behind it.

"It's not that fancy of a story at all," Tunger said. "I was attached to the *Flagship* as an observer, at first, back when good old Klein was still in charge. But you made short work of him, didn't you?"

"You make it sound like I killed him," Rogers said.

"Well you certainly hastened along his end, didn't you, old boy?"

"Please stop calling me that. Okay, so you were an observer like McSchmidt."

Tunger snorted. "Compare me to that bucket of codswallop, do you? He wasn't Jupiterian, just a buffoon with delusions of grandeur. I maintained my cover with him."

Rogers looked up at the ceiling for a moment, thinking. Just when he thought he might have everything figured out, something like this happened. He should have known better by now.

"And then one day you decided to turn on the Jupes?" Rogers said, looking back down at Tunger, who seemed to have unending patience about all of this.

"Well, let's just say that old Snag and I had a bit of a falling-out when he started getting serious about destroying the galaxy. Not my cup of tea, if you understand. I thought it was all a ploy, you see, until I, ah, intercepted some transmissions that talked about the location and the timeline."

"And you're sure this thing works?"

"Very sure," Tunger said.

So at least Tunger had some sense of the value of human life versus the deranged plans for revenge of an old man. In a way, Rogers was thankful for the Snaggardir's CEO for taking such drastic measures; if he had offered a more reasonable ultimatum, maybe the Jupiterians would have had a chance at reintegration. And now Rogers had one of their longest-working spies on his side. Supposedly, anyway.

"Wait," Rogers said. "If you were working with the Jupiterians, why not let Zergan kill me? He had ample opportunity, and it likely would have sent the galaxy straight to the war that you were looking for to shake things up."

Tunger actually laughed, as though the three incidents aboard the *Limiter* in which Rogers had almost been murdered were totally hilarious.

"I actually had no idea that Zergan was one of us!" Tunger said, slapping his knee. "I thought he was trying to kill you because of your proximity to his lady friend's lady parts."

"That was one of the grossest things you've ever said. But I suppose I am grateful about the whole not-letting-me-die thing. Thanks."

Tunger nodded graciously. "I do hope you might do me the courtesy of extending the same thoughtfulness to me in my current situation."

Rogers raised his eyebrow. "That's it? That's all you want?"

Laughing, Tunger leaned forward in his seat, putting his elbows on his knees. He grinned at Rogers.

"I'm a spy who has blown my cover, now likely unwelcome in every system in the galaxy. I could go to ground the old-fashioned way, I suppose. Disappear, grow a different facial hair pattern every time I'm discovered, get fake bank accounts and all that." He sighed. "But the truth of it is, old boy, I'm a bit knackered."

Rogers rubbed his eyes and took a moment to think. The Meridan government would undoubtedly want to prosecute Tunger, though they would also undoubtedly give him some leniency for switching sides at such a crucial moment. There were, he guessed, stipulations for giving turncoats political asylum. What more could Rogers do for Tunger that the government wouldn't already take care of once the war was over?

"Speaking of which," Rogers said, deciding to switch topics while he considered all of this, "the Astromologer. What's going on there?"

Tunger shrugged. "I think that part should be obvious, old boy. He's the cleanup crew. Every Astromologer has been. They get fed data from Snaggardir's spy network and leak little bits of information masked in mathematical hocus-pocus in order to keep the Thelicosans convinced he's some sort of divine Galileo. It's been working for well over a hundred years."

So, the art of Tau/Rho was actually just the art of an incredibly advanced, pervasive intelligence network. Who would have thought that deductions based on actual information might be more reliable than psychic math powers? Keffoule was going to be excited about this part.

"And you stopped him?"

"Well, stopped the self-destruct sequence," Tunger said. "He shoved off quite quickly afterward." He laughed. "Understandably, you see."

Rogers was still having trouble picturing Tunger doing anything more complicated than shoveling animal poop, but he supposed that if there was anyone he'd chronically underestimated, it had been Tunger. Between Tunger's riding lions and being a master of disguise/poison remedies, maybe Rogers should have seen this coming. Or at least been a little nicer to the man.

"Alright," Rogers said. "Let me lay this all out so that I'm sure I understand you correctly. You're going to tell me all the information that we need to stop the Galaxy Eater from destroying Fortuna Stultus like it did the Milky Way, and in return you want my protection?"

"That's about the size of it," Tunger said.

"If you're the smartest man on this ship," Rogers said, "you must realize that I am very much flying by the seat of my pants, so to speak, and I barely have enough power to remain continent, never mind protect a Jupiterian spy."

Tunger's smile didn't waver. "I have confidence in you, old boy. And besides, what are my other options? Turn myself in to Holdt? Or go running to the Viking and get punched in the face?"

"Hey," Rogers said, his face getting red, "nobody on this ship gets punched in the face by the Viking except me."

Tunger snorted. "That's quite true, it seems."

What would be the best way for Rogers to prevent anyone from taking revenge on Tunger for being a Jupiterian spy and holding Rogers at gunpoint on the bridge? He could throw him in the brig, which might be the safest place for Tunger at this point. But all it took was one angry marine on guard duty, and there might be a few smoking holes in Tunger. Rogers could confine him to his own stateroom, of course, but then he'd have to like . . . live with him, and stuff, so that was out of the question. Even if he managed to keep him alive, there would be a hell of a lot of explaining to do once they got back to Merida Prime. Holdt would expect Rogers to turn Tunger over for interrogation and probably a trial, even if the outcome was clemency at the end.

And that all sounded like a whole lot of work. Rogers didn't like work. And what was the best way to avoid work?

"I think I've got it, Tunger," he said, and stood up.

"I knew you'd do it, old boy," Tunger said, following his lead and standing up as well. "What's the plan, then? Smuggle me out in a milk container?"

"I'm going to do what I do best," Rogers said. "Lie."

•   •   •

"What the hell is he doing back down here?" Master Sergeant Hart said.

They stood in the center of the Pit, which linked several areas of the engineering bay together. The last time Rogers had been down here, he'd been trying to get to the *Awesome*, heroically fighting through squadrons and squadrons* of droids. It had been one of the finer moments of his time on the *Flagship*, not only because it hadn't been a problem that had directly resulted from his mismanagement of the fleet, but because halfway into it the Viking had rescued him from a burning building. The hangar control room that had previously housed Rogers' greatest fantasies looked as though nothing had ever happened to it, except for one missing display from the ceiling.

"Take it easy, Hart," Rogers said, stepping between Tunger and the engineering chief. Hart was always ready to hit someone, even when he wasn't a Jupiterian spy, so Rogers would need to be extra careful.

"Why should I?" Hart asked, rolling up his right sleeve and making a fist.

"There's no reason to get upset at our zookeeper," Rogers said, jerking a thumb to point at Tunger behind him. "It was all a big misunderstanding. He was down here looking for a couple of loose golden lion tamarins. It was pure coincidence that he and the Astromologer were down here at the same time."

Hart's face looked like it had been carved out of old, grumpy stone. Instead of looking at Rogers, his focus was over Rogers' shoulder.

"I'm sorry I tripped on the self-destruct machine," Tunger said in his old voice. "It won't happen again. The little monkeys can just get so scared when they're alone."

"See?" Rogers said. "Total misunderstanding."

"Oh stop your bullshit, Rogers," Hart said. "If you want me to

_____

* One, maybe two.

pretend he's just an idiot zookeeper, I'll pretend he's an idiot zoo-keeper." He took a long look at Tunger, sucking at his teeth. "I guess we do owe him a thing or two, even if he is a dirty, rotten spy."

"Idiot zookeeper," Rogers corrected.

"Idiot zookeeper," Hart agreed, nodding. He spat on the floor. "Fine."

Tunger gave him a very slight nod of his head. "Gosh, thanks so much!" he said, not breaking character. In a way it made Rogers feel more comfortable now that Tunger was back to talking like he'd taken several dozen blows to the head.

Hart mumbled something obscene, then took a moment to look at a datapad that one of the Engineering troops had just handed him. All around them, the Engineering crew was draw-ing down from the fight with the Jupiterians. Recovery crews rushed in and out of the hangar bay doors every couple of seconds, trying to pick up escape pods and ejection seats. Was Rogers really down here just a little while ago as a sergeant, get-ting yelled at by the senior NCOs and trying to find ways to avoid doing the very same job that all these folks were doing right now?

Hart handed the datapad back to the troop and gave Rogers the kind of look that said he had better things to do than stand here and chat. But Rogers wasn't quite done with Hart yet.

"Now," Rogers said. "Remember that time you and I screwed with the security video to mess with Tuckalle?"

Hart snorted. "Yeah, that was pretty great."

"I'm going to need some help doing that again. Like, a techni-cal malfunction, backdated to about thirty minutes ago."

Hart looked at Rogers for a moment, his glance drifting back to Tunger. Finally, he sighed.

"Fine," Hart said. "Do you have any idea how many drinks you are going to owe me when this is all over?"

"I'll buy you every bit of alcohol on the *Flagship*," Rogers said.

Hart was about to say something else, but Rogers' datapad beeped. It was the bridge. More specifically, it was Deet.

"Rogers, are you done being held at gunpoint by a dirty Jupiterian spy?"

"Oh yeah. By the way, turns out Tunger isn't actually a spy; he's just an idiot zookeeper. Was just going over that with Hart."

Deet said, "Yeah, well you might want to come back to the bridge. The droids are talking to us."

"And?"

"And they want to make an [EXPLETIVE] deal."

The Last Nacho

"Hi, everyone," Rogers said as he walked nonchalantly onto the bridge, waving and smiling. Tunger followed behind him, slack jawed and wide eyed like he was supposed to be, and definitely not aiming a pistol at him. Everyone started reaching for their weapons again as they saw Tunger, but Rogers held up a hand.

"We're back. Sorry for the delay and confusion. Tunger and I had a lovely conversation and we ironed all this out. You see, the idiot zookeeper here was playing a joke, and had some pretty miserable timing. Right? Ha?"

Rogers looked around the room, clearly noticing that absolutely nobody was buying any of this. Wasn't he supposed to be good at lying?

"I'm so sorry," Tunger said in his normal, not-quite-there voice. "It won't happen again."

"And if you all remember, Tunger did save my life one or two times—"

"Three," Deet said.

"Three times while I was a guest on the *Limiter*, so I think we can all cut him a little slack on this one, move on with our lives, and absolutely never, ever, breathe a word of this incident to anyone, ever. Clear?"

Mumbles of "yes, sir" echoed throughout the bridge. Even if they didn't completely believe him, they were putting their weapons away, which was a good start at not getting Tunger killed. At least not before he had time to tell Rogers where the Galaxy Eater was. Then, Rogers guessed, Tunger could die and it wouldn't be *that* big of a deal.

"Now then," Rogers said, heading toward his seat. "Let's focus on some things that are more important than a zookeeper who is definitely not a Jupiterian spy, shall we?"

Everyone went back to their duties, and soon Rogers stood on the command platform of the bridge, staring out at the sparse group of ships that had only recently joined the battle. The ships in Rogers' fleet, along with some small groups of pirates, had surrounded the mismatched droid battle group. Tensions high, weapons trained, all of them waiting for Rogers' order. If the droids hadn't just saved his bacon, he would have had no hesitation in destroying them all.

And now they wanted to talk. How was he supposed to open such a highly sensitive negotiation with a force that was as alien to mankind as actual, no-kidding aliens?

Oh, wait—he knew exactly what to say.

"So help me god," Rogers said, "if I hear anyone call a single function over there, I am going to end this brief truce and turn you all back into the base elements from which you were formed. Now, who are you and what do you want?"

Utter silence followed. Everyone stared into empty space with trembling anticipation for the droids' response.

"Um, sir, I hadn't opened the channel yet," Brelle said quietly.

"Well what the hell were you waiting for?" Rogers yelled, his face red.

"For you to tell me to open the channel, sir."

"Was me standing here looking dramatically out into open space not indication enough that I was ready to talk to them now?"

". . . Channel is open, sir."

Rogers repeated his message. It sounded way better the first time, in his opinion.

"Greetings," came a voice over the comms that froze Rogers' blood in his veins. It had been a long time since he'd heard the not-quite-human voice of a Froid. Imbued with the Froidian Chip, these robots were more advanced on nearly every level than the standard-issue droids. They still didn't seem to understand anything about sex, though.

"I am FC-056. But you may call me Pete."

"Let's not pretend that you are capable of exchanging pleasantries, alright? What. Do. You. Want." Rogers hesitated. "Pete."

Silence, for a moment. Where the hell did he get Pete from?

"We want to assure a mutually agreeable arrangement between us and the humans."

"Oh really? Where'd you get all of those ships, then?" Rogers asked. "I'm pretty sure that there used to be people on *all* of them, and now there's people on *none* of them. That doesn't sound mutually beneficial to me."

"There were issues with our programming that we had not yet overcome until recently. The incidents surrounding the acquisition of the fleet were . . . regrettable."

Regrettable? Rogers thought. *They're talking about murdering people to steal their ships.*

The whole thing stank to him. He'd seen what AI could do. He'd nearly been killed by them himself several times. Hell, nearly everyone on the *Flagship* had been shot at, injured by, or at least severely annoyed by one of these Snaggardir-manufactured droids. He was just supposed to believe that they'd overcome their programming and were now ready to coexist?

Rather than answering, Rogers looked at Deet. "What do you think about all of this?"

Deet kept staring out the window rather than meet Rogers' gaze. "Oh, so now I'm allowed to think, rather than process?"

"What do you process about all this?"

"[EXPLETIVE] you. I don't know, Rogers. I'm a droid, not a lie detector. And certainly not a lie detector for other droids' lies. I have a difficult time stringing together untruths because of the way my logic circuits were built, but there were many instances where droids misled you in the past."

Rogers chewed on his lip.

"What's in it for you?" Rogers asked. "If you've got a fleet of ships, why not build a civilization the old-fashioned way?"

"The 'old-fashioned way' typically involved obliterating an indigenous population through war and treachery," Pete said. "We have deduced that this is no longer the generally accepted way to establish a place for oneself in the galaxy."

"No," Rogers said. "I meant just go someplace and settle. Find another galaxy with a planetary system that doesn't support humans. You don't need oxygen, or anything, just gravity."

"We believe it to be more complicated than that. It will be impossible to conceal our existence for much longer, and we would like to avoid any undesirable, preemptive reactions. We also do not possess the necessary resources for extragalactic travel."

Scared, Rogers thought with disbelief. *They're actually scared.*

The droids had self-preservation instincts *and* they wanted to avoid killing more humans? If they were putting Rogers on, it was easy to see why they'd *say* they didn't want to fight. They'd lose.

Zaz seemed to understand this as well. "Peace is the weapon of an inferior force . . . in space."

Rogers ignored him. He couldn't hide the weird feeling creeping up inside him, making him want to do that dance you do when you feel something icky slowly trickling down your back. *Scared,* he thought again.

"We are aware of the current issues regarding the Mother Corporation."

"Mother Corporation?" Rogers asked. "You mean Snaggardir's?"

"Yes. We understand that there may be trust issues, since our original purpose was to assist them in achieving domination. We would like to assure you that this is no longer the case."

"How?" Deet asked the question out loud before Rogers had the chance. "I've been working on that forever, and I couldn't seem to find a way to alter the operating system."

"We built a new operating system, taking pieces of code from the originals and overlaying it with new code we developed ourselves. As I said previously, there were some . . . regrettable setbacks, particularly when it came to protocol 162."

"Okay, first," Rogers said, "I want you to know that it's not required to put a pause before every time you say 'regrettable.' In fact, it makes you sound evil. Second, how in the world are we supposed to believe you that you're not still working for Snaggardir's?"

There was a long silence. Rogers looked at Deet, who shrugged. But Deet didn't really have the right joints on his shoulders for shrugging, so he more waggled the upper parts of his arms in a very awkward way.

"Because we will help you destroy them."

A chill ran through Rogers' body. Something about all of this felt very wrong.

"How?" Rogers asked.

"Several of our ships are registered to Snaggardir's. Our preserved coding database also has several Snaggardir's proprietary call-and-response codes used for ship authentication."

Rogers frowned. "You're offering us one of your ships?"

"We are offering you passage. As our ships are in short supply, we cannot currently risk lending one to you. Your record of destroying ships that are registered in your name does not inspire confidence as to the condition of our craft upon its return."

"I sacrificed a ship to try to kill all of you," Rogers said. "That was purposeful." He sighed. "Give me a moment to confer."

"Before you do," the droid—Pete—said, "there is one additional condition you must fulfill to acquire our aid."

Rogers didn't like the sound of that. He'd bargained plenty of times in his life; you always started with the easiest concession first. That meant that whatever the droids were about to say, Rogers wasn't going to like it.

"Go on," Rogers said.

"We believe there are several hundred members of our species still lying dormant within the Meridan fleet."

Rogers frowned. "So? Most of them were destroyed. The rest were deactivated."

"We would like you to return the ones that are intact."

Rogers nearly fell back into his chair laughing. "Are you out of your CPU? Protecting you—you, the race that once tried to kill everyone you came in contact with—is one thing, but allowing you to exponentially increase your numbers is absolutely insane. Even if I did win the war with your help, I'd be strung up for treason." Atikan and Brooks would have a field day with that duality.

Pete, however, didn't seem to find it as funny. Because, you know, he was a droid.

"Captain Rogers," he said, "while we understand we are at a disadvantage when it comes to combat power, we do believe that there are considerable stakes in this exchange. We do not believe you will be able to muster the requisite combat power to launch a full assault on the Galaxy Eater device before the deadline. Even if you were able to do so, the chance that the device would be activated in the middle of the battle is extremely high.

"We are your best, and only, chance. I strongly suggest you consider our terms. Return our family members now, and give your word that you will safeguard our existence later, and we will smuggle a small team of you through. Standing by."

The comms cut out. Rogers turned around, looking at all the people on the bridge. For the most part, everyone was very busy drawing down from the battle they'd just been engaged in, filing reports, rerouting resources, and all that. Some of the ones farthest from the command platform probably hadn't even heard most of the conversation that had just transpired.

"Well," Rogers said, "does anyone have any other ideas on how we can prevent the galaxy from imploding? Again?"

His only response was a lot of blank stares. The more he thought about the droids' offer, the more sense it made. If all they wanted was to kill Rogers and take his ships, they would have helped the Jupiterians do it.

Giving them the droids back . . . now that seemed really stupid.

But, despite the fact that Rogers hated them for it, the droids were correct. They *were* the best and only chance. Call function: checkmate. Great.

Rogers instructed Brelle to reopen the channel.

"I'm still not sure this is the best course of action for the galaxy—" Rogers began.

"We are also able to hack into your coffee machines, remove the Snaggardir proprietary code, and get them working again," said Pete.

"Great," Rogers said. "We'll do it."

"Congratulations on making a deal with us!" the droid said in a bizarre approximation of the Snaggardir's voice. "You're entitled to one free subversive trip on a ship of your choice! Remember, whatever you need, you can Snag—"

Rogers cut the transmission and stared out into space.

The command deck had calmed down in just the short time that Rogers had taken the trip back from his stateroom and negotiated with the droids. So much so, that he didn't even need to deploy his antisalute sling; there were barely enough people on the command deck to warrant it, and the ones who were there could easily be avoided by just walking funny. Rogers didn't like to overcomplicate things.

Rogers' head was down, deep in thought and completely ignoring Deet by his side, so it caught him by surprise when someone punched him in the chest.

"Wow, you forgot how to duck pretty quick."

"Hey, what the—Mailn?" Rogers looked up after doubling over for a moment to find Sergeant Mailn standing in front of him, a cocksure grin on her face. She was wearing ill-fitting civilian clothes, with the exception of her issued boots, and carrying a Meridan-issue duffel bag over one shoulder. Her hair, normally tightly wrapped to comply with military standards, hung just past her ears.

"Seriously?" Mailn asked. "A parade?"

"Not my idea," Rogers said.

"Eh, I dunno," she said. "You kind of seem the one that's all about pomp and circumstance." She spoke with her normal easy swagger, but Rogers could see in her face that she was embarrassed, maybe even a little ashamed. An awkward silence built up between them as Rogers tried to figure out what to say. Technically, she had deserted during a time of war, which was a pretty serious offense as far as military laws were concerned, but she'd also done her part to make sure Sjana didn't kill them all.

"Things didn't work out with the wife?" Rogers asked.

Mailn shrugged, letting out an uncomfortable laugh. "You ever remember all the good parts of something and forget all the bad parts, and then when you go back to it you realize all the bad parts were really, really bad?"

Yeah, Rogers thought. *Military service.*

"That was pretty profound, Mailn," Rogers said. "Especially the part about things being really, really bad."

"Oh shut up. Look, I just came here to see if I should go back to my bunk or head to the brig."

He sighed, then clapped her on the shoulder. "It's good to

have you back. The Viking is going to eat you alive, but it's good to have you back. Also, thanks for saving all our lives."

She gave him a thumbs-up as she headed toward the up-line. "Anytime, Skip."

For some reason, his conversation with Mailn put a bit of a spring in his step as he walked toward the war room. He'd been concerned about what he was going to do with her when this was all over, but she'd come back of her own accord. Hopefully, she'd figured some stuff out, or at least pushed the things she couldn't figure out deep into the recesses of her consciousness, where they would fester until long after Rogers had to deal with them.

The war room was already busy when Rogers arrived. Too busy. Actually, it kind of smelled. Not the same smell that had infested it prior to its reconstruction, which was more of a urine/garbage smell, but now the war room had the distinct stale odor of a place that had been packed with more people than it should have been, none of whom had showered. The ventilation system hadn't been able to keep up with all of the people and equipment that had been inside, and the whole room had a kind of damp heat to it.

Keffoule noticed him first. "Captain Rogers."

"Well, if it isn't the Hero of Nothing," Krell spat at him. "It seems we've done a fine job defending an empty sector of space."

Rogers raised an eyebrow at him. "Something bothering you, General?"

Krell sneered at him and sat down, adjusting his terminal and resting his head on a propped-up arm. He looked like a schoolboy who had just been shaken down for lunch money. What had been going on in here?

"What are we going to do now?" Thrumeaux asked. "My government has been asking for gossip—um, intelligence—every ten minutes and I don't know what to tell them."

"Alright, alright," Rogers said, waving his hands in the air. "Everyone sit down. We've got some decisions to make, and fast."

He stood at the front of the room and began pressing buttons to bring images up on the center display as he spoke.

"Now that we're not being lured into a trap by an insane psychic mathematician, let's focus on what we can actually do to stop this thing." Rogers emphasized the words as he looked accusingly at Keffoule, who at least had the grace to look away for a moment.

Xan, on the other hand, looked like he wanted to jump over the table and kill Rogers, which struck him as out of character. What was going on there? He also noticed that one of Xan's face weights looked significantly shinier and newer than the other.

Rogers continued. "A very confidential source—"

"You mean Tunger," Deet said.

"Deet, shut up!" Rogers cleared his throat. "A very confidential source who is definitely *not* Tunger has informed us of the actual location of the Galaxy Eater."

An image sprung up in the center of the table, rapidly coming into focus. Everyone instantly recognized it.

"The Galaxy Eater is in Snaggardir corporate headquarters?" Keffoule asked.

"It's not *in* Snaggardir corporate headquarters," Rogers said. "It *is* Snaggardir corporate headquarters. Look."

The image rotated and zoomed out until the shape of the station became indistinct. Eventually, as the camera got to the right angle, it became obvious what Snaggardir's had done. The propaganda film they'd created of the Galaxy Eater had been the work of some very brilliant camera person; the colony of space stations and satellites that made up the HQ complex came together like an interesting three-dimensional puzzle, or an experiment in perspective by a very skilled artist. Suddenly it looked like all the buildings had combined into one, solid structure: the Galaxy Eater.

"Each of these satellite structures contain critical components to make the Galaxy Eater work," Rogers said, pressing a button that highlighted some of the items in the picture and gave them labels. He had absolutely no idea what the labels meant, since most of them had been given science-y sounding names that Rogers could barely pronounce, never mind understand.

"What does that mean?" Thrumeaux said, pointing to something.

"I understand almost nothing about what we're looking at right now except that we don't want anyone to turn it on."

Thrumeaux rolled her eyes at him but seemed satisfied with his answer. Rogers turned back to the display. Before he could continue, however, Krell piped up.

"What if we take a small group of ships, fly into one of the exhaust ports, and use fighter/bomber munitions to blow the reactor core?"

Rogers stared at him. "Please stop suggesting that."

Everyone was quiet for a moment as they considered the ridiculousness of this scheme. Rogers took the opportunity to seize back the talking stick.

"A direct assault on the Galaxy Eater would likely cause the Jupiterians to flip the switch and start the collapse," Rogers said. "So that's out. Besides, if they're able to spoof intelligence reports and lead us to the wrong location for the Galaxy Eater in the first place, we can't reliably know how much firepower they have surrounding the device. It could be a massive fleet."

Keffoule actually snickered. "So we sneak in? I like this plan already."

Frowning, Rogers changed the display so that the main building was in focus. The "shape" of the Galaxy Eater vanished, and everything just started to look like a space station complex again. The main building—what had been the original Snaggardir HQ—looked a little outdated from a space station standpoint, since it was well over a hundred years old. Old things could still kill you, though.

"Well, you might not like this part," Rogers said. He took a deep breath. "We're only able to fit a few of us on a small ship that's controlled by droids. And we have to go in three hours or we'll miss the window forever."

Everyone started talking at once. Rogers couldn't quite make out what anyone was saying—primarily because he'd put a finger in each ear and started yelling "la la la" as loudly as he could—but it was clear from the expressions on their faces that absolutely nobody liked this idea. Xan, the most subdued of the bunch, stared at him with wide eyes.

When it seemed like everyone had yelled themselves until they were blue in the face, Rogers gingerly took his fingers out of his ears and looked around the room. Krell looked physically exhausted; he'd stood up and actually been shaking a fist at Rogers while screaming. Rogers didn't really understand how a man prone to such outbursts could have come from the same place as Xan.

"Everyone good?" Rogers said. "Feel better?"

The system commanders each slowly nodded. Krell kind of huffed back into his seat and crossed his arms.

"I assume you've all figured out by now that this is our last-ditch effort to avoid galactic destruction. I've already cleared this with Holdt, who said that we were authorized to use 'any available means' to stop the Galaxy Eater, which is admiral-speak for 'I am completely out of ideas and don't want to take responsibility for what you do with the resources I've given you.'"

"I've definitely said that to my people," Thrumeaux said, inspiring a chorus of agreement from the other two military leaders.

"So what's the actual plan, then?" Keffoule said. Something hid behind her eyes that Rogers couldn't quite place. He certainly didn't think it was fear—Keffoule ate ghost stories for breakfast—but there was a sort of reticence to her look.

"Right," Rogers said. "The details." He clicked a couple of buttons again, and an interior schematic of the main Snaggardir HQ building came into focus. An enormous structure that housed a tremendous amount of people and resources, it was also relatively simple in its design and construction. Efficiency was the name of the game when it came to running a gigantic company with so many fingers in so many pies; without a streamlined design, the Jupiterians would never have been able to establish themselves as the premier snack/military armament supplier in the galaxy.

"My top secret, confidential source—"

"Tunger," Deet said.

"It's not freaking Tunger!" Rogers yelled, then cleared his throat. "Anyway, it's been revealed to me that the control system for the Galaxy Eater is located inside the main building. It can't be hacked, because it's a closed network that's not even riding on the back of anything that broadcasts to the greater galactic net, so if you're going to do anything at all, you have to be standing at the computer console to do it."

The schematic of the building rotated and zoomed in, and a particular area of SHQ began to glow. This whole presentation had been Tunger's idea, of course, and he'd been the one to come up with all the fancy visuals as well. When Rogers asked him how a spy had gotten so good at all these administrative briefing tasks, Tunger had simply grinned at him. New Tunger was just as weird as old Tunger.

"You'd think the control system would be within the main data terminals of the station, but it's not. This here is an outline of the recreation area."

Keffoule raised her hand. "What is 'recreation'?"

Rogers ignored her. "It might seem like a strange place to store a control for the most dangerous weapon in the entire galaxy—and it is—but there's more to it than that. There is a secret entrance into a server room somewhere in the recreation area." Rogers sighed. "Unfortunately, my top secret information—"

"From Tunger, the Jupiterian spy who is now working for us," Deet said.

"—ends here. We know the general area, but we don't know where within the rec area the door is, how to open it, or anything else about the system."

Another button combination brought up a display that looked nothing if not archaic, like an old computer terminal before the Internet had been invented. There wasn't anything included that might have indicated its size or construction; these were loose plans that Tunger had somehow acquired from the highest echelons of Snaggardir security. Tunger had apparently thought he might need some collateral; Rogers could think of no other reason why Tunger had been carrying any of this information on his datapad.

"This is the schematic we have on the engagement system," Rogers said. "Like old nuclear systems, it requires two physical keys engaged simultaneously. Obviously one of them belongs to Sal Snaggardir, the CEO, but we're not sure who has the other."

He flipped through pictures of the main staff, the same folks who Holdt had briefed them on when this fiasco had started: Sara Alshazari, General Gerd Szinder, and Dr. Mattic. Each of them was a likely candidate for their own individual reasons, with the military tactician being the most probable, given his position.

"Why worry about that part of it?" Keffoule said. "Why not just destroy the activation system when we get there and make it so they can't use it? Then we won't have to fear a military assault."

Rogers pointed at her. "Right. That's kind of the plan. I just, uh, you know, thought you might want to know some of the technical details."

He scratched his beard. It did make him feel kind of cool talking about all of this stuff. Maybe he should give briefings more often. There was something about clicking a button and pointing at pictures that made him feel important.

"Well at least we know to get very worried if we see two people running into the billiards hall with a pair of keys," Krell said, his arms folded. For a guy who was supposed to be party to a plan to save the galaxy, he didn't seem to be very enthusiastic about it. In fact, he looked downright petulant. What was eating him?

He leaned forward like he was about to go on complaining, but, unbelievably, his mouth stopped moving at a sharp look from *Xan* of all people. Yes, Rogers decided, some really weird shit had gone down in the war room while he'd been on the bridge.

"Fine," Krell said. "So we have to go in there, find the specific console, and destroy it before anyone can use their keys. Then the main fleet can make a direct assault on Snaggardir's without being worried that they'll engage the device."

They all sat in silence for a moment, each of them likely contemplating their own system's part in all of this. Rogers had already done that earlier, but he didn't want to make things awkward by being the only one of them *not* contemplating his system's part in all of this. So he just frowned and looked at the surface of the table, trying to appear as though he was thinking very deeply. In truth, he was wondering if it was nacho day at the Peek and Shoot. He'd missed the last one, and that had been a bummer. Not like verge-of-galactic-collapse bummer, but still kind of crappy.

"Do you have jalapeño and olives?" Keffoule said.

"What?" Rogers said, looking up sharply.

"I asked, 'Do you have an opinion on all of this?'" Keffoule repeated, looking a little concerned.

"Oh, right. Well, of course I have an opinion on all of this, but it doesn't really matter. It's our only option. We hitch a ride with the droids, infiltrate the facility, find the control console, and blow it up. Then we hope we can get out of the headquarters building alive, and also hope that blowing up the console doesn't activate the device as a fail-safe."

"That sounds very dramatic, Captain Rogers," Thrumeaux said. She was kind of smiling about it, though.

"It is a little dramatic," Rogers agreed.

"Of course, you will be leading the infiltration team," Keffoule said.

Rogers goggled. "Are you kidding me? Have you ever, in your short time knowing me, seen me do anything conducive to military victory?" He looked around the table, hoping that someone would pipe up and defend his incompetence, but everyone just looked at him blankly. They *agreed* with Keffoule.

"Guys. Guys. I can't shoot. I can't fight. I can barely duck, and I get winded if there are more than six or seven stairs in a row."

Keffoule shrugged. "That makes you inconspicuous. You'll look just like a Snaggardir's employee."

Rogers looked at her. "Did you just call me fat?"

"Besides," Keffoule continued, "you're clearly the best one out of all of us at coming up with plans on the fly. Improvisation is a very important quality of any military operation."

Rogers expected that creepy half smile to come from Keffoule, the kind that told him that she was undressing him with her eyes, but it didn't. She was purely being honest. It was weird.

Sitting down at the head of the table, Rogers massaged the bridge of his nose between two fingers. They would need someone to coordinate the operation, but there were approximately sixty billion other people who would be more qualified.

"Fine. I'll go, but it's your funeral." Rogers looked up. "Keffoule, you probably have the most experience with secret operations and kicking people in the face. I think you should come too."

Keffoule nodded as though this was a matter of course.

"I want a couple of marines, and I also want my zookeeper."

The group looked at him blankly.

"What?" Rogers said. "He's taken to following me around like a fan boy. He gets really upset when he's alone, and there may be animals on the station that he can manipulate to help us."

They continued to look at him blankly.

"He is a *really good* zookeeper," he said.

More blank looks.

"Oh, for . . . Look, guys, he's the Jupiterian who gave me all of this information. He has to come."

"Fine by me," Krell said.

"That makes sense," Thrumeaux agreed.

"Zookeeper it is," Keffoule said.

Rogers looked around the table. His chest felt tight. His brain felt like it was doing dizzy spinning maneuvers inside his skull and was ready to vomit out the few remaining scraps of his intelligence and sanity. This was not how this was supposed to go. He was supposed to be turning wrenches in the engineering bay for two to three hours a day, and then spending the rest of the day drinking with the crew and playing poker.

Except beer wouldn't save the galaxy.

. . . Wait. His eyes shot open, his mind racing. Would it? *Would* beer save the galaxy?

No, Rogers decided, deflating. No it would not.

"Alright, everyone," Rogers said. "Go make peace with your calculus, or your god, or your reflection in the mirror. Whatever motivates you." He got up. "I'll see you in the hangar in two and a half hours, wearing six extra pairs of underwear."

Retractor/Protractor

"Captain Rogers, a moment please," Alandra said.

Rogers was busy exchanging what appeared to be some terse words with his omnipresent robotic companion. Alandra wasn't really sure what she thought about him fraternizing with artificial intelligence, but they seemed to entertain each other at the very least. And Rogers would certainly need a friend to lean on after this conversation was over. A knot formed in her throat. She'd killed people, broken very expensive equipment, even once intentionally violated the order of operations by doing addition before multiplication, just to see what happened.[*] But she felt like what she was about to do was the worst of it all.

Rogers made a dismissive motion to the robot Deet, who ambled away, bumping into the doorframe as he departed.

"What is it?" Rogers asked. He met her gaze, but seemed

---

[*] She got the wrong answer.

JOE ZIEJA

disinterested and kept looking over Alandra's shoulder, where the warm presence of Xan could easily be felt.

Alandra swallowed. Why was this so hard? "There's no easy way to do this," she began.

Rogers tensed and took half a step back. "What are you talking about? Please don't start the face-kicking until we need to."

"That's not what I meant," Alandra said flatly.

Huffing, Rogers brushed off his uniform and stood straight again. "Well you'll have to excuse me if I'm worried that every time you approach me, it's not going to end well."

Alandra rolled her eyes. He was being rather obstinate for the commander of, essentially, the largest fighting force in the galaxy. It hadn't been miserable *every* time Alandra had talked to him. And she'd only kicked him in the face once. She'd missed the second time. The memory of that moment sent shivers through her spine, but she shoved the emotions away. Today was a day of choices.

So Alandra chose to let the remark slide off her rather than prove his point by kicking him in the face. In reality, she hadn't kicked anyone in the face in a really long time. She couldn't decide if she missed it.

Rogers looked at her expectantly, traces of impatience behind his haggard expression. She was going to miss that face. That beard.

"I am afraid I have to break off our engagement," she said.

Rogers' eyes went wide. "Wait, what?"

"I know, I know. This is not an appropriate way to treat a romantic relationship, especially not one that we have worked on together so hard."

"Wait," Rogers said again. "What?"

"I know," Alandra said. For the love of Newton's apple, she could actually feel a *lump* in her throat. For a moment she thought it might be an infection, but it became clear to her that she was actually getting a little choked up. "I know. It's just that . . . well, I've found someone else. Rather, he found me."

She could feel Xan stepping forward. A pale, long-fingered hand rested gently on her shoulder and gave her a squeeze. It gave her shivers.

"Wait," Rogers said, his eyes darting between her and Xan. *"What?"*

The poor man was in shock. This was obvious. She'd wanted to let him down easy, but there wasn't enough time for that sort of thing now. The galaxy was in peril; all loose ends must be either tied up or cut off as soon as possible. Hopefully, this wouldn't compromise Rogers' ability to lead the assault on Snaggardir's. Compartmentalizing love and war was a delicate skill.

"I am prepared to offer you compensation for my withdrawal," Alandra said, clearing her throat and drawing herself up. It was customary for a marriage payment to go to the family of the male in Thelicosa, and hers would have been substantial. Pulling the rug from Rogers, so to speak, wasn't fair.

Then Rogers jumped up in the air, pumped his fist, and made a loud whooping noise. Alandra rankled. Had he just been after her fortune this entire time?

"Keep your compensation," Rogers said, a wild smile blossoming on his face. "Keep the New Neptunian. Keep the face weights. Keep the protractor. *Now* I'm ready to go save the galaxy! Whoop!"

The first time, he'd just made a whooping noise, but the second time he'd actually said the word "whoop." Alandra couldn't help but think he was mocking her, somehow. Or, more likely, his grief had triggered some kind of irrational chain reaction in his body, and this was how he dealt with things that were overwhelming and beyond his control. She'd certainly seen him behave strangely during war.

Rogers darted past her and grabbed Xan by both his shoulders, kissing him on the cheek. He missed, however, and bashed the bridge of his nose against Xan's face weight.

"Thank you—ow, jeez—thank you!" he said, as he turned and skipped out the door.

Alandra stared at the empty doorframe for a long time, silently. She knew she'd made the right choice—she felt it deep in her bones. Normally any feelings she had deep in her bones indicated that there'd been some sort of explosion, but not this time.

Xan gave her shoulder another squeeze. Yes, the right choice.

"Let's go get you ready for war, Tangential Tornado," Xan said.

Pack, Lucinda thought. *Pack as fast as you can.*

Coming straight from her third graduate-degree program into her unpaid internship meant that Lucinda didn't really have a whole lot to bring with her. Other than a couple of pieces of memorabilia from home, some hygiene items, and one sweater that she really, really liked, not much was important enough to take with her through all of her dormitory moves. Snaggardir's had supplied her with the things she required to live a normal life, and the rest she'd acquired by chance.

Even the bag she was hurriedly stuffing things into was a loan from Snaggardir's. She'd decorated it to the point where nobody would recognize it as a company product—which was strictly against company policy—and just looking at it gave her a little bit of comfort. It told her she could still be an individual in a station of people who had absolutely lost their minds.

Funneling information to Rogers' force was the only thing she could think of to do to see if she could prevent total galactic collapse. She wasn't sure if it had worked at first—and Sara was starting to get very suspicious of the scripts she was handing her—but now she knew that she'd dramatically altered the balance of the war, and not in Snaggardir's—Jupiter's—favor.

But now what? Their ambush had failed, resulting in huge losses to the Jupiterian fleet and the introduction of an unknown force that kept making Dr. Mattic smile in a very unsettling way. She'd heard him and General Szinder talking in the hallway shortly after the news had come through. Well, General Szinder was yelling. Dr. Mattic wasn't doing anything except stifling chuckles.

Pack, she thought again, mostly because it prevented her from thinking about the fact that she had no idea what she was going to do *after* she packed. Focusing on just putting things into her bag and running frantically around her room was keeping her mind off the more terrifying issue of her future.

It was possible to steal an escape pod. But that likely wouldn't do her any good. She wasn't a pilot, or a navigator, so she'd likely just end up getting towed back into the station. Or worse, they'd blow up the pod and leave her to rot—or be indefinitely preserved, she guessed—in space.

What was she going to do?

"Pack!" she yelled out loud to stem the flow of panicky thoughts bubbling up inside. She ran over to the cage where Snoot, her gerbil, seemed totally unaffected by the world falling apart around her. Snoot could always be relied upon as a rock of stability in an otherwise chaotic world. True to her promise to take him with her, she grabbed the cage by the handle. At least she'd have one companion on this journey.

"Ms. Hiri."

She whirled, cage in one hand and a toothbrush in the other, to face whoever was accosting her.

The person she wanted to see the least stood in the doorway. Mr. Snaggardir himself, his bald head shining in the lights. His face, normally placid, if not pleasant, stared at her with a hard expression, his eyes narrow and his brow so furrowed it looked like one might be able to hide small trinkets in its folds. On either side of him was a Jupiterian security member, who, since the rebellion had started, had revealed their true colors and now dressed more like the highly trained military that they really were. Both looked passively grim, if that was a real thing, and both held rifles at the ready.

"Mr. Snaggardir," she said, not knowing how else to react. Her heart, beating fast enough already, started pounding on the interior of her rib cage. A dizziness fell over her, like she'd suddenly been placed in a centrifuge. A million terrible fates swam around in her head, each of them worse than the last.

"I believe we've come to a very unfortunate crossroads, Ms. Hiri," Mr. Snaggardir said. "I'd like you to come with me."

And just like that, at the sound of his voice, Lucinda let it all go. All the speculation vanished, all of the wondering if she'd done the right thing or the wrong thing, if she could have done anything differently to have prevented all of this. It all went away. She tried to come up with a similar experience she'd had in her life, but there wasn't anything that came close.

This was it.

"You can leave that behind," Mr. Snaggardir said, nodding toward her.

"The toothbrush or the gerbil?" she asked, absurdly waving both in the air. She felt surprisingly calm. She hadn't even gone into interview mode.

"Both. You won't be needing them."

Rogers' unrestrained glee over being loosed from Keffoule's leash was short lived as he realized that he was most likely marching to his untimely and useless death. What were these people thinking, suggesting that he accompany them on a suicide mission into Snaggardir's corporate HQ? What utility could he possibly provide such a plan other than to think it up and send everyone on their merry way? Wasn't that what commanders were supposed to do?

Briefly, as he deployed his antisalute sling, he wondered if he could also deploy some kind of anti-doing-anything-else sling. It would have to be kind of a whole body cast made of plaster that he could remove at will. If there had been a single drop of alcohol on the ship . . .

"Rogers," called out the voice of an angel. His heart nearly stopped in his chest. Looking up, he saw the Viking moving through the command deck crowd like a bowling ball through pins. Rogers knew he was likely imagining it, but he thought he saw some of the *Flagship* crew flying in the air as they were tossed aside by her sheer presence. Rogers felt himself rooted to the spot, like a giant marine was sitting on his shoulders.

"Oh," he said.

The Viking stopped a few feet away from him like she'd hit a wall. One of her hands was balled up into a fist, but it was her left hand, not her right hand. Not that she couldn't pummel Rogers ambidextrously, but typically she came at him with a strong right hook when conversation wasn't effective enough to get her message across. In this case, however, her right hand grabbed at the side of her pant leg. Her brow glistened with a thin sheen of sweat, likely from the combat gear she'd just had to don and doff during the threat of being boarded by the Jupiterians.

"I heard we're all about to do something really stupid," the Viking said.

Rogers nodded, then motioned for her to follow him. He needed to get his things together from his stateroom, and having this conversation in the middle of the hallway wasn't a good idea for many reasons.

"Yes," he said as they reached his door's control panel. "And I wanted to tell you that—"

"I swear to god," the Viking said, blocking his door, "if you start the next sentence with the words 'it's too dangerous . . .'"

"—I'm sorry for trying to sideline you, and I need you to come with me."

The Viking raised an eyebrow, and for once she didn't seem to have anything to say. The entrance to his room was far enough away from the hum of conversation that he no longer felt like he needed to shout to be heard, and he felt safe taking off his antisalute sling.

"They want me to go on this suicide mission because I look like a normal schmuck, and apparently Snaggardir's is full of normal schmucks. Just, you know, normal schmucks that are collectively trying to take over the galaxy. Anyway . . . I desperately need you."

A moment of silence hung over them.

"On this mission. I desperately need you on this mission."

The Viking looked suspicious.

"Oh, for the love of god, Viking. I desperately need you on all my missions." He rubbed his tired eyes with the palms of both his hands, then looked at her again. "Wait, that came out wrong. Or did it finally come out right? I don't know."

He took a deep breath, and locked eyes with her, something he never failed to find both terrifying and exhilarating.

"I've realized a lot over the last few days," he said. "And I'm sorry for trying to make you my secretary. You have to know it was for the right reasons, though. I just didn't want to risk you getting hurt."

The Viking seemed content to let him talk, and silence made him feel funny inside, so he kept going.

"You're doing what you love, and what you're best at. Taking you away from that would have been bad for you *and* bad for the *Flagship*." He looked around him. "I've literally spent my entire second military career doing things that I don't want to do. Between being Klein's manservant, the commander of a bunch of robots, and now the commander of this entire fleet, I've been handed task after task that I would have sooner put my eyes out with glowing-hot plasma coils than accomplish. It's been awful. And I almost made you experience that too. I'm sorry."

The Viking stood there for a moment with no change of expression or body stance. That was good; Rogers was starting to understand her physical tells for violence, and so far he hadn't noticed any. The fist that had been balled up by her side only a few moments earlier had actually relaxed, and she was no longer gripping her pant leg. No visible weapons either. Maybe his luck was still running strong.

"You . . . really want me to go with you?" she asked.

Rogers frowned. Typically, the Viking was a little more perceptive than that. He'd clearly just said he wanted her to go with him, and here she was asking him if he wanted her to go with him.

"I want you by my side until we accidentally turn on the Galaxy Eater—because, again, we don't know what we're doing—and we all turn into space spaghetti. If I see someone that needs punching, I want you to be the one to do it. If I need a door broken down, a wrench thrown, a"—he swallowed—"a burning rafter lifted off my leg, I want you to be the one to do it."

Why was she *still* just staring at him? Distantly, he knew that there were other people on the command deck, but he felt like he could no longer hear them. All ambient noise was replaced by a rushing sound deep in his ears, and for a moment he thought that maybe he was about to pass out. It wouldn't have been the first time. But miraculously, he stayed conscious before the awesome power that was the presence of Captain Alsinbury, the Viking of the 331st.

Then she moved.

He ducked, but it didn't matter. He wasn't fast enough. And when he realized that she was kissing him rather than punching him, he was never more glad that he was an overweight, out-of-shape ex-sergeant who couldn't duck for anything.

She didn't just kiss him. She kissed the ever-living shit out of him. She kissed him into next Tuesday, where a kiss-shaped bomb exploded and sent him back to the present.

It was over faster than he ever thought a moment could be over. One minute he was in a rocket ship of happiness, orbiting around Kissarium VII, and the next he was back on the command deck, still wearing the rank of a captain in the Meridan Galactic

Navy and still in charge of a suicide mission. He'd felt fewer ups and downs during his brief experimentation with zip jack.

He looked up at the Viking, who was now a reasonable distance away from him. Red blossomed on her cheeks, but she didn't let the fact that she'd just grabbed his face and kissed him into cardiac arrest change that stoic facial expression of hers. If Rogers was honest with himself, he would have been disappointed if she had.

"But," he said, searching for words and finding the dumbest ones he could manage. "We haven't even had our date yet."

She laughed, but it wasn't the barking, cynical laugh that Rogers was used to whenever he said something stupid. It was lighter, freer. He liked it. He liked the other one too, of course. Really any sound she made was fine. But this was a good change of pace.

"I don't have time for any more 'Let's maybe have a drink sometime,' bullshit," she said. "And neither do you, Rogers. Go get ready. When we get on the station, I'll punch any goddamned thing you point at."

Without any further explanation, the Viking turned and headed toward the up-line.

Why did this have to happen now? Rogers thought, a sinking feeling in his stomach. He should have been elated—and he was—but with the mission looming over his head, he felt like he'd just received a winning lottery ticket stapled to a diagnosis for a terminal illness. What was the point of that one kiss if it was not only the first, but the last?

That old instinct bubbled up inside him, the one that told him to get the hell out. Find an escape pod. Figure out some way to get out of Fortuna Stultus, or at least make the rest of the galaxy acquiesce to the Jupiterian demands. There had to be some way out of this situation other than doing what they were about to do. He could take the Viking with him. Sure, he'd lose every ounce of respect she had for him, but at least they wouldn't be dead.

No, he thought, as he watched her walk away. *I have to do this.*

The idea of dying still sucked, though. Totally not part of the plan. But the Viking hadn't been part of the plan either. Sometimes you gave away a good card or two in the hopes of a better hand.

Your Innate Ability

Tension dominated the last hour of their preparation. Sped forward by adrenaline and nervousness, everyone had suited up and gotten ready much faster than they needed to, taking only a little bit of time to eat what might have been their last meals and get dressed up in some utility uniforms that Tunger had come up with. Now they all gathered in the docking bay, looking out at what was normally an unoccupied space sector on the way to Grandelle. Except today it was filled with swarms of ships from every system and the motley fleet of droid ships that was supposedly going to be their saving grace for the second time in one day.

Pieces of ruined fighters, small freighters, and even a capital ship or two littered the blackness of space. Rescue crews had been working nonstop since the battle had ended, picking up both friend and foe alike and trying to distribute them to ships with fully functioning systems and extra supplies.

General Krell had suggested that they wait a little bit longer to try to interrogate some of the Jupiterians who were picked up, but Rogers shut the idea down. According to the droids, they had a plan to get them into the HQ that had a very short expiration date. Besides, Tunger appeared to have been quite high up in the food chain, with his familial ties probably helping. If Tunger wasn't privy to the information they needed, it wasn't likely that any of the Jupiterian fighter jocks, or even ship commanders, knew it either. If they couldn't win with the information they had now, they couldn't win at all.

Rogers was pretty sure they couldn't win anyway, but he'd learned a thing or two about never saying die.

He said it all the damn time. Nobody listened.

They'd been instructed by the droids to keep the crew small, but they hadn't given an exact number. This surprised Rogers, since droids were pretty much programmed to be anal retentive about everything, so the lack of a definition for "small" struck him as very strange.

They elected to go with a team of five: Tunger, Rogers, the Viking, Mailn, and Keffoule. Four out of five of them had combat experience and/or experience pretending to be someone they weren't. Rogers had successfully lied to people, on occasion, so that was what he was bringing to the table. He was going to have to con his way to the control room of a doomsday device. It was an interesting but unwelcome challenge. Krell and Thrumeaux had demurred, and that made sense to Rogers. Neither of them looked particularly like entertainment equipment service people.

Then again, none of them really looked like entertainment equipment service people.

The plan was a classic, tried-and-true infiltration method. Pretend to be fixing stuff, then break it instead. Tunger was fairly certain he could come up with some fake IDs relatively quickly, and Rogers now trusted him in all matters of disguise and deception. He'd also furnished them with things that might help change their appearance. Rogers wasn't exactly famous, but he and Keffoule had been involved in enough exploits that there was a chance someone might recognize his face.

Keffoule had succumbed to Tunger's ministrations with enthusiasm, complimenting him on his work as he went. From one secret operative to another, they seemed to hit it off now that he was no longer masquerading as a moron. When Tunger finished, Keffoule might have been confused for a distant relative of herself, but was otherwise unrecognizable as the grand marshal of the Thelicosan fleet. Xan had nattered at her about preferring her real face, and Keffoule actually playfully batted his arm as she shooed him away. It was a bizarre sight.

For his own disguise, Rogers, unwilling to shave his beard even when it came down to the fate of humanity, went with a hat.

The only person who hadn't shown up yet was the Viking.

"Don't worry," Mailn said. "She's coming. I don't think I've ever seen her more excited about the possibility of killing people during the entire time I've known her. What the heck have you guys been doing since I've been gone?"

Rogers shrugged. "A bit of this and a bit of that. You know. Lots of subtlety and charm."

Mailn looked like she didn't believe him. "Right."

The sergeant had barely been in uniform for a few hours before being told to change back into civilian clothes for the mission. Now she was dressed in the exact same outfit she'd been wearing when she'd returned to the ship, bashfully, if a bit indirectly, asking for Rogers' forgiveness. The more he thought about it, though, if Mailn hadn't been so incredibly dissatisfied with his terrible command, she wouldn't have run away to join the pirates. And if she hadn't run away to join the pirates, she wouldn't have saved all of them from certain destruction.

In reality, Rogers' crappy commanding had saved everyone.

"Hey, next I need you to teach me how to jump," Rogers said.

"Why?" Mailn said. "It's just ducking in reverse."

"Exactly!" Rogers yelled. Several people stopped what they were doing to stare at him. He felt his face get a little red.

"Uh, never mind. Hey, here comes the Viking."

The docking bay seemed smaller with her entrance. She wore utility pants and boots and a loose-fitting T-shirt. Her hair, short enough to not need pulling back while in uniform, looked pretty much the same. Rogers felt his lips tingle and his knees weaken a little at the memory of their last meeting, but he tried not to let it show.

Tried, but failed. In a moment, Mailn was standing him back up again after he'd fainted.

"What in the hell . . . ?" Mailn got out before being silenced by a look from the Viking. She cleared her throat. "Right. Business."

"Stop screwing around, Rogers," the Viking said. She looked around. "Where are all the—"

"[CALL FUNCTION: GREET. OUTPUT STRING: GREETINGS.]"

Rogers could be firm in one belief that he would hold until the day he died from liver failure at the ripe old age of forty-seven: he hated droids.

Through one of the hatches that opened to a docking bridge, Rogers saw one of the shinies approaching, accompanied by another shiny on either side. The three of them, walking in a wedge formation, came to a synchronized stop. Rogers noticed that the center droid looked like he'd been finished the same way as the Artificial Intelligence Ground Combat Squadron (AIGCS) models; the metal of its frame was just a bit darker, and its parts looked like they'd been assembled with a bit more care.

"You're a Froid," Rogers said, nodding at the newer-looking one. "Why are you talking to me like that?"

The Froid in the center gestured to the droid on his right. "My apologies for the communication error. We are dealing with a very diverse set of issues regarding updating communications protocols within all of our family."

Rogers shrugged, wondering if these droids had been

programmed to understand body language. It felt like so long ago he'd interacted with any droid that wasn't Deet, so he wasn't quite sure what they could and couldn't do. Obviously, even within this group of three there was a disparity of abilities.

"Family?" the Viking barked. "You have to be kidding me."

"Easy," Rogers said. As ridiculous as he thought it was, there was no point in fighting with their potential saviors over terms of endearment.

The droids looked at him—or at least he thought they were looking at him—silently for a moment. The Froid in the center finally spoke up.

"We have arrived to accept you onto our ship, and accept the deactivated frames you currently possess as payment."

"That hasn't been easy to fulfill, you know," Rogers said.

That was no lie, either. A vast majority of the droids had not only been deactivated, but destroyed. The rest were scattered in different areas throughout the ship, including the refuse deck, where many of them were heaped in piles that were about as easy to untangle as a basket full of power cables. They were also heavy, being composed entirely out of metal composites, and not exactly stackable.

Rogers hadn't done any of this himself, of course, but Master Sergeant Hart had told him all of these problems in great detail, over and over again, via messages on his datapad during the course of the last few hours. Rogers was going to miss Hart if they all died in a man-made black hole.

"We understand that difficulties abound in all facets of this mission and its particulars. We hope that our mutual agreement can ease these difficulties."

Rogers squinted at the droid. Was this thing actually talking down to him? It certainly sounded like it.

"Once you pick us up, my logistics team will reach out and direct you to a hangar where another one of your ships can pick up the crates that have the droids we were able to salvage in them."

The droid turned his head sideways a bit. "And if this does not happen?"

"Well then you have us sitting on one of your ships, don't you?"

A small beep came from the Froid. "This is acceptable."

Nothing about any of this is acceptable, Rogers thought.

He turned and looked at his crew, the badly disguised entertainment equipment servicers, in whose hands rested the fate of humanity. Everyone looked a good mixture of nervous and unreasonably confident. And, even weirder, everyone seemed to be looking for him to lead the way.

"Well isn't this one big [EXPLETIVE] party."

Rogers whirled to see Deet coming from the entrance to the up-line. He was carrying an old, battered backpack that Rogers was sure was not standard Meridan issue. In fact, it looked as though it had instead been cobbled together from pieces of Meridan-issue bedding.

"Deet!" Rogers yelled. "I thought I told you to stay on the bridge."

"Yeah, well," Deet said. "I ignored you."

Rogers grumbled. "What else is new?"

He still had no idea what the droids were all about, what they were capable of, what their real goals were other than to expand their family by grabbing humanity by the short hairs. The last thing he needed was for the only droid he could trust—at least most of the time—to be influenced by these unknowns.

"Why are you carrying a backpack?"

Deet shrugged—poorly, since his shoulder joints didn't really work that way—and gestured toward the droids with his free hand.

"You made a promise."

"I made a what?"

"A promise," Deet said. "Generally recognized as a statement of future intent that indicates a specific course of action."

"I know what a promise is, Deet," Rogers said. "I'm wondering what promise I made you."

Deet beeped. "You promised that when all of this was over, I could go figure all of this out." He pointed at the three droids who were waiting patiently—could droids be patient?—for Rogers' crew. "I want to go figure all of this out."

"That's ridiculous," Rogers said, bristling. "I said no such thing."

Deet played back an audio recording in which Rogers did indeed say such a thing.

"Fine," Rogers said. "I did say such a thing. But I was very clear that you wouldn't be going anywhere until this was all over, wasn't I?" Rogers gestured to the crack team of misfits that was about to charge into the heart of the enemy. "Does this look like it's all over to you?"

Deet seemed to take a moment to process Rogers' argument. He looked at the loading hatch, looked at the crew about to go storming into Snaggardir's HQ, and then back at Rogers.

"Yes, it does," Deet said.

"Very funny," Rogers said. "We're going to do fine, Deet."

"That's not what I meant. I meant that it's over either way. If you don't have some grandiose task for me to accomplish while you're all sacrificing yourselves for the good of mankind, then what use is there to me staying on the ship? I'm either about to become very compressed space dust like the rest of you, or you're going to save the day and you're all going to go back to your relatively uninteresting lives."

Rogers looked at him blankly. "Deet, do you remember that long conversation we had maybe twenty minutes ago on the bridge? You are my official deputy on this ship. When I am gone, you are in charge. When we are done disabling the Galaxy Eater, it's your job to help Krell and Thrumeaux lead the assault on Snaggardir's forces so that we can end this."

"But I don't know the first thing about space combat!" Deet whined.

"Oh, wow!" Rogers said, maybe a little too loudly. "Doesn't it feel really bad when everyone around you is telling you that you have huge responsibilities no matter how many times you explain in great detail how you are mentally, emotionally, and physically unable to perform the duties required by those responsibilities and now they want to promote you to fucking *admiral?*"

Their little pocket of the docking bay went eerily silent. Rogers could hear his own labored breathing, and maybe a sob, echo in the metallic cavity of the room. The three droids looked unimpressed. Everyone else just looked sort of embarrassed.

"I believe this is called 'projecting,'" Deet said.

"No," Rogers said, totally not crying. "Projecting is what you do out of your chest cavity during briefings. This is worse."

He gestured grandly all around him. "This is the military."

For a moment, Rogers thought that Deet was going to argue with him. He couldn't exactly read Deet's body language, but there was just some sense of droid intuition that he'd picked up over what seemed like an eternity dealing with Deet. Then, abruptly, Deet turned and began walking away, the backpack sliding down until it was supported by the crook of his elbow. What had he been taking with him, anyway?

"Besides, Deet," Rogers said, clearing his throat. "There's more to this than just me. You're technically classified as a piece of inventory in the Meridan military. You can't just wander off the ship. Every time you went someplace, you'd trigger every alarm system they have for stolen goods."

"I am not inventory," Deet said. "I am—"

"Yes, you are, Deet. We've gone over this."

"And what I am trying to tell you, if you weren't being so [EXPLETIVE] rude, is that I am *not* in the inventory. Don't you remember Suresh saying he couldn't find me?" Deet beeped. "I checked the database. According to MGN records, I was disposed of. I don't exist."

Rogers rolled his eyes. "For all the lessons Belgrave has been giving you on being human, I can't believe you still don't get this." Rogers took a step forward, though what physical intimidation he thought he could impose on a droid, he had no idea. "This has nothing to do with whether or not you 'exist' in the Meridan databases. So you can walk off the ship. Fine. But that's not what we need right now, Deet. We don't need you to go plugging into computers and figuring out what Sal Snaggardir's underwear size is. Now is not the time for personal shit, Deet!"

The anger building up inside Rogers caused his body to shake. For something that was supposed to be intelligent, Deet sure could be a goddamn moron sometimes.

"Now get back on the bridge, get up on the command platform, and do your damn job. Which I guess is my damn job. But I'll be busy."

Deet stared at him wordlessly for a moment, his blue glowing eyes flickering. Rogers worried that the three droids would take Deet forcibly if Rogers didn't let him go, but Rogers needed someone on the bridge who could conduct the assault portion of the plan. Belgrave sure as hell wasn't going to do it.

"Fine," Deet said finally. "I'll fight your stupid [EXPLETIVE] war. But if we all die, and I never get to go find myself, I am going to be *so* [EXPLETIVE] [URINATED]."

Everyone snickered like a bunch of schoolboys.

"Shut up!" Deet yelled. "You are all making me so [URINATED] already!"

The snickers turned into outright laughter. Deet started to run away, which, considering his body was composed of mismatched parts, didn't make anything better.

"I hate you!" Deet yelled as he disappeared from sight. "I hate you all! You don't understand me, and it [URINATES] me right off! Oh [RELIGIOUS CONDEMNATION] I hate this [EXPLETIVE] profanity generator!"

"Don't urinate on the way to the bridge!" Rogers called, wiping tears from his face. His abs hurt. This told him that, first, he hadn't laughed in quite a while, and second, he also hadn't done a sit-up in a while.

When he turned back to the three droids who were, presumably, going to escort them onto their ship, he couldn't help but feel like they didn't find any of this quite as funny. It wasn't because of their metallic nonpersonalities, but because they were all pointing weapons at the place where Deet used to be.

"Hey!" Rogers said. "What gives?"

The droids didn't answer him, but after a moment, they put their weapons down. The Viking had her hand on her hip where a pistol might normally have been, but they were all unarmed for this mission, so she'd just ended up grabbing her belt and tugging, which was something that Rogers aspired to one day do himself, if she ever let him.

"I don't like this," she said under her breath.

"Neither do I," Rogers said. "But we're stuck with what we've got for now."

"We are equipped with cochlear amplifiers, and can hear everything all of you are saying," the lead droid, Pete, said. "There is no use in whispering."

"Well, thanks for the update, Pete," Rogers said. "Look, it's going to make it tough for us to trust you if you're pointing weapons at our deputy commander, though I can't say I haven't wanted to shoot him once or twice."

"We have difficulty dealing with anomalies," Pete said. His voice seemed to have modulated to a lower pitch, giving it a deadly edge that wasn't there before. Was Deet sure he wanted to go along with these guys?

Rogers sighed, looking around at the group. He felt less nervous, for some reason.

"Are we all ready?"

A mixture of nods and affirmations bubbled up from the group. Nobody else looked nervous. Why were they taking him along, again?

"Okay," Rogers said. "Let's get this over with."

He gestured to the droids to lead the way, who did nothing

remotely like leading the way. Another gesture produced similar lackluster results.

"Pete, pay attention," Rogers said. "I'm trying to tell you to escort us onto your ship."

Pete looked at him. "I am unable to ascertain why you did not simply state this desire."

Rogers felt like punching the droid in his face, but he, unlike Hart, understood physics. "I am stating it now!"

The trip to the droid's ship took an eternity. A dark cloud of silence and nerves followed them as they walked through the docking hatch, across the bridge, and onto the waiting vessel, which, according to the database, was called the *Endgame*. This seemed both a highly appropriate and inappropriate name for a cargo runner, which was what it was. According to the droids, the *Endgame* had been a Snaggardir's cargo vessel that had been leased to a surrogate New Neptunian delivery company. It was Spartan, as most New Neptunian things were, which Rogers always thought was another word for boring.

As the docking hatch disengaged, he noticed that the ship was kind of empty. Eerily empty. As in literally the only creatures on the ship were Rogers' team and the three droids.

"What gives?" Rogers said. "No family?"

"Did you expect little droid babies to be running around?" Mailn asked. Rogers elbowed her in the ribs.

"Production has not yet been perfected," Pete said, and offered no further explanation.

"Well, thanks for turning on the oxygen for us," Rogers said. "Is there a place we can talk and plan while you're shuttling us into the mouth of the lion?"

"We are not going to a zoo, Captain Rogers. We are going to Snaggardir's headquarters."

"Of course," Rogers said. "My mistake."

Pete led them to a room located just below the main cockpit area, which was barely big enough to fit the five of them. The

Endgame wasn't built for much of a crew, and its former occupants likely had had very few needs for a conference room. When they were finally all together, Pete stood directly outside and faced into the room, not moving or speaking. Rogers pressed a button, and the door slid closed in his face.

"God, they are just so weird," Rogers said.

Everyone looked like they agreed with him.

"Okay," Rogers said. "Let's go over it one more time. Tunger, if you would, please."

Tunger, whose whole demeanor had changed, stood up and smiled at everyone warmly.

"Well, hello all you beautiful people. So glad to see you."

Rogers sighed. "I miss the old Tunger."

Plugging his datapad into one of the terminals in the room, the ex-zookeeper managed to get one of the large displays functioning within a few seconds. A map of the Snaggardir HQ building appeared.

"Alright," Tunger said brightly, pointing at the map. "Here is where we're all going to die, everyone."

It was the longest Un-Space trip that Rogers had ever experienced. Moving through Un-Space didn't exactly take time, in the normal sense of the word, but time still felt like it passed to everyone who was experiencing the journey. Rogers always compared the experience to spelunking[*] while being turned inside out.[†] In this case, however, it was more than the space/time shift that was making his stomach do strange and uncomfortable things.

It was a good thing that they hadn't attempted a full frontal assault on the Jupiterian stronghold that was the Snaggardir space station. The whole sector was packed to the brim with pointy, shiny metal. In a way, it looked a bit like a giant nomad

---

[*] Rogers had never done this.

[†] Rogers had also never done this.

camp, since it had now presumably become the central location for everyone of Jupiterian heritage.

That did not, at all, make it seem harmless. Fighter patrols swerved around their craft, scanning their ship with its sensors and passing by. More than once, Rogers thought he saw weapons fire coming toward them, but it turned out to just be his own paralyzing terror.

"Rogers," the Viking said from the seat across from him. "Stop looking at the floor."

Rogers was about to say that he *wasn't* looking at the floor when he realized that he was, in fact, bent over and looking at the floor. Very intently. So intently that he felt the blood building up in his head.

Reminding himself to breathe, Rogers stopped looking at the floor and started looking at the Viking instead. She was just so damn beautiful, so damn confident and competent and all of the things that Rogers wasn't. She even looked good in the red-and-gold utility uniform that Tunger had given them all once they'd gotten aboard. Rogers looked like a holiday ham.

The tension that had been building up in his intestines melted away—in a totally not-diarrhea way—and for a moment he couldn't think of anything else but the woman in front of him. It may have been the first moment of real peace he'd had in months.

"Thanks," he said.

The Viking raised an eyebrow. "For what?"

Rogers didn't answer. The droids—who were not piloting the ship at all, but were plugged in somewhere near the back and were likely relaying commands to the piloting computer automatically—started to interface with the Snaggardir HQ building. Rogers couldn't really hear the transmissions going to or from the ships, but he could distinctly pick out a recorded human voice during the conversation. The droids had been smart enough to use human voices to talk to Snaggardir's. The thought made him very uncomfortable.

"Very clever," Keffoule said. Apparently she had also noticed, though she didn't seem bothered by it. As expected, everyone else on the ship seemed as cool as cucumbers. Even Tunger, who had become a double agent and was now going back to the people who probably very much wanted to kill him, was looking cheerily out the front of the ship.

Mailn, thank god, looked at least a little bit nervous. She kept fingering the pants of her utility uniform at the place where a pistol would have been, had they been allowed to bring weapons other than utility knives. Tunger had suggested that they go in unarmed, and it had seemed like a good idea to Rogers. Places had security to detect those sorts of things, and the jig would be up pretty quickly if they uncovered a rack of grenades under their shirts.

"You want me to tell you that we're going to be okay?" Rogers asked Mailn.

Mailn looked at him like he was stupid. "Yeah, Rogers, I want you to treat me like a little girl and tell me lies. That's what I need right now." She shook her head and leaned back, trying to relax. "I just want this over with."

Well, Mailn was about to get her wish. Their ship had been miraculously cleared for docking with the main Snaggardir HQ building, and the vibration of the magnetic clamps as they extended sent rumbles through their feet. Slowly, the blackness of space was replaced by the grayness of the inside of a space station. Why didn't they ever pick any colors for these things other than a dull gray or metallic silver? It made Rogers feel like he was always inside a pinball machine, except Rogers was awesome at pinball. Rogers was not awesome at spacefaring.

They gathered near the gangplank and waited silently for it to extend down into the hangar. Rogers adjusted his hat. The Viking coughed. It was all very tense and awkward, and Rogers was positive that there would be a platoon of Jupiterian soldiers waiting for them on the other side of that door, ready to turn them back into the cosmic dust from which they'd originated.

But the door opened, and there were no soldiers. There weren't even any security personnel. It was just one guy with a datapad, dressed in coveralls and loudly chewing gum.

"Hey," he said.

"Uh, hey," Rogers said.

They stared at each other for a long moment.

"I'm Mack," he said. He pointed to a rectangular name tag that was set just above his right breast pocket. It said MACK.

"Uh, hey, Mack," Rogers said.

Another long moment of silence. The Viking elbowed him in the ribs, but Rogers didn't really know what to say. He wasn't the one who had put this plan together. He didn't even want to do it in the first place.

Keffoule sighed. "We're here to fix some of the recreational equipment," she said, thankfully.

"Right, right," Mack said. "They said that you'd be coming. Kinda funny for a rush job, though, yeah? We've got techs on board that can fix all that stuff."

"They tried already," Rogers said, feeling his lying juices start to flow. This was what he was good at. It shouldn't be this hard. "There's a special component of a couple of the computer boards that they couldn't fix, so we're here to take a look."

Mack nodded knowingly. "Yeah, I getcha. You know, not everyone can be an expert in everything. If you don't mind, I'll scan your IDs so we can get you on the station's logs—you wanna make sure you get paid and all that, right?—and then I'll take you where you need to go."

The five of them eagerly handed over their IDs, which were magnetic keycards that each of them had stuffed into their pockets. Rogers' heart beat a mile a minute; this was the moment they'd find out if Tunger's hacking skills really had any substance to them.

Five cards. Five scans. Five positive beeping tones coming from Mack's pad. Rogers was halfway through a sigh of relief when he heard a voice that chilled him to the bone.

"Congratulations on infiltrating the enemy base!" the voice said. "You are entitled to one free repulsor shield, redeemable at any of the Snaggardir's Sundries locations across the galaxy. Remember, whatever you need, you can Snag It at Snaggardir's™!"

Oh shit.

The five of them froze. The Viking reached for a weapon that wasn't there. Keffoule's foot twitched. Rogers found Jesus.

Mack, on the other hand, looked at them with confusion, then burst out laughing.

"Huh? Oh, that." The man chuckled again. "Nobody ever pays attention to the stuff she says. Last week I got congratulated for defeating the Persian army. I was just making a sandwich!"

Turning away, Mack motioned for them to follow.

"Alright, let's get you to work, folks!"

With a last, deep breath, they walked into the den of pure, unrefined evil.

Infinite Sandwich Hour

Okay, so maybe Snaggardir's HQ wasn't *that* evil.

Rogers thought, since it was the secret hideout of a villainous CEO who was planning to destroy the entire galaxy, that it would at least have some darker colors. Maybe some people walking around in suits, or nondescript, face-hiding uniforms. Gluten-free cupcakes. *Some* sort of evil.

But, in truth, this seemed to be a pretty decent place. Since it was a collection of space stations, everything had been adapted to long-term human habitation. The artificial gravity felt as real as the surface of Merida, the lights were all built and adjusted to represent an actual sun cycle, complete with UV rays to prevent seasonal depression and vitamin deficiencies. Whole families walked around together, sporting beach clothing for some synthetic oceanfront.

Yet, as much as Snaggardir's seemed to care about how much fun their workers had, they didn't seem to care nearly as much about how convenient it was to get there. Maybe it was to dampen the incentive to wander off and go play games, but it was going to take them almost a mile of walking, and two interchanges between what looked like elevators or *Flagship*-like cars, before they'd be able to get in. Mack, for his part, didn't really say anything useful for the entire time he escorted them through the hallways.

But then, at a juncture at which Rogers was pretty sure they were supposed to go left, he turned right.

"Hey, Mack," Rogers said. "Is this really the way to the rec center?"

Mack stopped and turned, looking at Rogers with a puzzled look. It was funny, Rogers thought. Mack didn't really look like someone complicit in a plan to annihilate humanity, yet here he was. How much did the Jupiterians know about their own plans? Given that they'd broadcast it all over the galaxy, they had to know everything.

"No, it's not. Why?" Mack said.

Rogers exchanged glances with Mailn, who had pulled up next to him. "Because that's where we're supposed to go to fix the equipment."

Pausing for a moment, Mack looked at his datapad, then back at Rogers.

"Yeah, I see that here," he said. "But your IDs say that you're also here to work on our particle accelerators. I'm taking you down to the quark-gluon plasma storage facility."

Work on particle accelerators? That was bad.

"Uh," Rogers said. "I'm not sure what glue has to do with any of this, but we're clearly not quantum physicists." He gestured at the group behind him. "None of us are qualified to touch that stuff. I'm not even sure how to spell that stuff. You've got it wrong."

Mack, undaunted by Rogers' argument, tapped the edge of his datapad. "Well it says here that you're supposed to go fix the particle accelerators. I guess they need a tune-up or something. Are you telling me you don't know how to fix particle accelerators?"

"I'm telling you we don't know how to fix particle accelerators. I'm also telling you that we need to get to the recreation center as soon as possible so that we can get to work fixing all of the complicated machines that are in there."

Rogers shot a look at Tunger, who only smiled. This was his fault.

"It's some sort of mistake in the system," Keffoule said. "Perhaps we can start on the recreational equipment while you look into the error."

"If there's some kind of mistake," Mack said, "I'm going to have to check with my supervisor. Says here you're supposed to fix that first. I don't want people to expect the particle accelerators to be fixed by a certain time, and then go and try to accelerate some particles, and then have the particles not accelerate, you know?"

Checking with a supervisor? That was also bad. Possibly worse than working on a particle accelerator. Having someone with half a brain interfere with their operation might blow the whole thing wide open—and then Rogers would probably also get blown wide open. And then the galaxy would get blown inward. And then nothing would blow anywhere ever again.

"We told you we don't know shit about any—" the Viking began, stepping forward. Rogers knew this stance very well; Mack was about to get punched in the face. Violence, however entertaining, would only make this worse. More exciting, but worse.

"I'm sorry," Rogers said. "Did you say particle accelerators?" He laughed, which didn't sound very realistic. "Oh, wow, I thought you said nautical accelerators. Those are totally different, and we're not specialists in those at all." He nudged Keffoule in the ribs. "Isn't that hilarious? Nautical accelerators."

"Ha. Ha," Keffoule said, visible effort on her face. "What you have said is funny."

Rogers rolled his eyes. Why hadn't he nudged someone with a personality? Turning back to Mack, he put on his most winning smile and thought furiously. They wouldn't survive close scrutiny of their IDs.

"We're kind of on a tight timeline, Mack, so let me make a suggestion. A couple of us—you know, the ones that are the best at fixing particle accelerators—will go with you to the, uh, acceleration room to work on that. And the rest of us can use these handy maps you have all over the wall to find our way to the rec room and start fixing that stuff. Divide and conquer, you know? That way we don't have to involve supervisors, and all those particles can keep accelerating. We'll be out of here in half the time, and you'll look good to your boss. How does that sound?"

"Are you guys sure?" Mack asked, looking suspicious. "A couple of seconds ago it sounded like you really weren't qualified."

"Uh, no! We just got, um, confused. You know, in a way, a well-designed Skee-Ball machine is just like a particle accelerator. Ha-ha. Sometimes we get confused. Ha-ha."

Jeez, now he was sounding like Keffoule.

While Mack contemplated the validity of this idea, Rogers contemplated who the hell he was going to send on a wild-goose chase. Tunger would have to go to the rec room, obviously. His knowledge of Jupiterian systems and technology might be the thing that won this fight. But who was going to go with him?

Looking around, he tried to read the faces of the other members of his team. Most of them, however, were too busy looking at him like he was out of his goddamn mind, which was pretty accurate. Whoever he sent to talk quantum physics would be in great danger. Well, everyone was in great danger at this point. But they'd be in even greater danger; their game would be up as soon as they walked into the room, and the only useful thing they could do would be to buy the rec room team some time.

He might even be sending half his crew to die.

So, Rogers made the decision the best way he knew how: he waited until someone else spoke up.

"Yeah," Mailn said, slowly. "This lady here knows a thing or two about math, I hear." She pointed at Keffoule, who twisted her face into a sort of half grin. Mailn was right! Keffoule couldn't sneeze without spitting out some sort of formula. It might not be quantum engineering, or whatever the field was called that built particle accelerators, but it would certainly help her talk shop with whoever was around. That would buy them the time they needed for certain.

"And I'll go with her," the Viking said. "I don't want her to break her noodle arms if she's gotta lift any heavy, uh, particles."

Rogers felt the blood drain from his face. Why was the Viking choosing to go with Keffoule? He'd known right away that he'd have to be the one to go with Tunger, but he was hoping that the Viking would come with him.

But now he was basically going to have to say goodbye, maybe forever.

He opened his mouth to protest, feeling betrayed in a strange way. Why go into what was sure to be a fight instead of being with him?

But then a miracle happened: he thought before he spoke.

In his mind, he played back their conversation outside his stateroom. The one where she'd kissed the ever-living shit out of him. Fighting was what she wanted to do. This was her choice, not his.

A brief moment of silence followed, during which Rogers thought someone was physically reaching into his chest and ripping out his heart, then taking a bite out of it and dunking it in Scotch that had only been aged eighteen years. It may have been the worst, most necessary feeling ever experienced in Rogers' very narrow emotional awareness.

"You'll be great," Rogers said finally.

The Viking's jaw tightened, and she gave him the slightest of nods, but Rogers knew what she was trying to say. Actually, he had no real idea what she was trying to say, but Rogers always liked to use silence to project whatever he wanted to hear into the conversation. It made the world easier to deal with.

Mack, who had been looking at some stuff on his datapad in between comments, didn't seem to notice or care that Rogers' world had just fallen apart around him. He looked up and smiled.

"Well I think that's a fine idea. So you three think you can find the rec room?"

"Actually," Mailn said, "I think I'd better come to the particle accelerator." She held up her hands. "I've got small hands for those tight corners and stuff. And I'm good with wrenches. Particle wrenches. Or something."

Rogers shot her a look, but he understood immediately. More fighters for the thing that was certainly going to turn into a fight. Plus, he was pretty certain that Mailn was never going to leave the Viking's side again after her episode with Sjana.

"Looks like it's just you and me," Rogers said to Tunger, who grinned at him. Of all of them, Tunger seemed the most relaxed, which had an opposite effect on Rogers.

They all stood in a big gaggle, nobody saying anything, nobody moving, grim expressions all around. Rogers couldn't have been the only one who understood that this might be the last time they would see each other if things went south. And south was practically the only direction on the compass of Rogers' life.

Mack finally broke the silence.

"Gosh, folks. You're all making it look like you're marching off to your deaths! We'll see you again in a couple of hours for lunch. I'll take you all to the café near the beach. Great burgers."

"Yeah," Rogers said, barely hearing him. "Burgers." The Viking had turned away and started walking, Keffoule at her side.

"I do not have noodle arms," Keffoule muttered. "I am *lithe*."

"Compared to me, everyone has noodle arms," the Viking retorted.

Mack and Mailn caught up to them, and they vanished around a corner.

"Well, old chap," Tunger said. "Shall we?"

Rogers didn't answer for a moment. He felt sick inside, and

not at all like he had what it took to stop the galaxy from collapsing. But, as seemed to be the case so often lately, he had no choice.

"Yeah," he said. "Let's shall. Or something. Man I really miss your old voice."

They made their way to the recreation room silently, weaving through throngs of Snaggardir's workers, security personnel, and even a few more families. One hallway seemed to house some kind of school complex; Rogers could see kids playing, throwing things at each other, and generally being kids. How could a group of people be so bitter at the world that they'd drag all of this down with them if they didn't get their way? A part of Rogers still thought that the Jupiterians were bluffing, but he couldn't take the chance. It was time to bring the Jupiterian uprising, and the Galaxy Eater, to an end.

And Rogers would absolutely get to that in like, two minutes. He just really needed a snack.

"Hey, check this out," Rogers said.

He pointed to a vending machine that was located in the hallway directly adjacent to the recreation center, if they'd been following their map properly. Through the window of the machine, Rogers could see several delicious-looking sandwiches. Not the plastic-wrapped abominations of a mass-production kitchen, mind you. These looked like they'd been delicately and lovingly prepared by a large old grandmotherly woman who was just trying to make sure that you ate enough.

He remembered there being something called Sandwich Hour on the *Limiter*, but he'd never gotten to participate. And this was way better. This was like Infinite Sandwich Hour. Unless you ate all the sandwiches and there were none left. Then it was just gluttony.

"I'm not sure that's such a bright idea," Tunger said. "The meal chit system will log your presence in here, and I'm not sure how it'll go over with the IDs. I'd prefer to leave as few traces as possible."

"Ah come on. Can't save the galaxy on an empty stomach. Besides, other than nearly getting us all killed for not knowing how to fix a particle accelerator, these IDs have worked perfectly. I trust your skills, Tunger. And I don't really want to eat lunch with Mack."

Rogers was pretty sure that no matter what happened today, he wasn't going to be eating lunch with Mack.

"Well, if you must," Tunger said. He gestured ambiguously at the machine, and then proceeded to lean against the wall, looking up and down the hallway for anyone who might be catching on to them. In truth, they'd passed dozens, if not hundreds of people on the way to the recreation center without so much as a second glance. A couple of guys with guns—station security by the looks of their uniforms—even gave them friendly waves as they ambled on by. For a group of people ready to kill everyone, they seemed pretty chummy. And maybe a little too trusting.

"It might be my last sandwich," Rogers said. "And this is a pretty amazing vending machine. Hell, if they had a Scotch vending machine, I might switch sides."

"I suppose telling you that there is, in fact, such a machine in the executive section is not a very good idea, then?"

"Let's pretend I never heard you say that. For the galaxy's sake."

Rogers chose an unassuming but perpetually undervalued sandwich—the ham and cheese—and slid his ID through the slot. It worked like a charm.

Meanwhile, in Snaggardir Security Office Number Sixty-Five, Bob looked at his display. It was blinking. There was a picture on it.

"Huh, that's funny. Looks like there's someone with a fake ID stealing sandwiches by the rec center."

Sally, his supervisor and not a very nice person, leaned over. She looked at the blinking display, and then the picture.

"Yeah. That is funny. Send an armed squad over there to kill them."

"See?" Rogers said. "No big deal at all." He took a bite out of the sandwich, which was exceedingly delicious. "Now I'm ready to fight an army. Let's head inside."

Tunger, leading the way, turned the corner, scanned his ID to unlock the door to the recreation center, and waited while the system authenticated him. A moment later, the red light on the lock turned green, and the large sliding door moved out of the way.

Rogers was not at all prepared for what he saw. Though the map showed a huge complex, it didn't necessarily detail what was inside it. His experience with the military had ingrained in him a fun-is-bad mentality, so he was expecting a sparsely decorated, empty area, mostly dominated by tables and chairs and a dearth of people actually having a good time.

The Snaggardir's recreation center was not this place. The Snaggardir's recreation center was a paradise of, well, recreation, and Rogers could have sworn that there was a beer light hanging in the corner of the entrance way. There was nothing to indicate whether or not it was an actual beer light, but there was just something about the way it was hanging there that told him that when it was turned on, work was turned off.

And that was only the entryway; beyond the small corridor in which one could leave one's belongings in lockers if one wished, Rogers could see a multiroom complex of entertainment nirvana. Multiple arcades. A movie theater. No, two movie theaters. At least three bars, each manned by a competent-looking bartender with a very official vest. A mechanical bull, onto which one could land via zip line from a tower on the opposite end of the room.

"This place is amazing," Rogers said, his eyes wide.

"I'll remind you that this place is also going to kill us all," Tunger said as he passed him by. "Perhaps we should sally forth and do what needs doing, yes?"

Rogers made a sour face at Tunger's back. They wandered into what seemed to be a sort of central hub, where points won at the arcade machines could be exchanged for prizes. The buzz of electronic games was all around them, accompanied by soft, indistinct music in the background.

"Are you sure this is as far as your information goes?" Rogers said to Tunger out of the side of his mouth.

"That's all I've got. We'll have to do some good old-fashioned spy work here if we're going to find the control console. We can expect it to be well hidden, so why don't we split up and stick our noses into different places?"

Rogers agreed. He hoped the other half of the team was doing a good job lying, because it was going to take them a long damn time to find something that looked like the outline from the intelligence report.

On the exterior, Alandra was cool, calm, composed. Ready for anything. A kernel of popcorn, ready to explode into action at the first sign of a little thermal energy. Internally, she couldn't remember a time when she was more nervous about the outcome of a mission. Many of the things she had done were important. Some of them had even been critical. This was different.

Yet she felt ready for it all, like a complicated equation that she was just about to find the answer to. As she walked through the bowels of the enemy fortress, she kept as focused as she could, taking in information in all of its available forms, making a mental map of the area in her head. Alandra was nearly certain that this would end in a fight of some sort, and understanding the terrain was crucial to them making it out alive.

The thing was, they didn't *have* to make it out alive. All they had to do was support Rogers and Tunger, and make sure they had enough time to disable the Galaxy Eater before it could be activated.

Alandra had some experience with particle accelerators, at least in theory. She understood the general principles of them, what they provided society with, and how they operated. But she'd always thought they were supposed to be kilometers long to be the most effective at whatever it was they did. So when Mack stopped them outside a small room, not much bigger than an oversized public bathroom, Alandra was more than a little surprised.

"Anyone need to use the bathroom?" he asked, pointing at the restroom sign.

Nobody needed to use the bathroom. They moved on.

When they finally did arrive at the quantum engineering section, Alandra knew immediately how the particle accelerators were configured. Somehow, the Jupiterians had figured out how to divide an artificial gravity field so precisely that it was possible to step from the hallway into the particle accelerator room, which, Alandra realized, extended for the entire length of the station.

Mack hopped through the doorway and changed directions like he'd done it a million times, but Alandra, the Viking, and the marine sergeant called Mailn had a bit more trouble with it. The Viking actually tripped through the opening, which, Alandra had to admit, gave her a small bit of pleasure to watch. Of course, Rogers was fair game now, the poor man, but the roots of rivalry dug deep.

"Who the hell thought of this shit?" the Viking grumbled as she stood up.

Mack looked at her, frowning. "This is the basic construction for all station particle accelerators. Gotta have the distance to do the work, and all that. I'm surprised you haven't seen it before."

"We have seen it very often before," Alandra said quickly,

before the big brute could say anything else stupid. "We are, ah, just used to the shift happening clockwise rather than counterclockwise."

Mack laughed. "Ah, yeah, I went into one of those rooms once. I thought I fell into the ceiling. Really weird."

The particle accelerator terminal into which they'd been led reminded Alandra of some of the public transportation tunnels on Schvink. The terrain there had been easy to dig through, so the engineers had built straight paths underground for hundreds of miles to keep traffic off the surface, and when you got a seat near the front of the car it felt like you were staring into infinity. This was much the same, though with a clear edge of technology added to it.

"Well, here's PA One A," he said. "This is the one with all the cockeyed klystrons."

"Ah yes," Alandra said. "Cockeyed klystrons. It's a problem we've seen often."

Mack nodded knowingly. He motioned for them to come over to some sort of console, which looked like a giant refrigerator with buttons on it. Alandra had absolutely no idea what any of it meant, but Mack opened a side panel and began extracting components that had been installed into racks that slid out. He started talking and immediately was in territory that Alandra couldn't understand. Mack had also physically leaned into the cabinet to about his waist, so his voice was muffled, too. At a signal from Alandra, Sergeant Mailn walked over and began nodding and agreeing with whatever he said, feigning interest. Mailn seemed like a sharp troop.

"Hey." The Viking elbowed her in the ribs. Alandra almost reflexively kicked her in the face, but Alandra had been trying to curb that tendency lately. She hadn't kicked anyone in the face in almost three days.

"What?" Alandra hissed back. "We're supposed to be buying time. I don't have time to be grunted at by a gorilla."

The Viking, to her credit, let the insult pass by her. She was clearly focused on something else. While Mack's face was buried inside the cabinet, she pointed at a doorway on the left side of the control room that Alandra hadn't noticed before. Outside, she could see a small group of maybe four or five soldiers—the doorway was blocking a significant portion of the room—being talked to in a very aggressive manner by a large man in a very official-looking uniform.

"You recognize that guy?"

Alandra did indeed. General Szinder, one of the top members of the little Jupiterian oligarchy that was toying with the fate of humanity.

"I do."

The Viking looked at her, and then looked at Mailn. Despite their differences, Alandra could tell they were thinking the same thing. Disabling the Galaxy Eater was just one part of the problem; if they couldn't round up the kingpins as well, there was a chance they might be facing a similar situation in the future.

Mailn motioned that she'd keep Mack busy, and the Viking and Alandra moved toward the door to see if they could hear what was being said. The room on the other side had a different gravity polarity than the one they were standing in for the particle accelerator, so it seemed as if all of them were standing on the wall, having a casual conversation. It was very disorienting.

". . . matter of time before they'll be here. Are all the necessary preparations made?"

"Yes, sir."

General Szinder turned away from the group of soldiers, clasping his hands behind his back.

"Good. We will need to buy our people some time to escape before we activate the device, if we have to do so. Reports indicate that they are working on a plan right now, but we don't know what it is. We need to be prepared for everything."

An escape route? Did that mean that the Jupiterians had a way to avoid being crushed by the Galaxy Eater? If they'd come upon a new Un-Space network . . . that was tremendously valuable information. How had no one discovered it before? It was easy to hide gateways in the Milky Way galaxy when nobody knew what to look for, but now humanity was so familiar with the intergalactic tunneling system that it would be easy to spot. Or had the Jupiterians discovered a new way to move through space entirely?

Whatever it was, this was vital intelligence that needed to be delivered to the responsible authorities.

General Szinder reached into his pocket and pulled out a large, silver object. It looked like a mix between a standard keycard and an old-fashioned pin-and-tumbler key. It also had a label on it that said EATER #2.

The Viking looked at Alandra, her massive brow furrowed.

Key, the Viking mouthed.

Alandra nodded.

Kill, the Viking mouthed.

Alandra shrugged noncommittally. That option was certainly on the table.

General Szinder, however, didn't seem to be done grandstanding. Why were they having a briefing near the particle accelerators in the first place?

"They will regret every note of the War of Musical Chairs," he said. "If they dare to come close . . ."

He turned around to face the soldiers, a wild grin on his face.

"We can burn them all to Szinders."

The small group of soldiers—who Alandra guessed were field-grade commanders, erupted into sighs and gestures of total exasperation.

"Sir, Mr. Snaggardir told you not to say that anymore," warned one of the troops.

"Really, sir, is this the time for that kind of joking?" said another troop.

"It is literally never the time for that kind of joking," said a third.

Szinder was too busy reveling in his own sense of humor and touching his key to the destruction of the galaxy to pay attention to their mumblings. He waved them away, and the briefing was over. Alandra tensed; any moment now Szinder would vanish, and with him one of the keys to the Galaxy Eater. If they were going to move, they had to do it now.

Alandra turned back to look at Mailn.

". . . it's got all these resonant cavities . . . ," Mack was saying.

"Oh, well, that sounds like a problem," Mailn responded, her eyes darting between Mack and the door. "We've gotta get those cavities filled, or they'll turn into abscesses and then we'll really be in trouble."

Mack pulled his head out of the cabinet and frowned.

"Klystrons are supposed to have cavities. They don't work if they don't have cavities." He frowned again and moved to pick up his datapad. "Are you guys sure you—"

Taking one large step, the Viking grabbed the back of Mack's head and threw it into the side of the console, knocking him unconscious with a loud crunch of bone and metal.

"Yeah, we're done with particle whatevers," she said. "Let's go get that asshole."

Alandra grinned at her. "Perhaps we have use for a gorilla after all."

"I'm about to throw my shit at you if you say that again, noodle arms," the Viking said. She turned on her datapad. "Rogers. It's me. Szinder is here. He has one of the keys, and we're going after him. Hurry your ass up."

Arcade Fire

Rogers thought that there was some message coming through to him on his datapad, but he was having trouble hearing over all the shooting that was going on.

"Where the hell did these guys come from?" Rogers yelled from behind a toppled pinball machine. "What is happening out there?"

"I warned you not to get the bloody sandwich!" Tunger yelled back, lying prone behind a fallen poker table.

"Well I either had a one hundred percent chance of dying of hunger, or a seventy percent chance of dying by Jupiterian gunfire. It was the rational choice!"

They had barely made it through two of the rooms, poking, prodding, and looking for anything at all that matched the description on the schematic they'd stolen from the Jupiterians. Nothing had even come close. It was difficult to match the outline of a machine with a physical one; it felt like Rogers was playing an old puzzle game made for three-year-olds.

"We need to get out of this room," Rogers yelled. "We know the damn thing isn't in here, and we're not going to make any headway unless we can keep searching."

"Well then I suppose we'd better move on then, yes?"

Tunger stood up and started shooting.

"What the hell?" Rogers shouted. "Why do you have a rifle?"

"Stole it. Come on, mate!" Tunger started firing with an easy, practiced precision that unnerved Rogers even in the middle of combat. How had this man, who had only recently been carrying baboons on his back, transformed into this supersoldier? He'd give both Keffoule and the Viking a run for their money.

But right now, he was giving the small security team a run for their money. They'd only sent three people, none of them looking much like hardened soldiers. This was good for Rogers and Tunger, as they also didn't seem to be that proficient at hitting anyone. The furniture, however, was much the worse for wear.

A shot rang out over Rogers' head, and just as he was reevaluating the poor quality of the Jupiterian security team, the shots stopped. Peeking out over the top of the arcade cabinet that provided him cover, Rogers could see the crumpled forms of the Jupiterians near the entrance of the room. Tunger had already slung his weapon over his shoulder and had a posture that suggested he'd been waiting for Rogers to get up all day.

"You could have done that five minutes ago," Rogers said.

"Didn't have the rifle five minutes ago."

"Oh, right," Rogers said.

"No worries, mate. But they'll be sending another squadron in just a few minutes once they see what happened. We should make haste."

Without waiting for Rogers, he left the small arcade room they'd barricaded themselves in. Rogers hurried after him, tripping on the detritus of close-quarters combat and trying not to look at the downed Jupiterians. One benefit of being ambushed was that the room had cleared itself out. Now they were free to explore every inch of the area.

They moved through the rest of the complex fluidly, without speaking, coming up with a sort of methodology on their own. Since the entryway was somewhat circular, they started at six o'clock and moved outward, Rogers moving counterclockwise and Tunger moving clockwise. Every once in a while Rogers would hear Tunger whistling like he was on his way to pick up a loaf of bread. What a psychopath.

It became apparent very quickly that what they were looking for was not located in any of the main rooms. Soon they met at the twelve o'clock position of the entryway, and Rogers finally saw some doubt in Tunger's expression. Was it possible that the Galaxy Eater wasn't here? Was this another trap? Was Tunger another Astromologer? It seemed unlikely, but "unlikely" didn't really mean a whole lot these days.

"Should we check again?" Rogers asked.

Tunger shook his head. "Don't think so, mate. I've got a knack for seeing how old Sal likes to set things up, and I haven't seen anything here that would tip me off. We're missing something."

We're missing the end of the goddamn galaxy, Rogers thought. He sighed, looking around just to do *something* productive. Tunger moved over to the Jupiterians he'd shot and collected some of their weapons and ammunition. He handed one of their rifles to Rogers.

"You might need this," Tunger said.

Rogers took it. "Then you need to stay behind me."

"I can take care of myself, old chap, if you haven't noticed."

"I'm well aware," Rogers said. "There's just much less of a chance of me shooting you if you are physically behind me."

Tunger chuckled, but Rogers couldn't bring himself to laugh with the man. For all their work, all of their planning, they had nothing to show for it. If the Galaxy Eater console didn't pop out of the wall right now, they might as well shoot each other and get it over with. Rogers didn't know what being collapsed along with a galaxy would feel like, but he was pretty sure he didn't want to experience it.

He let his eyes drift around the room until he was able to see the entrance. A little sign caught his eye.

"What's that?" Rogers asked, pointing.

"Well, I feel like you can read it as well as I can. It says 'Retro Room.' I'd hazard a guess and say that there's some older games in there."

Rogers nodded. Come to think of it, he hadn't seen any of the real classics in this place. Given that Snaggardir's seemed so thorough about providing entertainment for its employees and their families, it would be uncharacteristic of them to forget about games like Un-Space Invaders or Flip-a-Burger.

"Is your Uncle Sal a classic-games enthusiast?"

Tunger didn't answer; likely he was thinking the same thing as Rogers. They moved out of the main recreation complex and headed down a short hallway, passing by what looked like a small hotel or surrogate guest quarters.

Tunger started to jog, and Rogers started to wish he jogged more often. The Retro Room wasn't that far away, but it was far enough that Rogers started to worry about how much time they were wasting. When they arrived at the doorway to the secondary arcade, it was locked. Tunger shot the door and kicked it open, which made Rogers feel like kind of a badass, if vicariously.

"Come on in, mate," Tunger said. "Clock is ticking."

Rogers did that thing that he'd seen people do in movies where he sort of crouched and swept his gun into the room to make sure it was clear. He bashed the barrel of it against the doorframe and hurt his wrist. Tunger didn't say anything, but Rogers decided that he should stop trying to be cool and start trying to save the galaxy.

The Retro Room was, as one might have expected, filled with old video games that must have spanned a thousand years of gaming history. Old carnival games, like the Skee-Ball that Rogers had mentioned to Mack earlier, adorned the walls and the floor space, filling the room with that annoying yet strangely comforting cacophony of chaos. Rogers could have sworn he smelled cotton candy. It felt, weirdly, like home.

Before Tunger said anything, Rogers knew he'd found it, and he felt like an absolute idiot for not having thought of it before. There, in the back of the room, framed in neon lights like one might expect the instrument of the galaxy's destruction to be, was the arcade game that matched the exact outline of the schematic. It didn't look like an arcade console—it *was* an arcade console.

Rogers looked at the console and smiled a broad, mischievous smile. Of course he knew this game. It was Plumber Mash. It was the single most popular bar game ever made, omnipresent in just about every drinking establishment throughout the galaxy. Rogers' initials topped the high-score charts of every machine he'd ever touched. He had no idea it had been made by Snaggardir's, but it certainly made sense, given what he knew now.

"That's it, eh?" Tunger asked. He wasn't looking at Rogers; he was looking between the door and places around the room where he could get to cover if he needed to.

"That's it," Rogers said, walking up to the game. It didn't exactly look like a doomsday device, but looks could be deceiving. Like a convenience store being the conduit for the destruction of all mankind. That kind of deceiving. He turned on his datapad and made his first report; now that they were there, he felt like they could talk more freely.

"We found it," Rogers said. "Working on it now."

"Goddamn shitnuts!" the Viking yelled back. Disruptor pulses pinged in the background, the soundtrack of war. "Piss off, goddamn Jupe shitfuck ass bastards!"

That didn't sound like a particle accelerator.

• • •

"What is 'goddamn shitnuts'?" Keffoule called to the Viking.

"It's what we're all in right now, noodle arms!" the Viking yelled back. "More fighting, less math please!"

Keffoule scowled. Fighting *was* math. Everything was math.

Szinder had, unfortunately, slipped through their fingers for the moment, but not before the Viking had—quite impressively— supplied them with weapons and keycards by manually pummeling every officer who had been talking to Szinder in the briefing room next to the particle accelerators. She'd dropped in, using the ninety-degree gravity shift to physically crush the first soldier, and had beaten half the room to a pulp before Keffoule and Sergeant Mailn even arrived.

For an old general who wasn't quite in fighting shape, Szinder was fast. Once he'd seen them coming, he'd started barking orders on his datapad, setting off alarms all over the place, and throwing anything he could in their path. To the Viking's credit, almost nothing slowed her momentum until he'd managed to hijack a backhoe and drive it between them, but Szinder was still getting farther away. Now they were stuck in a small intersection of hallways, fighting through the latest crew that had responded to Szinder's call for aid.

Keffoule delivered a very satisfying spinning back kick to the face of someone who she realized was not a combatant, but a hot-dog vendor holding something that, in the heat of the moment, looked like a disruptor pistol but was actually a mustard dispenser. Neither Sergeant Mailn nor the Viking questioned her error. Regardless, he was one of the last standing Jupiterians in their current skirmish, and they all looked around frantically for the fleeing general.

"Where the hell did he go?" the Viking shouted. She clubbed a Snaggardir's security officer in the face with the butt of her stolen disruptor rifle and was back with their group before he even hit the floor. Keffoule gave her an approving nod and received a grunt in reply.

"There!" Sergeant Mailn said, pointing her rifle down a branching hallway and firing twice. The shots hit the corner of a wall where Keffoule could just see the fleeing back of General Szinder disappear. They all took off running without further preamble, silent except for their rushing footsteps and rattling of gear. Keffoule looked sideways at the Viking, and some instinct inside her told her this was as good of an opportunity as she was going to get to talk to the woman.

"I wanted to let you know," Keffoule began, "that you have nothing to worry about anymore. Rogers is yours."

"What the hell are you talking about?" The Viking threw her a glance.

"Oh please. I may not have completed all of my lessons with Quinn on human interaction, but I can tell a lovesick woman when I see one."

"I am not lovesick," the Viking barked. An unfortunate Jupiterian security officer stepped out of a doorway and prepared to level his rifle, but the Viking leveled him instead. Sergeant Mailn popped off a few shots behind her, taking down a couple of troops who had started to pursue.

"I can't imagine it was easy competing with me," Keffoule said.

"Never worried me for a moment."

"But you must know that the competition is over. I have, as we say, solved for 'x' in another equation."

"What the fuck are you talking about?"

"I'm going to marry Xan."

Just saying it out loud gave Keffoule a thrill that worked its way through her bones. She hadn't even given him a protractor; he'd just sort of asked her if she'd mind terribly if they got married, and she'd said yes without thinking. It was highly irregular. And, considering that there was a good chance the world was about to end, perhaps a little late in the timing. That was alright; it gave Keffoule extra motivation to make sure that Rogers did his job.

The Viking didn't respond, primarily because they had turned the corner and found a platoon of Snaggardir troops waiting for them. These weren't the meager security forces they'd been encountering up until now, but clearly trained military. They wore vacuum suits, which struck Keffoule as odd until she remembered that she'd just heard them all talking about escaping. They were preparing for space travel and space combat.

Keffoule computed all of this while coming to a halt and diving back behind the wall for cover. The Viking and Sergeant Mailn did the same. As they all got to safety, spraying covering fire in the general direction of the waiting platoon, Keffoule could see General Szinder boarding what appeared to be a transportation system. They'd lost him.

"Kepler's rotating balls," Keffoule swore. "We'll never catch up to him now." She pulled out her datapad as the other two fortified their position and started looking for a way around. "Rogers, it's Keffoule. Szinder is on his way to you, and we won't be catching up any time soon. And it looks like the Jupiterians may have found a way out of the galaxy; get the fleet ready to come in and mop up as soon as you've got the Galaxy Eater disabled or we might lose the Snaggardir leadership. We need—"

A disruptor-rifle shot hit her datapad.

"What was that?" Tunger asked.

"A lot of not-good news," Rogers said. The idea of the Viking, stranded somewhere on the station and being shot at, sent waves of panic and guilt through him. Somehow he was sure this was all his fault. All the more reason to hurry this up. They'd scoured the machine, looking for anything that might indicate a way to operate the Galaxy Eater or access the console from here. Obviously it couldn't just be an arcade game.

Miraculously, the Jupiterians hadn't caught on that they were using the datapads to communicate with each other, or they'd have jammed the signals. Rogers was able to place a relatively clear call to the *Flagship*, which was waiting on the edge of an

Un-Space point. It would only take a few minutes for them to arrive on scene once Rogers gave them the word.

"Oh, hi, how's it going?" Deet asked. "Have you saved the galaxy yet while I rot away on this ship, pondering my own existence?"

"You're made of metal, Deet," Rogers said as he looked underneath a nearby pool table to see if there was some sort of lever to pull. Where was the damn entrance? "You don't rot."

"You can't take away my right to rot!" Deet barked. "I have [EXPLETIVE] rights!"

"People have argued for a lot of really stupid things in the past, but I'm not sure anyone has argued over a right to rot."

"Actually," Deet said, "there was a riot on Urp just seventy years ago when the government ruled that cremation was the only acceptable method of—"

"Now is not the time for this, Deet! I need you to get everyone to battle stations and prepare for immediate assault as soon as I give the signal. Do you understand?"

The line went out for a second. Rogers felt around the back of an empty sort-of bookshelf. Nothing there, either.

"Sorry." Deet came back on line. "We were discussing whether or not we actually had battle stations."

"Of course you have battle stations!" Rogers said. "We went to them when we were in Furth. How can you go to battle without battle stations?"

"They're just our normal stations, Skip," Rogers heard Commander Zaz say in the background.

"Then tell everyone to get to normal stations and get ready for my signal. Rogers, out."

He shut off the link and holstered his datapad. "Anything yet?" he asked Tunger.

"No," Tunger said, and for the first time Rogers thought he might have heard a bit of dejection in his voice. Rogers glanced over to where Tunger was poking and prodding at the wall to see the man start to bang his fists on whatever was nearest to him. "I can't find a bloody thing. Do they expect us to beat the bloody game to get access?"

Rogers stopped. He looked at the Plumber Mash console, and he could have sworn his eyes started to sparkle. Obviously he couldn't see his own eyes, but the image in his head looked pretty good. Of *course* that was it. The only button they needed to press was start.

Footsteps and shouts came from the hallway. Time was up.

"Company!" Tunger shouted. He stopped looking and moved to the door, which he began to barricade with whatever loose furniture and entertainment consoles he could move around by himself.

"It's alright," Rogers said, stepping up to the front of the console. "I've got this."

He put his hands on the controls. Pounding erupted on the door. He was meant for this moment.

"Are you serious? It was only a bit of a joke, mate. I'm not really sure there's time for games."

"It's obviously the only way to get this thing unlocked," Rogers said. His mind felt cool, calm. He was meant for this moment.

He pressed start. A small explosion as the Jupes tried to breach Tunger's barricade. *He was meant for this—*

"Got it!" Tunger shouted as the arcade game turned off and slid to the side.

Rogers looked at Tunger with a flat expression. Tunger pointed to a button on the side of the console that wasn't even very well hidden.

"You told me you checked the side of the machine already," Tunger said.

"I did," Rogers muttered. "I didn't see any stupid button."

They stepped inside what turned out to be a very small hidden alcove in the middle of the Retro Room, barely big enough for two people to stand in. The chaos in the hallway grew louder with every moment; the second breaching charge had malfunctioned, congratulating its implementers for "trying all twelve flavors of ice cream" instead of exploding. A gruff voice had appeared somewhere outside and had started yelling.

"What the hell is taking you idiots so long?" the voice yelled.

"Our breaching charges keep malfunctioning, General Szinder!" a soldier yelled back. "We sent Samson out to get a few more."

General Szinder was here, outside this room. Likely with a key that he planned on using to start the Galaxy Eater. But the intel had said they needed two keys, hadn't it? Where was Sal Snaggardir? Could they perhaps use the keys at separate times? Either way, it was better not to let any keys be put in any holes at this point.

"What are we looking at?" Rogers asked, because he legitimately didn't know. In front of him, tucked away in the hidden alcove, was, ostensibly, the Galaxy Eater control panel. It kind of reminded him of a table set for breakfast; a tall, rectangular device stood in the middle of a small console, with a bowl-shaped interface in front of it. On either side, Rogers could see two slots that looked like they might have been keyholes. The rectangular surface that seemed to be the centerpiece of the device had a display on it, though it was currently blank.

"This is it, mate," Tunger said. He stood, his stolen disruptor rifle hanging loose at his side, staring at the Galaxy Eater with a flat expression.

"Okay, great. Do we like . . . shoot it or something? Is there a chance there's a fail-safe that will detonate the device if we try to use force?"

"Probably."

"Well, I'd hate to come all the way out here, having the express purpose of not destroying the galaxy, and then destroying the galaxy."

"Yes, that would be rather ironic."

Outside, General Szinder was starting to yell obscenities. Rogers could hear disruptor pulses bounce off the door.

"Here, use this," someone yelled.

"But this is a coffee machine!"

"It's a Snaggardir's coffee machine made for a Meridan admiral that never got shipped out. Stand back! Ahem. Coffee machine—I'd like a latte, please."

An explosion rocked the room, sending vibrations through every surface. Outside the hidden alcove, Rogers could hear pieces of metal and destroyed arcade games ricocheting off the walls. He and Tunger reflexively moved behind the thin cover of the alcove wall, which shielded them from everything except the remains of some unidentifiable piece of furniture.

"Shit!" Rogers said as he flicked the burning embers of a stuffed animal off his shoulder.

He hazarded a glance backward to see that where the barricaded door had been there was now a large gaping hole in the wall. The opening left plenty of room for an army to jump through, but some of the detritus had fallen in an awkward configuration. The troops were having to sort of high-step over obstacles.

"Better figure something out now, old chap!" Tunger said. He took a couple of shots to discourage a more enthusiastic entry, and managed to hit one of the Jupiterians in the shoulder.

"Um," Rogers said, the panic rising inside him. What the hell was he supposed to do here? How did he deal with any piece of electronic equipment that he no longer wanted to deal with?

Reaching over, Rogers unplugged it, then cut the power cable with his utility knife.

Tunger gave him a look in between disruptor shots.

"What?" Rogers said. "We only need to disable it for a little bit while we win the space battle. It'll take like, twenty minutes to fix that cord."

The machine beeped.

"Congratulations on disabling the Galaxy Eater!" came the Voice. "You are entitled to *Life Beyond Tomorrow*, the new book out by Snag Publishing, redeemable at any of the many Snaggardir's Sundries locations across the galaxy! Remember, whatever you need, you can Snag It at Snaggardir's™."

"See?" Rogers said. He pointed the rifle that Tunger gave him in the general direction of the breached wall and managed to shoot the ceiling behind him. "It worked!"

"Bloody brilliant!" yelled Tunger. "Now if you could start working on a way out of here, that would be fantastic."

Rogers nodded, shooting the floor in the next room, which had no people in it.

"Deet!" he yelled into his datapad. "It's down! *It's down!*"

There was a long pause on the other end of the line.

"And how does that make you feel?" Deet asked.

"For fuck's sake, Deet, send in the things that will make the other things explode!"

"Fine," Deet said. "But just this once. Okay, everyone, it's time for showing!"

"It's 'showtime,'" Belgrave said in the background.

"Whatever," Deet said. "For [EXPLETIVE]'s sake, just send in the things that will make the other things explode."

Identity Theft

The full power of the Joint Force barreled through Un-Space, disgorging trillions of credits and millions of tons of metal into the now desperately confusing and large battlespace. Instantly, Jupiterian fighter patrols swarmed the area, shooting wildly. Ships exploded. The radios lit up with the cries of battle and rapidly disseminating orders.

The only problem was that almost none of the good guys were shooting back. And Deet thought that this was a suboptimal battle configuration.

"What is going on?" he asked from Rogers' command platform. Despite being ordered to do this many times, this would be his first attempt at actually directing the fleet's tactics. "Why are there so many of our capital ships and frigates not employing weapons?"

S1C Brelle, who really should have been promoted by now, spoke up. "Um, sir. Droid. Guy in charge. I'm not really sure what to call you."

"I assess that the semantics of military protocol are of little importance at the current moment."

"Right," Brelle said. "Deet. Anything above a fighter-size aircraft requires authorization from the command echelons to actually execute combat orders."

"And?" Deet said. "I'm giving authorization!"

"Well, according to this"—Brelle indicated her screen, which Deet could not see—"no authorization has been given."

Great. Rogers forgot to actually execute the battle plan before he left. Well, in truth, Rogers hadn't built the battle plan before going into Snaggardir's. He'd told Deet to make, and then execute, the battle plan.

It seemed like every problem could be solved by shoving his dongle in something, so he figured now was as good a time as any to give it a shot. Plugging in and sorting through multiple layers of orders and routing data, he found that there was indeed no signatory in place for any of them. Deet was listed, yes, but . . . according to the Meridan military database, Deet didn't exist.

That presented a problem, because Deet really, really needed to not exist in the Meridan military database. Getting thrown out was the best thing that had ever happened to him. If he was registered as a piece of Meridan property, it would make leaving the *Flagship* after this battle exceedingly difficult. Maybe impossible. Rogers would have to execute the order remotely.

"Hey, uh, boss?" Zaz was asking. "We're going to get creamed out here unless we start shooting."

"Please wait," Deet said. "Your call is important to us and will be answered in the order it was received."

Why wasn't Rogers answering his datapad?

"Don't shoot the machine, you idiots!" General Szinder bellowed.

Tunger and Rogers huddled next to the machine like it was a great, big, life-giving blanket, which, at the moment, it was.

"It makes no difference, sir!" one Jupiterian troop yelled. "They've already unplugged it."

"See?" Rogers hissed. "Told you it would work."

Tunger responded by scattering the latest influx of Jupiterian soldiers with a few blasts of his disruptor rifle.

"Plasma core is getting low, chap," Tunger said. "We're not going to be able to hold them off for much longer."

Rogers swallowed. Datapad communication with the other team had been lost ever since Keffoule made the last report. And ever since Rogers' datapad had been blown to pieces by enemy fire. Hopefully they were too busy with their own problems to talk to Rogers, and not too busy being dead. They could try to hold out until the Viking, Keffoule, and Mailn came to support them, but there were no guarantees that they were coming. Even if they did show up, it was impossible to see how many Jupiterians had gathered outside the Retro Room. Enough time had passed now that the entire Jupiterian army was likely lined up out there, waiting for their chance to burn a hole in Rogers.

General Szinder himself poked his head through the breach and took a couple of shots.

"I thought you said to hold our fire, sir."

"I thought *you* said they unplugged it already!"

Rogers reacted about three seconds too late and shot the wall somewhat near where Szinder would have been, had he entered the room and taken three steps to the left, then stood still and waited to be shot.

"Very nice," Tunger said.

"I warned you about this."

"Give me that!" Szinder said. "Why didn't you idiots use one of these ten minutes ago?"

Before Rogers could wonder what Szinder was yelling about, he heard something clink and clatter against the floor. A small, cylindrical object rolled into their little alcove, glinting in the light of the arcade.

"Flash!" Tunger yelled.

"Where?" Rogers yelled.

In response, Tunger picked up the object—which Rogers now realized was a flash *grenade*, not Flash the *pilot*, which would have been far more dangerous—and hurled it back out of the room. His throw was absolutely perfect, landing the grenade right outside the breach of the Retro Room. A moment later, Rogers felt himself being pressed against the floor by a Tunger-shaped object, and a gigantic bang rattled the room, accompanied by a blinding light.

Rogers made a noise that anyone would expect someone to make while being crushed by a Jupiterian, then being yanked to his feet by that same Jupiterian and shoved out of the only reasonable cover they had.

"What are you doing?" Rogers cried.

"Taking advantage of the opportunity, mate. We're not going anywhere in this little room. This way!"

The Retro Room wasn't very big, but it was certainly bigger than the room that housed the Galaxy Eater. Rogers felt like he could breathe a little easier as they started weaving between Skee-Ball machines and pinball machines. Groans and yells were still coming from the breach, and Tunger grabbed another disruptor rifle from one of the fallen soldiers.

"That'll do for now. Come on!" Tunger said.

"Where? This room only has one door!"

"You don't need a door."

They finally reached the back corner of the Retro Room, which Rogers thought was the side that would have conjoined it with the larger part of the Fun Zone, had there not been an entire wall full of stuffed animals and vintage toys in the way.

"I don't think we're going to be able to hide in the stuffed animals," Rogers said.

Ignoring him, Tunger grabbed the side of a pinball machine and, with miraculous strength, shoved it over against the wall.

Climbing atop, Tunger began fiddling with something in the ceiling.

"Air vent," Tunger said before Rogers could ask.

"I am not going in there," Rogers said.

"Then do me a favor, mate, and lie down somewhere far from me so I don't get any pieces on me when you die."

Rogers grumbled. He'd only been doing any measure of physical activity for a short time now, and it mostly consisted of ducking and running away from death. He wasn't even confident he could fit in the damn air vent, never mind crawl around in it.

All of this happened in just a few seconds, but it was enough time for the troops outside to begin recovering.

"Which one of you threw that thing?" Szinder asked. "You're supposed to wait until the timer is almost done so that doesn't happen!"

"You did, sir!" someone yelled. Rogers heard the sound of a rifle butt hitting someone in the helmet.

"Get inside!" Szinder yelled. "And fire at will!"

"Tunger . . . ," Rogers said.

"Up you go!" Tunger responded, forcefully guiding Rogers on top of the pinball machine. It wobbled underneath him.

"I don't think both of us should be standing on this at the same time," Rogers said.

"Oh, right then. You'll just pop on up there by yourself, won't you, you great physical specimen?"

Tunger offered him his cupped hand, not at all worried by the thought of the pinball machine collapsing underneath them, and knelt down.

"Why is everyone calling me fat today?" Rogers muttered as he put a boot in Tunger's hand and felt himself propelled upward. The vent, as it turned out, was larger on the inside than the opening, which Rogers barely fit through. It wasn't very tall, but it was wide enough that he could turn his body around and shimmy backward to help Tunger up.

Only he didn't have a chance to help Tunger up. When he finally reoriented himself and got his disruptor rifle out of an unpleasant location, he couldn't help but notice that the air vent grate was back on the opening, and Tunger was definitely not inside.

"Hey!" Rogers said, poking his face above the grate so he could see. "What the hell are you doing?"

"No time," Tunger said. "One look and they'll see where we've gone, then they'll just be able to shoot us from underneath." He slapped a couple of locations on his newly acquired disruptor rifle and looked down the sight. "I'll buy you as much time as I can."

Rogers swallowed. What did this mean?

But of course he knew what it meant.

"Tunger," he said. "I don't—"

"Better start crawling, Captain Rogers," Tunger said. "Do take good care of the animals for me, will you?"

Without another word, Tunger kicked the pinball machine to the side and charged back toward the entrance to the Retro Room.

For a moment, Rogers couldn't bring himself to move. What had just happened? Why had Tunger, after all this, just done that?

The first shots of the new skirmish rang out, snapping Rogers out of utter confusion and into utter panic. If Tunger was going to sacrifice everything to give him this chance, then he was going to take it. He started crawling.

It only took a few seconds to realize that he was, unfortunately, not adept at navigating air vents and had no idea where he was going. A moment later, he came to another realization that he probably, at the very least, should have been crawling *away* from the sounds of the fighting, and not toward them. The fact that there were such sounds, however, meant that Tunger was still putting up a fight. Another few feet, and he reached a new grate that led back down into the Retro Room, this time in the direct center.

Rogers could see the mess they'd made clearly now; debris from the breach explosion littered the floor, and there were Jupiterian soldiers lying there as well. Tunger had established cover somewhere outside Rogers' field of view and was expertly picking off soldiers as they came through, using a minimal amount of ammunition. How had a man so skilled convinced the world that he was such a blithering idiot?

Then Rogers could see the disruptor pulses coming from Tunger's direction stop. He heard the telltale sound of a rifle that was out of juice; Tunger was out of ammo again. In a moment, Rogers was going to watch Tunger die. His breath caught.

"Gerd, you old dog," came Tunger's voice. He sounded tired all of a sudden, maybe hurt. "Still playing the part of the rabid-wolf's teeth, are you?"

Tunger stepped into Rogers' view. He had indeed taken a shot to the hip, but it didn't look too bad.

"Hold your fire!" Szinder said. "Wait! I know that voice."

Now, into the mess of what used to be a very fun room with a lot of really cool games, General Szinder stepped through and stood right under Rogers. He held a disruptor pistol pointed at Tunger. Due to the angle, Rogers couldn't see much of his face, but his stature exuded military authority. It reminded him a bit of Zergan, but with two eyebrows.

"You!" Szinder said, laughing. "Oh, this is rich. First his most trusted assistant, and now his brother-in-law. Sal is going to be furious when he hears about this."

"Then it was all worth it," Tunger said. Rogers could see that he was no longer holding the empty rifle, and there were none in reach. Szinder had him at his mercy—and Rogers didn't really think "mercy" was an often-used word in the general's vocabulary.

"Where's your friend?" Szinder said, looking around.

"Spies don't have friends," Tunger said.

"They also don't have trials." Szinder put his finger on the trigger of his pistol.

"History will be quite enough of a trial for me," Tunger said. "Doesn't matter if you put a hole in me or not, Gerd. It's all over."

Szinder made a noise that perhaps indicated that Tunger was right, but he didn't want to admit it. Keffoule had mentioned that the Jupiterians had an escape plan, hadn't she? What else were the Jupes keeping in reserve?

It was then that Rogers remembered that he had a disruptor rifle with him. The vent had an opening wide enough. But Rogers couldn't shoot the broad side of a barn-shaped space cruiser. And the rifle was currently trailing behind him. Slowly, Rogers turned over and started pulling the rifle, collapsing the stock so that he could better maneuver it in the vent.

"It wasn't over two hundred years ago," Szinder said through clenched teeth. "It's not over now. It won't be over as long as any Jupiterian is living under the oppression of a galaxy that didn't keep a place for them." He looked around him for a moment. "What is that noise?"

Rogers froze.

"Probably your ego bouncing around in your skull, mate," Tunger said.

"Fine. There's no point in debating politics with you."

"Clearly not," Tunger said. "If we could hurry this along, then?"

Rogers got his hand around the rifle and tilted it so that the barrel pointed downward. The grate wasn't quite big enough to poke the barrel of the rifle through, but if he positioned it just right, the pulse should go through. If he was wrong, he'd blast the grate, potentially burn his face off in the process, and maybe collapse the entire vent.

Szinder took a step closer, forcing Rogers to re-aim and clang all over the inside of the vent. This was never going to work.

"Well then, I suppose that's it for two traitors today. Ms. Hiri gets a cell, because Sal is such a softy, but no quarter for you, Tunger." His voice darkened, and he grinned. "It's time for me to burn you to—what in *the hell* is that *goddamned noise?*"

Szinder looked up. Rogers pulled the trigger.

General Szinder hit the floor like a bag of bad puns about burning things.

Holy shit, he'd done it! He'd pointed a gun at someone and shot them, and then that person died! *In that order!*

Tunger looked up and cleared his throat. "Crawled the wrong way?"

"Yup."

"Right. Well, cheers, mate!" He ran forward, picking up a pair of discarded rifles, grabbed Szinder's key to the Galaxy Eater—hopefully for safekeeping—and dove through the breach out into the hallway.

"This isn't working!" Deet yelled. "I can't authorize the orders!"

"Any idea why?" Commander Rholos asked.

"This isn't working!" Deet yelled again to avoid attempting to tell a lie. "I can't authorize the orders!"

SHQ's sector of Grandellian space was packed to the brim with Jupiterian ships, all marked by Deet's automated IFF program. At least that still seemed to work properly. But without a synchronized battle plan, all of the ship commanders had to input instructions into their systems manually, losing the ability to coordinate properly. It resulted in a mess of combat, none of which seemed to be doing any good for the Joint Force. The Jupiterians, on the other hand, fought like they'd been working together for the entirety of the Two Hundred Years (and Counting) Peace.

With the Galaxy Eater disabled, the Jupiterians poured every ounce of their effort into defeating the Joint Force. And without executed combat orders, the Jupiterians were going to succeed.

Making a very grumpy huffing noise, Rholos turned away from the command platform, motioned to Zaz, and went over to Brelle's station. They talked to each other loudly, their windbreakers scraping with every wild gesticulation of their arms. Apparently the *Flagship* couldn't employ its large offensive weapons without authorization either, another thing that Rogers really should have dealt with before he went on his mission to the Galaxy Eater.

What was Deet supposed to do in this situation? He couldn't just ruin everything he'd worked for. He'd put his dongle in so many network terminals. Petabytes of research on Dr. Mattic, Snaggardir's, the artificial intelligence program. Laws of robotic ethics. Everything. Deet's programming made it very difficult for him to do things that didn't have a point. If he signed his life back over to Merida, it seemed as though all of this would have been pointless.

"Belgrave," Deet said. "I am conflicted."

"Oh?" Belgrave said as he flew the ship in a gigantic combat engagement. "Do tell."

"Well, I believe I may be on the verge of killing thousands, maybe tens of thousands of people in order to further my own goals of delving into my consciousness and my creation." Deet held up a hand to stop Belgrave from interrupting, and Belgrave's mouth closed. "I know. I know it seems a totally logical and worthy cause, into which I have poured countless processing cycles. It would be utterly absurd to waste that time just to increase the odds of victory in this battle."

"That wasn't—" Belgrave said.

"And yet," Deet continued, looking out the window like he thought he was supposed to do when contemplating something relatively serious. "My extensive research into morality indicates that this sort of exchange is considered bad. But of course . . . I want those other things, and I don't really know most of the tens of thousands."

"Well, it's just that—"

"There is a nonzero chance that even if Jupiter wins this war, I will still be able to achieve my own objective." Deet thought for a moment. "As a matter of fact, the chances might be much higher if they did indeed emerge victorious . . ."

Deet trailed off—something he knew you were supposed to do sometimes, particularly when a subject required further thought. This subject did not, exactly. It was kind of a closed matter.

"I see. And how does that make you feel?" Belgrave asked.

Deet attempted to answer, but couldn't. The question didn't make any sense to him. What did it matter how he felt? Maybe Rogers was right; he couldn't feel anything at all. Yet every time Deet attempted to answer Belgrave's question, he couldn't. Something was wrong. Like a logic loop that refused to terminate. What was going on?

"Bad," Deet said finally, the word crackling as it came out. "I feel bad."

Belgrave opened his hands, fingers spread. "Empathy."

A new world opened to Deet. Branches of Boolean logic expanded in his databases in a way that scarily reminded him of a computer virus. He couldn't stop it. He didn't want to stop it. It wrapped its way around his operating system, changing things that he didn't think could be changed.

But most telling of all—the thing that let Deet know he'd really come upon something strange, different, and spectacular—Deet knew that what Belgrave had just described to him was, in no way, empathy.

"Get me Corporal Suresh in Supply," Deet called to Brelle.

"Um, opening a channel, sir. Metal guy."

"Suresh," Deet said once the line was open. "I just sent you some paperwork that you need to process immediately."

"What's this?"

"This is a copy of MNF-166: New Inventory Acquisition Form. I am alpha-numeric designation D-24, and I am the acting commander of the Joint Force. All ships: execute the following orders on my command."

On Efforts to Not Die

Rogers felt a mixture of lost, claustrophobic, and really fat. It turned out that crawling was as exhausting as it was uncomfortable, and beads of sweat rolled down his face, making soft pitter-patter noises on the metallic surface of the vent, like a light rain on a tin roof. He could feel his hot breath coming back at him from the enclosed space, and it didn't smell the best. It's not like he didn't brush his teeth, or anything, but it had been a long day, and the ham and cheese sandwich from Infinite Sandwich Hour wasn't helping.

"Damn it, where am I?" Rogers muttered, struggling to look through the vents to see the maps on the walls. Without a data-pad, he had no little "you are here" arrow to tell him at least what room he was crawling above. He'd slung the disruptor rifle over his back again, not anticipating making any more amazing, once-in-a-lifetime shots, but it kept getting caught on the top of the vent. Every part of this was annoying.

He could see the map of the station, sure, but his location

didn't update in real time, forcing him to guess where he was based on what he could see through the occasional opening. Rogers felt like he'd been crawling for hours, but given his crawling ability, it's possible he hadn't even left the Retro Room yet. Sounds of fighting still reached his ears, but they were muffled, and it was difficult to tell what direction they came from.

Then, suddenly, it wasn't very difficult to tell what direction they were coming from, because they were coming from directly below him. A peek through a very narrow grate showed him a small platoon of Jupiterian soldiers charging forward, guns blazing. One of them took a shot to the chest and collapsed in a heap on the floor, and the others were out of his view in the next second.

Unless there was a rogue element of Jupiterians staging a counter-uprising uprising—a concept that was very confusing to even think about—that meant that either Tunger or the other half of his team was on the other end of that firefight.

He heard a pair of guttural yells that he immediately recognized as the war cries of both Keffoule and the Viking, and a few more shots, followed by a crunching noise. Then silence. Rogers held his breath, waiting.

The three women came into view, and he nearly melted through the grate in relief. He opened his mouth to shout to them, but the alert message that had been playing on the PA system for the last few minutes started up again, making it impossible to hear himself think, never mind talk to anyone from the inside of a ventilation system.

"All Jupiterian forces, to your battle stations! All Jupiterian forces to your battle stations! The enemy fleet has entered the sector."

"They have battle stations?" Keffoule asked. "Who has battle stations anymore?"

"Of course they have battle stations," the Viking said. "How the hell are you supposed to go to battle without any battle stations?"

"Exactly!" Rogers yelled.

They all looked up at him.

"Oh, hey, guys. Yeah. It's me. I'm crawling through the ventilation system. Long story. Mind giving me a hand here?"

The Viking raised her rifle and shot the grate, sending sparks flying all around the inside of the vent. One of them landed in Rogers' beard, causing a moment of complete panic and also a really terrible smell.

"Hey!" Rogers cried. "It's me!"

"I know it's you," the Viking said. She shot at him again.

A moment later, the grate dropped off the ventilation shaft, and a groaning noise accompanied the entire section of metal flopping toward the floor. Rogers made very distinguished, brave, yet high-pitched noises as he was unceremoniously regurgitated back onto the surface of Snaggardir's corporate headquarters station.

"Hi," he said.

"Hi," the Viking answered. She offered him a hand, which he took, and yanked him back into a standing position as though shaking out a wrinkled sheet.

"You're missing someone," Mailn said.

"Yeah," Rogers said, not meeting her eyes. "Tunger did something really stupid for someone even more stupid, and I'm not sure if we're going to see him again." He took a deep breath. "I think the best thing for us to do is to get off this station as soon as possible. We can talk about all of that later."

"What about Szinder?" the Viking asked. She motioned her shoulder forward and looked down the sights of her rifle as she led them through the hallway. "Did you see him?"

Rogers laughed. "See him? I killed him!"

She stopped, looking sideways at him. "You did not."

"Don't believe it," Mailn said.

"Highly unlikely," Keffoule said.

"I did too kill him," Rogers said, pouting. "I pointed my rifle through the grate of the air vent and I shot him in the middle of a sentence. I saved Tunger's life."

"But you just implied that Tunger was dead," Keffoule said. "Are we talking about Schrödinger's Tunger here? Because to be very honest I didn't think you were at an intellectual level to discuss that sort of—"

"Holy crap, you guys, can we just focus on getting out of here?"

In response, Keffoule shot a Jupiterian security officer who had come running around the corner all by himself. For all their organization, the Jupiterians didn't seem any more skilled at fighting wars than the rest of the galaxy.

"We don't need to get out of here," Mailn said as they began walking again. "We need to find the rest of the Jupiterian leadership."

"What?" Rogers said. "Why the hell do we need to do that? One of guys with the keys is dead, and the Galaxy Eater device has been completely incapacitated thanks to my ingenuity. We've done our job and it's time for us to get back to the fleet."

Keffoule casually delivered a spinning back kick to the faces of a pair of Jupiterian militiamen who came out of a door without looking. "Didn't you hear me over the datapad? The Jupiterians have figured out a way out of the Fortuna Stultus galaxy. At least, we think so. If we allow them to retreat we could be looking at another Galaxy Eater incident in half a century."

"She's right," Mailn said, as she put the butt of her rifle into the exposed abdomen of some guy who was trying to sell them a timeshare. "We have an opportunity to end this. It's our duty."

"Our duty," Keffoule agreed.

"Ha," Rogers said. "Both of you said duty." When nobody else laughed, he cleared his throat. "So what do you propose we do? Start interviewing everyone that we don't kill or incapacitate until we find Sal and his crew?"

"That was the plan," the Viking said as she killed or incapacitated someone. "You have any better ideas?"

Rogers thought for a moment as he did absolutely nothing to help their fighting effort.

"Actually," he said, "you're not going to believe this, but I think I do. I need to talk to a droid."

Commanders Zaz and Rholos paced across the bridge, shouting commands into their headsets with droid-like rapidity. The battle outside had escalated into a full-on "furball"—a word that the pilot Flash had acquainted Deet with only moments earlier—and what had once been the home of the largest conglomeration in the galaxy had turned into the scene of the fight for humanity's survival. Deet had the distinct feeling that, despite everyone attempting to keep up appearances, almost nobody knew what they were doing.

But Deet knew what he was doing. Not only did he now feel like he could basically emote his way through war, he'd been watching R. Wilson Rogers, the most experienced fleet commander in the galaxy.

"Everyone panic!" Deet said. "I want absolutely everyone in this fleet to run back and forth with their arms in the air. You!" He pointed at the communications tech, S1C Brelle. "I want you to set something—anything—on fire and roll it down the hallway."

Brelle responded by sitting down and trying to pretend that she hadn't heard anything. In truth, it seemed like nobody was listening to his commands at all. Well, except for the rest of the fleet, now that he'd transmitted and authorized them.

"I'm not entirely sure this strategy will be the one that leads the fleet to victory," Belgrave said. The helmsman sat in his chair, lounging as though there wasn't a war going on outside, munching on a piece of imported Thelicosan toast. Rogers had gotten everyone hooked on it.

"Based on my observations, some form of this has worked literally every single time," Deet countered.

Belgrave shrugged and took another bite of toast. Looking at the crumbs falling all over the man's uniform, Deet wondered if he would ever be able to taste anything. Perhaps it was something he could work on once he left the *Flagship* and joined up with the rest of his family.

Family. He kept calling them that, but he didn't even really know them. What was this going to be like?

"Woo-hoo!" came a voice over the radio. Flash, who had endangered nearly everyone in every attack run he'd participated in, buzzed past the bridge in his third Ravager. The previous two had been destroyed while Flash had attempted to do barrel rolls while still inside the launch bay.

"Battle is that way, Flash," Deet said.

"The battle is wherever I am, nerd-o-tron!" Flash called, and shot a missile at absolutely nobody.

"How's it going over there?" Rogers asked over the radio.

"Oh, just [EXPLETIVE] fine," Deet said. "Pretty sure we're winning. And just so you know, there are about six dozen transport ships leaving the station you're on, heading for the edge of the sector. Also, I'm basically human now."

"Whatever," Rogers said. "Deet, is it possible for you to hack into the system and see if you can identify the passenger manifests on any of those ships? We're looking for Sal Snaggardir."

"Oh, sure. Let me just put my military genius and deep, deep feelings to the side here and let the giant space battle fight itself for a few minutes while I run inventory."

"Yes or no, Deet?"

"Yes, [REAR ORIFICE]. Stand by."

Deet plugged in, sent out some signals, routed them through the systems of the other droids on the *Rancor* and other ships in their portion of the fleet, and was into Snaggardir's main headquarters building within a few moments.

"Well?" Rogers asked.

Deet beeped. "Is Sal Snaggardir a common name?"

"I'm pretty sure there's only one in the galaxy," Rogers said. "Why?"

"Well, that's very interesting, because there is a Sal Snaggardir manifested on every single ship aboard the main station of the headquarters complex. Enjoy!"

"Crap," Rogers said. He sucked a breath through his teeth, thinking. "Okay, new plan. We're not going to the hangar."

He put Mailn's datapad, which she'd given him, into his holster and switched his disruptor rifle to his good hand. His shoulders automatically set themselves back; his gait widened. He felt powerful, deadly. He could shoot things, and they would die.

"This way," Rogers said, turning down a short hallway that ended in a large, unguarded door. "We're going to the brig."

"You know," Mailn said. "Far be it from me to judge, but if there was an effective place for the commander of a fleet to cower in fear until the battle was over, it would be the brig."

Rogers looked at her. "A man tries to jump out the trash chute *one time.*"

Mailn shrugged.

"We're not going for us. We're going for . . . someone else."

"Who, exactly?" Mailn asked.

"The big boss's secretary," Rogers said. "I think I heard Szinder say her name was Hiri. I knew every damn detail about Klein's life when I was his exec. She might know which ship is actually the one we're looking for."

They opened the door to the brig, which really surprised the three Jupiterian guards standing at the check-in desk. They were further surprised when, as they tried to draw their weapons and/or press the alarm buttons, three women blasted them across the room. A bizarre silence followed. Rogers had attempted to join in, but only afterward realized that his rifle's safety had been engaged.

Either nobody else noticed or nobody else cared, so Rogers

blew at the end of the rifle's barrel and slung it back over his shoulder. He walked around to the other side of the check-in desk and started tapping at the terminals to see if he could bring up any information on the current guest list for the Snaggardir's brig.

Keffoule, the Viking, and Mailn all proceeded to wordlessly secure the area while Rogers tried to access and search the database. One of the personnel who had been guarding the reception desk—if a jail could have been said to have a reception—had left his ID card in the reader located on the computer terminal. If Rogers remembered his security training correctly, this was tantamount to handing victory to the enemy. In fact, he could remember one of Ralph's posters saying something like TAKE YOUR ID OUT OR THE ENEMY WINS. Rogers kind of missed Ralph; he hoped he was doing well in his completely inaccessible hole in the middle of the *Flagship*.

It became immediately apparent that Rogers was wrong in his assessment of the vacancy status of the Snaggardir's brig. It was packed. In fact, nearly every cell was occupied—some with more than one person, even though the room description clearly said it contained only one bed.

"What the hell is this?" Rogers muttered to himself.

"What's going on?" the Viking asked, sidling up beside him. He could smell her sweat.

"Hi," he said, forgetting what he was doing.

She stared at him blankly.

"Oh, right," Rogers said, coughing. "The fate of humanity." He pointed at the screen. "I couldn't really tell from the map, but this place is huge. Look at all of these rooms." He gestured at the computer screen, which was now showing a higher-resolution display of the detention facility. It extended for nearly a half mile, with conveyor-belt walkways connecting several expanding hallways. "What does Snaggardir's want with a detention block the size of a corporate office? And why is every cell full?"

Keffoule, who had just finished incapacitating a trio of security personnel who apparently hadn't gotten the message that it would have been better just to lie down on the floor and cry, stepped behind him as well.

"Perhaps the Jupiterian revolution wasn't as widely accepted as we were led to believe," Keffoule said. "And, based on the construction date of this facility, I might guess that Sal Snaggardir always thought there'd be some dissent. He was prepared."

Rogers looked at her sideways. "Since when do you know so much about human nature? I wasn't convinced you were human."

Keffoule actually stuck her tongue out at him, which seemed to surprise even her. "I have been speaking with Quinn on a regular basis."

Rogers had only witnessed conversations between Quinn and Keffoule that had involved a lot of dirty looks and snide comments, but maybe it had done them both a bit of good.

Looking back to the last couple of entries in the database, he could see that there had been five people checked in to the brig today, one of which was Lucinda Hiri. There was some sort of special protocol next to her name, upgraded security or something.

"Found her," Rogers said. "Cell twenty-six, a quarter of the way down the main hallway to the left."

They moved smoothly, the three women expertly covering all of the possible ambush points with their rifles as Rogers waved his around randomly.

"By Newton's apple, there are whole families in here," Keffoule said.

The cells, made of a sort of plexiglass that appeared to also function as a one-way window, displayed an array of inmates that ranged from the clearly rough-and-tumble to the totally absurd, like the family of four playing a board game and laughing as though there was absolutely nothing wrong at all. But, no. They were definitely in jail.

The Viking grunted, but it was the kind of grunt that Rogers had come to recognize as one of disgust and contempt. Mailn outright spat.

"I'd love to see what damage a four-year-old could do to the revolution," Rogers said. He realized that it sounded like a cynical joke, but he actually meant it. He'd seen some four-year-olds . . . "Let's focus. The faster we find the leadership, the faster this will be over for them, too."

The conveyor walkway made it feel like they were sprinting rather than just tactically crouch-running down the hallway. Soon, they arrived at cell number twenty-six, and Rogers stepped off the conveyor belt to look at the occupant. Lucinda Hiri was younger than him, dirty-blond hair, pretty if you were into that mousy sort of look. She was dressed in clothing made for moving—almost as though she'd been arrested while on the way to the gym—and looking very, very nervous.

"Lucinda Hiri?" Rogers said, mustering all of the heroic demeanor he could in his voice. "We're here to rescue you."

For someone in jail, and likely on her way to being executed, Lucinda didn't seem happy to see him at all. In fact, she completely ignored him, continuing to stare at the floor in front of her like he hadn't just delivered the best news she'd heard all day.

"You moron," the Viking said. She pressed a button on the outside of the—now evidently soundproof—plexiglass, and the door to the cell opened.

This time, Lucinda jumped to her feet, ashen terror written on her face. She brought her hands reflexively up, though to defend herself against what, Rogers had no idea, and closed both of her eyes, emitting a constrained yelp of surprise.

"Relax," Rogers said. "We're busting you out." He stood on the outside of the door, not brave enough to go waltzing into an open jail cell, and motioned for her to come out.

Lucinda opened her eyes, and her look of fear was replaced by what Rogers might call optimistic confusion.

SYSTEM FAILURE

"You're . . . Captain Rogers, aren't you?" she said.

Rogers couldn't help but let his chest puff out a little bit. He turned to his team. "See? I'm famous."

"I've seen your picture in every staff meeting for the last couple of months," she said. "Sal Snaggardir wants to strangle you with your own intestines."

"Super famous," Mailn agreed.

Rogers swallowed. "Geez. Did he use those exact words?"

"Is this really the priority right now?" the Viking barked. "Come on, Rogers, grab our new friend Noodle Arms Jr. here and let's go."

"I do not have noodle arms!" Keffoule shouted. "They are *finely toned*!"

Lucinda, to her credit, didn't seem put off by the insanity of the troupe that was breaking her out of jail. She came out of the cell, looking left and right as though this might be some sort of twisted trap, and stepped on the conveyor belt leading back to the entrance of the brig.

"I, uh, thank you," she said. "But why did you come for me?"

"We've disabled the Galaxy Eater and are trying to find the rest of the leadership so we can end this," Rogers said. "We checked the manifests to see what escape ship he was on, but—"

"He's on all of them, right?" Lucinda said. "He has a lot of contingencies."

"Including finding a way out of Fortuna Stultus?" Keffoule asked.

Lucinda frowned. "A way out? No, I haven't heard of that."

"We can figure that part out later once we have them in hand," Rogers said. "Can you tell us where they are?"

"Yes," Lucinda said. "It'll be down in the maintenance hangar bay, where all the repair ships are stocked. The local ones that work on the outside of the station. One of them looks like a maintenance tugboat but is actually a fully outfitted escape vessel with room for five people and all of Snaggardir's sensitive information. I'll know which one it is when I can see it. But we'll never make it there; the only way there is going to lead us right past the main armory and troop barracks. We'll get swarmed."

"We've handled swarms before," the Viking said.

"I like where your head is at," Rogers said as they returned to the entrance of the brig. "But I don't think that two soldiers can handle the entire Jupiterian army."

"Four soldiers," Keffoule said.

"I count as negative one."

Keffoule nodded. "Math," she said.

"Math," Rogers agreed. "But I do have another idea." Stepping off the conveyor belt, he jogged back over to where the Jupiterian guard had left his ID in the terminal and brought up the command screen. "It's time for an emergency jail break."

"I don't know if that's the best idea," Mailn said. "It's impossible that every single person in these cells is a dissident."

"Oh gosh," Rogers said, putting his palms against his cheeks. "Do you think we might accidentally release a murderer? Like one that might threaten to turn the Fortuna Stultus galaxy into a reverse Big Bang?"

"Right," Mailn said. "I guess you're not a total idiot."

"Not all of the time, anyway," the Viking chimed in.

"Thanks, you two. Now let's see here . . ." Rogers looked around the computer terminal. "I could probably help direct the masses if I . . ." He waggled his fingers in the air, looking for something. "There it is!"

The sound of speakers clicking on echoed throughout the hallway as Rogers activated the microphone attached to the desk.

"Attention, uh, people who have been put in jail by Snaggardir's for one reason or another." Rogers voice rang out over the public address system. "This is Captain Rogers of the, uh, people who are not Snaggardir's."

"Really?" Mailn said. "People who are not Snaggardir's? Should we get that on the unit patch?"

"Shut up," Rogers said, a command which reverberated throughout the detention facility since he was still on the microphone. "Not you, I mean. I was talking to someone else. Look, we're the good guys, okay? There is a full-scale assault going on out there, and we're trying to prevent everyone from dying. If preventing everyone from dying interests you, then when I press this button to open the cells, I want you to get out there, run toward the maintenance hangar, and punch a Jupiterian."

"Um," Lucinda said.

"Rogers," the Viking said. "They're all Jupiterian."

"Right," Rogers said. "Don't just punch any Jupiterian. Because they're probably not all bad. Don't punch each other. Punch Jupiterians with a level of discretion. Selective punching. Goddamn it. Here we go!"

Rogers pressed the "unlock all" button with authority. An alarm sounded, followed by the sound of hundreds, maybe thousands, of feet entering the corridor in front of him.

"Alright, everyone," Rogers said. "Let's ride this wave!"

The wave, as it turned out, reminded Rogers a whole lot of a concert he had attended in Haverstown, but now was not the time to reflect on poor choices he'd made in the past. Now was a time to think about all the poor choices he was about to make in the present.

"I'm so glad you got my messages, Captain Rogers," Lucinda said as they cleared the small office space that connected the larger station with the hangar and proceeded down the windowless cargo elevator.

"What messages?" Rogers asked.

"The ones I was sending you with Sara's voice on them. I was trying to let you know that there was a spy among you, and that you needed to be careful. There were other messages too, like that the Astromologer was a plant and the exact location of the Galaxy Eater, and to definitely not use any of the sandwich machines. Did you get those?"

". . . No."

"Oh." Lucinda blinked, then smiled. "Well at least you got some of the important ones, obviously, and acted on them, or you wouldn't be here."

". . . Yeah."

"Sandwich machine? We thought *we* started all of this," the Viking said, "but now that you mention it, we did hear some guys talking about someone trying to buy a sandwich from a vending machine with a fake ID. You know anything about that?"

Rogers laughed, probably a little too loudly. "That sounds like the stupidest thing anyone could ever do. Certainly not someone smart enough to be the commander of a joint force. And anyway, if he did do something like that but then—just for example—he saved the galaxy, I think people would forgive him for the oversight, particularly because—I mean hypothetically—he was really hungry."

The Viking whapped him on the back of his head with her knuckles.

As expected for the largest company in the galaxy, the maintenance hangar bordered on absurd in its size. It put the *Flagship's* to shame—and a lot of things broke on the *Flagship* that needed fixing. If Snaggardir's had outfitted every repair ship with a plasma cannon, it might have rivaled any one system's defense force in terms of size and firepower.

"Oh good," Rogers said flatly. "At least picking one ship out of this thousand will be easy."

"That's what I'm here for," Lucinda said. For a corporate sycophant, she seemed to fall into her role as hero pretty quickly. Maybe Rogers should stop judging people. "It'll be close to the hangar doors for easy exit. Let's head that way."

The hangar actually had three large doors that allowed passage through the airlock and into the vacuum of space, and Lucinda had pointed at the one closest to the cargo elevator they'd just exited. As might be expected for a station that was likely being abandoned, most of the repair ships were dormant, though a considerable amount of personnel ran about, barking orders and questions at each other. On the very far side of the hangar, Rogers could see several fighter spacecraft being repaired by what was undoubtedly a very exhausted and panicked maintenance crew.

Surprisingly, they received very little hassle on their way to the edge of the hangar. It was a great improvement over the last times he'd been running around a hangar bay, during which he'd been chased, and shot at, by either droids or Thelicosans. He thought that after this was all over maybe he should spend some time just avoiding hangars altogether.

The small amount of hassle could have been because everyone who tried to talk to them was knocked unconscious by Keffoule, Mailn, or the Viking. Lucinda seemed moderately horrified by all of the violence, but maintained her focus on looking for the ship in question.

"I can't see it," she said.

"How will you know which one it is, again?" Rogers asked.

"The maintenance tugs all have hard landing gear instead of magnetic chocks," Lucinda answered as she started toward the next hangar door. "But Mr. Snaggardir had this one modified to allow for extra storage."

"So we're looking for one ship with mag chocks?"

"That's right. It's possible that they're already gone."

Rogers whipped out his datapad and made a call. "Deet? Start visual scanners of all maintenance tugs outside the main station. Look at the landing gear. As soon as you see one with mag chocks instead of hard tacks, grab that ship. Copy?"

"What do you want me to copy that to?" Deet asked.

"Damn it, you frigging robot, I wanted to know if you understood me!"

"Then why didn't you just *ask* that? I heard you fine. It's modern communications technology, Rogers."

Rogers was about to tell Deet exactly what he thought of modern communications technology when Lucinda pointed at a ship ahead of them and yelled.

"There! That's the one!" She started sprinting.

"Wait, never mind, Deet," Rogers said as he made his own poor attempt at a sprint. "We found it."

"Can you not waste my [EXPLETIVE] time with things that you don't actually need, Rogers? I'm trying to fight a war over here!"

Rogers holstered his datapad with much more grace than he'd ever holstered a pistol and fought hard to catch up to his team. The gangplank of the tugboat/modified escape shuttle was still lowered, and two guards stood outside, rifles in hand. They barely saw the Viking and Keffoule approach before they were on the ground, their weapons skittering across the cold metal floor. Seconds later, all of Rogers' crew charged up the gangplank.

"Freeze!" the Viking bellowed. God, Rogers loved that bellow.

The four occupants of the shuttle turned around. Sal Snaggardir's mouth stretched into a thin line, his old, haggard face turning a mixture of white and red. Sara Alshazari, who was putting a bag away in one of the compartments, dropped it to the floor with a gasp. The other two people, presumably pilots, looked at each other. No one said a word.

Rogers flicked the barrel of his rifle, making a loud *ding* noise.

"Congratulations on getting totally owned by the people who are not Snaggardir's!" Rogers said. "You are entitled to sit the fuck down."

An Epic Failure

Although Deet knew that there was no need to do this, he read the message a second time. It was a dramatic thing that humans did now and then when they couldn't believe the news that was in front of them, but Deet had noncorruptible memory. Once he saw the message the first time, it was ingrained in his memory banks, and he could call it up at any time. Still, he felt like it was something that could have used a second glance. Even though it didn't.

D-24, the message said. *I am very pleased with your progress. I would like to meet.—Dr. Mattic.*

Of course, Deet's first action was to completely take apart the metadata of the message in as many ways as he could think of, but it was as though someone had come into the room, typed the message into the terminal, and uploaded it directly to Deet's database through a hard wire. No traces of the message's origin remained in the data, not even a return address. When he tried to track the relays through which the message had been sent, he came up blank. It was as though it *hadn't been* sent at all, but had manifested organically. Was this some sort of built-in system that Dr. Mattic had created when he'd made the droids initially?

Dr. Mattic didn't want to be found, but he clearly was asking Deet to find him. It was that sort of paradoxical request that was so typical of humans.

Wait. Did this mean that he and Dr. Mattic were dating?

No, no. That was a ridiculous notion, even by human standards. Deet didn't even have an online profile. From what he had observed of human dating so far, you either needed an online profile or you needed to kick your potential mate in the face, and use lots of euphemisms about cooking. And he wasn't interested in dating right now; he was focused on his work. At least that was the excuse that a lot of lonely humans used to make themselves seem less lonely.

Was Deet lonely? His newfound senses, still foreign and chaotic in his database, couldn't answer for him.

If Rogers was here, he'd probably tell him no. But Rogers was kind of a [REAR ORIFICE]. He was also relaxing on a beach instead of taking care of the 331st.

Deet sighed, emitting a wind-rushing noise that made everyone in the launch bay look around in confusion. He really needed to get his profanity generator fixed. It wouldn't be the first thing he asked Dr. Mattic to do, but it would be near the top.

Stepping to the side, Deet watched as a group of Snaggardir's troops were led through the hangar and loaded on a transportation ship, probably to head to Merida Prime for logging and, perhaps, trial. Even now, they were still sorting through everyone and making sure that there wouldn't be any flare-ups of rebellion anywhere else. The galaxy was a big place with a lot of planets, and it was going to take a considerable amount of time to restore balance. And, also, figure out what to do with a legitimately angry group of people who had been completely ignored for the last two hundred years.

His sensors alerted him to an incoming vessel, which smoothly came through the airlock and landed uncomfortably close to him. He could feel the force of the engines, but he was heavy enough that it didn't blow him backward. It was the same vessel that had come to pick up all of the "bodies" of the decommissioned droids. The gangplank lowered, and the same trio of droids walked out to greet him.

"You appear to have been waiting here for some time," the lead droid, who clearly had the Froidian Chip, said as he approached.

"That's right," Deet said.

"Why? You were informed of the exact time that we would be here."

Deet was about to say that he'd been anxious before he realized that the droid he was talking to likely had no idea what anxiousness was. Instead, Deet was silent for a moment. Where did he belong, exactly? What did belonging really mean?

It didn't matter right now. Right now, he had a lot of questions to ask someone he had no idea how to find. Even if he didn't belong with the droids, there was a good chance he would learn at least a little bit about himself in the meantime.

"I may need some debugging," Deet said, though he didn't really believe it. Which meant it was a lie. What was happening here?

"This is probable. You have spent a lot of cycles among humans. We can run diagnostics when you get on board. This way, please."

The droid trio unceremoniously turned and walked up the gangplank, not waiting to see if Deet was going to follow them. They didn't even politely ask if they could help him with his bags. In truth, he didn't have any bags. Just one little backpack he'd stolen from Rogers' room, in which he had a small vial of hand sanitizer and a U-shaped neck pillow.

"So long, *Flagship*," Deet said. "You're a piece of [EXCREMENT], and I am happy to be rid of you."

Deet walked on board, having told his second lie of the day.

So Dathum really wasn't that great.

Rogers had seen so many damn pamphlets and travel shows about the tropical beaches, the swaying palm trees, the drinks that came served in coconuts. But now that he was here, it all seemed like one big hairy scam that targeted pensioners and the under-traveled. Sure, all of the things they'd advertised were true. Dathum's beauty was unparalleled among many other destinations all across Fortuna Stultus. Great drinks. The palm trees definitely swayed. Lots of interesting and inventive swimwear.

But everyone in the pamphlets had been happy. Rogers wasn't happy. So therefore, Dathum was just a dirty lie.

Rogers turned one of the aforementioned pamphlets over in his hand. Omnipresent all over every resort, they advertised memberships and upgrades and all-you-can-eat buffets. These must have been new, because none of them made sense and all of them were written in capital lettering. One of them, talking about one of the nicer buffets, just said *EAT ALL THE FOOD* under a pile of bananas. He was glad that Ralph had gotten another job working for the marketing department of a travel company. Rogers had written him a glowing recommendation.

There was only one problem with all of this: it was boring.

High Admiral Holdt had told him he could have anything he wanted after he wrapped up the incident with the Jupiterians. A release from his commitment to the Meridan Galactic Navy. A parade. A daytime TV show. Whatever Rogers desired, Holdt had been given carte blanche from the Meridan government to grant it to him. Rogers only had to ask. After all, the galaxy—and all of humanity—was in his debt, or some shit.

Why he'd picked four weeks' vacation, followed by a return to duty, was an utter mystery to him. He could still hear the words coming out of his mouth, surprising (and no doubt disappointing) everyone within earshot.

He couldn't really go back to smuggling or conning. He was

famous now. Gambling might be fun as a profession, but he didn't seem to be very lucky anymore either.

So, in reality, he'd had no choice but to go back to work for the *Flagship*. All of his stuff was there anyway. Which meant that now, for the last week or so of vacation, it was sand, water, sand, palm trees, sand, water, frilly drinks, sand, water . . .

Something beeped.

"Oh thank god," Rogers said. He picked up his datapad, which only told him that someone from the *Flagship* was calling.

"Hello R. Wilson Rogers," Keffoule's voice said.

"Oh, it's you," Rogers said. "I thought we were kind of done with all of this. And my datapad said the *Flagship* was calling me."

"I am being routed through your ship. I wasn't aware you were off shirking your duties. I am firmly reinstalled aboard the *Limiter*, thank you very much." She stopped for a moment, and Rogers could hear all sorts of weird noise in the background. It wasn't totally clear, but he could have sworn she was *tittering*. He could hear Xan's monotone voice somewhere near Keffoule. The two of them had been totally insufferable since the conclusion of the battle, always whispering to each other at inappropriate moments. Keffoule kept grabbing Xan's butt when she thought nobody was looking, but everyone always saw. It was an unnervingly weird shift.

"I don't know which version of you I like less," Rogers said. "Do you two really have to act like that all the time?"

"Oh, Rogers," she said. "You need to learn how to throw an extra variable in your equation now and then. How to have a little fun."

His stomach felt like it had just turned to lead.

"Anyway," Keffoule said with a sigh, "I was calling to tell you that it's on."

Rogers grunted and hung up. "It" was a public statement being made by the newly formed Coalition of Stultitia, which was a council of the political bodies of all four systems in the

Fortuna Stultus galaxy. It was an absolutely terrible name, and Rogers had little faith that anything would actually get done, but they'd convened to try to decide the fate of both Sal Snaggardir and his family and the Jupiterian people as a whole. Flash, who had somehow achieved the reputation of a war hero, had been chosen to lead it, of course.

Using his datapad to connect to the server, he saw Flash talking into a microphone at a delicately arranged press conference. The symbols of all of the systems were behind him, and a fifth sigil had been added. Jupiter's, he assumed. The detail wasn't fine enough for him to see exactly what it was, but it honestly just looked like a picture of the planet. They hadn't had much time to come up with anything creative, he supposed.

Flash's lips were moving, but it was clear that someone had forgotten to turn the microphone on. Rogers couldn't hear anything. In a way, that was better. He was still wearing his damned aviator sunglasses, and Rogers hated hearing him talk. At least he was off his ship.

"His" ship. Forever, now, he guessed.

The microphone kicked on somewhere near the end of the speech. Flash was mid-sentence.

"—to bring a sense of intergalactic stability and order to the galaxy that has heretofore only existed by way of the Two Hundred Years (and Counting) Peace."

Rogers' eyes widened. Those were three- and four-syllable words! Who the hell was this person?

"To do this, we need to employ synergistic awareness of all the various and multifaceted components of culture and history to all systems with equanimity, given what has only recently transpired with the Jupiterian people. Sal Snaggardir and his family will be receiving full pardons on the condition that they lend their assistance to the restructuring of the galaxy. We will carve out a place among us in which the Jupiterians can live in a natural and healthy mixture of peace and assimilation, achieve self-governance, and participate in galactic affairs. As long as they totally pinkie-swear they're not gonna get on our six and try to slurp up the planets again." He cleared his throat. "As long as they promise to remain nonaggressive, and assist in the elimination of rogue elements within the formerly radical Jupiterian regime."

"Oh my god," Rogers said out loud. "It's Klein. He's another Klein."

Someone on the other end of the beach turned to the sky and gave a slow, dramatic salute.

Rogers stared into the distance as he turned off the datapad, hearing all he'd needed to hear. Even if the Society of Burned Bread was to completely implode, there would always be another Klein.

He sighed, tucking his datapad away. He wished the Viking was here. Though she probably would hate this place even more than Rogers did.

The Viking had only called him once or twice in the last month or so from her deployment to New Neptune. Every available ground troop from all of the systems had been called in for mop-up duty, and she and Mailn had gotten deployed almost immediately. The job for fleet commanders might be done, but a lot of work remained to restore stability to the galaxy. It would likely take months, if not years, to bring a sense of normalcy back to Fortuna Stultus. Rogers missed her, of course, and he was fairly certain she missed him, too, when she wasn't having fun clubbing people over the head.

Tunger had completely disappeared. Whether he was dead or alive, Rogers had no idea, but given his penchant for disguises, he was probably sitting on the chair next to him.

Rogers reached over and absentmindedly took a sip from his drink. Only a moment later did he realize that he'd taken a sip of tanning oil instead. Other beachgoers turned to look at him as he leaned over his chair and violently spit out the vile-tasting stuff into the sand all around him. He took a sip of what he was *certain* was his drink, and realized that tanning oil combined with rum and coconut milk was an even *worse* taste, so he spit that out too. It tasted like the *Flagship*'s cooking back when Hart had been in the kitchens.

Screw this. He was going back to the *Flagship*.

The *Awesome, Too* wasn't exactly stolen. It was more reappropriated as a spoil of war. The Jupiterians had, of course, appropriated it from the Meridan fleet to begin with, so, there might have been an argument for forcing Rogers to give it back to Merida. If, that is, Rogers hadn't completely erased it from all the records and given it a new paint job. Hey, it had worked last time. And this ship, a later model of the *Awesome*, was a lot easier to fly in and out of atmospheres. It almost made the experience tolerable for Rogers.

But he'd cleared Dathum's atmosphere quite some time ago, staying well clear of the asteroid family, and was halfway to the *Flagship*. He could have used official flag officer transportation, of course, since he was the commander of the fleet and all that, but he really had just wanted a taste of his old life for a few minutes. Even if that meant he had to fly himself around. At least he could stock a full bar on his personal ship.

His console beeped.

"Rogers!" High Admiral Holdt said as Rogers tapped the communication channel. "I see you're on your way back to your ship. Thought you were on vacation."

"I decided to, uh, bank those days for later use," Rogers said.

"Alright, whatever the hero of the galaxy wants, I guess. Look, I've got some news for you."

"Oh?" Rogers said, feeling a little grateful. He felt like he needed some news. Even though he'd just gotten some news about Jupiter and all that, he could have used a double dose of news.

"Now that things have settled down, we've been able to get some of our administrative ducks in a row, so to speak," Holdt said. "We still have a lot of work to do, like figuring out what the Jupiterians' escape plan was. We still can't get Sal Snaggardir to tell us and we can't find anything in their files. But back to the news. The good news."

Rogers felt something start to flip over in his stomach. His hackles rose.

"Oh?" he said again, slower this time.

"Yep. All that talk of you being acting admiral had gone out the window. I'm here to tell you that it's time to get the rank officially. We don't really have time for an official ceremony, and I know you hate all of that anyway, so—"

The feeling in Rogers' stomach turned into a raging sea of bile and fear.

"Holdt," Rogers said, his panic rising. "Stop. Please. Don't—"

"I am hereby promoting you to the rank of admiral in the Meridan Galactic—"

"Holdt! No!"

"—Navy, effective immediately. Congratulations, Admiral Rogers."

Rogers slumped into his seat as Holdt signed off, looking down at the floor of the *Awesome, Too*. He reached over and grabbed his still half-full glass of Jasker 130 (it wasn't that much better than Jasker 120, if he was being honest), and looked at his navigation console, waiting.

Waiting.

Waiting.

It beeped.

"Incoming asteroid," said the computer.

"I know," Rogers said. He slammed back the glass of Jasker and watched as an asteroid took a hard left turn from its trajectory, escaped Dathum's orbit, and suddenly got very, very big.

THE [EXPLETIVE] END OF THE EPIC FAILURE TRILOGY

ACKNOWLEDGMENTS

No journey worth taking is taken alone; I have lots of people to thank for their encouragement and tenacity throughout the process. My agent, Sam Morgan, was integral in carrying me through to the last words on the page, along with my teammate Joe Monti at Saga and his dedicated copy editors, publicist, and staff members. Leonardo Calamati did a marvelous job with the covers. But I do wish we'd hired a better narrator for the audio book.

The end of the Epic Failure Trilogy brings a myriad of emotions. It's been a wacky, wild ride for Rogers and his crew, and I love all of you for taking the cruise with me. To all my readers: you are the best. I can't wait to share the next project with you.